THE GAME OF LIFE

THIRTEENTH BOOK IN THE BRIGANDSHAW CHRONICLES

PETER RIMMER

ABOUT PETER RIMMER

~

Peter Rimmer was born in London, England, and grew up in the south of the city where he went to school. After the Second World War, aged eighteen, he joined the Royal Air Force, reaching the rank of Pilot Officer before he was nineteen. At the end of his National Service, he sailed for Africa to grow tobacco in what was then Rhodesia, now Zimbabwe.

The years went by and Peter found himself in Johannesburg where he established an insurance brokering company. Over 2% of the companies listed on the Johannesburg Stock Exchange were clients of Rimmer Associates. He opened branches in the United States of America, Australia and Hong Kong and travelled extensively between them.

Having lived a reclusive life on his beloved smallholding in Knysna, South Africa, for over 25 years, Peter passed away in July 2018. He has left an enormous legacy of unpublished work for his family to release over the coming years, and not only they but also his readers from around the world will sorely miss him. Peter Rimmer was 81 years old.

ALSO BY PETER RIMMER

~

The Asian Sagas

Bend with the Wind (Book 1)

Each to His Own (Book 2)

~

The Pioneers

Morgandale (Book 1)

Carregan's Catch (Book 2)

~

Novella

Second Beach

PART 1

MAY 1993 — THE MILE-HIGH CLUB

1

A month after his brother Randall's marriage to Meredith, Phillip Crookshank arrived back at Harare Airport, too late in the day to drive up to the valley. He was feeling lonely. All his three siblings were either married or living with a girlfriend. At turning thirty-seven he was the only one on his own. With his mother dead, his father now living in England after having been thrown off his farm by the Mugabe government for not being indigenous, the only relation he had left in Zimbabwe was his half-brother, Craig. Walking out to the parking lot where he had left his truck before flying over to England, Phillip made up his mind. He would drive to his brother's flat in the Avenues and sleep the night in Craig's spare bedroom, then drive up to his safari camp the next day. His partner Jacques had handled the business while he was away. There wasn't a problem. He would do the shopping for supplies in the morning and then drive the five hours up to the Zambezi Valley. Having made up his mind, he felt less lonely. Craig's girlfriend, Jojo, wouldn't mind. He would take them to dinner. Jacques was just as capable as he was of showing the new group of Americans the African bushveld. The rains had finished. It was the perfect time of the year for an African safari.

With his lone suitcase in the back of the truck Phillip turned on the ignition, pulled out the choke and pumped the accelerator pedal three times. Jacques's well-tuned engine fired immediately. Half an hour later, with the suitcase in his hand and the car parked outside, Phillip walked up the one flight of stairs and along the corridor to Craig and Jojo's flat. The light had gone. They would be home from work. Phillip rang the bell. The door opened to a smiling Jojo, behind her a beaming Craig.

"You two look so damn happy. Mind if I spend the night? The wedding was great. You should have come over. Your mother and Dad send you their love... Well say something. If you smile any wider your faces are going to crack."

"Jojo is pregnant. We found out this morning. We're going to get married. All I have to do now is get her father's permission. It's an old Shona custom. We're going up to the village over the weekend. Come in, Phillip. Of course you can stay."

"I'm very happy for you both. Congratulations. Do you want me to take you out to dinner?"

"Don't be silly. You must be tired after the flight. We'll make supper in the flat. Traditional African cooking with *sadza*. You'll love it."

"How's the job going?"

"Trying to help people isn't always easy. The donors are performing well. It's using the money properly to help the impoverished which is difficult. Delivering what you promise. A lot of it's politics. We have to balance everything. Come in."

"So when are you two getting married?"

"When Craig gets my father's permission and Dad accepts the *lobola*. We love to keep up with our traditions. They are so important to us. Makes us Shona who we are."

"Welcome to the Crookshank family, Jojo."

"Thank you, Phillip. Want a beer?"

"I'd love a beer."

The brothers stood looking at each other while Jojo went to the fridge in the kitchen.

"Tell me about your brother's wedding. What does my sister's baby look like?"

The questions flowed. By the time Phillip went to bed he was exhausted. Lying awake, he could hear them talking. Laughing. They were so damn happy. It made him jealous. A reaction that was wrong.

Making himself think happy thoughts for Craig, Randall and Myra, Phillip finally fell asleep.

They all left the flat at the same time the next morning, Craig and Jojo to go to work, Phillip to do the shopping. Craig and Jojo had tried to look excited about going up to Jojo's village at the weekend to tell her family the good news. In the old days *lobola* was paid in cows. Now it was paid with money. When Craig had said they were driving up to the village on the Saturday, Phillip had been watching Jojo. There was fear in her eyes. Nothing in life was simple. Whether the problem was her being pregnant and unmarried, or an interracial union, Phillip wasn't sure. He wasn't even sure if the father knew his daughter was living with Craig.

Phillip drove to the Farmers' Co-op to shop for supplies, an old habit from growing up on a farm. With the truck full from the list he had made before leaving camp on his journey to England, Phillip drove out of Harare. At the end of the north road was the border with Zambia. To the left of the road, Lake Kariba; to the right, Mana Pools and Chewore, both in the Zambezi Valley. The drive was long, the road free of traffic, the dirt road bouncing the truck when he turned off the tarred road. He was back in the Zambezi Valley, the place he loved most in the world. Across the valley, down from the high escarpment, he could see the tall riverine trees. Behind, to the right over the escarpment some hundred kilometres away, was World's View, the farm once owned by his father and where Phillip had grown up. From what he had heard, the farm was now unproductive, a man in Mugabe's government having been given the land. The farm was now used as a place for the man to enjoy at the weekends. Phillip had tried to find out what had happened to his father's workers. No one knew. No one cared. For a lifetime of supporting the right political party the man had received his just reward. It made Phillip sick to the stomach. But that was life. One man's fortune was another man's disaster. Or in the case of World's View, hundreds of people's disaster. But life went on. To the end. It always did.

An hour down the dirt road that ran along the side of the big river, Phillip saw his camp through the trees. One of the fifteen-seater buses was parked next to the ablution block, the only brick building in the camp. Everyone lived in tents. Square, frame tents with an awning in front and three compartments. The sun was going down behind the riverine trees, and people were moving around the camp. His staff were working the cooking fires, getting ready for the evening *braai*. When Phillip got out of the truck he could hear the birds calling from the trees on both banks of the Zambezi River. Taking a deep breath of pleasure into his lungs, Phillip smiled.

"How was the trip, Phillip?"

"Good, Jacques. How's it going?"

"We found a pride of lions for them this morning. Everything's fine. Good to have you back."

"You have no idea how good it is to be home. Wherever you go in England there's traffic and people. You breathe petrol fumes. There's noise all the time. This is paradise. And there isn't much left of it in this brave new world."

"You can say that again. My name is Martha. I'm part of the group. You must be Phillip. Kansas City, Missouri. That's where I come from. We got to save this world, Phillip, or one day it will be gone."

She was in her thirties and smiling, wearing shorts and an open shirt with two of the top buttons undone. It had happened to Phillip before. When they went hunting with guns on safari, the trophy was a dead animal. When they came on safari with cameras, Jacques and Phillip were the trophies. Either for their bodies or their stories of the bush. Giving an inward sigh of pleasure mixed with the feeling of having been pimped, Phillip walked with the girl and Jacques towards the group of tourists sitting in square canvas chairs round the open fire. As the sun went down, the temperature began to drop. One of Phillip's staff was handing out beers and glasses of wine. Putting on his smile of welcome, Phillip joined his clients. Behind them, out on the flowing river, a fish rose out of the water. Phillip took a beer from the safari driver Sedgewick and drank from the bottle. The questions began.

"It's a Zambezi bream. The river is full of them."

"We saw lions this morning."

"I'm glad to hear it."

Sedgewick had put a side of venison on the spit over the cooking fire. The gas lights on their poles were lit. It was the dry season, no chance of rain. The guests had all been told to use the anti-mosquito lotion and take anti-malaria pills. The sunset was brilliant, fading fast. As they drank, the talking increased. The girl called Martha had sat next to Phillip. It was all part of the business. After the third beer, Phillip relaxed and began to enjoy himself. Maybe he wasn't a trophy. Maybe she liked him. Phillip let her talk. Let her tell him about herself. There were worse ways of making a living. His mind drifted, only half listening. America was far away, another world. When the woman put her hand on his bare knee Phillip concentrated. Another middle-aged woman was chatting up Jacques. Martha, making her living in advertising, had joined the group of singles on the safari. The tour was breaking up in five days' time. Martha, stroking his knee, was trying to make the most of it. Instead of taking a beer from Sedgewick, Phillip took a glass of red wine. Sedgewick turned the spit and locked it at a different angle. The meat had to cook on all sides. Munya, Sedgewick's assistant, was preparing the salads at a long trestle table. Another long table was laid for the guests. The firelight took control, climbing up inside the branches of the riverine trees.

"Can we walk down to the water, Phillip? Bring your glass of wine. I love your accent. It's so different. How old are you if you don't mind me asking? Your camp is so perfect. We had a marriage out of our last singles tour. In a big place like Kansas City it's difficult to meet new people. There are people at work. People in bars. A long tour like this is much better. Lets people get to know each other."

"I'm turning thirty-seven next week."

"Have you ever been married? I've had two husbands. No children. I like being free. Husbands can be so demanding. They only think of themselves. But don't get me wrong. I love men... You're not married, are you?"

"No. I've never been married. Two brothers and a sister and I'm the only one single. My sister lives in America. Married to an American. They live outside Los Angeles in a beach house."

"What does he do?"

"He's an actor. A film actor."

"What's his name?"

"Julian Becker."

"I don't believe it. He's famous. And he's your brother-in-law? I loved him in *Masters of Vanity*! Saw it twice."

"My brother Randall wrote the book it was based on."

"Wasn't the author's name, Randall Holiday?"

"His pseudonym. His real name is Randall Crookshank. He's just got married. Why I wasn't here when you arrived. I went over to England for the wedding. Randall lives on a farm on the Isle of Man. Writing books. Not a bad life."

"My goodness. That is something... Doesn't the river look beautiful?"

"Yes it does. There's an old saying that if you drink the water of the Zambezi, you will always be drawn back to Africa."

"Can you drink the water?"

"It's safe to drink out in the middle of the river where there is no bilharzia. The bilharzia worm likes shallow water. It's a parasite deadly to humans. We're safe up here on the riverbank. Nearer the water are crocodiles and hippo. Never forget you are in the African bush."

"You'll protect me, Phillip."

"That's my job. My gun over there leaning against Munya's table is loaded."

"Oh, it's so exciting. Let's go back to the fire... Do you like me, Phillip?"

"Of course I do."

"I'm so glad. We've five whole days... And nights."

Taking Phillip's free hand, Martha giggled. Phillip thought what the hell. You never knew in life what was going to happen next. He had drunk enough not to care. Go with the flow, he told himself. In five days the woman would be on the other side of the world. Sedgewick had begun carving the kudu, the meat cooked to perfection. Sedgewick was good. The guests were moving to the long table close to the fire. The nearer the fire, the fewer problems with mosquitoes. So far, Phillip had seen none. It was all part of the African experience. Phillip sat down at the table, Martha next to him. A fresh wine glass stood at each place setting. Munya put a plate with three slices of venison in front of Martha. People were passing round the salad bowls. A buck barked from the other side of the river. The animals were coming down to the water to drink. There were no hi-fis, a strict rule of Phillip's in the bush. It was all about feeling the night, listening for the wild animals. Waiting for the owls to call. Talking to each other about the day's experience, not listening to some rapper explaining his problems. It didn't suit everyone. But rules were rules.

After supper, most of the guests went to their tents. They were tired. The first game drive began at sunrise.

"Do you have your own tent, Phillip?"

"No I don't. I share mine with Jacques."

"What do you do with the gun?"

"Take it to bed."

"What a pity."

They talked about saving the African wildlife and drank more wine. Munya had stoked the big fire with long lengths of wood. Wild animals were kept away by the flames. Martha went to bed on her own. Another day running a safari was over for Phillip. They all had to make a living. You could sit in a cubicle and work on a computer like Martha, or you could entertain tourists in the African bush. It was how life went, creating a product. Sighing inwardly, Phillip took himself off to his tent. Far away downriver a lion roared. The lion was hunting for his food. Animals. They were all animals. He was drunk. Thinking rubbish. Maybe tomorrow he would make a pass at Martha. In the tent, Jacques was asleep. Phillip could hear him snoring from inside his compartment. Lying down under his mosquito net, Phillip went to sleep.

When he woke with the dawn he had not turned once in his sleep. Outside the tent he stretched, yawned and looked around. There were buck not far away drinking from the river. They moved away one by one and disappeared through the trees. A fish eagle looked at Phillip from its perch on the branch of a tree. There was no threat to the big bird, it was king of its castle. Only the fish would find the bird a problem. Munya was moving around tidying up from the previous night. A big kettle, hung from a tripod over the fire, was letting off steam from its spout. As the guests came out from their tents they would be offered tea or coffee. Breakfast would come later, after Phillip had taken the bus on the morning game drive. Martha was standing by the side of the fire, drinking a mug of coffee. She smiled at Phillip.

"Did you sleep well?" She was giving him that knowing look that spoke of expectation. She had emphasised the word sleep. Phillip knew what she meant. He smiled. It was all part of the game.

"We're nearly ready to go, everyone. When you're ready, take your seats in the bus. This morning, I'll be your guide. We're going to drive away from the river towards the escarpment."

Jacques had not come out of the tent. It was his day to lie in. To relax. The stories about the African bush were now up to Phillip. Jacques called it the entertainment, what the clients had come for. Stories they could take back to their suburban lives in America. Something to look back on. All the wildlife films in the world could never create the feel of being in the bush.

They drove off. Two of the guests had drunk too much the previous night and had not come out of their tents. All that journey from America wasted. Sedgewick was driving. Phillip, close to the window next to Sedgewick, scanned the bush with his binoculars whenever the vehicle paused. The Zambezi Valley was seventy kilometres wide. Immediately, Phillip picked up the vultures. They were circling a kill. Something had died in the night so that others could live. It was the cycle of life. Phillip told Sedgewick where to go. They drove on through the long grass, skirting the tall red ant hills. During the bush war that had concluded with Mugabe forming a democratic government, ending colonial rule, one of Phillip's friends had hidden in an ant hill during a terrorist attack on their farm. As they drove on, the vultures came lower. There were twenty or thirty birds, beautiful in flight, ungainly once they landed. A bit like revolutionary politicians. The thought made Phillip smile. He went up and down the bus, pointing out the circling vultures. Ten minutes later, Sedgewick pulled up close to the kill. There were no signs of lions, which was strange. The carcase, whatever it was, was hidden from sight by the tall grass.

"Everyone stay in the bus while I go take a look. Something made the kill so it won't be far away. You can photograph the vultures through the window."

The birds were still circling, taking no notice of them. Phillip made his way through the grass, his loaded rifle at the ready. Then he saw it. Lying on its side with its horn cut from its head was a black rhinoceros. The animal was slowly bleeding to death. The predator was human. The animal had been darted by poachers, the horn cut off while the animal was still alive. It was highly treasured for medicine in Asia, and worth a small fortune. Seven kilos of rhino horn could buy you a mansion. The horns were sold on the Chinese market where they were ground into powder, mixed with water and used to treat rheumatism and a host of other problems, including chasing away the devil. Phillip fired one shot into the animal's brain. He was crying. Above, the shot made the vultures fly higher. There were so few black rhinoceros left, they would soon be extinct.

"I hope you all enjoy your medicine." He was looking up at the sky, past the circling vultures, wiping the brief flush of tears from his cheeks.

Regaining his composure, Phillip walked back to the bus. It was enough to make a man an activist. To fight for the animals. To stop the last of nature being destroyed by predator man in his pursuit of personal gain. But who did you blame? The poacher trying to make a living in a country where the economy was floundering? Or the people who bought the medicine they thought was going to cure their rheumatism or chase away demons? Not sure how far away the poachers were, Phillip told Sedgewick to drive on. Probably they had crossed the river into Zambia. The men worked in groups, skilled hunters armed with rifles. Phillip told the tourists there was nothing left to photograph. Sedgewick looked at him, his eyebrows lifted. Phillip said nothing. There were three elephants over to the right. Sedgewick drove away from the kill towards the big animals. The photography went on for five minutes. Phillip had climbed up onto the luggage rack of the bus to scan the bush with his binoculars. The poachers were nowhere to be seen. The panic he'd felt began to subside. The Americans were chatting away taking pictures of the elephants while the great animals browsed the green shoots on the tops of the trees. Everything seemed peaceful. Life was like that and then all hell would break loose. Smiling, unaware of danger, the tourists got back into the bus. Sedgewick drove back to the camp. It was time for breakfast.

Out of the bus and away from the clients, the driver looked at Phillip.

"What happened? Why did you fire the gun?"

"They'd cut the horn from a living animal. I had to shoot it."

"Poachers. I told them in the bus you were scaring away the vultures."

"As a boy there were so many black rhinoceros in the valley you found them everywhere. Now the whole of Southern Africa is down to thousands. One day we'll all become extinct. Too many people on the planet. My dad says that when he was born in England, there were around two billion people on this earth. There are nearly six billion now. It's unsustainable."

Phillip could smell the bacon frying as he walked away on his own.

He went down the slope to the water. One day it would all be gone. Everywhere in the world, the people were moving into towns to live in concrete jungles. To Phillip, looking out over the beauty of the Zambezi River, it didn't make sense. Man wasn't born to live his life in a hutch, his only access to the world through television.

"What happened back there, Phillip?"

"Have you had your breakfast?"

Martha had put her hand on his shoulder. They stood side by side looking out over the flowing river.

"Nothing for you all to worry about, Martha."

"When you came back to the bus you looked scared."

"It's good to be scared when you're surrounded by wild animals."

"You're not going to tell me."

"It wouldn't help. We're safe. There isn't a problem."

"Can we go for a little walk?"

With the rifle slung over his left shoulder, they walked up to the top of the bank.

"Have you ever been to America? Would you like to come over? There can't be much of a future for you here."

"Maybe not. But it doesn't matter. I'm going to live in Zimbabwe for as long as they'll let me. I was born here, though as the son of a British colonial my rights are tenuous. Who can blame them? The tables have turned. We'll be allowed to stay for as long as they can use us. That's life."

"We could make love in the bushes."

"And then we couldn't."

They both laughed. The tension had broken. Phillip could hear the birds singing. Hear the flow of the river. For now, there was peace on earth. Back at the camp, Jacques was showing the guests how to catch tiger fish. They were the predators, the sport of fisherman, some of them were as big as thirty kilos. It was like fishing for shark in the sea. An hour after breakfast, a man hooked one. He was a skilled fisherman, letting out his line, playing the fish. Twice the big fish jumped out of the water and the fisherman reeled it in. When it tried again to get away, the fisherman let the line run. This time when he reeled it in there was no resistance. The fish was exhausted. Three of the guests ran down to the water's edge as the fish came out of the water. Its eyes were alive, the tail just flapping. The fisherman walked down the bank to claim his catch. He clouted it with a piece of wood he found in the mud. Then he held the fish up by its gills, its eyes now dead. Phillip stood high up on the bank with his rifle, scanning for crocodiles. The man was smiling for the cameras, all the guests clambering around, everyone taking photographs of the man and his fish. Back home, when he showed the photograph, he would be a hero. Jacques went down with a scale to weigh the catch.

"Just over twenty-eight kilos."

Everyone was clapping and smiling. When the man was told he couldn't eat his fish because there were too many bones, he threw it back into the water. The fun was over. Especially for the fish. Phillip, looking down on his happy tourists, wondered if a man should feel sorry for a dead fish. He ate meat and fish, so the idea was probably ridiculous. But he wasn't sure. By the time lunch came, a platter of grilled river bream caught by the guests, Phillip was still thinking of life's anomalies. They tucked in, the food delicious. By now, Phillip thought, the poachers would be far away, carrying their prized horn on the start of its journey to Asia. When he got back on top of the bus for one last search for the poachers, there was no sign of the vultures. They had landed. Among the tall grass that obscured Phillip's view of the kill, the birds would be flopping all over the carcase, tearing at the flesh with their beaks. It was hot in the midday sun on top of the bus. Most of the tourists had gone into their tents for an afternoon nap, the tents shaded by the big trees that sucked their water out of the river. A few of the Americans were sitting in canvas chairs under the trees, most of them reading. One woman just sat. It was Martha. She was looking at him. Gave him a wave. Phillip smiled and climbed down the ladder on the side of the bus. There was an empty chair next to her. Phillip walked across and sat down. Neither of them spoke. Jacques, Munya and Sedgewick were taking a nap in their tents. Everything was peaceful.

"What you are thinking, Phillip?"

"Of that dead fish he tossed back into the water."

"Tonight, when everyone has gone to sleep, come to my tent. There was a good moon last night so you won't have to use a torch... Did you hear me, Phillip? Please. You have everything I love in a man. You're caring. You love animals. You love your Africa. I want to take away one last big memory of your Africa. I want to take you. Your African magic.

To remember forever. The soft side of life. I just want one tiny piece of you. Is that too much to ask? I see the way you look at me or I wouldn't be asking. Who knows, maybe there's more for us than a night in a tent under the African moon. Come to me, Phillip. We can comfort each other. We need love. Mental and physical. Usually it starts with the physical. You don't want to end up on your own for the rest of your life. Tonight. When the moon is up and everything is quiet. No one else will know. I've never asked a man to make love to me before. It usually just happens. There are only four more days. If you don't try for love it may never come."

"You want me as a trophy?"

"No, I want you as a man. You don't have to give me an answer. Just come... Now, what happened this morning?"

"Poachers darted and dehorned a rhinoceros. Poachers are dangerous."

"So that's what you were searching for just now."

"My job is to protect my clients."

"You think they've gone?"

"I hope so."

"Tell me all about yourself, Phillip. About your life. You've heard about mine."

"It's been pretty ordinary. I'm the eldest son of an English tobacco farmer who emigrated to what was then Rhodesia just after the Second World War. My mother died when I was very young. She was attacked by a pride of lions after she got lost in the bush after drinking too much. My mother was an alcoholic. Randall and I have missed her every day of our lives. We have a stepmother who is wonderful. But, however hard she tried, she was never our mother. Then there's Craig and Myra, our half-siblings..."

Martha took his hand as the words flowed out. When Phillip finished talking, people were coming out of their tents. Munya was preparing the bar. It was almost time for sundowners.

"You've lived through a lot, Phillip. That bush war must have been terrible."

"It was. The threat of attack on the farm was always there. Most of the farmers drank to get away from it... You want a drink?"

"Are you coming to my tent tonight?"

"Certainly. When the moon comes up." He was smiling gently at her.

That night, they made love in Martha's tent under the mosquito net. They said nothing, not wishing to be heard. Mutually satisfied, they lay on their backs. Leaving the tent as quietly as possible, Phillip walked through the trees back to his tent. Everything was quiet. Before opening the flap of his tent Phillip looked out over the moon-washed flow of the river. The night was quiet, no sound other than the crickets and frogs. Phillip, wide awake, went to bed. He couldn't sleep, thinking of Martha. What was life all about? Was it just mutual satisfaction in a tent under an African moon? Three more nights and she would be on her way back to America, far, far away. The thought made Phillip feel lonely. She was right. On his own at almost thirty-seven he was going to go through the rest of his life by himself. He had never had a mother. Now the chances were, he would never have his own family. What was the point of a life without a family? Craig and Jojo were lucky. They were going to have a baby. A child that would be with them for the rest of their lives. In the next compartment, Jacques snorted in his sleep and made a noise that sounded like a chuckle. He was dreaming happy dreams. Making love to Martha was mutually satisfying. It was a roll in the hay. Maybe a four-night stand and then nothing, their lovemaking in a tent under the African moon no more than a dream. Feeling lonely but contented, Phillip drifted away into sleep.

2

The day before the tour was due to break up Martha asked if she could stay. It was five days before Phillip's thirty-seventh birthday, a birthday he had expected to spend on his own.

"We can't leave it now, Phillip. I'll tell the office I'm sick. Or ask for a month's unpaid leave. We're all friends in the office. Like family. They'll understand. You can show me more of Zimbabwe than the Zambezi Valley. When does your next tour arrive?"

"Not for a month or two when it's the northern hemisphere summer season. Then the tours are back-to-back and we operate both our buses."

"There you are, you see. Plenty of time for both of us. We make love so well together. You're not selfish like so many men. You wait for me to be satisfied. It's a great start. You could fly over to America. Do some promoting for your business. There's always a travel expo going on somewhere in America. It'll be good for business. Good for us. I can pay your airfare. I know you Zimbabweans can't use your money out of the country. What I love most about our relationship is you can't say I'm after your money. Can you get money out of the country?"

"Not a cent. Unless you do it illegally. Exchange control is strict. And the exchange rate on the black market is ridiculous. But you don't have to worry about paying my airfare. Have you heard of Ben Crossley?"

"Wasn't he a Hollywood actor?"

"He was also my maternal grandfather. For years he lost touch with my mother after he left his wife and family and drifted across to America. Randall traced him after going back to England in search of his roots. When Grandfather Crossley died after a long illness he left the two of us his fortune. My half is in a well-managed trust in Jersey, an island owned by the British crown in the English Channel. I've never touched any of it. The money just accumulates. Why I can carry on living in Zimbabwe without fear of being penniless when I grow old."

"How much have you got in your little trust, Phillip?"

"A couple of million. Haven't checked for a while. You don't broadcast to Mugabe you have money overseas or he'll force you to bring it into the country, or kick you out if you don't."

"A couple of million Zimbabwe dollars won't look after your old age."

"A couple of million pounds will. Four million US dollars."

"That is a fortune."

"Grandfather Crossley said the most difficult thing with money was not to make it but hang on to it. He was careful with his money. He asked us to look after it for his descendants. Which I will. Money gives you the feeling of security. Gives you freedom, its only true advantage. Leaving us his money was part of my grandfather's atonement for abandoning his family."

"So not only are you a good lover, Phillip. You're a rich lover."

"Why are you laughing?"

"I thought I was giving you a way out by going to America... Can I stay for a month?"

"Nothing would give me more pleasure."

And a week ago he had not even met Martha Poland. Sometimes life went so fast it took your breath away.

"What's so funny?"

"Life. You never know what's coming."

They broke camp at first light. Munya and Sedgewick were to stay on site. There was a chance of another tour being booked before the high season. Jacques drove the bus with the tourists to arrive at Harare Airport three hours before the flight to America. Phillip and Martha took the truck. They had all eaten breakfast. The grand tour for Phillip and Martha started at Lake Kariba with a slow trip down the lake on the car ferry to the Victoria Falls. They were beginning to get to know each other. Phillip had seen the Falls many times but they were still spectacular. An ocean of water going over a lip that was more than a mile long into the gorge. The sound of thunder. By the time they drove into Harare to see Craig and Jojo they both knew there was more to their affair than a run around the African bushveld. Each day they found more in common. Music: both enjoyed classical. Books: both liked reading a good novel that made them think. But most of all they both had a passion for nature. It was all going to be one big surprise for Craig to find his older brother with a girlfriend who was taking him to America.

When Jojo opened the door of her flat in the Avenues, Phillip knew immediately something was wrong. Both Craig and Jojo had long faces. They looked tired. Agitated. As if they hadn't slept properly for a week. Phillip introduced Martha.

"Can we both stay the night?"

There was silence. Jojo began to cry.

"I'm sorry. Have I done something?" Martha, standing next to Phillip, looked uncomfortable.

"He won't let us marry. Won't accept *lobola*. Wants me to get rid of the baby."

"Why, Jojo?"

"My father is old-fashioned. Doesn't want me to marry out of the tribe."

"Is it racial?"

"Probably. My mother is beside herself. She's his fourth wife. My father is nearly eighty. He doesn't understand the modern world. Doesn't want to understand it. Wants everything to stay the same. Be what it was in the times before the Zulus conquered Mashonaland, before you English came to our country. He won't accept the world has changed. All his four wives are still alive. They all do what they are told. And that is meant to include us children."

"What are you going to do?"

"I'm not going to have an abortion. Phillip, my father wants me to kill my baby... I'm sorry. Come in. Of course you can both spend the night. How did the tour go?"

"So what are you going to do, Craig?"

"We're thinking of going to live in England. Do the fundraising instead of looking after the people. It all starts with money, so we'll still have jobs."

"Won't he change his mind?"

"Never. He'd rather die than see me married to Craig. He always said my good education would end in disaster. My mother persuaded him. She was younger then. When she could get her own way. I'm sorry. Would you like some tea? Are you American, Martha? I recognise the accent."

They walked through into the lounge and all sat down looking at each other. Phillip looked from his brother to Jojo, who seemed to be in despair. Martha looked uncomfortable. There was nothing to say. The pregnancy was forcing Jojo to choose between her family and Craig. To choose between Shona culture and the culture of the colonials, a world she had found through her education that had finally taken her to university and her meeting with Craig. Phillip got up and rested his hand on Jojo's shoulder. She was a small, fragile girl with a beautiful face.

"I'll go and make us all some tea. I know my way around your kitchen."

"Would you, Phillip? My mind is numb. I can barely think... What's it like in England?"

"Cold. Wet. And very small. Green. Very green. The countryside is beautiful. You'll love England, Jojo. It'll be a whole new experience... There isn't any milk." Phillip had gone into the small kitchen and was looking around.

"You'll have to use powdered milk."

"You won't have any trouble getting yourselves married in England. Your mother and our father will love it, Craig. Give them something to do. Dad's biggest problem, now he doesn't have the farm, is boredom. He says he never has anything to do. Nothing to think about. Nothing to plan. Each day exactly the same. Your child will be born in England with British citizenship. Which, with all the chaos in Africa, isn't a bad thing. If he's born in Zimbabwe he won't be able to claim British citizenship. He'd be a second generation Crookshank not to be born in England. The world is so damn volatile... Tea or coffee for you, Martha?"

"Coffee. And one spoonful of powdered milk. When's the baby due, Jojo? I so envy you. I'm thirty-seven and childless. Life is pointless without children. Is it a boy or a girl?"

"We don't know."

"Doesn't matter so long as the child is healthy. Has all the right toes and fingers. It's a great void in my life having no children. You don't know how lucky you are. It'll all work out. Life always does. Think positive. It's your life and the child's. Not your parents'... I shouldn't be interfering. I'm sorry. We Americans are far too full of our own opinions."

"Don't worry. I like what you say. You will stay with us? You can tell a Shona girl all about America. Take my mind off my father. Why is life so difficult?"

"Because it is life. And being Shona or American doesn't make the slightest bit of difference. Don't you agree, Phillip?"

"Why don't I take all of us to dinner at Meikles? You two are going to get married whatever happens. You're going to have a baby. Let's celebrate. If your father is eighty years old the future isn't his problem. Things change. King Lobengula of the Zulu Matabele lost out to Cecil Rhodes and us British. Now the colonials have lost out to Mugabe and you Shonas. Africa will be a very different place when your child is grown up. So will the world. Whether for better or worse no one knows. It's all part of evolution. Who knows, greedy man will most likely blow himself to pieces. So let's enjoy ourselves while we can."

When they reached Harare's premier hotel two hours later, it was half past seven in the evening. The main restaurant was half full as they went in from the adjacent bar to claim their table. All of them were hungry, smiles back on their faces, and the chit-chat and banter began.

Martha Poland looked from Phillip to his brother Craig and to Jojo, not sure what to make of the situation, careful not to voice an opinion on a subject that had nothing to do with her. It was the first time she had heard of *lobola*. The idea of a man paying the father for the daughter was foreign to Martha. In her way of life a father gave away his daughter. In British history the father had to pay a dowry to his future son-in-law if he wanted her to have a good marriage. Cultures were different. The man had four wives which made Martha wonder. Four women, married to the same man, all with their own agendas, sounded like a recipe for permanent discord. Martha's late father would have said the man was out of his cotton-picking mind. In the Poland family, with a mother and father both with short tempers, the result was bad enough with two of them. Growing up, Martha always remembered her parents bickering. Poor Jojo, growing up with a father and four women, all of them rivals.

"How many brothers and sisters did you have, Jojo?"

"Thirty-two, of which twenty-three are still alive. Two were killed in the war of liberation. The other seven died of AIDS-related illnesses."

"I'm sorry to hear that. AIDS is terrible."

"They think a quarter of my people are HIV positive, though most of them have not been tested. It's worse than any war of liberation as we can't see the end of it."

"They'll find a cure. They find a cure for every illness."

"They haven't found one for cancer. Anyway, at least I don't have the fear of my child being HIV positive. Craig and I are faithful to each other. And we've both tested negative for HIV. That's something I tried to explain to my father but he wouldn't listen. His mind wanders. What's it like living in America?"

"Much the same as anywhere, I'd guess. Crowded in the cities. Beautiful in the countryside. We Americans sell our culture through television. You must have seen it. All our stories have been written for the world to see. One of our major exports comes out of Hollywood and the television studios."

"Have you enjoyed your visit to Zimbabwe?"

"Even more since I met Phillip."

"I'd like to visit America."

"You never know. You and Craig may one day come over for a visit."

Martha, to make her point, smiled at Phillip and held out her hand on top of the table. Phillip took it, stroking the palm with his index finger. The small black girl with the tragic face looked from her to Phillip and back again. She was different, making Martha wonder what a child born to two so different cultures would grow up into, the thought strange and vaguely uncomfortable: the old racial divide rearing its ugly head. Travel was an eye-opener in more ways than one. She brought her right hand back towards the food on her plate, picking up her knife and fork. The steak was as good as anything she had ever eaten.

"You're right, Phillip. Zimbabwean beef is the best tasting beef in the world."

The compliment made Jojo smile, the hand moment forgotten. Martha ate her food in silence, sipping at her wine. She was wondering what Phillip would find in America, a man of English origin who had grown up in Africa, speaking Shona as well as he spoke English. Could there be a future for her with Phillip? Was it not too late for a third marriage with children? What she wanted most was a family. To grow old with a man, surrounded by their children. Grandchildren. A life fulfilled. All the money she made in her world of advertising meant nothing without a real home and family. And the girl opposite her at the table was pregnant. Martha's envy was a physical torture. Life was a bitch. Thirty-seven, two marriages, both gone bitterly sour, and not a child to show for it. Every time, the men had said wait, neither wanting the responsibility of children while they were in their twenties. Faithful to their agreement, Martha had diligently taken her contraceptive pill and look what had happened. Both of them, once they had fucked her out of their system, had turned to other women, lying, cheating behind her back until both marriages had exploded into nothing. Sitting at a dinner table in the middle of Africa, Martha wondered what life was all about. A meal, a few drinks was so temporary. Smiles and laughter but nothing tangible. A brief moment to escape from the multitude of life's problems. She was getting old. Her biological clock was ticking past the hour. And what was Phillip thinking? Was she just another lay? Another conquest soon to be forgotten?"

"Penny for your thoughts, Martha."

"You wouldn't even want to know."

At the end of the long dining room a band was setting up their instruments. Craig was telling a story about how much good the Non-Government Organisation he worked for was doing. Martha smiled, enjoying his enthusiasm. The NGO was the new big career to follow in a troubled world where people gave to charity to assuage their guilty consciences for being better off. Giving made people feel good. There was nothing wrong with it. From Craig's story the problem was in the distribution, getting the money to where it was needed without wasting too much of it on overheads and corruption. When food was given to Mugabe's people it had to look as if it was coming from his government, not some foreign charity with a hidden political agenda. By the sound of it, even giving was complicated. When Jojo picked up on the story, Martha's mind wandered away into her thoughts. The day-long trip down Lake Kariba; the stay at the Victoria Falls hotel; their passionate lovemaking; the pleasure of mutual satisfaction. After a few more days of it, would Phillip want to see more of her? What did either of them know about the other? Just a few weeks ago neither of them knew the other even existed. Was there ever more in life than a day-to-day existence? When Martha put down her knife and fork she had cleaned her plate. Phillip was telling a story about an evening at the Centenary East club, when it was attacked by terrorists. Jojo looked at Phillip with something close to hatred, making Martha concentrate on what was going wrong. Craig was squirming in his chair.

"My brother was killed in that action. And they weren't terrorists, Phillip. They were freedom fighters. Were you in the club yourself that night?"

"Fortunately not. I'm sorry. I had no idea. A good friend of mine was killed that night. I hate war. It's so pointless. No one wins when you look back."

"Can we change the subject?"

"By all means."

Martha excused herself and asked the waiter to show her the way to the bathroom. The future of Craig, Jojo and their child was going to be full of conflict. Martha took her time. When she got back to the table the tension had gone. The conversation was back to trivia, all of them treading carefully. The band was playing. On the surface, the replay of what Jojo had called 'the war of liberation' was over. Mentally, Martha wished both of them luck. But it had made Martha think. Would the girl go back to her family in the village and marry who she was told to marry? Abort the child? Or would the two of them go to England and make a happy family? Anyway, she told herself as the waiter put down the pudding in front of her, it was none of her business. Thankfully. Homogenous societies were much easier. The world, with all its emigration, was creating a host of new problems. Among them religion, race and the disparity of wealth. Martha shook her head, glad she wasn't a politician. On the trip down the lake, Phillip had told her that in Africa the best way to handle politics was to keep the hell out of the way. Despite the apparent banter at the table, Martha could feel the undercurrent of friction between Phillip and Jojo that was making them all uncomfortable. To Phillip, the brother was a terrorist who had attacked and killed his friend without provocation. To Jojo, her brother was a hero who had fought for the liberation of his people from the yoke of colonialism. What was right to Jojo was wrong to Phillip. Most of the colonials had packed up and gone somewhere else to live, according to Phillip. The thought made Martha smile.

"Can we book our flights to America tomorrow? We can go to the American embassy with your passport and get you a multiple visa. You've shown me your country. Now it's my turn to show you mine. The Midwest is perfect in any direction you look. We're in the middle. That was a lovely dinner, Phillip. All the travel has made me tired. What I want most of all now is a long, peaceful sleep and a cuddle."

The party broke up. Phillip paid the bill with his credit card and they all went home. Back in the flat, they quickly went to bed. In the dark of the night, they lay on their backs, neither of them speaking for a while.

"That was just terrible, Martha. I wasn't thinking, bringing up that story. I had no idea her brother was a terrorist, let alone killed in an attack in the Centenary. There were two clubs in the Centenary, exclusive to the white farmers. My family used both of them. Squash and tennis at the East club, cricket at the West. They were part of my upbringing."

"Wouldn't it be better for you to leave Zimbabwe? Leave it all behind?"

"Probably."

"You'll love America. The Midwest is so peaceful. You could get a job. Your grandfather was an American citizen. You could start a tourist business. There are so many options."

"If they want to be together they'll have to go and live in England. That was ugly. For a moment, she wanted to kill me."

"Or she could abort the baby and go back to live among her people."

"What a terrible decision... Can we get on the plane tomorrow?"

"Hopefully. Come here. Hold me."

"I don't think I can make love."

"We'll see... There. How does that feel? You can't worry about other people's problems. They'll have to sort themselves out."

"I need comforting."

"That's what I'm here for, Phillip. We both need comforting. It's part of life."

They were up early in the morning. Martha packed just in case. She wanted to go, as soon as possible. When they arrived at the table for breakfast Jojo was waiting for Phillip.

"It wasn't your fault, Phillip. I shouldn't have jumped down your throat. He was my favourite of all the brothers."

"We're all manipulated by other people. Especially politicians. They say everything will be better if we follow their cause. In the days after the Second World War the British were short of American dollars. They had to pay back all the money they had borrowed in the three years before the Americans came into the war. In those days, most of the tobacco was grown in America, payable for in US dollars. Little Rhodesia grew some tobacco but not enough. My father's generation was encouraged to go out to the self-governing colony of Southern Rhodesia to grow tobacco. Rhodesia was part of the sterling block. No need for US dollars. Dad was told that after a five-year apprenticeship to teach him how to grow and cure tobacco he would be offered a Crown Land farm at seven and sixpence an acre. Thousands of acres. A young man's dream in England where they all live on top of each other. A young man just out of the navy had no idea he was being used. Or the land when he got it would cost him ten pounds an acre to stump out the trees and prepare the bushveld for cultivation. There was just the land. Nothing else. No dams were required, unlike Zimbabwe, where it didn't rain for six months. No roads. No barns. No housing for himself or his labour force. Everything had to be done from scratch. It took Dad seventeen years to make World's View profitable and pay back the debts he had incurred building it up. Then the place looked good. Along with three thousand other tobacco farms that had been dug out of the bush. And then came your people's manipulation, Jojo. People like your brother were recruited into a liberation army, promising the people prosperity, promising them the newly productive land. But now, who is prospering? Are the people of Zimbabwe better off than they were? Freedom isn't much good to anyone when they're starving. And if they confiscate the rest of those three thousand farms, God help them. A few politicians, the ones who survived the assassinations and did what Mugabe told them, have prospered. But the economy, without the white man's knowledge, is headed for destruction. Yes, in the end it will come back again. People survive their politicians. Your brother died to make a few people rich. My father was persuaded to leave England so that Britain could pay its tobacco in sterling and further the British Empire. Who was right and who was wrong is a matter of opinion. I was a damn fool last night. I wasn't thinking of your feelings. I should have been. I can't expect you to accept my apology for what I said, any more than I can apologise for colonialism. Good and bad came out of it. The right answer is most likely for us whites to leave Zimbabwe and get out of your way. Let you run your own country. Let you have your pride back again. But it happened, Jojo. And we can't change what happened. You two love each other. Don't let my stupidity last night come between you. You both have a child to think of. I was lucky to inherit a fortune from my mother's father, a mother I have missed all my life. If some of my money will help you and Craig to settle peacefully in England, you only have to ask. That's what money is for. Helping friends and family. I'm sorry, Jojo. Truly sorry. You have every right to hate me."

They tried to smile, tried to look happy, tried to enjoy each other's company. But hanging over all of them was the Damoclean sword of racism. Martha finished her coffee and looked around the room. It was time to go. For all of them.

"First stop the American embassy and your visa, Phillip."

WHEN AN HOUR later Phillip proved to the girl in the embassy his grandfather was Ben Crossley, he was given his visa. There was nothing like fame, particularly the fame of a Hollywood actor, to make things easy. The girl gushed at meeting Ben Crossley's grandson. Martha gave the address of her apartment where Phillip would be staying and they were out the door with the visa stamped into Phillip's British passport. The next stop was the travel agent. The plane leaving that night for London was only three-quarters full, the main tourist season not having started. From London they would fly to New York and then on to Kansas City. A long journey but it didn't matter. Getting Phillip to come as soon as possible to America was what was important. They were smiling when they left the travel agent. Martha's return ticket had been changed for the flight. Back in the centre of Harare, the streets teeming with people, they found a coffee shop and went inside. Neither of them wanted to go back to the flat in the Avenues. They took a table close to the window.

"One thing I wanted to ask you. When your father was recruited to go out to the colonies, why was tobacco so important to the British?"

"Dad says the tax on pipe tobacco and cigarettes paid for the British national health service brought in by the new Labour government that had replaced Churchill's Conservatives."

"Didn't they know tobacco was bad for the health?"

"If they did, they didn't care. They knew smoking was an addiction. They could tax cigarettes to the heavens and people would still buy them. Much better than income tax. The more the people smoked, the more the government made, and people didn't moan so much as they did at income tax. If they had increased lower income tax that would have made the Labour Party unpopular with the emerging middle class. Ironic, don't you think? You let people smoke and make themselves sick so you can give them a free health service."

"The world is nuts."

"You can say that again."

"I notice you don't smoke, Phillip."

"Of course I don't. My father was a tobacco grower. The toxic smell of nicotine in the grading shed when the tobacco came out of the curing barns was enough to put you off smoking for life. Another irony. Sometimes life is just plain stupid. That tart on the counter looks good. Let us eat tart and forget about sin tax and the French Revolution."

"Maybe it was downright hypocrisy using the tobacco tax to fund the health service."

"I doubt it. Politicians aren't that clever. They can only see what is right in front of them. What will further the party. Further their careers. The one thing politicians crave more than anything is being popular. Except for people like President Robert Mugabe whose craving is for power. I hate politicians of all shapes and sizes, the way I hate lawyers. They all twist the truth to suit themselves, the lawyers to make money, the politicians to get power. And all in the name of democracy and the rule of law. Winston Churchill said democracy was a dreadful way to elect a government to run a country. He just couldn't think of a better one. There are theocracies where the state is run by the church. Hereditary kingships. Dictators of all stripes. In history some of the best rulers have been hereditary benevolent kings able to lead their people and their armies from the front. And then you have one man one vote that goes by the name of democracy. Government of the people by the people. The average man electing a government to give the average man as much as possible. Or so he thinks. The reality is we have no idea of the capabilities of those we elect to govern. Take your pick. What does the average man with his average elected politicians know about the pitfalls of running a multi-billion economy or keeping us safe? It's why man plunges so regularly into arguments, wars and financial crises. We haven't found honest people to govern us and never will. Just look back at the twentieth century: two world wars; a great depression; communism fighting capitalism in Korea; Vietnam for you Americans. And who knows what's coming next? I ran away from it all, Martha. Ran away into the African bush. To the peace and quiet of the Zambezi Valley. But I won't be able to hide forever. The quiet of the big river. That's been my paradise. But once the new government confiscated my father's farm I knew it wouldn't last. So, here we are, going to America, the adopted land of my grandfather. But, whatever happens to me in the future, I will always long for Africa, the place of my birth. So will Jojo and Craig."

"Who was it who said, 'let them eat cake'?"

"It was supposed to be Marie Antoinette, talking about the starving peasants in France who the aristocracy that ruled the country was ignoring. So the people took over and chopped off their heads."

Sad at Phillip's melancholy, Martha watched him walk up to the counter and come back with two small plates of tart.

"Lots of cream on top, Martha. Can we make a rule, you and me? To never again talk of politics."

"We can try. You must have read a lot of books during your stay in the Zambezi Valley."

"You can say that again. The only form of entertainment. How's your tart?"

"Perfect."

"You've got cream all over your mouth."

"You want to lick it off?"

"Not in public!"

Martha used her tongue slowly to gather the cream, all the time looking at Phillip, both of them thinking of sex.

"Are you a member of the mile-high club, Phillip?"

"Not yet. When the lights are dim in the cabin tonight we can sneak into one of the toilets."

"Is that a promise?"

"As sure as I'm eating this tart."

They smiled gently at each other. They were happy. More than anything else, Martha wanted to fall in love, before it was all too late. Dimly, at the end of the tunnel, she was seeing a light. Their ages were right. The sex was right. They both had money. In America, Martha could offer Phillip sanctuary. From what she had seen of Zimbabwe, the white settlers were no longer wanted.

"Do you want children, Phillip?"

"Yes I do. Someone's got to inherit Ben Crossley's money. You know, she couldn't believe he was my grandfather."

"Why don't I stop taking the pill?"

"Aren't we jumping the gun? A month ago we didn't even know each other."

"Don't you feel something special? They say you know straight away when you meet the right person. We have the right chemistry. Oh, and if you think I'm after your grandfather's money I'm not. I own my apartment free of mortgage. I have a strong share portfolio spread right across the market. Like you, I don't waste my money flying first class. A few more years at my current salary and I'll never have to worry about money. Which makes me comfortable for both of us in this world where people want you for what you've got, not for who you are. People with ulterior motives. I've met a few of those lately, some much younger than myself who see me as a financial opportunity. On that score neither of us has to worry... Say something, Phillip."

"You want some more tart?" He was smiling at her, his eyes twinkling.

"We're not going to make love in the toilet?"

"Probably not. We'll leave the mile-high club for other people."

"I shouldn't have brought up going off the pill."

"Why not, Martha? Let the gods decide. Maybe we can't have children."

"So you don't mind?"

"As I said, let the gods decide. If I was concerned, I would have been using my own contraceptive. To make sure. As you were inferring with the money, can we really trust anyone? We think we can. We hope we can. But we only find out later when things go wrong."

"Do things always go wrong?"

"They don't have to, but they usually do. And no, I'm not a cynic. Just a realist. An appreciator of the human condition and how life works. You take the good with the bad and hope for the best. Too often we try and make things happen the way we want. Which is what you're doing. You want children. So do I. So we'll let the gods decide our fate. We're not naïve children anymore, which is good. Maybe we've both found a little wisdom by the age of thirty-seven. I hope Craig and Jojo have a little wisdom to dig themselves out of their predicament. But life is one big chance. If my mother had not been killed by a pride of lions my father would not have married Craig's mother, and neither Craig nor my sister Myra would have been born, and Jojo would not be pregnant. A friend of mine once said that if in the year fifty thousand BC someone had said 'not tonight thank you, darling' most of us, if not all of us, wouldn't be here."

"Will you want to visit Myra in California?"

"Of course. She's my sister. Blood is always thicker than water... We'd better go back to the flat and do what we can for Craig and Jojo before we go to the airport."

"You don't think they went to work?"

"They said they were calling in sick."

Phillip used his finger to get the last of the cream off his plate, sucking his index finger as he looked into her eyes.

"Waste not, want not. My father's words. During the war, everything was scarce in England. They learned as children never to waste food. He said it was the best lesson of his life."

They left the coffee shop and walked around Harare, ending their walk on a bench in the gardens of Africa Unity Square. When they drove back to the apartment there was no sign of Jojo or Craig, not even a note.

Three hours later, when Phillip was planning to drive himself to the airport and leave the truck in the airport garage, they heard the key going into the lock of the door. Jojo and Craig came in, both of them smiling.

"Did you go to work?" The worry on Phillip's face had turned into a smile.

"To resign. We've both resigned. We're going to England. We're leaving tomorrow before this whole mess destroys both of us. I phoned Dad. He's going to meet us at Heathrow Airport. Sorry, you'll have to cut your visit short."

"We're booked to fly to America tonight."

"Well, there's a thing. Let's have a drink to celebrate."

"Jojo can't drink being pregnant with my nephew or my niece, but we can. Who knows when we four shall meet again? In thunder, lightning, or in rain? But all is going to be well."

While Martha joined in the celebration, her feeling of guilt at fibbing to Phillip began to wane. She had been off the pill the first time she made love to him, having stopped taking it months before during a long period of drought without a lover. He had not used a condom so why should she feel guilty? She had brought up the subject. Cleared the air if she should fall pregnant, her next period due at the end of the week. She had covered her tracks. That was what was important. Life was never plain sailing. A girl had to use her brains. The most important thing was to get herself pregnant before her age made it all too late. But it wasn't easy, the lie coming back to flip her stomach each time her mind thought of a pregnancy. It wasn't only a question of 'not tonight thank you, darling', fifty thousand years ago. In all their histories there would be subterfuge. Life, when Martha thought about it, was pretty basic. All the fancy stuff like love, honour, duty, righteousness, was made up by man to cover his sinful tracks. The only basis of life was procreation. Making another generation to carry on the same old game. And then she asked herself another question. Did she want a child for companionship or to look after her when she was old? Were children just an insurance plan for the future? Was the fundamental basic instinct of needing children one's own self-preservation? The selfishness that Martha tried never to think about. Was caring about other people a ruse to make sure people cared for her? However much she tried to think her way round it, she had still lied to Phillip. In her moment of truth she hated herself. Despised who she was.

"What's the matter, Martha? Having second thoughts? I don't have to come with you if you don't want me to."

"Of course I do. I was miles away. There's so much to think about.

Introducing you to all my friends. Showing you the sites of Kansas City. There's so much to be done."

Smiling happily, Phillip turned away to carry on the conversation with his brother. For a moment Martha had panicked: to tell him or not to tell him she had lied. That was the question. If she kept it to herself and at the end of the week she found out she was pregnant, she would have to live with her guilt for the rest of her life. Jojo looked miles away. It made Martha smile to herself ruefully. If she thought she had a problem, what about Jojo? Thinking of leaving her parents, her country and her culture for the rough and tumble of modern Europe. It made Martha feel sorry for Jojo, countering her own moment of despair; other people's bigger problems making her feel better with herself. She drank down her drink and held out her glass for another one. Craig filled it up with wine, not missing a beat in his conversation with his brother. They were talking about their father in England. About Craig's mother and Phillip's stepmother, a woman with the name of Bergit.

"Was your mother German, Craig?"

"No. Not at all. She was named after a German. Something to do with my grandfather before the war. How's the wine?"

"Perfect."

"We're all going on our travels."

"Certainly looks like it."

"When I said we would raise money for the charity they were happy to let us go and work in England. It's all working out just fine. Cheers, Martha."

"Good luck to you both, Craig."

"It's all going to work out just fine."

"I hope so. I really, really hope so."

3

_W_ hen they left later in the truck to go to the airport Phillip was thinking to himself. Did he really want to father a child with a woman he barely knew, a woman from a different country? They had a common language but that was about all. The only thing Phillip knew about America was what he had seen on television. And that wasn't often. There was no television in the Zambezi Valley. Just books. Chats round the campfire at night with passing strangers. Customers who would most likely never come again. Holidays abroad for most of them were 'been there, done that one, don't have to do it again'. Once they had seen wild elephants they wanted something else to add to their list. It was all about impressing their friends back home; another place to say they had been to, to add to their bragging list in a fast-paced world that was all about spending money, about showing off. The odd visitor was more interesting but most of them weren't. They drank themselves into a stupor at night around the campfire, something they could have done just as successfully back home at a fraction of the cost. And now Phillip himself was going to America. To a big city where they all lived on top of each other. Would a child make any difference? Even with all his grandfather's money, did he want the responsibility of bringing up a child now he was approaching forty? She had asked him if he wanted a child and he had answered spontaneously. On impulse. Not giving himself time to think through the reality, the everyday effort of bringing up a child. Anyway, he thought, his mind relaxing, if Martha hadn't got herself pregnant by the age of thirty-seven she probably never would; not after two husbands. Going to America was going to be fun. Martha was going to be fun.

When the loudspeaker called the flight they all stood up. Phillip shook hands with his brother.

"Give my love to the family in England, Craig. Let me know the date of your wedding. Who knows, big brother may just pitch up. You two have a happy life together. That's all anyone can hope for. It's you two and your children. I'm sure at your age you'll want more than one. Look after my brother, Jojo. Once you're married and the kid's born your father will relent. Mark my word. He'll want to see his grandchild as much as anyone. And thanks for looking after us. The world's a small place these days, so we'll all keep in touch."

In among the bustle of people, they got on the plane. They had two seats next to the window, Martha sitting furthest from the aisle. The door to the Boeing 747 closed. The flight attendants took their seats. The big aircraft rolled out onto the runway.

"Do you think I should have told Dad we were touching down in England? Seems silly to ask him to go to the airport just to say hello."

"Don't worry. You'll be going over for your brother's wedding."

"And if you get pregnant?"

"Then we'll have to see... Are you excited?"

"About what?"

"Going to America, silly."

Phillip smiled. Tried to relax. The aircraft took off. Whatever was going to happen it was now out of his hands. 'Let the gods decide, Phillip Crookshank.' Feeling better, he took hold of Martha's hand. It was warm and comforting. A small, soft hand. Maybe, just maybe, their life together had just begun. At that moment, the Zambezi Valley seemed far, far away. Was the African adventure that had been his life up to now finally over? Was cricket, the sport that had captivated his youth, a thing of the past? No one in America played cricket. It was all baseball and American football, sports that for Phillip had absolutely no appeal. When he thought back to his years at Rhodes University in South Africa studying for his degree in history, it was all so far away. It made Phillip smile. A history degree. About as much use in the world of making money as a sick headache. At least he had learned about American history in among the rest of the history of the English-speaking world, the common bond that had brought Martha into his life. And history, like life when you looked at it properly, was pretty ordinary. What was the difference between George Washington and Robert Mugabe? They both wanted to get rid of the British. Free themselves in their own pursuit of wealth and power. And both of them had succeeded. Like countries and civilisations they all came and went, leaving behind their progeny to make a new mess. The British had come and gone. Now it was the Americans. Who in the world was going to be next?

"What are you thinking about, Phillip? You're quiet as a mouse."

"The irony of flying from one ex-British colony to another one. You want some of those dinky bottles of wine on that girl's trolley?"

Phillip put up his hand to catch the eye of the flight attendant. On a long flight in Phillip's experience one either slept or drank. Flying was boring; pinned in a chair with the back of someone's seat you couldn't even see to stare at. In the old days they went around the world sedately in ships. His father had gone from England to Rhodesia by ship, the journey taking a glorious six weeks of fun and games and getting to know people with a common purpose in life.

"Red or white, sir?"

"Make it four small bottles of that Nederburg Cabernet."

The bottles with the glasses were passed over the passenger sitting on their right.

"Enjoy your flight. Dinner will be served in an hour."

Phillip unscrewed the cap on the small bottle of wine and poured a little glass for Martha, and one for himself. He had let down both of the flap tables at the back of the seats in front of them.

"Cheers, Martha."

"Cheers, Phillip."

The wine tasted good. The best of South African red. They were smiling. They were happy. What else, Phillip asked himself, could a man want in his life: a glass of good wine, a woman he found attractive, and nothing, hopefully, to worry about. They were high in the sky. In a world of their own.

"You're grinning your head off. Are you thinking of that mile-high club?"

"Not really. But I was thinking of us. Let's get tipsy. Makes the journey go quicker."

"Why ever not?"

By the time they finished their fourth glass of wine they were having a giggle. The old man sitting on Phillip's right was fast asleep. Through the peephole of a window they could see the wing of the aircraft that was holding them up in the sky. Martha had put up their tables so Phillip could lean across her to look out of the window at the stars. The stars felt close, a beautiful sight. It made Phillip feel part of a great universe, something vast: he could see the moon; the Milky Way, like a bucket of fresh, frothy milk spread over his view of a perfect night. In the cabin, the main lights had been dimmed. Up the plane, the occasional reading light shone above the seats. During the flight attendant's last visit with the drinks trolley, Phillip had taken four more dinky bottles of wine, enough to see them far into their journey.

"I've got to go to the bathroom. How do we wake up the old man?"

"We try to slide round his knees."

"Is that possible?"

"Must you go?"

"Unless we want a puddle."

"I'll go with you... Excuse me. My lady has to go to the toilet."

The old man moved his feet, squashing his knees against the side of his seat. Phillip got up and pushed past him. He smiled sleepily at Phillip as he passed.

"Won't be long. Sorry to wake you."

"When you got to go, you got to go."

Phillip reached the toilet first and opened the door. Martha went inside. Phillip looked round to see if anyone was looking. When he looked inside, Martha was sitting on the loo. She was smiling at him. Phillip slid inside. With the door closed behind him, Phillip waited. They both knew what they were about to do. They had drunk just enough wine to lose their inhibitions. When Martha had finished she stood up and washed her hands in the basin, Phillip took her from behind. At first they were giggling until it became serious. Full of alcohol, it took both of them a long time to climax. When it was over, Martha turned round to Phillip. They hugged and hugged.

"We've just joined the club, Phillip."

"You can say that again."

"How long have we been?"

"I have no idea."

They went back to their seats. The old man was half asleep. They slipped through without saying a word.

"You want some more wine?"

"Of course I do, you idiot."

"Stop grinning like a Cheshire cat."

"That was perfect. Absolutely perfect. We'll drink the rest of the wine and then we'll sleep."

"Pass out more likely."

"What took you two so long?"

When Phillip looked round the old man was grinning at him.

"You have no idea how much I would give to have my youth back. To do it all over again. You two love each other. An old man can tell."

Feeling guilty, sheepish, caught with their pants down, they tried to contain their giggles. They were so happy Phillip thought he was going to burst. They touched glasses, drank, all the time looking into each other's eyes. Then they kissed, softly, their mouths tasting of wine. When Phillip turned off the overhead light, the wine was finished. Holding Martha's right hand in his left, Phillip drifted away into sleep. He was back in the valley. He was young. The girl was running ahead of him through the bushes. Phillip ran and ran. Before he could see who it was running away from him, Phillip woke with a jolt. His knee had knocked the flap-table, rolling the last dinky bottle of wine into his lap. His pants were wet from the remnants of the wine. Martha was fast asleep, her head tucked up to the drawn flap of the window. The old man was snoring contentedly. None of the lights were on over the seats, all the passengers sleeping. The whole aircraft was asleep. Outside, on the other side of the covered window, fire would be powering from the jet engines. Hoping the pilot was wide awake, Phillip drifted back into his sleep. There were no more dreams. The Zambezi Valley, along with the girl, had gone. When Phillip woke, the girl with the trolley was offering him tea or coffee. His pants were still wet from the wine. Two hours later, after breakfast, the plane touched down at Heathrow Airport for refuelling. They both had mini hangovers, about the size of the small wine bottle that had tipped in the night over Phillip's trousers. When they got off the plane, the red wine on his dark trousers was not visible. It was strange for Phillip to be so close to his father. He went to a phone booth and dialled his home. There was no answer. Back in the plane, they waited.

"Do they give you a certificate or something?"

"What for, Martha?"

"Membership of the mile-high club."

"I can ask the flight attendant."

"Better not."

They were whispering. Smiling. Getting the giggles. The plane took off. Next stop New York. The old man had gone. The seat next to Phillip was vacant. Sitting in the aisle seat opposite was a young girl. She smiled at Phillip.

"My word, you've got a good tan. You didn't get that in England."

"The Zambezi Valley. I live in Zimbabwe."

"It's my first trip out of England. My fiancé lives in New York. He's an investment banker. We're going to get married when his divorce becomes final. He's a bit older than me. You mind if I move and sit next to you? I'm scared of flying."

Phillip looked at Martha, twisting his nose. It never stopped. When he looked round the young girl was sitting in the seat next to him.

"This is my wife, Martha. She's from America."

"Pleased to meet you."

The girl looked from Martha's left hand that was on the armrest and back at Phillip, her eyebrows now slightly raised.

"So, tell me, what do you do with yourself in Zimbabwe? If I talk, I'm not so frightened."

"Is he rich?"

"Oh, yes. Very rich. Why do you think I'm going to America when I'm frightened of flying? I'm just joking. My name is Libby. I'm a model. I model hats."

"How old are you, Libby?"

"I'm nineteen."

"This is Martha, Libby. I'm Phillip. I'm sure you'll enjoy the flight. You'd better move back to your proper place. They don't let passengers change their seats."

"Are you sure?"

"Absolutely certain."

The girl got up and moved back to the aisle seat, sitting down and staring in front of her.

"She was trying to come on to you. Can you believe it, Phillip?"

"She's just frightened of flying. I'm old enough to be her father."

When lunch was served two hours later the girl had struck up a conversation with a young man across the aisle. It all made Phillip smile. He pulled out one of last night's empty wine bottles from where he had stashed it in the pocket in front of his knees.

"You want some more wine?"

"It's daylight. We're not alcoholics."

"Just passing the time. Flying goes on and on. I hate being locked into a seat. Are you going to see any of the others?"

"They'll all be back at work. It was fun to be with them in Zimbabwe. I'll leave it at that. People are different when they get home. One more stop and then it's home sweet home. Born and raised in Missouri. My father had a farm. Cattle and sheep. There's nothing sweeter than being raised on a farm."

"Is he still farming? Both of us raised on farms. No wonder we get on so well together. There's so much to find out about you."

"He died. Cancer."

"I'm sorry. Was it lung cancer?"

"He smoked forty cigarettes a day. No one accepted smoking was such a big problem in those days. A long, horrible death. Mom sold the farm and moved into the city. By then I had started working in Kansas City. The boys had moved off. Gone on their travels. Haven't seen much of either of them for years. Strange how you are so close as children and then you go your separate ways. They're older than me. I was my mother's late surprise. Just the three of us."

"Does she see them?"

"Sometimes. Hugo flew her to Tokyo last year."

"What does he do?"

"A civil servant, you call it. Why he's always somewhere else. He never married. Ford has two kids but doesn't live with them. Why are there so many broken marriages? No one commits for life anymore."

"Our modern world has lost the plot, according to Randall. He wrote about it. He hates the modern world. Why he ran away to the Isle of Man to write his books."

"What's he writing about?"

"Our story. The history of Rhodesia told through the eyes of people. That kind of fiction is more factual than a history book. He's happy. So is she. All that counts."

"What does she do all day while her husband sits and writes books?"

"Writes children's books. Artists marry artists if they're lucky. He misses Africa but not the politics. We can have one small bottle with lunch. One glass won't hurt us."

"That's the trouble. Good intentions turn to two. Then three. Then we're back in the toilet. It's chicken or beef. What you having?"

"The chicken. I wonder how many times in her life the flight attendant has asked 'tea or coffee', 'chicken or beef'. She must be in her late thirties. Another of those jobs that seem glamorous until you try them. On your feet dealing with people."

"What's the perfect job?"

"Randall says it's the life of an artist. Being creative. Making something that will last. He says most lives come to an end and that's it. And if you haven't produced any children no one thinks of you again. Or cares a damn... Thank you, kind lady. The chicken looks delicious."

"Thank you, sir."

"My pleasure."

"What are we going to call him?"

Taken by surprise, Phillip looked from the small tray the attendant had passed him and back to Martha. Then he smiled.

"We'll call him Miles. At school they'll call him mile-high Miles."

"Don't be silly. Children don't want to be told where their parents made them. They can't even imagine their parents having sex. Have you ever thought of your parents in bed together? The idea is horrible."

"Oh, but we know they were or we wouldn't be made. Anyway, I can't remember my mother."

"It must have been terrible."

"It was. Bergit did her best. But growing up without a parent leaves a gap so big it is never filled. It made me something of a loner. I enjoy being by myself in the quiet of the African bush. Listening to the doves. The bark of a buck at night. An owl calling. I always translate what the birds are saying into English. The African dove calls 'how's father, how's father'. I'm not kidding. It's in the bird book. Another bird sounds like she's saying, 'you're cute, you're cute'. Why, when I hear it, I know the bird is a lady... Why are you smiling, Martha?"

"Miles. We'll call him Miles. On one condition. We never, ever mention we're members of the mile-high club."

"Miles is a very nice name."

"Promise?"

"I promise. We will never tell him how he was made. He can find out that sort of thing in school."

"Do they teach sex in your schools?"

"All the time."

"You're kidding. All right. One glass of wine."

London to New York from the banks of the Zambezi River. The world had become so small. It made him think, the drone of the aircraft's engines in the background of his mind. When Phillip was growing up on World's View the thought of going to America would have blown his mind. Like the idea of flying to the moon. And now, when he looked at the moon it just wasn't the same. Bergit was telling the younger children, the Americans had been to the moon. They were sitting out round the fire next to the swimming pool in the cool of a winter's night. The coals were not yet ready to cook the steak. Craig was then five years old and Myra three. The whole family were having a *braai*, a tradition Phillip still cherished. The moon was big, with not a cloud in the night sky. Three layers of stars twinkling in the heavens. It was the most beautiful of sights for Phillip, until Bergit had reminded him an American astronaut had walked on the moon, and that had shattered Phillip's dream as a young boy. Since then Phillip had learned that wherever man was there were problems. The whole world, except South Africa, had applied economic sanctions against Rhodesia following Rhodesia's Unilateral Declaration of Independence from Great Britain that had left Rhodesia with a white government in a country where the whites were only ten per cent of the country's population. Phillip was fourteen years old. He had turned to his father as they all looked up at the bright moon.

"Was there any fighting over the moon?"

"There is. It's a competition between the Americans and the Russians."

"It doesn't look so beautiful anymore."

"You're nearly a man, son. You'll get used to it."

"I preferred not knowing."

"There are a lot of things in life you'll wish you didn't know."

"How big are the heavens?"

"Forever. Probably, people live there. It's conceit to think we are the only inhabited planet. It's better to live in ignorance. If there are people out there they probably won't like us."

"Why ever not?"

"People don't like each other unless they are getting something out of them. Why the whole world hates us Rhodesians. Buying our tobacco in sterling isn't important to the British anymore."

"Will we win?"

"Probably not."

And now, as he sat thinking back, he was almost in America. He would always remember Bergit talking about the man on the moon. He had known from school. Only looking up at what he had thought was an untarnished moon on that perfect September night had he realised the implications. It was in that moment that he had lost his innocence.

"What do we call her if it's a girl, Phillip?"

Phillip shook his head, bringing himself back to the present to his seat in an aeroplane, his wine glass in his hand.

"That's easy. We call her Miley. Miles or Miley. Cheers, Martha."

"Promise it's only one glass."

"I'll try. To Americans on the moon."

"What's that got to do with it?"

"It's a long, sad story of growing up... Why do people always want to fight with each other?"

When Phillip glanced at Martha she was no longer smiling.

"Are we about to have a fight, Phillip?"

"Not with you, silly."

Martha picked up her glass that Phillip had filled with red wine and drank. Phillip still had that faraway look on his face, a sad look. The girl at the end of the row was looking at him, making Martha wonder why young girls were so often interested in older men. It had to be for their money. If the girl knew Phillip had four million dollars of his grandfather's money in the bank it wouldn't even be a contest. Men, whatever age they were, preferred young, attractive women. If she got pregnant and had a baby, how long would she be able to hold on to Phillip? Would a Miles or a Miley keep him? Or would he stray like the rest of them? Probably. But she would have a child. Something that would always be hers. A part of her that no one could take away. Two hours out of New York, the thought of getting home was agitating. The break from work and life's responsibilities was about to be over. All those hassles. All those fights with people, trying to get her clients the most economic advertising. Advertising was all about getting results, increasing the client's profits. All the links in the chain that made the client's business grow. Get it wrong and you were out. Gone. Finished. Advertising was full of stress. Full of expectations and disappointments. The best of advertising programmes didn't always work. Sell, sell, sell. That's what the clients wanted.

"What are you looking so worried about, Martha?"

"Work. The constant stress of work. I'm almost home. We change planes and the next stop is Kansas City."

"Don't you enjoy your work?"

"Some of it. Most of it. It's the constant fear of getting a campaign wrong and costing my clients money. It's one big fight for market share. Keeping ahead of the competition. But it keeps me busy. Stops me thinking about myself and what I've done in this life. Do you ever think of what you are doing in life? What it's all about?"

"It's about enjoying each moment. Enjoying the present."

"She's still looking at you."

"That's her problem. I'm looking at you. Looking forward to seeing Martha in her own home surrounded by her own things. I want to get to know you better. To get to know Martha the person. Enjoying each other has to be more than outward appearances. This is the last glass of wine I shall ever have before visiting America."

"I wasn't on the pill when we first made love."

"Are you pregnant now?"

"I'm not sure. I'm sorry. I lied to you."

"Neither of us took precautions. We are both equally responsible. Smile, Martha. You're nearly home."

"You're not mad at me?"

"Whatever for? Let the gods decide. When are you due?"

"In a few days. Maybe a week."

He was smiling at her, one big grin on his face, making Martha happy, the young girl at the end of the row no longer a threat.

"How long do you think you'll be staying in America?"

"That depends on whether you're pregnant. If I'm a father of an American child they might let me stay. Stay in the present, Martha. Let the future take care of itself. It's much too early to judge if we love each other, a word with so many meanings."

"Be kind to me, Phillip."

The sweet smile he gave her made his eyes half close.

"I'm going to take a nap. Wake me when we're coming in to land."

Martha sat staring out of the window. There was nothing to see. The sky went on forever. And even if she was pregnant, would he want to join her and make a family? He ran a safari company in the heart of Africa, the bustle and stress of living in a city as foreign to him as the night sounds of Africa had been foreign and frightening to her. They were poles apart. Her desperation at getting pregnant had got the better of her. The chances were, if she did have a baby she'd end up a single mother like so many others in the wonderful new world of women's liberation. And when the child grew up she'd be left alone, a lonely old woman, of little or no importance to anyone. Sitting staring into space through the small, round window of the aeroplane made Martha wonder what life was all about. The old days of marriage for life were long gone. The moment one of them grew bored they looked for someone else to screw and moved on, the same old pattern of self-destruction in a world that only had one value, the value of money and what it could bring. If you had money, you could buy your way out of a problem, or so people thought. But did it make them happy? Life in the fast lane. Everyone in America wanted it. It was the American dream. But what had that dream given them? Materialism without feeling; life with people you called friends; everyone using each other the way she was using the man with his head on her shoulder, who she had picked up for pleasure on the banks of an African river; having sex; getting pregnant; having a complete stranger's baby. There were so many unanswerable questions.

But when Martha looked back, the other two husbands hadn't been much different. Just the place of the meeting with the same immediate mutual sexual satisfaction that had had them hopping into bed. And when they both found the sex was good they wanted more. They didn't want more of each other, just more of the sex. She had married both her husbands in the hope they wouldn't run away. Wouldn't leave her. But both of them did. One big affair after another without meaning. Showing off a husband to her single friends. And where had all that led to, she asked herself? Sitting looking out of an aircraft window, hoping or not hoping that she was pregnant. The former meant life with a meaning. The latter meant she'd be alone for the rest of her life as she moved forward into the horror of middle age.

Was there, or had there ever been a purpose in life, she kept asking herself, each moment of her thought leading her nowhere. Phillip, the new man in her life, was snoring, a fluting sound just below Martha's right ear. Martha was not sure what to make of the sound: was it making her happy or was it threatening, the rumbling of thunder for an uncertain future? There was an old saying her brothers were fond of repeating: 'Leave it in the bar. Don't bring it home.' Should she have left him in his safari camp instead of inviting him to America, the last straw to clutch before men stopped looking at her? Thirty-seven sucked. Seventeen, when she had first had sex, had been so different. At seventeen the world was her oyster. Men were everywhere, most of them giving her the look. At seventeen, Martha had not known the meaning of being lonely. Life was a constant whirl, with singles clubs or blind dates not in her lexicon. Phillip coughed in his sleep making her shiver. Who was this man? What would his family have in common with a bunch of Americans? When Martha looked down out of her right eye, Phillip's mouth had shut. The fluting had stopped. The drone of the engine went on. Maybe Phillip was right: 'Let the gods decide.' The thought made her begin to feel better. A baby would be nice, whether they called it Miles or Miley. Martha closed her eyes, looking for sleep. 'Let the gods decide.' Within a minute she was fast asleep next to Phillip.

When Martha woke from her troubled sleep the dreams she had dreamed were gone. The seatbelt light was on. They were about to land.

"Phillip! Wake up. Fasten your seatbelt. Welcome to America."

"Why'd you wake me? I had almost caught a tiger fish. A real big one."

"You were snoring."

"I'm sorry. Sleeping sitting up is a bugger. My word, life is exciting.

Who'd have thought this a couple of months ago? Poor Jacques. It isn't fair making my partner do all the work. Ever since grandfather died and left me his money, I've been getting lazy. Having a good nest egg takes the panic out of having to make money."

Two hours later they were back on a plane with a whole new load of passengers. Three and a half hours later, when they landed on Martha's home soil of Kansas City, it was half past five in the afternoon.

"I'm going to cook you supper. We'll get the cab driver to stop at the grocery store. Aren't you tired? All my bones are aching."

"I'm so excited at being in America my mind's going to explode."

"I want to eat a good meal and sleep for a week."

"My nap sorted me out. Wasn't it Dagwood in the comic strip who said the best thing in life was a nap between naps?"

"You're nuts. Come on. Let's get our cases."

"Everything looks and sounds so different and yet everything is just the same. Airports and people don't change. Here, it's just more of everything. Will I see the Mississippi?"

"No you won't, but you will see the Missouri which Kansas City straddles. There's Kansas City Missouri where I live, and Kansas City Kansas on the other side of the border."

"When do you go back to work?"

"Monday. We have three days to sleep and relax. You want to go out on the river?"

"I certainly do. My life is rivers. Are there any fish?"

"Plenty. We can hire a small boat and go downriver. It'll make you feel at home."

"You don't have lions or elephant. Or hippo floating nose-up in the river. You don't have vultures."

"Oh, but we do. There are more vultures in the big cities of America than there are on the whole Zambezi River."

"Let's avoid the vultures. A trip down a big river sounds just my cup of tea. Have you got a fishing rod?"

"We can always hire one."

"America. I love it already. There's always someone who's got what you want."

Happy she was making progress with Phillip, she helped him load their luggage onto a trolley and he pushed it out to the line of cabs.

Martha gave the driver her address in the city. She was happy to be home. It was always the same when she went on a trip. The best part was getting home. It took them an hour to reach the centre of the bustling city. Phillip put the suitcases on the pavement in front of the twenty-storey building. Martha's apartment was on the tenth floor.

"You gave him a good tip. Where'd you get the dollars?"

"Periodically, we get dollars from our clients. Fifteen per cent. Isn't that the right amount in America?"

"You've done your research, Phillip."

"Of course I have. America's all about being a good tipper. Keeps the wheels turning. So, this is you. City life at the centre. I've never stayed in a building so tall in my life before. How many people must there be in this building living cheek by jowl?"

"I have no idea. When I close my front door and turn on the television it all comes down to me and my apartment."

"Now it's you, me and your apartment. And who knows, by the end of next week we'll know if we have a visitor. Have you got a good view from your window?"

"Not really. Don't look out much. Just more buildings. I live in the centre of a city. But it's good for work. Takes me ten minutes to walk to the office. The price of the apartment was high but it cuts down the stress. Launching an advertising campaign can keep me in the office until midnight. Time, Phillip. That's what's expensive. If you want to make money in America you have to work late hours. With my home close to the office I can work till I drop and still have time for a proper night's sleep."

"And if you get pregnant. What then?"

"I'll cross that bridge when I get to it. There are good places with day care. Nannies. You can get what you want in America if you have money."

"Growing up in a city must be horrible."

"People get by. If you don't know what it's like to grow up on a ranch you don't know any difference."

"Lead on, Macduff."

"Who's he?"

"Someone I think in Shakespeare. Just a saying. One of my stepmother's favourites. Wow. What a building. So this is your home."

PART 2

JUNE TO JULY 1993 — A THREE-DAY BENDER

1

*S*he was home, everything familiar giving Martha a deep feeling of contentment. She touched the wood carving of a small cow she had been given by her father when she was ten years old. Phillip was looking around the apartment, the luggage left in the small hallway between the toilet and the kitchen. In the lounge, she opened the curtains and looked out at the building across from her balcony. The old woman Martha had never met waved at her. Martha waved back. Next door, the television was on. The moment she opened the door she had heard the couple below arguing as usual. The familiar smell of cooking wafted up when Martha opened the lounge window. Down below to the left she could see the passing traffic, hear the blare of a police siren. On the tenth floor, she was high enough not to smell the fumes of the petrol. As she stood, thinking where to take Phillip for the evening, she could hear the sound of an aircraft.

Back inside, she turned on the television. It was time for the news, not that it mattered. It was habit. Much of Martha's life on her own was routine and habit. Instead of listening to what was being said on the news, she played back her messages. Most she flicked through. The important messages would be on her office answering machine that she would hear on Monday morning. Phillip was standing on the blue rug, in between the settees. He was looking at an abstract painting she had bought from the local art gallery. Martha still had no idea why she had bought it, other than to fill up the blank space on her wall. It meant nothing. The artist was famous. When the old man died, the woman in the art gallery had told Martha the painting would be worth a fortune. Martha's attention was drawn back to the television. There was trouble being reported on the news. There was always trouble somewhere in the world. Martha was not sure what the newscaster would have to say if somewhere, someone did not have a problem. Americans liked to hear about problems in other people's countries. Other people's problems made people feel happy about themselves. There was a brief shot of the new president, the Democrat Bill Clinton. The man had an engaging smile. She left Phillip walking round the room looking at the rest of her paintings, a puzzled look on his face, and walked into the main bedroom. The bed was a double bed she had taken with her after her second marriage. The room was stuffy, the curtains closed. Martha opened the curtains and both of the windows. The neighbours had stopped arguing. The old lady was still on her balcony. This time neither of them waved. She pulled back the bedcover and fluffed up the pillows. The news from the lounge had turned to the weather. Tomorrow was going to be a perfect day for a run down the river.

"You want the cases in the bedroom?"

"Thanks. We forgot to go to the grocery store. We'd better go out to dinner."

"Fine by me. I can use my Jersey debit card. Did you know you can't buy foreign exchange in Zimbabwe? Unless you're a member of Mugabe's government. They all have bank accounts overseas in case there's another revolution. Politics is all about getting your hands on the money."

Phillip walked through with the cases into the bedroom, smiling at Martha. He was always smiling.

"Do they know about your Jersey bank account?"

"Don't be silly. I like your flat. Who carved the cow in the lounge?"

"My father."

"It's the best of the lot. Don't understand any of the paintings."

"Neither do I... I'll make some room in my cupboard for you. Then you can unpack."

"Is it nice to be home?"

"I love coming home. Everything is so familiar. How do you like Kansas City?"

"Different. Very different. I've lived in the bush most of my life. City life takes a while to get used to. Well, here I am. You must have some food in the house. Can't we cook up some bacon and eggs? Make some chips. Jet lag is catching up with me... This room looks really nice. A good-sized bed. Let's cook ourselves something while we're having a drink and then climb into bed. We've had enough running around. Didn't you want to phone your mother? She must get lonely. I'll cook. You phone your mother."

"Do the British eat anything else but bacon and eggs?... Put your dirty clothes in the bin in the bathroom."

For the first time in a long while Martha had a man in the house. She watched Phillip unpack his things into the cupboard, leaving his dirty clothes on the floor. They walked together into the kitchen where Martha kept her whisky.

"Don't you people buy frozen dinners and put them in the microwave? You want me to take the ice out of the fridge? This is one smart kitchen. Where are the glasses?"

"There's probably something in the freezer box. TV suppers, they call them. Been there for months. How long is frozen food edible?"

"Years. Hundreds of years. They found food and booze in the arctic left by the early explorers, frozen into the ice. When the food was unfrozen it was perfectly edible. The whisky tasted just fine... The weather forecast for tomorrow is sunshine with a little cloud. Pity you can't see the river from the balcony. Oh, I forgot my washing. How naughty of me. Hang on a second while I put it in the bathroom. I'm not used to living with a woman."

"You don't really want to cook?"

"Not if I can use the microwave. This is America."

"Are you going to miss Africa?"

They were talking through open doors that faced each other across the hallway.

"For the rest of my life if I have to go. It's a bug everyone gets. Spend two years in Africa and you'll never willingly live anywhere else."

"Wouldn't me being pregnant make it willingly?"

Phillip walked back into the kitchen.

"Mugabe won't last forever. Countries come to their senses. Maybe one day we'll be a family living in Africa. Maybe Dad will get back the farm. Nothing stays the same forever. The farm's produced bugger all since Mugabe's crony took it over. If they do that with all the farms there won't be any food in Zimbabwe and that will be a real bugger. For everyone... Do those two in the flat below always argue with each other? Are they married?"

"Willy and Beth. They never stop."

"Are you friends?"

"Only in the lift. I never socialise with the other owners and tenants. If you fall out with them you can't get away from them."

"Wise girl."

"I'll go and phone Mom."

"Are you going to tell her you've brought an African into your home?"

"Not exactly in those terms."

"Ah, racism. Always comes up. Why, just because some poor sod looks different to us, do people get so upset about it? Doesn't ever worry me. Most of my friends are black. Look at Craig and Jojo."

"And all their problems."

"People. It's always other people. Cheers, Martha. To your health. To hell with your wealth."

"Have a look in the freezer."

"They'll be happy. It's just a bad period in history. Aftershock of colonialism."

"For their sake, I hope you're right."

"I'm always right... God knows what this is. Says dinner for one. No, on second thoughts, where are the eggs? I've now found a pack of frozen bacon. If we put it in water it'll thaw quickly. Got any spuds? Bread?... Forget it. Two frozen dinners for one."

"You're nuts. We're going to have fun together."

"We already are. I love America."

"I hope so, Phillip. I really hope so."

"Why are you feeling your stomach?"

"Just in case."

"Then I'd better give it a feel."

"We'll end up not having our supper."

"Does that matter?"

"Let's eat."

"Let's eat. There's a story of some mystic in India who hasn't eaten for years. Gets his energy from the sun. They put him in a room and watched him eat nothing for a week. Came out just fine. What's that show playing on your television?"

"A sitcom. They record laughter and laugh at their own jokes."

"Can the neighbours hear?"

"Probably. You'll get used to all the noise."

"At home, all you hear are the birds and the animals. The wind in the trees. Everything here is man-made. You know they say by the turn of the century half the people on earth will be living in cities. They're piling into cities in China. Why?"

"They must like living in cities. More opportunities."

"What better opportunity than being able to grow your own food?"

"Too much like hard work. If you have a job and money in the city everything is at your fingertips."

"Ah, money. The all-powerful god... How does that washing machine work?"

"You turn it on."

"Silly of me."

They drank a second glass of whisky. Martha pulled the dinners out of the microwave and tipped them onto plates. They sat down at the small kitchen table and ate their supper, both of them quiet. In the lounge, the programme on the television had changed to a debate on the economy. Martha only half listened. The whisky was sending her to sleep. With the food finished she put the plates in the sink and led Phillip through to her bedroom. They got undressed and climbed into bed. They were both too tired to have sex. The curtain and window were still open, the noise from outside blurring as Martha fell asleep.

In the middle of the night Martha woke to the sound of people talking in her lounge. Phillip was still sound asleep. The immediate panic turned to annoyance. She got up, went into the lounge and turned off the television. She walked across to the window. There was still some traffic on the road. Mouthing 'sorry' to her neighbours, Martha closed the window. Most of the lights in the apartment block opposite were out. She drew the curtains and went back into the bedroom. Phillip was fluting, the same sound he had made on the aeroplane. She lay awake thinking, unable to go back to sleep. She was lying on her back. She could hear a police siren not far away, the noise of her city familiar. She was content. Nowhere could she hear the sound of a television. Slowly, the light came up at the start of a summer day, Phillip now quietly sleeping. She had a companion. She was happy. Her thoughts blurred as she fell back into sleep.

When she woke, Phillip was no longer next to her. She could hear the tap running in the bath. Feeling guilty, she walked naked into the lounge, picked up the phone and dialled her mother. On the third ring her mother picked up the phone.

"Hello, Mom."

"Martha, where've you been? You said you would phone me the moment you got home. I've tried many times but all I get is that damn answering machine."

"We got back last night."

"Who's we, Martha? Oh, you mean you and your singles club."

"No, it's Phillip."

"And who, may I ask, is Phillip?"

"A man I met in Zimbabwe."

"He's a Zimbabwean? Martha really. How low can you sink? And you brought him home? Where is he?"

"In the shower."

"I don't know what this world has come to. Bringing back an African."

"His parents are English. Have you heard of the actor Ben Crossley?"

"Naturally. Everyone has heard of Ben Crossley. What's that got to do with it?"

"Ben Crossley was Phillip's grandfather. Left Phillip and his brother a fortune."

"How much?"

"Four million dollars."

"Ben Crossley's grandson is in your shower?"

"He just shouted to give you his love."

"Are you two lovers?"

"Yes, we are."

"You've got my attention. Tell me everything."

"How are you, Mother?"

"As well as can be expected. I'm seventy next year. What does a woman on her own do at my age? No one is interested in an old woman. I go to the book club once a month. Not for the books but for the company. But they don't want to talk to an old woman. I've been on my own since I was fifty-two. The boys don't care about me. When they phone it's just duty, not because they want to talk to their mother. And old Mrs Crabshaw is ninety-four and perfectly miserable. I just hope I don't live that long. My arthritis is terrible. Do you know how terrible it is to always be in pain? All that gallivanting around the world, you don't have time to think of your poor mother all on her own..."

For ten minutes Martha listened to her mother's problems, the same old problems that never changed.

"You children have abandoned me. That's what it is."

"We'll come and visit you tomorrow."

"What's wrong with today?"

"We're hiring a boat and going out on the river. Phillip lives on the Zambezi River. Runs a safari business with a partner. I want him to feel at home. Got to go. Call you soon."

"Goodbye, Martha. And don't abandon me."

When Martha looked round, Phillip was sitting on the settee watching her.

"Sorry about mentioning your grandfather and his money."

"I understand. I'm flattered your mother remembers my grandfather. I had no idea he was that famous."

"All she does is watch old movies on the television. She's so lonely. My poor mother. But if we tried living together she'd drive me insane. Always talks about herself. Always moaning. Being alone in old age can't be any fun. Let me have a quick shower and then we'll go to the grocery store. She wants to meet you tomorrow."

"It'll be my pleasure."

"It's going to be hot today. We'll hire a boat with a canopy... Oh, God. They're at it again. Willy and Beth. It never stops."

"You didn't talk much yourself."

"She's cooped up on her own day after day with no one to talk to. I like to let her talk. Gets it out of her system. She's been so lonely since Dad died. She says a big city on your own, surrounded by people, is the loneliest place in the world. I've said many times she should get out more often but there's nowhere she wants to go other than her monthly meeting at the book club. I don't know what to do with her. The boys have their own lives to live. They don't help. We're all selfish, I suppose."

"And all I ever wanted was my mother."

"Life isn't all what you want it to be. Most families quarrel. Just listen to those two in the apartment down below. All they do is argue."

"Go get your shower. I'm hungry."

They walked to the grocery store and back, ate breakfast and went down in the lift to the second-floor basement. To Martha's surprise her car started first time. They drove out of the city. Half an hour downriver they found the small marina Martha was looking for. They had packed a sandwich lunch. The sun was shining, and Martha didn't have a care in the world. Only twice, before and after making the ham sandwiches on the kitchen table, had she thought of being pregnant.

"Do you have fishing rods to hire?"

"Sure, lady. You know how to run a motorboat, mister? Don't want no accidents on the river. Looks calm enough but all rivers have problems."

"I live on the banks of the Zambezi River."

"Where the hell's that?"

"In southern Africa."

The man gave Phillip a look that said he didn't believe him and walked them down to the boat. Phillip had given the man his Jersey card.

"You really know how to run this thing? You want some worms?"

"Worms would be good."

"You sure have a weird accent. Which country you say you live in?"

"Zimbabwe."

"Does that debit card work?"

"Try it. You'll have no problems."

They waited on the boat while the man went back to get the rod and the worms, the key to the boat's engine still in his pocket.

"It works. Here's the receipt and your key. Have a nice day."

Phillip took the boat out on the river, Martha in a chair under the canopy watching him where he stood holding the steering wheel. For ten minutes neither of them spoke as they chugged downriver. When Phillip found a spot he moored the boat and picked up the fishing rod. With a worm wiggling on the hook she watched him gently lower the line into the water.

"I have no idea what I'm fishing for. But it doesn't matter. The pleasure of fishing isn't in catching the fish. Unless you're hungry."

"You want a sandwich?"

"I'll have one of those beers in the coolbox. I'm impressed. You have everything you need in your flat."

"Got to be organised."

"Once, I travelled miles down the Zambezi looking for Randall. He'd gone AWOL to write a book. Camped by himself on the banks of the Big River. Said it was the only way he could write, without people around him. Spent a day searching for him."

"Did you find him?"

"In the end. An American publisher had accepted *Masters of Vanity* with an advance that was going to blow his mind. Randall had no idea. You know, he was born in the back of a truck when Mum and Dad got stuck in a rainstorm between two rising rivers. They were on their way to Salisbury to the hospital for Mum to have the baby. There's something about rivers that are in our blood... I think I'm getting a nibble. What kind of fish do they have in the river?"

"I have no idea... You know, we could have brought Mom."

"A bit late now. Come along, little fish. Take the bait... Does she fish?"

"She'd have talked non-stop."

"We'll leave that until tomorrow. Where's my beer? He's nibbling again."

"Sorry."

"A fishing rod with a line in the water. A sunny day under a canopy in the shade. A cold beer. A lovely woman. What more could an old bugger like me ever want?"

"A child."

"Of course. A child. I've got him! Hook, line and sinker as they say in the classics. Hold onto the beer. This lad wants to run... Now look at that. The little bastard unhooked himself. These American fish are good. Good luck to you, lad. Who wants to die?"

Smiling, Martha went to the coolbox for Phillip's beer. It was all part of men's image. A fishing rod and a beer. She gave him his beer and sat down again. Neither of them spoke. There was no need for talk. In midstream, the great river flowed and flowed, all that water moving down the length of America. On the other side of the river the wheat crop had been harvested leaving great tracts of stubble as far as Martha could see. She was more at home in the country than she was in the city, the thought of town and Monday twisting her stomach: all those people and problems about to submerge her in the modern world of commerce. But you had to have money. Lots and lots of money. There was no pleasure without pain. Even if she did get pregnant, would he want to stay in America in an apartment in the heart of the city? He would probably go back to Africa and leave her alone to look for another man. There were always men without money looking for a woman to pay their bills. With women making so much money in industry and commerce, the game had reversed itself. Now men were looking for successful women to provide them with a comfortable living. There was always a catch. Men would tell you anything when they wanted something. People called it charm. But it wasn't. In the old days they wanted to get into her pants, promising anything in pursuit of sex. As they grew older, especially the failures, they were looking for money and a lifestyle they couldn't provide for themselves. It was all far too complicated for Martha: everyone, including her mother, had an angle.

"Got him! I swear I've got him. This time the hook has gone right down his throat. There we go, mate. Take some of the line. That's it. Now we reel you in. It's a big one. Blimey, we don't have a net. How do we bring him on board? You want to come and help, Martha? Look for something you can put under the fish when I bring him to the surface... Oh, never mind."

The fish, when Phillip pulled it slowly from the water dangling on the end of his line, wasn't that big after all.

"They feel a lot bigger when they're fighting. Another one like that and we'll have enough for supper. Poor bugger. Just look at him flapping."

"That's why I prefer to buy them frozen. On the farm, I hated watching Dad wring the neck of a duck or a chicken. He used to stroke the neck from bottom to top and then snap it with a jerk. They say chickens can still run with their heads chopped off. Can't you hit him with something?"

Phillip picked up his fish and pulled out the hook. As she watched, the life went out of its eyes. Their supper was dead.

"Don't worry, Martha. We all have to eat."

"Enough to make you a vegetarian."

"Vegetables have life. Make seed to reproduce themselves. What's the difference?"

"You got to be kidding?"

"Sadly, I like a good steak and a nice piece of fish. We were meant to be carnivorous. Why we've lasted so well so long. All part of man's evolution."

The sun moved with the day, making Martha move her chair away from the heat. There were birds in the tree close to the boat. Later, the trees gave shade to the boat. The coolbox was empty of beers, now filled with dead fish. Phillip had got the hang of fishing. With enough fish for a week, Phillip dismantled his rod and started the engine, puttering out into the stream. They had talked about their lives all day, filling in their backgrounds. Family life wasn't much different whether you lived in the heart of Africa or the heart of America. Humans growing up were all much the same. Phillip took the boat into shore and helped Martha onto the bank. He made a small fire. When the coals were hot he made an improvised spit, gutted four of the fish and cooked them over the fire.

"Quite delicious, Phillip."

"Fresh fish over a *braai*. Nothing better. You Americans call it a barbecue. Doesn't matter. I suppose we'd better take him back his boat before it starts to get dark. A perfect day. I love chatting to you. I don't notice your American accent anymore. Strange how quickly we get used to new things."

Martha watched Phillip douse the remnants of the fire with water from the river. He was strong, his movements easy. There was not an ounce of fat on his body. The rich suntan of Africa gave his skin the look of perfect health. If he stayed, she was going to love him with all of her heart.

"What have I done to deserve that look, Martha?"

"We'll have to see."

"Here we go. The engine's as sweet as a nut. That man knows what he's doing."

When they reached the marina, Phillip gave half of the fish in the coolbox to the man who had rented them the boat. Everything else went in the car. Martha drove them back to Kansas City. Back to the lights and the noise of the metropolis. She made supper which they ate in the kitchen, taking their coffee into the lounge where they sat in front of the silent television. It was hot in the apartment. Martha got up and turned on the air conditioning and closed the windows. There was no sound from Beth and Willy. The woman across the way was out on her balcony, the light from her lounge making a silhouette. Martha waved. The old lady waved. One day, perhaps, they would meet each other. When Martha went back to sit down and drink her coffee, Phillip had fallen asleep in his chair. Gently, Martha kissed his lips. For a long while she watched him sleeping before turning on the television. Her coffee had gone cold. She watched the programme, not taking it in. It was a film. Without having watched the beginning Martha had no idea what was going on. When Phillip woke they went to bed. This time Martha had turned off the television. The apartment was now cool.

2

The next morning Martha left Phillip reading the Sunday newspaper and went to pick up her mother. Growing up on the farm, Sunday lunch with the whole family had been the best time of the week: they had all eaten too much, her mother and father taking an afternoon snooze. It was a family tradition. For Martha's mother, lunch with one of her children and a stranger wasn't the same. Mostly, she ignored Phillip and talked about herself. Every now and again, Phillip tried to join the conversation with little success. Her mother was being a right royal pain in the buttocks, but Phillip didn't seem to notice. Then he smiled and slipped in the dagger.

"Martha and I are trying to have a baby, Mrs Poland. Before it's too late for both of us."

"You've only just met! You're not even married."

"After two false starts I thought it better to get pregnant first."

"Are you pregnant, Martha? Oh, my God!"

"Maybe. Hopefully. We'll know if the gods are on our side in a few days' time. If not this time, we'll try again. We both want to have a child before I'm too old."

"I don't know what this world has come to."

"We'll probably be saying exactly the same to our children."

Phillip, having brought the conversation back to the present with a jerk, was smiling. For the first time Martha could remember, her mother looked uncomfortable.

"Are you going to live in America? Is that the reason you want to get my daughter pregnant?"

"It was Martha's idea, though one I heartily concur with. And by right of my parents' birth I have right of residence in Britain. So, no, it's not an escape from Zimbabwe and our current political problems."

"You run a safari business Martha tells me?"

"I do indeed. Me and Jacques. Oh, and we're going to call him Miles if he's a boy and Miley if she's a girl."

"What are you laughing at, Martha?"

"Sorry, Mother. It's a long story."

"Tell me."

"It's a secret, Mrs Poland. Never to be divulged."

Trying to control her fit of giggles, Martha watched as Phillip and her mother smiled at each other. The ice was well and truly broken.

"Come and sit next to me, Phillip, and tell me all about your grandfather."

"It will be my pleasure..."

The story of a film actor's success kept Martha's mother enthralled, barely interrupting Phillip's monologue. For a moment, before she got the giggles, Martha thought Phillip was going to tell her mother they were members of the mile-high club, not a subject to bring up with a parent.

"And he left you a lot of money?"

"Luckily, it has not affected our lifestyles. My brother Randall is a novelist. He says the process of writing, the satisfaction of writing, is far more important than money. That true self-satisfaction can't be bought with money. I have the same passion for the African bush. We are both extraordinarily lucky that our passions give us a living. Grandfather Crossley's money is a safety net for both of us but it won't change our lives."

"If you have a child and marry my daughter, what will you do?"

"The new people who are taking over South Africa from the Boers are talking about an African renaissance. With luck, we'll all learn how to live in harmony with each other. Martha came to Africa. I didn't go to America. It's all in the lap of the gods."

"She'll be gone like the boys."

"You can come and visit. Why not? A whole new experience."

"I get so bored on my own."

"I'm sure you do."

"The same old routine day after day."

"You're lucky not to have to worry about money. Martha told me about selling the farm. Now, why don't I get you a nice cup of coffee? When I come back from the kitchen I want to hear about your life. Enough about mine and my grandfather's."

"I loved his movies."

"So did I. He gave people pleasure. That's real satisfaction from a life. You brought up three successful children. That's your satisfaction, Mrs Poland."

"Please call me Aggie. I was christened Agnes but my friends call me Aggie."

The mention of her mother's Christian name gave Martha a warm glow. It was all going better than she expected.

"He wants to live in Africa."

"What we want and what we get, Mother, are often two different things. From what I heard there's trouble brewing with this man Mugabe. He hates the white man for putting him in jail, according to Jacques. Jacques thinks Mugabe will take his vengeance out on the white farmers."

"But he can't last in power for ever, Martha. No one lasts forever. I believe in hope. Hope for everyone in Zimbabwe. The whole economy depends on the success of the white farmers. In the end, we'll teach the blacks how to farm commercially but it will take time. Who knows, Aggie?... That's a lovely name."

"Not really. I made the best of it."

They laughed as Phillip filled up their cups with coffee. Afterwards they took her mother home. Phillip had put two of the fish in a plastic bag. Back in the apartment, Martha went to the spare bedroom that was her study. The files she had brought from the office were on her desk. With the door closed, she sat down to work.

The next morning when Martha went to the office she had no idea what Phillip was going to do with himself during the day.

"Don't you worry about me, Martha. You have a job to do. I'll keep myself amused. Take a walk round the town. Have a drink in a pub. Read a book. Watch your American television. When will you be back?"

"That depends."

"You want fish for supper?"

"You got to be kidding."

"Eat what you got. It's a rule in Africa."

"I'll give you a ring if I'm going to be late."

AT THE OFFICE, Martha walked straight into a minefield.

"Where the hell have you been, Martha? Your clients don't take kindly to being left without their advertising executive. You crossed the line."

"Am I being fired?"

"Get to work. Your clients pay us to work. They expect service."

"Sorry, Franklyn."

"Why did you extend your holiday?"

"A man. I met a man. I may just be pregnant."

"All I need right now from one of my executives is maternity leave. I don't have time to analyse the ins and outs of your accounts. Who's going to look after them?"

Feeling guilty, Martha walked down the long, open office to her cubicle. As she walked, no one even waved at her. They were all heads down, absorbed in their work. Quickly, Martha was sucked into the vortex.

WHILE MARTHA WAS on another planet absorbed in the fictional world of advertising, making products into stories to catch the attention of customers, Phillip was walking the streets of the city, everything concrete and tarmac, everything hard and unyielding. Africa to Phillip felt like a million miles away. The only animals he could see were people. No dogs, not even a cat. Around him were people and traffic, everything moving determinedly, a city where life was business. He could smell the fumes, taste the petrol.

"I suppose they get used to it."

A passing woman gave him a look.

"I must stop talking out loud to myself."

This time a young man looked at him oddly. Phillip smiled to himself. Thinking out loud was part of his life when walking the African bush. In Kansas City, no one strolled. They all strode as if their lives depended on it. Just in case he got himself lost he had written Martha's address down on a piece of paper. From both directions, people were peeling off into a shopping mall. At the entrance, on what looked like a small bandstand, a lone guitar player was singing a song. There was no cup in front of him. He wasn't a beggar, the music all part of a plan to draw in customers. On the pavement at the entrance were two-piece triangular billboards announcing the day's specials. It made Phillip think of Martha and her business. America revolved around advertising, everyone competing to push their products. Phillip walked on, the sound of the guitar player lost in the noise of the traffic. When he glanced up, looking for the sky, there were neon signs on the sides of the buildings, flashing more of the wares, causing Phillip to bump into a passer-by.

"Watch where you're going!"

"Sorry."

Further up, on the side of the pavement, an old man was sitting hunched on the ground. He looked soulful and unhappy. In front of him stood a tin can. Round his neck hung a sign that said 'homeless'. The pedestrians took no notice. When Phillip looked at the old man the eyes were empty. Nothing inside. No emotion. No feeling. Nothing. Phillip took ten dollars out of his wallet, bent down and put it in the old man's can. He was now close to the man's grizzled face, the lank unwashed hair and the unkempt beard. The old man, deep in his own misery, didn't look at Phillip. Phillip walked on. Somewhere, sometime back in history, the old, crumpled body sitting on the pavement had been someone's child. A boy growing up. A man with expectations. Now, all there was had gone. On the old man's breath Phillip had smelt cheap alcohol, the man's only solace. In among all this wealth was abject poverty. In Africa, in the rural areas, a man built himself a mud hut by cutting poles out of the bush. The small rondavels were thatched with grass. People were never homeless. The thought made Phillip homesick for Africa. Thinking of the old man made Phillip realise how lucky he was. Born to a family with wealth, wealth that had been in the family for generations, the knowledge and money passed from father to son. Had the old man lost his parents? Did he have any children who cared? Did he get a bath? Clean those blackened teeth with the dreadful gaps in the middle? Did light ever show in those eyes? It was all a world outside of Phillip's experience. He walked on, quickening his pace.

A clock on the corner of a building struck one. People were coming out of their offices for lunch. What to do was Phillip's problem. Walking the streets was going to make a long day. All that time to kill. For the first time since school, he found himself bored. He was one stranger among all the teeming masses. He tried a coffee shop and sat up on a stool and tried to order a cup of tea. The man behind the counter looked at him as if he was stark raving mad. Phillip smiled at him and changed his order to coffee.

"What kind of coffee?"

"Whatever you've got."

"Look, mister. I haven't got all day."

"My mistake."

Phillip walked out of the shop and back onto the pavement. It wasn't even possible to stand and look at the people. The heat was becoming worse. In Africa, the heat was clean, not so suffocating. Ahead he could see the sign of a bar. Inside, the bar was pleasant and cool. He walked across the room. Up at the bar, he ordered a beer.

"What beer you want?"

"Whatever you got. There was a beer advertised on your sign. Make it one of them. Can I sit?"

"Do what you like. You want a glass?"

"Please."

"You want to run a tab? You do have a credit card?"

"Of course. Would you like to see it?"

"How it works, mister. Enjoy your beer."

Behind Phillip's back, people were eating lunch at the tables.

"Can I order a sandwich?"

"You can have a hamburger."

"Thank you. One hamburger. The beer is nice and cold. We drink cold Castles in Africa."

The man looked at Phillip's card and handed it back. Halfway through the beer, a small plate with a hamburger was put in front of him. Phillip ate his lunch. No one took any notice. Next to him, a man was telling his companion a joke. They both laughed at the punchline, an old joke Phillip had first heard years ago in the Centenary East club. The two men were enjoying themselves.

"How do jokes that have never been written down travel round the world? Make it another beer. You make a good hamburger."

Instead of striking up a casual conversation, the barman walked away. The third beer when it came tasted better than the first. It was lucky he had eaten the hamburger. Drinking on an empty stomach was never a good idea. The joke teller and his friend had gone. The lunch hour was over. Despite the food, the beer was getting to him. Some days he could drink all night and walk home sober. To get drunk, a man needed a drinking companion. A drinking companion without a memory. When drunk everyone talked rubbish, all part of the escape from a troubled world. And then, the next day, instead of pleasant memories, came the hangover. At thirty-seven Phillip told himself he was getting old. At just gone three by the clock on the shelf above the rows of bottles behind the bar, two women took the empty stools next to him. They were well dressed and plastered in make-up. Phillip was bored, and to pass the time, found himself eavesdropping.

"I'm sure he's having an affair. He's a pain in the ass. After a couple of years of marriage they all have affairs."

"You're not exactly an angel."

"Sometimes you have to use your sex appeal to do business. Men are such fools."

"I think he's listening."

"I don't give a damn. It's rude to listen to other people's conversations."

"Are you going to leave him?"

"Whatever for? They're all much the same. It's good for the image to have a husband."

"Darling, you really can talk rubbish. I've done far better at work since I divorced Jim."

"It was the settlement, not the divorce."

"Maybe."

"How much did you get?"

"None of your damn business. Has Bert got any money?"

"He's always spent what he earns. Says with inflation there's no point in trying to hang on to your money."

"He's a fool."

"And ten years younger and quite insatiable."

"What you going to do?"

"I don't care as long as I get my share. He won't leave me. I earn twice what he does. And the house is in my name."

"Did you make him sign a prenuptial contract?"

"Of course. Now, what are we going to drink? Let's order a bottle of wine."

"Aren't you going back to your office?"

"Maybe. Maybe not."

"That smile says you're coming on to me."

"Do you mind? You really are beautiful."

"I really do need your business."

"I know you do, darling. Let's get tiddly. Then I'll make up my mind."

"He's still listening to us."

"Good luck to him."

Phillip picked up his beer and walked down the bar before there was an argument. Apart from the two women at the end of the bar and two still occupied tables in the dining sector, the place was empty. The barman had sat himself on a stool opposite Phillip. The older woman with the younger husband was holding the other one's hand. Phillip tried not to look. He drank down the third beer and ordered a fourth. The barman put his beer along with a clean glass on the bar counter. The top had been taken off the bottle.

"As a barman you see everything. She can't be after her. She's got a husband."

"She's bored and rich. Comes in here a lot. Works across the street. Either a man or a woman. Never the same. She's a lot older than she looks. Plastic surgery."

"I'm killing time until my girlfriend gets back from work."

"You were wise to move down the bar. That old girl's got a foul mouth and a temper. All part of her frustration. I can't work out your accent."

"At least we both speak English."

"On holiday?"

"I'm not sure. It was all spur of the moment. What does the other girl do?"

"She sells office equipment. You'd be surprised what salespeople will do to get business. So, where is it?"

"What?"

"Your home?"

"Zimbabwe. A small country in southern Africa. I run a safari business. How I just met my girlfriend."

"Here they come. The early drinkers. There's an hour between the last of the lunchtime crowd and the start of the evening."

"Thanks for the conversation."

"My pleasure. Raise a hand when you want another of those beers."

On both sides of Phillip people sat down on the barstools. It was coming up for what people in Zimbabwe called sundowners, the time when the sun went down at six o'clock and people started drinking. Near the equator, the time of sunset never changed much. Instead of listening to other people's conversations, Phillip finished his beer and waved his card at the barman.

"Add fifteen per cent for yourself."

"They've gone off together. The salesgirl is going to get screwed."

"You think so?"

"I know so. In the end, everyone gets screwed."

Phillip signed the bill and left the bar. A young girl on her own took his seat. Outside, Phillip tried to remember which direction he had come from. He had no idea when Martha was coming home. There was more time to kill. Outside it was hot. Even with the hamburger, he was thirsty for alcohol. He found another bar and walked inside.

"A glass of white wine."

"Coming up."

There was nothing much else to do but get himself drunk. From his wallet he took out the piece of paper on which he had written Martha's address. There was nothing sillier than getting yourself lost in a strange city. The five o'clock crowd were much younger. They all looked happy. Without being asked, Phillip showed the young girl behind the bar his card. Just to make sure. She was pretty. A dark, pretty girl showing her breasts. Why the young crowd up at the bar were all men. The wine was sweeter than Phillip expected. The man next to him was trying to hit on the girl without much success. She was used to it. All part of the marketing. The music was loud. Comfortable on his barstool, Phillip sipped at his wine. Two glasses of wine later he knew he was happily drunk. It didn't matter. He had nothing to do. On both sides of him they had turned their backs, busy with their own conversations, the music drowning out most of their words. After the fourth glass of wine, Phillip paid the bill and walked outside. No one had taken any notice of him, a process Phillip repeated in another bar down the road. He was drinking himself sober. Alone, in another man's town. It was better in the Zambezi Valley with his friends. Hoping Martha was home by now, he went outside and found a cab. He gave the cab driver the piece of paper.

"You know where that is?"

"Sure I do."

"Home James and don't spare the horses."

The man shook his head, with no idea what Phillip meant. American traditions were different to British. When Phillip got up to the apartment, the flat was empty. Across the way, the old lady was out on her balcony. Phillip waved. Below, Beth and Willy were arguing as usual. Phillip poured himself a whisky and sat in a chair. If he was going to stay in America for any length of time he would have to find himself something to do. He couldn't spend every day waiting for Martha. In every relationship, there were always problems. Probably why he had never been married. Alone in the chair he could only think of Africa, his home, the place of his birth. It made him smile. When Martha let herself into the apartment, Phillip was fast asleep, the glass of whisky on the table in front of him untouched. He woke to her kiss on his mouth.

"I'm exhausted. They suck it out of you."

"What time is it?"

"Just gone midnight. I've just time to get into bed, have a night's sleep and start all over again. Did you have fun?"

"Never been better."

They went straight to bed, Martha falling asleep. Phillip lay awake wondering what he was doing. From outside, he could hear the constant noise of the traffic. An aircraft went overhead, followed by another. He couldn't sleep, his body clock not yet used to American time. On both sides of the apartment he could hear the neighbours' televisions. He was in America. He would have to get used to it. Phillip cuddled up to Martha and fell into a trouble-free sleep.

3

The morning came with Martha at full speed – taking her shower; getting dressed; putting on her make-up; having her breakfast standing at the kitchen table. She gave him a kiss and dashed for the door. Phillip was still in his pyjamas. Boredom, like a thick cloud, descended. He walked to the window in the lounge and looked across the way. A man in one of the flats was peering through a telescope mounted on a tripod, looking across at Martha's apartment block. Phillip wondered what he found so interesting. In a city there was no privacy. As he looked, he heard a crash of thunder that managed to transcend the noise of the traffic. Soon after, it began to rain. Buckets of rain. The thunderstorm brought back thoughts of Africa. The trick in an African thunderstorm was not to stand under a tree. Trees, rather than people, attracted the bolts of lightning. In his mind, Phillip was running through the tall grass, his face up to the thundering heavens. Why, instead of living in the beautiful countryside, had half the world moved into cities? To Phillip, it made no sense. Living in the bush, a man had everything he wanted. A home he could build. Fruit and vegetables he could grow. Long-legged chickens for meat and eggs. The forest to gather mushrooms. A life of gentleness free of stress and all of life's pollution. The man with the telescope had gone when Phillip brought his mind back to the flat. The rain was easing up. He was still standing in his pyjamas.

"You're a lucky bastard, Crookshank. You don't have a hangover. Now what the hell do we do all day?"

Feeling like a fish out of water, Phillip walked through to Martha's kitchen to make himself a cup of tea. Back in Africa, it had all seemed easy. He had found a girl he really liked who wanted to give him a baby. In Africa, he thought it was just about the two of them. But it wasn't. With the tea made and the storm over Phillip took his tea into the lounge. In the lounge was a hi-fi and Martha's store of classical and pop music. Smiling, Phillip worked his way through the tapes until he found what he was looking for. Slipping in the tape, Phillip sat himself down and let the music of Haydn flow over him. It was the Twenty-Eighth Symphony, one of Phillip's favourites. When the tape stopped, Phillip felt flat. He had long finished his tea. He was still dressed in his pyjamas. He got up and went to the window. The rain was coming down. He was trapped between four walls in a strange country. They spoke the same language but that was about all. He was not a city man and never would be. They would have to see.

In the apartment, the temperature was constant, controlled by the air conditioning. He turned on the television and flipped the programmes using Martha's remote control. What he found was of no interest: local news for local people. On the television, everyone seemed happy. Over in the corner was a small bookcase. On top was a copy of *Newsweek*. Phillip flipped through, found nothing about Africa, and put it back again. He looked through the four small shelves of books, but he was not in the mood for reading. He had developed a creeping hangover that was giving him a headache. Back at the window, it was still raining. Phillip opened the window and closed it again. The air was hot and humid. It was wise to feed a hangover so Phillip went back to the kitchen. He made toast, fried some bacon and cracked open three of Martha's eggs. The food tasted good. He made two more pieces of toast and smeared them with marmalade. Back in the lounge, he sat on the couch and twiddled his thumbs. Apart from Martha, everything he wanted was thousands of miles away.

"Pull your finger out and do something."

The words dissipated around the room. He had a bath instead of showering and got dressed. He had been out of his mind to give up everything on the spur of the moment. There was nothing worse than boredom. A man had to have something to do that was constructive, or he might as well be dead. Blaming the creeping hangover for his depression, Phillip went out to the lift, the spare key in his pocket. In Africa he had had the intention of promoting his safari business. Of talking to the American travel industry. But where to begin? And if he found a travel seminar, would they want some obscure person from the African bush to address the meeting? As Phillip dashed to a cab, the rain came down, half drowning him,

"Are there any travel agencies in Kansas City?"

"They're all over the place."

"They got a Thomas Cook?"

"Sure they have."

"Is it far?"

"Two blocks."

"Thank you. I can't walk in the rain."

At the travel agent Phillip got out of the cab and ran for cover. Inside Thomas Cook no one knew what he was talking about. They were all far too busy selling tickets. Back outside, Phillip stood under the awning while the rain pelted down. Next door was a bar. Keeping out of the rain, he edged his way under the awnings. It was ten o'clock in the morning and the bar was open.

"You'll end up a bloody alcoholic, but what the hell?"

Inside, men on their own were dotted down the barstools like something from a Wild West film. One of the men was wearing a broad-brimmed hat. So far as Phillip could see, no one was talking. It was the morning run for hard drinkers. With empty stools on either side of him he joined the rest of the men.

"Make it a Scotch."

The whisky came and Phillip looked at it. As he picked up the glass his hand was shaking. He couldn't bring the glass up to his mouth. He put his head down towards the bar counter and took a drink. The whisky was strong. His first instinct was to leave it alone and order a coffee. The long day alone loomed as the alternative.

"Oh, what the hell?"

"You got the shakes, my friend?"

The man an empty barstool away on his right was smiling at him. It was the man with the wide-brimmed hat.

"You can say that again."

"A couple of those will sort you out. I'm on a three-day bender. Then it's back to the ranch. Got to make the best of what you have. No point in half measures. What's your name? My name is Clem. I run the ranch. Don't own the place. Just run it. Suits me fine."

"Phillip. Phillip Crookshank."

"We don't use last names in a saloon."

"No, I suppose you don't... I grew up on a farm. A tobacco farm. It was recently confiscated by the Mugabe government. When Dad found the land after the war there was nothing on it. Just bush and wild animals."

"We do cows and horses. A few pigs. Twenty thousand of them. Plenty of space. A week in the big city is enough for me."

"You don't have a wife?"

"Good-looking women don't want to live on a ranch. They want to live with their friends in a city. Kids are the same these days."

"I know the problem. Don't I know the problem."

Phillip dipped down again to his whisky. When he came up the man was smiling at him.

"Got hooks in it," Phillip said ruefully.

"I know the feeling. Drink it down and have another one. Africa. Never been to Africa. Never been out of America. Missed the war in Vietnam. Told me I had a heart murmur. Only time my heart said anything. It was towards the end. Didn't want me, I suppose. Luck of the draw. Life's full of luck... It's a woman, isn't it?"

"How do you know?"

"Women drive a man to drink."

"It's not her. I don't want to give up my safari business."

"If she wants you enough she'll go where you say... Solly, give the man one on me... You mind if I move up?"

"Be my pleasure. We had cows and horses on World's View."

"Was that the name of your ranch? Strange name for a ranch."

"From the main house on the ridge you could see all the way to the escarpment above the Zambezi Valley. Best view in the world."

"What happened to your old man?"

"Went back to England with my stepmother. Dad says you have to take what comes."

"And your mother?"

"She was attacked and killed by a pride of lions."

"Lions?"

"She got drunk, drove into the bush, ran out of petrol and tried to walk home. She's buried in a grave on the edge of the escarpment, overlooking the valley. I work in the valley. Where I have my safari business. How I met Martha... Thank you. Cheers. Down the hatch... Why do we drink so much?"

"Man's best friend."

"She's from these parts. Grew up on a farm in Missouri. We're trying to have a baby."

"Good luck to you."

"Before it's too late."

"They say it's never too late. You want a cigar?"

"Don't smoke."

"That's classic for the son of a tobacco farmer."

"We were called tobacco growers."

"Whatever... Still got hooks in it?"

"Getting better."

"That's the way to go. Alcohol kills a lot of us in the end. Make the best of it. Can't stay sober the whole of your life."

"You're right, Clem. Nice to meet you."

"Nice to meet you too."

"Do they still call you cowboys? People who run cattle?"

"Not really. That was back in the good old days. Now we're a ranch hand. A ranch manager... I love animals. They never answer you back. Never pick an argument. They say us humans are animals. But we're not. We're different. We're always arguing with each other. Petty bickering. Trying to get our own way. Why I like to live on my own. Make my own food. Do the dishes. Peace and quiet with the animals."

"You need kids to pass it all on. To make sense of it. Or when you die, all that passing down through history, the ancestral heritage, comes to nothing. Why Martha is trying to have a baby."

"I knew a Martha once. I was nineteen. I wonder what happened to Martha? The last I heard she was going out with some guy... Years ago.

How the years go by. I've just turned fifty. Anyway, that's how it turned out."

"Did you love her?"

"Probably. At nineteen you don't know what it all means. Sad really. The most important time in a man's life and you don't know what you're doing. Have you been married? These days they get married and divorced. Met a man who divorced his second wife in three months. She was working for him in a restaurant. He fired her. They got divorced. He married again. And divorced her too. He was getting himself drunk right here in the saloon. People like to tell strangers their life story. Why we drink alone. There are no repercussions spilling your heart out to a stranger."

"You can still get married at fifty."

"They're only interested if you got a lot of money. No, when the old urge gets the better of me I find a woman who gives a little and takes a little if you get my meaning. I don't like calling them whores. They're just making a living. What's the difference? In my day, the man always paid. Now the women are making money and young men are taking advantage. The world changes and everything stays the same. Three marriages. Makes all those promises one big lie."

"Was he happy on his own?"

"Didn't ask him. Just got drunk. Never saw him here again."

"Let me buy you the next one."

"That's my man. Never met a man from Africa before. Ain't you white men got problems?"

"Big problems. But whoever rules, Africa will stay the same. Those of us who stay will blend in eventually. In many ways, Zimbabwe is better now than it was. Man to man, we get on better with each other. We're getting to know each other. Teach each other what's good and what's bad... Mr Barman. Give us both the same again."

"Will Martha go live in Africa?"

"I have no idea."

"And you don't want to live in America?"

"I'm an African, Clem. I may have a white skin but I'm an African. A Zimbabwean. It's the same in America. People came to this country from all over the world. But they all call themselves Americans... Cheers, old boy."

"Now that sure the hell does sound colonial. 'Old boy.' Only ever heard that expression in a movie. I like you, Phillip. To a good day's drinking. How does that sound?"

"Sounds good to me."

"When's she coming home?"

"Last night it was midnight."

"Then we got time. Oh, yes, we got time. You want to tell me about Africa, Phillip?"

"It would be my pleasure. Now where do I start? The highveld of southern Africa is the most beautiful place on this earth, the views, the climate, the great rivers. And of all the rivers in the world the most exciting is the Zambezi..."

Phillip talked on and on. Clem was a good listener. The hooks had gone, the whisky going down smoothly.

"I must be boring you. We all love to talk about ourselves. Tell me more about your Martha. Your life on a farm in America. Where were your family from before they came to America?"

"England and Ireland. Several generations back, according to my father. The first Wesley ran away. Had done something wrong. The Irish side, my mother's side of the family, came out of Ireland because they were hungry. There was a famine. When you've always had enough food it's difficult to imagine going hungry. So they came to America."

"Do you know anything about your ancestors?"

"Not really. Just that they came to America. Ordinary people. Just ordinary people."

They talked. They drank. They became friends. The day went by with the whisky. When Clem fell backwards off his barstool, Phillip helped him back to his feet. The barman suggested they went home. Outside, the rain was still coming down. Phillip put his new best friend in a cab and Clem gave the driver directions, his voice thick, his words slurring.

"You got that, driver? My friend's had a few too many drinks."

"We'll get him home."

Phillip gave the man fifty dollars to make certain. The cab drove off leaving Phillip standing in the rain. Surprisingly, he felt quite sober. The watch on his wrist which he had changed to American time said it was half past two in the afternoon. All that time still to be wasted.

Before he fell off the barstool, Clem had said he was going to look for his Martha.

"I'm going to find her, my African friend. She must be somewhere. What if she's as lonely as me? We could make our lives together at the end instead of the beginning. No children. Just the two of us growing old together. Sitting round the fireplace in the winter. Riding horses. Martha loved to ride a horse. We can have dogs and cats. A talking bird in a cage... Where are you, Martha? I need you, Martha. There's no point without you, Martha."

It was then, throwing his arms back over his head, that Clem had fallen backwards off his barstool and cracked his head.

Back in the bar, Phillip went to where he had started. Silent men were still on their barstools.

"I put him in a cab and paid the driver."

"He's been looking for Martha for years. You think she exists?"

"Does it matter? Give me one of those cups of coffee. I need to eat. Luckily, I had a good breakfast. Am I still all right in your bar?"

"You want a hamburger?"

"Hamburger and coffee. I'm also waiting for Martha."

"We all are, chum."

"No, mine is real. She's at work. Why I'm sitting around drinking."

"Just take it easy. Don't want no accidents. No trouble. That's my job. To make sure there's no trouble."

"You're most kind. You can start another tab."

"Be my pleasure. You have to get the balance. Without customers, I ain't got no job."

"He gave the man the name of the hotel."

"Stays same place every time he comes to town. A few times I've had to put him in a cab. He's a good customer. All part of the service."

When Phillip finished the food and the coffee, he paid the bill. Outside, thankfully, the rain had stopped. He was at that stage of having another drink and going the same way as Clem. At home in Zimbabwe it would not have mattered. The pavement was crowded with people. Trying to concentrate, he made his way home. Twice his feet got in the way as he tried to avoid the oncoming people. The lobby of Martha's apartment was empty.

"Was her name really Martha?"

Shrugging his shoulders as the lift door slid open, Phillip stepped inside. The apartment was empty. In the bedroom Phillip dumped his clothes on the floor and got into bed. When he woke it was dark. There was still no sign of Martha. Phillip dressed and went into the lounge and across to the bookcase. Howard Spring's *I Met a Lady* caught his eye. The title was so appropriate. On the couch, he began to read. Soon he was deep in the story, the author drawing him into a world as real as the one he had left in the bar. He was in England, the place of his parents' birth. The home of his ancestors. When Martha let herself into her apartment it was just after midnight. Phillip was sober. The day had passed. Back in bed, Martha was too tired to make love. The girl was stressed out and exhausted. All she wanted to do was sleep. It was well into the night before Phillip found his dreams. When he woke, Martha was up and motoring.

"Sleep all right, Martha?"

"Thank goodness. Got to go. Meeting at eight. Have to prepare."

"Is it worth it?"

"Don't be silly. Of course it's worth it. How I make a living. Afford this apartment. If you want things in life you've got to work for them. Everything costs money."

"I'm bored stiff."

"Got to go."

"When you getting back?"

"Who knows? It's all go. You don't stop running in advertising."

It was Wednesday. Another day to kill. In the kitchen, Phillip made himself a good breakfast to line his stomach. At ten o'clock he walked back into the bar. Clem was sitting on his barstool, his hat on his head. It was the second day of Clem's bender.

"Well, if it ain't the man from Africa. Come over here. Did Martha come home?"

"Did you find your Martha?"

"Not yet. Give the man a whisky. Let's get started."

"How's your head?"

"Never felt better."

Along the bar from both sides of them, the barstools were dotted with lonely men staring silently into their drinks. Like yesterday, the first drink had hooks in it. Phillip's mouth felt like the bottom of a parrot cage. On the second drink, like the first, they clinked glasses.

"I owe you fifty dollars."

"You owe me nothing. I wanted to make sure you got home. What drinking companions are for."

"Today, Solly, put all the drinks on my tab."

"My pleasure, Clem."

The man left them to serve a new customer.

"Don't know what I'd do without him. There's nothing better than a saloon with a barman who looks after you. Most bartenders are only interested in the size of their tip. Not our Solly. Right, Solly?... You know tomorrow is the first of July. I'll be back safe on the ranch by the fourth, away from temptation. It's good to be American on the fourth of July. All across America we celebrate."

"Do you ever take off that hat?"

"Only when I go to bed. You know what, my African friend, we're going to start celebrating."

They clinked glasses, downed their drinks and waited for Solly to refill them. By the fourth of July, Martha had said she would know if she was pregnant. Trying not to think of the consequences, Phillip picked up his drink.

"To life, and all its twists and turns."

By lunchtime Phillip had forgotten all about babies. They were both on the slippery slide to congenial drunkenness. Clem was having a good time. So was Phillip.

"Hamburger time, Solly. Got to stay in control. Don't want no accidents."

"Coming up, Phillip."

"On my tab, Solly."

"No, Clem, this one's on mine. It's hamburger time."

"Whatever you say. You coming in tomorrow?"

"Of course I am. It's a three-day bender."

They were both silent, thinking of the consequences. Drinking had its problems. They were part of the line of silent drinkers staring into their glasses, not a woman up at the bar.

"What made your family go to Zimbabwe?"

"In those days it was called Rhodesia. It all began with Sebastian

Brigandshaw, an ivory hunter. He started the dynasty that led to his son Harry running a tobacco farm. My grandfather was an aeronautical engineer and Harry, who'd been a pilot in the First World War, flew the Short Sunderland seaplane on its first test flight with him. When my grandfather was killed during the evacuation of Dunkirk, Harry Brigandshaw became mentor to my father and my Uncle Paul, and after learning how to grow tobacco for five years working on other people's farms, my father was given a Crown Land farm. A tract of bush. When the farm was flourishing decades later, along came Robert Mugabe, the first black president of what they then called Zimbabwe, and tossed us off World's View without compensation. Which is where we are now. Luckily, when growing tobacco was highly profitable, Dad had invested some of the profits in England through my Uncle Paul, which eventually went into a block of flats in Chelsea, a London district on the River Thames. Like so often, there was a woman involved. Her name was Livy. A bit like me and my Martha. If my grandfather hadn't met Harry Brigandshaw I wouldn't have been born in Africa, met Martha on her safari, and be sitting with you in a bar in downtown Kansas City."

"So here we are, my African friend. Solly, give us another one. Let's get started."

"I thought we were started?"

"Really started. That hamburger was good, but now I need a drink."

"It was all due to the Brigandshaws, my being in Africa. Let's drink to Sebastian and Harry Brigandshaw, father and son. Without them my father would never have gone out to Africa and met my mother, and my life would never have begun."

"It's all one big chance."

"Maybe, just maybe, there's another chap on the way. His one big chance to join this big and wonderful world."

"And if she's pregnant you have no idea what you will do?"

"Let the gods decide. And don't forget to look for your Martha. The big chance for you, Clem, is your Martha. And right now out there somewhere she's waiting for you."

"To our Marthas."

"To life."

"To the chance of life, my African friend. To the chance of life."

They clinked, smiled at each other, and drained their glasses. Phillip knew he was drunk. And by the time they helped each other out of Solly's Saloon, arms over each other's shoulders for support, they were staggering drunk. With Solly's help, they fell into the back of a cab.

"First we drop my African friend at his Martha's."

"You two are drunk."

"You can say that again."

"And you, sir. Where you want to go?"

"The Alameda Plaza."

"You two got money?"

"As much as you want. My African friend here's grandfather was Ben Crossley, the famous Hollywood actor."

"You got to be kidding."

"Left him four million dollars."

"You got Martha's address on that piece of paper? Home James and don't spare the horses. Here is one hundred of your beautiful American dollars. My friend paid for the drinks. You can keep the change."

At the apartment, the cab driver helped Phillip to the lift.

"You okay now, mister?"

"You are a scholar and a gentleman. I shall never forget you. Please look after my friend. He's a little tipsy."

With difficulty, Phillip pressed the right floor button. The lift door closed. When it opened, Phillip got out and stumbled to the door of Martha's apartment, fumbling the key into the lock. Inside, he bounced off the walls of the small passage on his way to the bedroom. Luckily, there was no sign of Martha. Phillip, fully clothed, fell face first onto the bed. He was asleep the moment his head hit the pillow.

HE CAME out of his drunken sleep into the darkness. There were noises. Voices he did not understand. Panic changed to fear. There were no animals. No birds. Just distant voices that made no sense. Phillip pulled himself up. He was on top of a bed. All his clothes on. The voices stopped. The sound of a door opening brought back reality. Quickly, Phillip took off his clothes and climbed into bed. When Martha came into the bedroom and switched on the light, he pretended he was fast asleep. Quietly, gently, Martha got into bed and brought her naked body up against his. She leaned over him to turn off the lights. Her body was soft, her fragrance sweet. Phillip smiled with contentment, the hangover not yet begun.

"Sleep well, my lover. Now we are three... I'm pregnant... Are you awake?"

"I am now."

"I'm so excited. The test was positive... How was your day?"

For a while Phillip lay still, his mind racing, his body tense.

"You want to talk about it, Martha?"

"Not now. I'm so tired. And happy. We have a whole lifetime together to talk about it. We're going to have a child. Oh, Phillip, I'm so happy I could burst... Did you have a few drinks?"

"And then some. The second day of Clem's bender."

"You must get bored with nothing to do all day... Are you going to look for a job?"

"I'm in between a drunk and a hangover. Better I don't think."

"You can think tomorrow."

"Maybe not. It's the third day of Clem's three-day bender. I promised him."

"Never break a promise... Goodnight, my lover."

"Goodnight, Martha. Sweet dreams."

"Oh, they'll be sweet... Did you have any supper?"

"A hamburger. Better than nothing."

"Are you happy for us, Phillip?"

"Of course I am. It's just my head. Man, can that Clem drink."

Unable to sleep, his mind in turmoil, Phillip lay awake. The rhythm of Martha's breathing changed as she fell asleep.

WHEN PHILLIP WOKE to the day, the bedroom curtains were still drawn. He could hear Martha in the kitchen. His eyes were wide open. He was going to be the father of a child. When Martha came into the bedroom and opened the curtains he was doing his best to smile. Next to him on the small table she had placed his morning cup of tea. They smiled at each other and kissed.

"Got to go. Work calls. Enjoy your day with Clem."

"He's going to look for his Martha."

"Good. Let's hope he finds her."

"Are you going to be late again tonight?"

"Probably. I'm trying to catch up from my holiday. Have you got a hangover?"

"You don't even want to know."

"Naughty boy. You're lucky to have found a friend so quickly."

"Maybe one day all four of us will meet."

Phillip waited for Martha to reach the door.

"We could always go back to Africa. Live in the bush."

"With a child?" She had stopped. She turned round to look at him.

"It's a great place to grow up, living with nature. How it was once upon a time. He can go to boarding school. Learn to ride horses. Know the name of every bird by the sound of its song. Breathe clean air into his lungs. Urban stress would never enter his life. His friends would be the animals and the birds. Many in America would love the chance of such a lifestyle."

"Got to go."

"That's my point. Urban life, the pursuit of money. Never gives us time to enjoy each other. Are you happy, Martha?"

"I try to be."

"There's a big difference. In the Zambezi Valley I have a business and the perfect lifestyle to enable us to be close to our child. Watch him growing up right in front of us. We'd be at peace with each other. None of this bickering. Just listen to them."

"That's Willy and Beth. They always argue."

"But why?"

"I must go, Phillip. I have a meeting."

"And when you have your baby, will you still have daily meetings? Between us we have more money than a family will ever need. What's the point in making more?"

"We'll talk about it tonight."

"At midnight? When you're so tired all you want to do is sleep?"

"It's not going to be easy."

"It can be if we make the right decisions. Not just for me. Not just for you. For all three of us. For all of our children."

"Are you scared of being a father? Is that it?"

"No. I'm scared of leaving my life in Africa and joining the rat race in pursuit of money that's worthless."

"That's just stupid talk."

"Think about it. I'm different, Martha. You've never known a person like me. I grew up differently. Better we leave this discussion for the weekend. We can take the boat out again and go fishing."

"You're a strange man."

"Just different. A product of the peace and quiet of the African bush."

"I should never have got myself pregnant."

"That's no longer the point. You are pregnant. Off you go. We'll work it out. We both want a child to give us a future. That's what's important. Life never was simple. We're not children anymore. We've learned to think ahead. If we concentrate, we can see what's coming."

"You never know what's coming."

"It's still better to think. To look at all the possibilities. And yes, three months ago the idea of my becoming a father never entered my head. Tomorrow's Friday. We have all today and tomorrow to think through our options without getting into an argument. And most importantly we can't be selfish. There's another life on the way."

Martha turned and walked out. He heard the front door open and close. Exhausted, mentally and physically, Phillip lay back on the bed. The discussion would have gone better had he not been drunk the previous day. Women wanted their own way for their children. He was trapped. Whichever way he thought of it he was trapped in Martha's world. He had a degree from a South African university in history, as much use in America as a hole in the head. His life had been surrounded by nature since the day he was born. Now he was going to have to live in a concrete jungle. On top of his jumbled thoughts about Martha he tried to think through the politics of Africa, where many a white man was considered the enemy. Wouldn't a son or daughter have a better chance in America? He got up, went to the kitchen and made himself breakfast.

"Now what the hell do I do?"

He made the bed, tidied the apartment and ran the vacuum cleaner round the lounge and bedroom. He was not used to doing housework. Outside, the sun was shining. Another day that was now so different. To clear his head he wanted a walk. Clem would have to wait. Poor Martha. It was all so exciting and so complicated. Commitment. A lifetime of commitment.

· · ·

OUTSIDE IN THE street it was hot. Phillip walked and walked. Whatever he thought of it he was going to be a father. Only that part was clear. He walked for two hours, coming round in a circle. He was outside the saloon. There was nothing else for him to do. Inside, Clem was up on his barstool, the hat on his head.

"What's the matter, my African friend? You look harassed."

"She's pregnant."

"Oh, my goodness... Are you going to marry her?"

"I have no idea. For all intents and purposes we only just met."

"How it happens. Solly, give him a drink. We got another reason to celebrate."

"I don't want to live in a city."

"You could always buy yourself a ranch."

"Now that's an idea I hadn't thought of."

"What would you do without your friends? Make yourself comfortable. It's the last day of our bender. We got to celebrate."

"You think Martha would like to live on a ranch?"

"Why don't you ask her? She grew up on a ranch. You can grow yourself some tobacco. Run cattle. Have yourself some horses."

"Will you help me on the farm?"

"Of course I will. Cheers, my old friend... That's better. Now you're smiling. To the third day of our bender. To our good health."

"Let the gods decide."

"That's better, my friend. One day at a time. What my mamma always told me. One step at a time. One drink at a time."

"Are you drunk, Clem?"

"Getting there... Smile. You're going to be a father. One day you're going to get drunk with your son. What's better than that?"

"What do you pay for a ranch?"

"Depends how big it is."

"Will they give me a residence permit?"

"Probably. If you marry her. Your grandfather was an American citizen. Your sister Myra is married to an American. You have a niece born in the States. Julian Becker, now there's a big Hollywood name. And he's your brother-in-law. Don't you worry. They'll let you stay. And you got money. That's the one that really counts."

"How did you remember so much of my drunken ramblings?"

"'Cause I listen. I drink, sure, but I listen. And your future mother-in-law's name is Aggie. You're a lucky man. You got everything."

"I never think of it that way."

"That's the trouble in life. We take too much for granted."

"So what should I do?"

"Get yourself drunk. It's the last day of our three-day bender. The start of a long friendship. You see that man over there looking so damn miserable? His wife just left him. Now he's got no family. You've found yourself a family. Propose to the lady. Buy her some jewellery. Make all those wonderful plans together for the future."

"You got a phone number on the ranch?"

"Course I do. Solly, give us a pen and some paper. And pour us another drink... What kept you this morning?"

"I went for a walk to clear my head."

"Did it help?"

"Not much."

They laughed. A good, long chuckle. Phillip was feeling better, not sure if it was the walk, Clem or the drink. The idea was finally sinking in. Whatever else happened, he was going to be a father.

"Where do we start looking for your Martha? America is a big country."

"Put ads in newspapers?"

"My Martha will be able to help. We'll advertise for your Martha. She's sure to have friends. With luck someone who knows her will stumble on our adverts."

"The world she is a-changing."

"You can say that again... If I found a ranch with the homestead up on a hill I could call it World's View."

"Guess you could."

"We almost had an argument this morning."

"That's family. Goes with the territory. Among all that love and joy is a whole lot of bickering... They tell me there's this new thing, the World Wide Web. It's going to be the next big thing."

"How do you know all this, Clem?"

"I told you. I listen to people. You pick up a lot in a saloon. Back home on the ranch I think it through. Chew it over. You got to get something positive out of a drink."

"You mind if I take it easy today?... I think they're calling it the internet"

"You got to think, my friend. I understand. Been a pleasure meeting you, Phillip."

"When do you drive home?"

"The moment the sun comes up tomorrow. Then it's work, work, work. I love my work. I love my life. All I want is my Martha. And you're going to help me find her."

"Certainly am. Got your number and address in my wallet."

"Hamburger time, Solly. Bring the man a hamburger. He got to think."

Keeping his drinking under control, Phillip waited for Clem to finish his bender. At the end, he saw his new friend to a cab. They shook hands. For the next three hours Phillip walked around the streets of Kansas City. Back in the apartment he made himself supper and went to bed and tried to lie awake while he waited for Martha. His eyes closed. Phillip moved gently into his dreams. He was on a horse in country he had never seen before. He was happy. When he woke it was Friday morning. Next to him Martha was still asleep. He sat up and watched her sleeping. She was smiling, enough light coming through the drawn curtains for Phillip to see her face.

"Good morning, honey."

"Good morning, Martha."

"You got some sleep?"

"The best sleep of my life."

"I took the day off. Told my boss I'm pregnant. He understood. They've all got a kind heart when you get down to it."

PART 3

JULY 1993 — PEACE BE WITH YOU

1

*M*artha left the apartment without having breakfast. She took the lift down to the second-floor basement where the cars were parked, having told Phillip she was going to do the shopping before they went fishing. She drove instead to her mother's apartment on the outskirts of Kansas City.

"What on earth are you doing here on a Friday morning? Aren't you meant to be working?"

"I'm pregnant."

"You'd better come in. Ford just phoned. There's another argument with Elizabeth about him seeing his children. Why can't you people marry and just get on with your lives? So who's the father, Martha Poland? Thank goodness you changed back to your maiden name after you divorced that dreadful man."

"Phillip."

"Are you certain?"

"I hadn't slept with anyone for months and months."

"How pregnant are you?"

"Enough to be certain. The doctor took a blood test. I was in a hurry to find out."

"Is he going to marry you?"

"I'm not sure. He wants us to go back to Africa."

"That's plain ridiculous."

"Franklyn gave me the day off. We're going fishing. I booked the boat. Fishing and talking."

"You can't bring up a child in Africa. One revolution after another. They shoot each other and they hate white people for all that colonial oppression... You want some coffee? You barely know the man."

"I wanted to get out of my apartment before we started an argument."

"He didn't take it so well?"

"He went very quiet when I told him."

"I thought you said he wanted a child?"

"An idea is one thing. Reality another. He calmed down as the idea sank in... I don't want to be a single mother along with the rest of them. I want a family. I want to stay at home in America. I don't want to run off and live in the African bush. And I like my job. Full of stress but it's interesting. Exciting. What would I do with myself in the bush? Mom, what do I do?"

"Have you had breakfast?"

"No."

"Then we'll make ourselves a nice breakfast and sit round the kitchen table and talk. Where's Phillip?"

"In bed. He met some man called Clem in a saloon and joined him on a three-day bender. Phillip had nothing to do when I was at work. Says he'll need a week to recover."

"How long have you known him?"

"A couple of months."

"And in that time you met, matched and got yourself pregnant?"

"Something like that."

"Oh, my goodness. What are we going to do with you, Martha?... Do you want sausages?"

"I'd love some sausages... Why are you laughing?"

"My children. They never fail to amaze me. At least he's got money. Or so he says. You can never be sure with men. Your father was an exception... Do you want a boy or a girl?"

"I don't care so long as the kid's healthy."

"Have you checked Phillip's genes?"

"Of course not."

"Why doesn't he want to live in America?"

"He loves Africa. He has a passion for Africa."

"Just remember, however it works out you won't always get your own way. Marriage is give and take. Remember that, Martha. Pancakes. We're going to have some pancakes smothered in maple syrup. You've loved pancakes since you were a child... He'll have to get a job. Do something constructive. He can't just sit around living off his grandfather's inheritance. Listen to what Phillip has to say, but now you're pregnant with his child you have an unbreakable bond. Nothing can ever change it... Africa is far too volatile to bring up children."

"He says politicians, like governments, come and go, but the people stay behind. Mugabe is in his late sixties now and everything will change for the better when he's gone."

"He's rationalising... But what on earth is wrong with America? He should be grateful he can get into our country when you marry him."

Martha sat on the kitchen chair watching her mother make the pancakes, her mind in turmoil. After two childless marriages she thought she was sterile, despite all the tests. In her mind there had been no point in a third marriage. Under the table she felt her stomach, trying to imagine the new life growing in her belly.

"I want a child of my own so badly."

"I know you do, darling. Now, eat your breakfast. It's all going to turn out just fine. Don't they say it's third time lucky?"

"You're laughing, Mother."

"Why not? I'm going to have my first granddaughter. Eat up. You can't leave him alone."

"He's such a nice man."

"We can only hope so."

Her mother had that knowing look on her face. When they had finished the pancakes, Martha fried four eggs with rashers of bacon. Her mother was watching with that same faint smile of hope mixed with sadness she so often gave her children. Martha put the eggs and bacon on the plates with the sausages and put them down on the table. They sipped at their coffee. Martha was hungry. They ate in silence, deep in their thoughts.

"That was just what I needed. Better go... Why is life so damn complicated?"

They kissed at the door. Downstairs her car was where she had left it.

Martha drove to the supermarket and did the shopping, buying what she needed for a picnic, the problems playing through her mind. By the time she reached home the prospect of living in Africa seemed better than spending her life alone as a single mother without a husband. Phillip was standing barefoot in the lounge, wearing nothing but a pair of shorts, giving Martha a surge of sexual excitement. He was looking across at the opposite block of apartments, the windows closed, the air conditioning humming above the noise of the traffic. He turned to her and smiled.

"We could buy ourselves a ranch."

"Or we could go back to the Zambezi Valley. I could help you and Jacques run your business. Do the marketing. Do your advertising... I booked the boat. We can go when you're ready."

"You were a long time. Did you go and see your mother?... I thought you would. That's something I haven't been able to do in my life... What did she say?"

"That I mustn't be selfish and only think of myself."

"She sits there half the day. She looks so damn lonely."

"Did she wave at you?"

"The odd wave across the street is all she has... We'd better pack the picnic basket and go... How is she?"

"Lonely."

"Why didn't you live with her after your second divorce?"

"She didn't want me to. Thought it would cramp my style... Come here, please. I want you to make love to me. I want us all to be so damn happy. If we love each other, nothing else will matter."

"And the ranch?"

"Let's think about it. There's no rush."

Hand in hand, they walked through into the bedroom.

ON THE MONDAY, Martha went back to work, at peace with the world. Franklyn's door was open. She put her letter of resignation on his desk.

"Are you sure you know what you're doing?"

"Do we ever know? I'm going out to live in Zimbabwe."

"When?"

"As soon as possible."

"I'll need time to replace you, Martha."

"Once you find the right person it won't take long for both of us to introduce her to my clients. A new, fresh brain can often be advantageous."

"You'll need a month to clear your desk."

"Maybe. I do have an assistant. What's wrong with Jasmine taking over my clients?"

"She's twenty-five years old."

"In the modern age it's all about youth. The computer age... I do so want a baby."

"Kids can be a pain in the arse. I know from experience."

Through the day Martha ran from one task to the other, concentrating on her work. Having made her choice she didn't want to change her mind.

The day finished with a drink in Franklyn's office.

"How old are your children?"

"Fifteen and seventeen. The girl, Tildy, is fifteen and thinks she's grown up. Her mother says she lost her virginity when she was thirteen. Her body matured fast. Likes to wear clothes to show it off. Had to happen. Her mother put her on the pill. By the time she's twenty she'll be bored with the lot of them. Men don't marry promiscuous women. They like to play around with the likes of Tildy but they don't marry them. I have no idea what we're going to do with her. The boy can't make up his mind what to study to get into a good university. Keeps changing his mind. Says he wants to be a rock star. Who's he kidding? I can't even imagine their pointless lives in twenty years' time."

"Like me, Tildy will get herself pregnant from a nice man and go live far away. At least she attracts men. And boys of seventeen never know what they're going to do with their lives. Most of it happens by accident. You can only try and plan your future. My mother just gave us that look and shook her head. The three of us have done all right. Not much good at marriage. But that's the modern world. Women these days have careers and don't have to rely on their men. They are financially independent. Much better. You never know a man until you've lived with them."

"You're losing your career."

"But not my experience. I'm going to apply it to Phillip's safari business. Extend his business to general tourism earning a commission from the other operators and the hotels. Tourism in Africa has never been better. It's different. Where else do you meet a lion in the wild? I'll always be an American. The world's a global village and that's not going to change any time soon. I've found a travel expo that's taking place in Los Angeles next week. I want Phillip to go and talk to them. A man just out of the African bush will blow their minds. He has a sister living just outside LA. Give him something to do while I'm handing over to Jasmine. She's so excited. Has all the energy."

"You sure she can do it?"

"Only time will tell. Give her a chance. She deserves it... Don't worry about your daughter. None of us are saints. Got myself knocked up at the age of thirty-seven."

"Wasn't it intentional?"

"Of course it was. Some would call it entrapment. Not quite the old school expected by our parents... Thanks for the drink."

"You going home?"

"It's seven o'clock in the evening. I've resigned. Give a girl a break... Thanks, Franklyn. It's been good working with you."

"Hope it all works out."

"So do I. So do I. Tildy is a lovely name."

Feeling lightheaded from the day's excitement and the drink, Martha walked from her boss's room. A few people in the main office were still in their cubicles, their heads down. She stood, a solitary woman approaching her middle age, and saw their lives as they really were. It made her sad, the thought of going to live in Africa giving her a new hope. There had to be more to life than just making money, tarting oneself up with the proceeds of that money trying to impress people. It was all showing off. The clothes, the smart apartment, the plastic surgery, all to make a person feel important, washed by the self-satisfaction from other people's envy and praise. No one took any notice of Martha as she left the office. Jasmine had gone home to tell her boyfriend about her promotion. Downstairs in the basement her car was waiting in the company parking lot, one of the privileges of being an account executive. It made Martha smile into the rear-view mirror ruefully. She was throwing it all away to make a life with a man she barely knew in a country in another hemisphere.

"You're out of your mind, Martha Poland. Gloriously out of your mind."

Back in her own basement she went up in the lift. At her door, as she put the key in the lock, she could hear the lovely sound of classical music. The music was Haydn's Twenty-Eighth Symphony, one of her favourites.

"You didn't go to Solly's Saloon?"

"You came home nice and early... Isn't it beautiful? You must bring all your music. We won't mind the sound of classical music playing to the African bush. We don't like loud music with all those bass drumbeats... How did it go?"

"A lot better than I expected. Franklyn's agreed to give Jasmine a try at my job. We'll be out of here by the end of the month... You had supper?"

"Made a curry. A friend of Dad's was in the Indian Civil before he came to Rhodesia. Always called it 'a damn fine curry'. Showed me how to make it."

"There's a travel expo in LA next week. You should go. I've got you an invitation. You can stay with your sister."

"And you can fly down for the weekend."

"Will Julian Becker be there? I've always wanted to meet a film star."

"Probably... Can we book our flights to Harare? I'm worried about leaving Jacques without my help."

"You call running a safari work!"

"Some tourists can be a pain in the arse."

"Franklyn says that of his children."

"You want a drink?"

"Why not?"

"First, the future Mrs Crookshank, give me a kiss. Are you excited?"

"About what?"

"Both, you idiot. You always turn me on."

With a satisfied smirk on his well-tanned face, Phillip poured them both a drink. The lovely music was still playing. Martha, for the first time since she could remember, was completely at peace with the world. All the usual worries from work had flown out of her head.

"An expo. Just what I was looking for. You're a genius, Martha."

"I know I am... When do you want to eat?"

"Oh, there's plenty of time. All I have to do is put on the rice and warm up the curry. I found all the right spices in the supermarket. And a nice bottle of South African red wine. Your shops are good. I'll phone Myra tomorrow. Everything in my life is suddenly fitting in."

"I've got some big ideas for marketing your safari business."

"I'm glad. You'll have something to do before the baby is born... Where do you want to get married? We can go to Vegas or wait until we get to Zimbabwe. I think it should be Las Vegas. It'll be done. No argument. No waiting around. Just the two of us and a couple of witnesses."

"I like it... I'm going to rent out the apartment fully furnished. Selling for the right price takes too long."

"I like it."

"Stop smirking."

"I like it... Why don't we pay a visit to your bedroom?"

"You're incorrigible... Do you love me, Phillip?"

"Love's a word with too many meanings, too many parts to it. There never was an all-consuming love in the way girls would like it to be. Men get love and lust muddled up. Do I love the idea of spending the rest of my life with you? Of having a family with you? Yes I do. Do I love your body? I'll prove it until you are a very old woman. Do I love the way people like to think of love without any conditions? I probably don't think so. There will be good days and better days. Life is a changing habit. Within us all are so many mixed feelings that ebb and flow. We will have to trust each other. Something people these days in the corporate and political world are not very good at. The old English school of my father and the Brigandshaws was built on trust. An Englishman's word was his bond. In those days if a gentleman lied or cheated he was ostracised from society. Thrown out on the rubbish heap. They didn't need lawyers to punish the thieves and cheats, it was done by their own families and friends, a far more terrible punishment. Let us try and go back to the old way so we can trust each other to behave and teach our children to behave. That's what's important in our lives together. It will bring happiness and tranquillity. We will always know what is going on between us. None of that uncertainty that is so much part of modern stress that makes so many people miserable... Have I said too much?"

"I love your mind as well as your body, Phillip."

"Good. Let's get to the bed. My hormones are screaming."

They laughed, finished their drinks and went into the bedroom, the great cloud of life that had so often smothered Martha blown away. The Haydn symphony had finished. All they wanted was love.

---

*P*hillip flew off to Los Angeles at the end of the week. Martha had said she needed the weekend to start going through her things. Handing over to Jasmine, taking her to the clients with Franklyn to explain she was pregnant and leaving the business was easier than she expected. People were happy for her, the women excited. The idea of leaving America was not mentioned. Jasmine, to Franklyn's surprise and satisfaction, had many positive ideas for the clients' advertising, often dominating the conversations. After work they went out for a drink. Jasmine's boyfriend joined them.

"The clients were impressed, Jas. Where did you get so many new ideas?"

"As your assistant I kept my mouth shut. The ideas are meant to come from the account executive. I listened to you, Martha. You've been a wonderful teacher."

"Are you two getting married?"

"One day, maybe. We're happy living with each other. I'm too young to settle down and have a family. We want to have fun without too many commitments..."

"Is his brother-in-law really Julian Becker? That's so awesome. I loved him in *Masters of Vanity*. Corporate America with all its warts to a T.

Some of those greedy bastards on Wall Street would steal their grandmother's pension," said Noah.

"His brother is Randall Holiday, the author of the book. Holiday is his writing nom de plume."

"You've got to be kidding me. Talk about the rich and famous..."

"Where are you and Phillip getting married?"

"I think it best to wait until we get to Zimbabwe, Jas. Wait until I'm six or seven months pregnant. Women of my age have miscarriages. We should be certain we are going to have our child before the complication of marriage."

"Makes sense to me," Jasmine said.

"By the end of next week I will have gone through every file. I want to fly to LA and be with Phillip and his sister. From there we want to fly to Africa. Will you be ready to take over?"

"Just say the word."

"To happy lives, Jasmine."

"To happy lives, Martha... You mind if I give you a hug?"

"So, Noah. What do you do for a living?"

"I work for a medium-size telecom company and head up their communications department. We supply large corporates throughout the States where they operate. One day soon I'm going out on my own. If you want to make money, real money, you got to own your own business. I like money. So does Jas. Wow, what a salary increase she just got. You want to marry me, Jasmine Fairbanks?"

"Not this moment, Noah Hughes... Are you after me or my money? And don't be too hard on those bastards in Wall Street. They're the cornerstone of our economy. Your clients won't like to hear you rubbish them. The system works. America is the richest country in the world. Nothing wrong with a financial system that makes our dollar the choice reserve currency for every other country. We dominate the world financially from Wall Street... I love this singer. If he had the right agent and publicist he could go places. Forget about having to make his money in bars, singing for his supper. I should talk to him. Horst and Maples can help him to become famous."

Martha smiled as the lovers talked on. They were so comfortable with each other. Youth in all its happiness and blissful ignorance of life's realities. The young man could play the guitar and sing, no doubt about it. A lounge singer, happy with his music.

"Maybe he doesn't want to be famous, Jas."

"Everyone wants to be rich and famous, Noah."

"Some just like their music. Mozart just loved his music."

"And he died a pauper."

"But his music stayed behind. His music will live forever. Money gets spent. His music was far more important than any amount of money. I love beautiful music... Are you going to marry me?"

"Is this a proposal on the back of my new salary? Just because I'm now earning more money than you it doesn't mean you have to marry me."

"Do you fancy the singer?"

"He's nice. This is my favourite bar. He sings in the happy hour on Tuesdays, Thursdays and Fridays... You going to buy me a ring?"

"There's no point in buying the ring until you agree to marry me... Don't look so serious, Jas. I'm only kidding.... Same again, everyone? Good. I'll get them."

"Look, I've got a lot of packing to do at home. You two lovebirds enjoy your evening together. And Jasmine, so far as I'm concerned, you are now the account executive."

It all made Martha inwardly smile. People always liked to talk about themselves. The last Martha heard of their conversation as she left the lounge bar, Jasmine was talking about her, thinking she was no longer within earshot. Noah was waiting to get his own story back into the conversation as Martha gave them a last look over her shoulder. The man was barely listening to what Jasmine had to say, making Martha hope with all her heart that Phillip was different, that marrying late in life would prove to be an advantage. Hitching up with other people always had its problems. Jas and Noah were going to find out, all part of life's process.

She walked back to the offices of Horst and Maples and back down to the company parking lot. She drove herself home. In the apartment it was quiet without Phillip. No music was playing. The old girl was not on her balcony. Willy and Beth were not arguing with each other. She had the weekend alone and a last week in the office before flying to Los Angeles. She felt lonely. Sad. Her mind empty of happy thoughts, the gnawing pain of uncertainty back in the depths of her stomach. Was it all going to work or had she made the worst mistake of her life? But life went on. From day to day. Only time would tell the outcome of all three of their lives. She was going to have the baby. There was no real thought in her mind of a miscarriage. Martha Poland and daughter in the African bush. Or was it Martha Poland anymore? She would have to get used to Martha Crookshank, wife and mother in the African bush. As she worked through her cupboards and drawers the niggling feeling of fear in her stomach disappeared. She was again confident. Thinking positive thoughts. She put on her favourite Haydn symphony that Phillip had played so often. Poured herself a glass of Phillip's South African wine. The beautiful music flowed over her. There was no turning back. She knew that the moment she found out she was pregnant in the doctor's rooms. She sat thinking, knowing she should phone her mother, tell her she was going to be left all on her own in Kansas City, all three of her children scattered.

When she got up to go to her bed, Martha was crying. Not for herself. She was crying for her mother. All that work and love bringing up a family coming down to two rooms on her own in a city where no one cared a damn about Aggie Poland. But that was the way of life. Each generation forced to look out for themselves in a world that had gone global. No longer families living on the same ranch for centuries, passed down from generation to generation, or living in a small village, generation after generation, buried next to each other in the same churchyard as had happened for centuries in the old countries of Europe where so much of America had come from. It was a brittle world, a harsh world, a world dominated by the pursuit of money, no longer a place for lasting happy families. As Martha stopped crying and tried to sleep she kept thinking. Of life's purpose. Was there going to be a happy future for her baby, with love and family? Was her daughter going to marry and divorce twice before she was forty, brief relationships so quickly discarded? A life that was empty of everything other than materialism? There was no point lying in bed worrying her guts out as there was no sure-fire solution. There was evolution, the core process of life. Maybe it had never been any different. Maybe many had stayed married but hated each other, their lives worse together than being separated. Late in the night, from sheer mental exhaustion, Martha fell asleep. After she had breakfasted the next morning after a long lie-in, the phone rang. It was Phillip.

"You're up early! How are they?"

"I'm at the beachfront house on the cliff. It's so beautiful. How's it all going?"

"I'm worried about leaving my mother all alone."

"She can come and stay with us. She'll love the big river and all the animals and birds. All she has to do is lock up her apartment and go to the airport. Myra is so pleased I'm getting married and having a son. How are you, Martha? We'll pick you up at the airport next Saturday afternoon. The weather is just perfect. I'm about to go down to the beach for an early morning swim."

"Just had breakfast. Jas is taking over. All on schedule."

"Got to go. Julian is calling me. We're going far up the beach to his favourite spot... He's just called 'hi'."

"Enjoy your swim."

"We will. See you soon."

"I miss you, Phillip."

The line went dead. Martha went back to bed with a cup of coffee. Phillip had sounded so excited about going for a swim in the sea. The nearest sea to his camp on the banks of the Zambezi River was hundreds of miles away. She finished the coffee, had a shower and dressed to go out and see her mother. When she arrived her mother seemed surprised to see her.

"I was just going out to see Mrs Crabshaw. At ninety-four she doesn't have many visitors."

"I feel as though I'm abandoning you by going to Africa."

"Don't be so silly, Martha. If you're happy with Phillip and a baby then I'm happy. I want all my children to enjoy their lives. Don't worry about your old mother. I'm quite happy on my own. I enjoy a good think lying in bed in the morning. Going back over my life. Remembering all the lovely bits. This morning I was thinking right back to when I was six. We had a cat called Smokey. Mostly grey with white paws. I loved that cat. Don't you worry about me. I enjoy cooking my own supper. Eating in front of the television. We're so lucky in this modern age to have so much television at the press of a button. There's always something to watch. I never get bored. Old Mrs Crabshaw gets bored as her eyes are going and she can't watch the television. Just listens to the sound. Her ears are still good. I count my blessings every day... Have you had your breakfast? Of course you haven't. I'll make us some of your favourite pancakes. Is Phillip in Los Angeles?"

"He's just gone swimming in the sea with Julian Becker."

"Lucky man. I'm so happy for you, Martha. I hated the idea of you growing old without having had a family. Now you've started you must have three children. One after the other. Children keep each other company. Help each other growing up. You remember how it was with Hugo and Ford. They loved their little sister. I loved so much the sound of happy children playing. There were always kids visiting the ranch. The sound of children's voices playing in the garden is one of life's true joys."

"You're amazing, Mom."

"I know I am. Give me a hug. Wherever you are, I'll always be thinking of you."

"And I'll be thinking of you."

"Now don't get all sentimental on me, Martha. Mrs Crabshaw can wait. She doesn't know I'm coming for a visit. That's the trick in life. Never keep people waiting. Make it a surprise. You look all worked up about something. What's the matter? You can tell your mother."

"I'm scared. What happens if something goes wrong? If we fall out with each other and I'm stranded all alone with a baby in a far-off land? Who could I turn to for help? Ford or Hugo couldn't come running."

"Of course they can. In this day of jet aeroplanes help is only a day away."

"We'll be stuck in the bush. How would they find me?"

"Your singles group found him without any problems."

"They met us at the airport."

"That's my point. Keep some American dollars in your purse. Money can always buy you transport to the airport however far away it is. These days there are always airports close enough, or places like Zimbabwe would not have a tourist industry. Only in the distant past did people get lost in the wilds of Africa. You're just a phone call away from me and the boys."

"They don't have landline telephones in the camp. And they don't have a wireless connection."

"Then how do they conduct their business?"

"I don't know."

"Take it one step at a time. Don't let your imagination get the better of you. You worry too much."

"I'm going to have a baby."

"When do you leave?"

"Saturday for LA. We do the long flight a few days later."

"Have you left the company?"

"Next Friday."

"My poor Martha. Don't cry. It'll all work out perfectly. Help me with these pancakes. I've got another idea. When we've eaten, we'll both go and visit Mrs Crabshaw. It'll take your mind off your problems."

"You're a wonderful mother."

"My mother was a wonderful mother. You are going to be a wonderful mother."

"He did say if Zimbabwe does collapse we can always come back to America."

"So stop worrying, darling. Everything is going to work out just fine... The maple syrup is in the cupboard. Ninety-four. Now that's a ripe old age. She wants to reach a hundred and receive a cable from the Queen of England. She came to America from England when she was a young girl. Born in the last year of the nineteenth century. She met an American soldier at the end of the First World War and followed him home to Kansas City. She was a nurse looking after the wounded. What was almost a tragedy for her husband turned into a perfect life for both of them. He recovered completely, thanks to Mabel. Funny how something so awful as being blown up in the trenches can turn out to be a blessing."

Martha poured on the maple syrup and ate her breakfast, the syrup trickling down the side of her mouth.

"Did she have any children?"

"Four of them. One died in the Second World War. They visit when they can."

"And grandchildren?"

"They don't come by so much. She loves talking about them. She can go on a bit but I always listen without interrupting. Talking about her life makes her smile with pleasure. Do you want any more pancakes? She had a full and colourful life."

"Will the Queen of England really send her a telegram?"

"Who knows? Probably. She says she may be an American citizen speaking with an American accent but underneath it all she is still English. She says her roots are English, her life American."

"Through Phillip, Julian Becker said 'hi' to me."

"Did he now?... They say that kind of fame can be more of a burden than a pleasure. I prefer two nice rooms in obscurity and a visit from my pregnant daughter... Have you finished? Good. Let's go visit Mrs Crabshaw. And whatever you do, don't interrupt... Wipe your mouth, Martha. It's covered in maple syrup."

The old lady herself opened the door, using her walker. She peered at both of them without any sign of recognition. When Martha's mother spoke a big smile spread over the old woman's face.

"It's Aggie. How nice of you to pay me a visit. Judith says she's coming to stay with me for a week but good intentions are often just good intentions."

"This is my daughter, Martha."

"Come in. We'll make a nice cup of tea, or would you prefer coffee? I can't see too well but I can still work my little kitchen. If I get up close I can read the gauges on the oven. Poor Judith. She's always on the run. If it isn't her husband who needs her, it's one of her children. She's sixty. She should slow down. Still works in the office five days a week. They were going to give her a week's holiday. We shall just have to see. What brings you to my little abode, Aggie?"

"We thought you might like some company. And coffee, please."

"Come in. Sit yourselves down. I'll put on the kettle. I know Americans drink coffee but my English upbringing gets the better of me."

The old lady shuffled away through the open door into her kitchen. Martha followed her mother into the lounge. On the shelves were numerous photographs of children. In the centre of the shelves, in pride of place, was a photograph of an old man. His hair and beard were white. In a corner all by itself was an old photograph of a young man in a uniform unfamiliar to Martha. The room was comfortable, all the furniture old like most of the photographs. Martha sat herself down on an old sofa, sinking deep into the cushions. Opposite her the young man in the strange uniform was giving her a piercing stare. Her mother had followed Mrs Crabshaw into the kitchen. Looking round the room, it was as if time had stopped fifty years ago. When the tea tray was put on the low table in front of Martha's sofa she was thinking she should have let her mother visit Mrs Crabshaw and gone home to start the packing. There was so much to do and so little time in which to do it. After a cup of Mrs Crabshaw's coffee she would make an excuse and get on with it.

"Who's the young man in uniform in the corner, Mrs Crabshaw? He has piercing eyes."

The smile on Mrs Crabshaw's face faded to sadness. She slowly walked over and picked up the old photograph, holding it close to her chest.

"This is Jimmie. I've never told your mother about my Jimmie. He was killed in the Second Battle of the Somme before the Americans came into the war. The honourable James Hallingham. He was my fiancé... How do you like your coffee?"

"Milk and one sugar."

"Aggie, sit you down and make yourself comfortable. It's so nice to have a visitor once in a while."

The old lady put the photograph back on the shelf, a faraway look on her face. Martha's mother added the milk and sugar to the coffee. No one spoke.

"His father was the seventh Baron Hallingham. Their home was Hallingham Hall. Jimmie was his son and heir. We had known each other since our early childhood. The Hallinghams and the Wintertons had been friends for many generations. Marrying Jimmie was my destiny from birth. All part of that old aristocratic tradition in England that doesn't exist anymore. Old Lord Hallingham never recovered from Jimmie's death. Jimmie was the end of the line. The Hallinghams had had a long history of girls in the family, each generation struggling to have a male heir. English titles can only be passed down from father to son. With Jimmie dead and his wife too old to have any more children, Lord Hallingham lost all interest in life. He had no purpose. No one to leave his name and estate to that had been passed from generation to generation of Hallingham for three centuries. In today's world all that history doesn't matter. In those days it was everything, the foundation of the British ruling classes. Then came the great Depression in the thirties and the old man lost most of his capital. There was just the old estate.

Right to the end of his life he was selling off pieces of land to make ends meet. He died with just the big house and twenty acres. The house was falling down according to Jimmie's sister. Whenever she came to America she paid me a visit. Been dead these thirty years has Jennifer. She never married. Neither did either of her other sisters. With Jennifer's death the family died out. Much like so much of the old England. When Jimmie was killed I became a nurse and went to the front. The casualty clearing stations behind the fighting where they brought the wounded. It didn't matter if the wounded were French or British. When the Americans came into the war in 1917 we had American wounded to look after. Bert was blown up by a German artillery shell. We became friends. When the war was finally over in 1918 I accepted Bert's invitation to go out to America. I wanted to run away from all the pain. In America, we became more than friends and we married. He said I should never forget Jimmie. That he was the lucky one as the shell hadn't killed him. It is my only photograph of Jimmie, taken after receiving his commission in the Royal Dragoon Guards. I had the most wonderful life with Bert but we never forgot Jimmie. Men like Jimmie died saving their country. Saving the English-speaking world. I would have been Lady Hallingham. And then we lost our own Jimmie on the beaches of Normandy... But enough of me, Martha. Tell me about yourself. Those old English families have practically all died out now. They created the empire. The greatest empire the world had ever known. And now look at it. Nothing. They've shrunk back to that beautiful little island. That island of Shakespeare set in its silver sea. Peoples and countries come and go. Now it's up to America. I just wonder if we are up to it. All that responsibility. All those problems of other people... I do hope the Queen sends me a telegram on my hundredth birthday. An old tradition, sending her subjects a telegram if they live for a hundred years. She's all they've got left. When she goes I wonder if even the Royal Family will survive. It's all gone so quickly. Happened to the Greeks. Happened to the Romans. Now it has happened to the British. Will there be an American empire? We shall just have to wait and see... I'm sorry if I'm boring you. The ramblings of an old woman. So much has changed. I wonder what life will bring for my great grandchildren. And what is your daughter's story, Aggie?"

"She's pregnant and going to live in Africa."

"My goodness. Whereabouts?"

"A small country called Zimbabwe."

"That they once called Rhodesia. It was the last British colony in Africa. The last vestige of the old British Empire. How interesting. Even now I'm nearly blind I still have books in my life. Audiobooks I can listen to. I've had a passion for reading all my life... Why are you going to Africa?"

"My boyfriend is Zimbabwean of British descent. One of the few left in Zimbabwe. Most of his family have gone."

"And you are not married?"

"Not yet."

"The world has changed."

"I have to pack. We fly out at the end of the month. Thank you for the coffee."

"Run along. And remember, enjoy your life. Despite all those wonderful promises made by the world's religions, it's the only one we are going to get. When we are dead, we are dead as mutton."

Tears of sadness appeared in the old lady's eyes.

"How will the Queen of England know where to send you her telegram?"

"I hold dual citizenship. Governments know all about us, Martha. Now, run off and do your packing... Rhodesia. They say it was a very beautiful country to live in. I'm sure it still is. You have your whole life ahead of you. The one thing I truly envy at the end of my life is youth. I'd love to be young again. Live my life again. Maybe I will. Just maybe I won't be as dead as mutton... Are you going to marry him?"

"Before the baby is born."

"What's his name?"

"Phillip Crookshank."

"Goodbye, the future Mrs Phillip Crookshank. Thank you so much for your visit."

When Martha stood up to leave the apartment, the eyes of the young man in his dress uniform were still looking at her from the photograph back on its shelf. She gave the man a smile.

"Mom, you'll be all right taking a cab back to your apartment? I'll see you before I go."

"Run along. Stop dithering. Mabel and I have lots more to talk about."

"I'm sure there's a more beautiful life waiting for us when we die, Mrs Crabshaw."

"I hope so, Martha. It's all a matter of faith. I should go back to my church and pray. Maybe I will. All this cynicism isn't good for an old woman. Age removes our optimism. Suffocates our hope. We've seen too much pain. But then again I should be grateful for so many wonderful moments. May you have many happy moments in your life. Treasure them. The bad parts are best forgotten. I wish you luck with your baby. You will be the lucky one having your own child. You have a nice voice. I'm sure you are just as beautiful... Going out to Africa. Now there's an adventure."

"Goodbye, Mrs Crabshaw."

"Go well with your life."

Feeling sad, melancholy but strangely excited, Martha drove home to pack, the sense of guilt at leaving her mother to catch a cab coming back to worry her mind.

"I'll phone and go collect her... And stop talking to yourself, Martha Poland, it's a bad habit."

All through her packing, she thought of the life of Mrs Crabshaw, an idea growing in her mind. If Phillip's brother could write books, why couldn't she? The idea of a romantic novel based on the life of Mabel Crabshaw was appealing. She would have to do her research. Go back in history. Get the feel of the early years of the twentieth century. At the Chewore camp on the Zambezi, she would have all the peace and quiet she could ever want to sit and write. It would give her something to keep her mind occupied. Or should she try and write a book about herself and the people who had passed through her life, the good and the bad of them? Maybe Randall would come to Chewore for a visit and she could pick his brains. Ask how he did it. Find out the secret of writing a book. When she phoned her mother she was happy to bursting, the ideas cascading through her mind. Instead of sitting doing nothing in her new African home, she would do something constructive. If it was any good, Randall Holiday the writer would find her a publisher and she'd have a career for the rest of her life, no changing jobs, no need for retirement. She would always have something to do.

"Are you ready, Mom?"

"Whenever you are. Have you finished packing?"

"Not yet. I'm going to be a writer."

"What brought that on?"

"Mrs Crabshaw."

"One minute you're having a baby and getting married to a perfect stranger. Now, out of the blue, you're going to be a writer. I give up. You're all nuts. The whole pack of you. All my children."

"I'm on my way."

"Thank you, Martha."

"I'm never going to forget Mrs Crabshaw. In life you have to have a purpose. She wants to live a hundred years so she can receive a telegram from the Queen of England. I want my babies and I want to write a novel. Maybe lots of novels... Why have you gone silent?"

"I'm just smiling, Martha. Just smiling."

Mrs Crabshaw was still asleep when Martha picked up her mother. She would have liked to ask the old lady more about her life. She dropped off her mother and drove home. By the end of the week she was ready, her stuff packed, her accounts handed over to Jasmine Fairbanks. With her hand luggage in the taxi she was taken to the airport, her journey begun. For most of the flight she slept. No worries. Nothing to regret. At Los Angeles Phillip was waiting for her at the airport. A beautiful girl was standing next to him. Next to the girl was a tall man, his face familiar. They were all smiling. Some of the passengers off her plane were staring at Julian Becker. Myra gave her a hug.

"Welcome to our family, Martha. You'll love living in Zimbabwe. Fancy that. Both Phillip and I are now part of America. Did you tie everything up in Kansas City? You'll get used to it in Africa as I did when I came to live in America. This little girl is Shoona. Say hello to your Aunty Martha... She is a little shy with strangers but there again she is only a baby... We have three days to get to know each other and then you're on your way. Phillip met so many people at the expo. Lots and lots of new business."

Only after touching the side of the child's face and shaking hands with Julian Becker did she hug Phillip. They hugged for a long time, both of them clinging to each other. She was happy. She was going to be married. Going to have a baby. And if luck and fortune came her way, she was going to write a successful novel. What more, she asked herself, could a woman of thirty-seven years of age ever want for a happy future?

"I love you, Phillip," she whispered.

"I love you, Martha. We're going to be so damn happy together."

NOT SURE WHETHER lust was the more appropriate word, Phillip, hand in hand with Martha, followed his sister and brother-in-law from the terminal. He had never seen Martha so bubbly, all smiles and happy talk. Something else had come up he would have to find out about. Julian had hoisted Shoona up onto his shoulders, holding his daughter by both of her hands, the child towering above the throng of busy travellers, looking every which way in her excitement, the heels of her little feet kicking her father's big chest. The man was taller than anyone in the terminal, his hair long, his blue eyes sparkling with the joy of holding his daughter. Outside they found the car.

"How's Kansas City, Martha? Spent the first seven years of my life in that city... Can you hold Shoona while I open the car?"

"Good memories, I hope?"

"Not really. When I was six years old my father had an argument in a bar with a man, went home in a cold rage, picked up his gun, went back to the bar and shot him. Dad was executed the following year."

"Does the media know that story?"

"Not yet. Please don't tell them."

"Of course I won't."

"Being famous isn't all it's cracked up to be."

In the back seat with Myra, Phillip listened, keeping his mouth shut. Everyone had a story, not all of them good. Shoona, good as gold, was sitting next to Martha strapped into a child car seat. Despite his wealth and fame, Julian liked to drive himself. No showing off with a chauffeur for Julian Becker. Phillip liked him. All that fame and fortune had not gone to his head. His niece next to Martha made Phillip feel comfortable. Martha was going to be a good mother. After a long drive they arrived back at the beach house.

"Take your wife-to-be down to the beach, Phillip. I'm sure you have lots to talk about. We'll have a barbeque when you come back."

They walked down the garden past the swimming pool that commanded the most beautiful view out over the ocean that Phillip had ever seen and took the long winding path down to the beach. It was the holiday time of the year, the beach in front of the cliff with the houses, crowded with swimmers. They walked away from all the people. When they were out of sight of the crowd, Phillip led Martha to a rock where he sat, patting the smooth surface of the rock next to him. Martha sat down. She was still smiling.

"What's up? If you don't tell me, you're going to burst."

"I'm going to write books."

Silent and smiling, Phillip picked up a pebble from next to his feet and slung it towards the sea.

"It'll give me something to do when you and Jacques are on safari."

"What are you going to write about?"

"Mrs Crabshaw. The ninety-four-year-old friend of my mother. She wants to live to a hundred and receive a telegram from the Queen of England... Are you listening?"

"To every word... Do you know how difficult it is to write a book?"

"Not yet. Oh, Phillip, I'm so happy. I've got everything planned for us. And I'm going to write lots and lots of books... I like him."

"Who?"

"Julian."

"Everyone loves Julian Becker. He just hates all the attention... Let's walk down to the water's edge. I want to see if I can skip these flat pebbles over the water. If it works we'll come back and make love behind the rocks."

"Don't be ridiculous!"

"Just kidding... Race you to the water."

The first pebble sank, the second skipped three times over the still surface. A couple, hand in hand, were walking slowly towards them down the beach. A seagull, its wings back, dived into the sea and came up with a fish.

"The fish eagles do that in the Zambezi."

"You really love that place don't you?"

"Yes I do. There's something so unique about Africa. Gets under your skin. Remember me saying, once you've drunk the waters of the Zambezi River you will always want to come back again?"

"We can register the birth with the American embassy just in case. What we want in life doesn't always work out."

"All those other people."

"You've got it. I'll make notes so if we have to run from politics I can write about it and hold onto all our memories forever. We're going to make some lovely memories, Phillip."

"Of course we are."

THE THREE DAYS passed them by in a dream, a happy dream for all of their memories. As the plane took off, Phillip, on his way home, felt the relief surging through his body. He had enjoyed himself. Enjoyed meeting Clem. Glad to see his sister and Julian. But when it came to it there was no place like home. At Harare Airport, both of them tired from the endless journey, Jacques was waiting, the back of the truck filled up with supplies. The sun, as always in July, was shining. Jacques sat in the back and let Phillip do the driving.

"Give me a rundown of what's been happening while I was away."

Concentrating on the road and to what his partner was saying, he took the road that would end at the Zambian border where they would turn a few miles short into the Zambezi Valley along the dirt road to Chewore. By lunchtime they were back at the camp. The frame tents with their comfortable compartments were up, the ten German tourists eating their food under the shade of the riverine trees. Munya and Sedgewick were all smiles.

"Welcome home, boss."

"Glad to be back. You remember Martha? Martha's going to be staying with us. We're getting married. I'm going to be a father... How are they, Jacques?" All four of them were looking across at the tourists.

"Having a good trip. We took them out this morning as the sun came up. They leave tomorrow. New tourists arrive on Friday."

"Never stops. Business is good."

"How was America?"

"Lots of new business. This year is going to be the year of fat bonuses for all of you."

They all smiled. Even in the peace and seclusion of the Zambezi Valley, it was still all about money. It made Phillip sad. There had to be more to life than just money. Thinking of the fortune left to him by his grandfather, Phillip told himself he was being an idiot. With so much money in the bank, money to him was unimportant. For others without money their future lives were always vulnerable. Only money gave them security. If Mugabe threw all the remaining whites out of the country what would happen to Munya and Sedgewick? Could they start and run their own safari business? Phillip doubted it. Where would they get the capital to buy the buses, the contacts to find the clients?

"Let's go for a walk. I want to feel the bush. Listen for the songbirds."

With his .375 rifle in one hand and Martha held by the other, they walked in the shade of the trees along the bank of the river. Phillip smiled with the joy of pure contentment. The big river flowed past them, past small islands, flotsam taken with the heavy run of the water. From below in the small bay, tall reeds grew out along the sides of the water. They found a fallen log and sat themselves down in comfortable silence, the river in front of them a poem of flowing beauty. In the middle of the day the birds were silent. There were no crocodiles or hippo visible in the river, the far bank more difficult to see. Hippo, just the tops of their heads and their bulging eyes showing, had the habit of watching hidden among the reeds. He put the gun down next to him against the log where the bark had broken from the fall from the tree. There was consummate peace on earth. Martha, a wistful smile on her face, was holding both of her hands over her stomach. Phillip gently stroked the back of her hands.

"I brought my cassette player and classical tapes."

"Did you bring a typewriter?"

"I'm going to write in longhand. In a place like this who wants a clacking sound? Without electricity, you can't very well use an electric typewriter."

"You seem to have thought of everything."

"A girl has to be prepared. Where am I going to have our baby?"

"In the Harare private hospital."

"It's so strange being here so soon after the noise and bustle of Kansas City. One minute we were in civilisation, the next in the wilds of Africa. The change so quickly is freaky."

"You'll soon forget all those shops and people. Take a while. Did you bring lots of pens and paper?"

"Reams of it... You think the rhino poachers have been back again?"

"Probably. There's too much money in it to stop them."

"Living in a tent. Whoever would have thought it? One big, glorious whirl in my life. That's the exciting part about life when you don't know what's happening next."

"A cold shower under a tree from a hoisted bucket."

"How does that work again?"

"You pull the bucket with its underneath hose up into a tree by a rope and turn on the tap."

"Of course. It was only yesterday."

"With all that pressure in America obscuring your view."

"You think we could lie down on the ground and take a nap? I never sleep on planes."

"Why not? In the bush, I always sleep with one eye open. Welcome to your new home, Martha Poland."

"It's all so beautiful."

"Nature. There's nothing more beautiful than nature. Are you going to be all right living in the wilds?"

"I hope so. Nothing has yet sunk in. You, the baby or living in Africa without a computer and the constant attention of people. I suppose this was how it was for everyone centuries ago. How our ancestors lived."

"Where is your book going to start?"

"I don't know. I want to think. Look back at America from so far a distance and see what we were all about."

"Not Mrs Crabshaw? Randall always says its best to write about one's own experiences unless you want to write fantasy or sci-fi and all that escapism."

"Maybe I'll write the story of an American woman approaching her middle age who gets herself pregnant by a safari operator on the banks of the Zambezi River."

"Are you hungry?"

"I'm starving."

"Let's walk back and get some food. I'll ask Munya to put up a special tent where you can write in perfect solitude. Welcome to the rest of your life. Wherever it takes us. With a child we'll be bound to each other forever. In the end it won't matter where we've lived, we will always be drawn together through the bond of our children."

"You're a romantic, Phillip."

"And I'm practical. Both our lives changed forever the moment you conceived our child... Look! Floating with that log out in the middle of the river. It's a hippopotamus. There. Can you see it, Martha?"

"I think I can. Yes. I see its bulging eyes."

"You know that animal can snap a boat in half with its jaws? It's as dangerous as an elephant or a lion."

"You're trying to frighten me."

"Warn you, Martha. This is Africa. In the wilds, man does not control everything. To that hippo floating downriver we are just two animals. He doesn't know about guns."

They walked back to camp. The fire was low, the coals still red. From the tree where it was hanging, Phillip cut two steaks from the carcase of an impala. Munya had made salads for the tourists, some of which was left over. The rule at Chewore camp was to never throw away food. The venison was quickly cooked. They ate at the folding table in the shade of a towering tree. In the water, all Phillip could see was the dead flotsam. The hippo had sunk back under the water. Munya had brought them a pot of tea with some powdered milk and a bowl of sugar. A butterfly, each wing the size of Phillip's hand, was fluttering close to where they were sitting. The butterfly was yellow, the top of its wings jagged, black spots dotting the thin membranes. There were red flowers under the tree. The butterfly flitted from flower to flower, opening and closing its wings as it gorged on the nectar.

"That butterfly is so beautiful, Phillip."

"Unusual at this time of year. This really is peace on earth and good will to all men."

"Peace be with you, Phillip."

"And you, Martha. And our child. Would you care for a cup of tea?"

PART 4

SEPTEMBER TO OCTOBER 1993 — NO PLACE LIKE HOME

1

$\mathcal{M}$artha's writing desk was a white folding table made of metal. There was a hole in the middle to take an umbrella. For six frustrating weeks she sat with a ballpoint pen and a sheet of white paper trying to write a story. Every morning, under the awning in front of her writing tent, the river flowing down in front of her, she tried her best. Each morning she read back the previous day's writing and threw it away. Groups of tourists came and went, some pleasant, some demanding. Jacques and Phillip did their best to satisfy them, Martha watching from a distance, trying not to be involved. Most of them were urbanites hoping to alleviate the boredom of their mundane lives. They wanted to take something back from all the money they were spending.

Seeing her sitting doing nothing, Phillip walked across to her tent.

"Why are so many of your guests so damn difficult?"

"Most of them enjoy the memory of their safari more than watching the animals. They demand to see everything in a few days: elephant, lion, buffalo, giraffe, leopard, hippo, and rhino, to say nothing of all the different species of buck. We do our best. Some people are never satisfied. They've paid their money and expect everything. What's the matter, Martha?"

"I can't write."

"It took Randall years. He says you have to get to know your characters and get into their heads."

"Why is it so hot?"

"Next month is October. They call it suicide month, it gets so hot and humid in the valley. This is our last tour of the season. By the end of November, the rains will break and we won't come back to Chewore camp until the end of March. By then you will have had our baby and you and I will be married. Next week we will go up into the Chimanimani mountains, six thousand feet above sea level where it's cool at night. I have a cottage on a lake."

"You never told me."

"You never asked me." Phillip was smiling. "One step at a time."

"Why is writing a story so difficult?"

"Never tried."

"What do you do all day by a lake?"

"Go fishing. Read a book. Walk in the cool of the morning. I cook and keep the place tidy by myself."

"All alone?"

"When I needed company, before you came into my life, I drove into Mutari. Took a room in the hotel next to the pub. A bit like Clem."

"You're a strange creature."

"I grew up on a farm. You get used to amusing yourself. Come and say goodbye to our guests. Jacques is taking them to Harare Airport."

Not sure if she could take the solitude in a cottage by a lake, Martha followed Phillip to where the last guests were standing round the bus, waiting to start the journey home. They were all Americans. She was homesick. She wanted to go with them. Even make a run for it.

"Are you bored, Martha?" Phillip was looking at her, a quizzical look on his smiling face.

"Just a little."

"It'll all change once you have our baby."

"I know it will. It's all so strange to me. You think I'll get used to it?"

"Only time will tell."

Life never had been simple. Martha smiled to herself. Not everything good in life came all at once. There were the good bits and the bad bits. There was Phillip and the baby growing in her belly. There was missing her old friends.

"You can't have your cake and eat it."

"You want to go back with them?"

"Part of me."

"And part of me wants to stay in Africa."

"But you have all that money!"

"Money doesn't make you happy. Look at them. They're more excited today than they have been all week. They're going home."

THE NEXT MORNING when Martha woke there was complete silence. Munya and Sedgewick had left in the truck for their three-week holiday to see their relatives in Harare. There were no sounds of birds. Not a plop in the river. A wind came up and brushed the tree that shaded the tent. Phillip was still sound asleep lying on his side. He had rolled up the tent window the previous evening leaving the mosquito gauze to protect them from the night. The big mosquito net that hung over them from the centre pole of the frame tent was being brushed by the soft wind. Martha could see the river through the window, the fine mesh of the gauze dusting the water of the river soft brown. The sun was shining, casting shadows of the tall trees across the flowing water. A big bird flew past her line of sight, gliding, making no sound. Martha was glad she had stayed and not run away with the American tourists.

She got out of bed and walked from the sleeping compartment with its double mattress on the floor, through to the living area, a perfect veranda looking out from the high bank above the Zambezi River. She was naked. The sun, dappling through the leaves of the trees, played on her soft white body. She walked down to the small bay. There were tall reeds on either side. The water from the river was just lapping the muddy sand. She looked around for any sign of animals, the sun now washing her body. Smiling, Martha walked forward into the river, her feet squishing the mud and sand. The water was cool. She sank forward onto her knees. On hands and knees, face down, she sank below the surface. She turned onto her back, her mouth full of water and squirted. On the bank of the river, Phillip was standing with his rifle. He let out a chuckle.

"This is perfect, Phillip."

"Doesn't get any better."

"Can we stay here alone for a week? Just the two of us?"

"I don't see why not... You want some breakfast?"

"I wouldn't mind... Can you see anything?"

"If I could you'd have heard my gun."

"I thought you were asleep."

"The slightest sound when I'm sleeping brings me awake. My subconscious is always alert. You want fish for breakfast?"

"I want you."

"That's possible. You'd better come out of the river. No point in tempting fate. We're not the only creatures looking forward to eating our breakfast."

Martha sat with the water up to her hips. She turned onto her knees to get a grip. From the reeds, a frog was watching her. She winked at the frog.

The heat was stifling. There was no breeze. Only the water out in the river was moving. The insects had stopped singing early in the morning. Kansas City and her previous life were as far away as the moon. Without Phillip and his gun she knew she would have felt frightened. She walked up to the steep bank of the river, her naked body dripping with river water. On the ground next to Phillip was his fishing rod. She walked past towards the tent and felt a slap on her bare bottom. Instantly, Martha wanted to have sex. When she looked back Phillip was casting his line deep into the small bay where she had been swimming. She stood watching. Phillip was whistling. The urge to have sex slowly subsided. By the time Phillip caught a fish her body was dry.

"That should do. A four-pound bream."

"You don't feel the heat?"

"I'm an African, Martha. I may look like a European but I'm an African. Your swelling belly is so damn beautiful."

"Don't you want to make love to me?"

"First let me gut this fish."

"Men!"

"Someone has to be practical. Just kidding. Go into the tent and lie down. I am always at your service, madam." The last words were spoken with a bad French accent.

When they made love, Martha's uncertainty evaporated. She was alone with her man on their 'tropical island' and all was well. He had his hand on her pregnant belly. Martha dozed off. When she woke, she could smell the smoke from the fire where Phillip was cooking their breakfast. She got up from the mattress and put on her pants, not bothering with her top. Her small breasts were still firm. The fish smelt delicious. She walked out and kissed him on the back of his neck: Phillip was kneeling, tending the fish as it cooked. He had made the toast. A breeze came up. She was happy. In that moment she had never been happier.

They ate the fish at the camping table under the canopy of their tent. Her writing tent was away to the right. Looking at her writing tent she felt empty. There was nothing there. No story to write to give her comfort, to bring back her old life and her friends. She ate her half of the fish thinking about her mother. A picture of Mrs Crabshaw came into her mind. She could almost hear the old lady talking, the story Mrs Crabshaw had told about her life beginning to niggle in the back of Martha's brain. Maybe writing about someone other than herself and her own experiences would be easier. She was going to try. There was nothing wrong with trying. The soft breeze coming up from the big river was cooling, making her mind concentrate. It was easier to think.

Phillip finished his fish and smeared marmalade on a piece of buttered toast. He looked happy. He was where he belonged. Sometimes in Kansas City he had looked to Martha like the proverbial fish out of water. If she wanted a happy family she would have to stop thinking only about herself. Making sure not to swallow a bone, she finished every piece of her fish, smiling with contentment.

"That fish was perfect."

"Told you. Life doesn't get better."

"I'm going down to my writing tent. What have you got on your agenda?"

"Paperwork. Jacques leaves it to me. He takes them to the airport; I do the paperwork."

"Has this year made any money?"

"You'd be surprised. Why Munya and Sedgewick were so happy with their bonuses. We run a tight little ship. Nothing gets wasted. No unnecessary overheads. I bought the cottage before I inherited from my grandfather. A small bond from the building society. What I have in Zimbabwe is mine. There's something about making your own money."

"Don't I remember."

"Write well."

"I'm going to try."

"You'll love our cottage."

"Is it ours?"

"It is now."

When Martha reached her writing desk Mrs Crabshaw was in her mind. The saga began. Within minutes Martha was deep in a story, the tent, the Zambezi River, all gone. Two hours later Martha came out of her imagination into the physical world. She clipped the written pages together, turned them over and left them on the white table. She was smiling. She was satisfied. Like eating the perfect meal.

"How did it go today?"

"I'll know tomorrow when I read it back."

"You're all smiley. Got to be a good sign. This afternoon we're taking the boat upriver. See what we can see."

"I thought you hated the noise of the outboard motor."

"I do. But I'm not going to row. Downstream is fine. Trying to row back against the power of the Zambezi is real hard work. You haven't played your music. No sound of Haydn."

"Maybe in the cottage."

"Ah. The perfect cottage for two by the side of a lake."

"Why don't you try writing?"

"Maybe I should. Maybe I will. We'll both make ourselves famous."

"Do you want to be famous?"

"Not in the slightest... Tea, and then we go out on the river. Venison for supper with a bottle of wine. Life's tough down by the river."

"All sounds good to me. Except I can't drink the wine."

"Shame. I'll have to drink for both of us."

"For all three of us, Phillip."

The old boat had been bought for the tourists to let them be part of the river. The bank of the river was perfect. For Martha, out in the middle was all-consuming. A complete world of flowing, powerful water. Tall trees on either bank a distance away. Islands in the stream. Animals standing motionless on a small sandbank watching. When the boat passed and Martha looked back, the buck and giraffe were browsing and grazing, the head of the tall giraffe visible above the trees. They were far away from the world. It was all so beautiful. For half an hour they putt-putted up the river before stopping in one of the small bays. Phillip's gun, loaded, was at the bottom of the boat.

"You can see where the elephant have been. That tree's been pushed over. Look deep into that tree over there and you can see an owl, eyes wide open. A spotted eagle owl. They call to each other at night. He's fast asleep with his eyes wide open."

"Why doesn't he fall off his perch?"

"The powerful claws stay clamped on the branch even while he's asleep. What would we do without a flask of tea?"

The afternoon passed in mutual harmony. As the sun sank behind the distant escarpment, the flowing river turning to red in the glow of the sunset, they arrived back at Chewore camp. Phillip made the fire. He cut a hindquarter from the buck still hanging high in the tree, the netting over the carcase having kept away the flies to prevent them laying their eggs. The light went quickly. Within half an hour it was dark, their world shrunk to the two of them sitting round the campfire on canvas chairs, Phillip drinking the wine. Martha took a sip and gave back the glass. The South African red wine tasted good.

"You could probably have one glass."

"Never break the rules."

By the end of the evening, their stomachs were full. Phillip had drunk the bottle of wine. He was tipsy. It made Martha smile.

"Sorry you couldn't join me. When people drink together they don't see the difference. They talk on, nineteen to the dozen. Stop giving me that knowing smile. I know I'm getting a little drunk. It's the purpose of drinking wine. You look so beautiful in the firelight. There he goes again. Far upriver. It's another spotted eagle owl. Now, that's his mate calling back to him. The night is so alive. The crickets are singing. The owls are calling. And the moon is coming up. My perfect Africa. Nature. Just nature. Nothing forced on us by man. This is how we were meant to live. Not suspended up ten storeys in a concrete prison. No wonder they need all those therapists."

"I miss it."

"I know you do. I'm being rude about your old lifestyle. Let's give it time. If you can't adjust we'll have to think again. You know that old saying: 'What's good for the gander isn't always good for the goose.' I'm as pissed as a newt and loving every minute of it. A whole bottle of Nederburg Cabernet all to myself. And there he goes again. The perfect sound. An owl calling to its mate. They always sound so damn happy. To the tent, my lady. 'Tis time to sleep. Perchance to dream."

Phillip doused the fire with a bucket of water he had brought up from the river. They went to bed. Within a minute Phillip was sound asleep. The moon was playing through the gauze of the tent window, the canopy with the zips on either side now shutting them into the tent. Martha lay awake thinking. Would there really be a future for them in Africa? Minorities were invariably persecuted when they had money and property. It was all politics, the constant fight for power. In America they all had an equal say in what was going to happen, or so they were told by all the smart politicians. Could a family stay in the wilds and not be a part of the modern world? Martha doubted it. Phillip was snoring, a soft fluting, followed by a snore and a grunt. He had told her many times she was beautiful but did he really mean it? Or was he saying it to make her feel good? She was thirty-seven years old, no longer so gullible. And how was a baby in the wilds going to get educated? Would the child be sent away to boarding school in America? There was no future in Zimbabwe's educational system. To be competitive children had to have the best of education. They would grow up apart from their parents, fostered by teachers, so what was the point of it all in the first place? Life for her in a tent while her children grew up on the other side of the world, coming home for holidays, and soon going off again. Was that a life? They would never be able to truly know each other. Halfway into the night Martha was still tossing and turning. Next to her the father of her child was sleeping peacefully. The cicadas were still screeching outside the tent. Not far away a lion roared three times thrusting fear into her belly. Phillip did not wake, the loaded gun next to him on the groundsheet beyond Martha's reach. On the farm growing up she had once fired her brother's shotgun and hurt her shoulder from the recoil. She had never even picked up a rifle. In the dark of the night, washed by an eerie pale moon, Martha wished she was back in her Kansas City apartment with its solid concrete walls and all the safety a pregnant mother-to-be could want.

"He's a good mile away. Sounds a lot closer at night."

"I'm frightened, Phillip. I thought you were asleep."

"Trust me. I've spent my life in the bush. There's plenty of food for him. Anyway, when they're hunting they don't make a sound."

"Now I'm even more frightened."

"The roar of a lion in the African bush. Now that's a real sound. Nothing artificial about that. I'll bet the only time you heard a lion roar before was at the start of an MGM movie."

"Stop laughing at me. My whole body is shivering with fright."

"Come to me, Martha."

"Oh, Phillip. What's going to happen to us?"

Slowly, gently, Phillip calmed her down, his hand stroking her body. After a while she became aroused. Fear was mingled with lust as she made passionate love. After climaxing twice she was satisfied. The fear had gone. Within minutes she was sound asleep, deep in her dreams. When she opened her eyes it was light, the dawn chorus of birds bringing her awake. She was no longer frightened. A new day had begun.

"That was a lion last night?"

"Oh, yes. That was a lion, Martha. The next time you won't be so frightened."

Martha got up and went outside the tent. The river was flowing, everything just the same. She made a fire and boiled the kettle, making tea for Phillip and a mug of coffee for herself.

"I'm going to try and write. Enjoy your tea. How's your head?"

"Not so bad. I love it when you walk around naked."

Martha put on her clothes and walked down to her writing tent. She put the mug of coffee on her desk next to the pages she had written the previous day. She took a sip of coffee, braced herself, and turned over the pages. She began to read the previous day's writing. The language was jumbled, the sentences difficult to read. None of it flowed. The story she had hoped was so good was as dead as a dodo... She sat back, her hopes of something to do with herself in the wilds of Africa shattered. She couldn't write a story to save her life. Nothing had come alive. The people weren't real. The pictures she had been trying to draw with her words not visible. She could write advertising copy, short phrases to capture the average person's short attention span. Writing a story and bringing it alive was outside her capabilities. She felt flat. She pushed away the useless pages and drank her coffee. There was nothing for her to do. If she stayed in the wilds of Africa she was going to be bored out of her cotton-picking mind.

"Oh, Franklyn. What have I done?"

After half an hour of negative thinking she walked out of the stifling hot tent. The heat of the sun was overpowering. She wanted a life. Good sex and a happy relationship just weren't enough. Neither, most likely, would be a child, despite all the instinctive longing without which the human race would have been extinct.

"Didn't work?"

"I can't write. Business words but not stories. What the hell am I going to do with myself, Phillip?"

"You want to go home?"

"With all my heart. Thank God I didn't sell my apartment or get rid of the furniture."

"How long's the lease?"

"There isn't one. They took it monthly. He wasn't sure about his job. Probably renege on paying his rent. Out here I can't even check my bank account. What are we going to do?"

"Take my fifteen-seater bus and go up to the cottage. Treat it all as a holiday."

"You mean that? You've got all that money. You could start a business in America. Life could go back to normal. Jacques can take over the camp. Find himself a black partner and do what Mugabe wants."

"Was it the lion?"

"It was the bloody awful writing. I thought this new one was so good yesterday. Today it's just horrible."

"Let's pack up and go. Munya and Sedgewick will be back in three weeks to look after the camp. The worst that can happen is an elephant knocking over the ablution block. I'll pack the tents into the bus... Don't look so sad. Dreams are just dreams. Reality is something quite different. We whites have lived in a fool's paradise in this country for over a century. Maybe it's my turn to face reality. Can't live in the past. Do you want to get married here or in America? You don't have to make up your mind now. What a shame. I thought we'd get away."

"From what, Phillip?"

"That dreadful, terrible, ugly modern world."

"I can always have the child on my own."

"It's my child as much as yours. My future."

"Yes I know. I should have been on the pill. It's all my fault."

"It's life, Martha. How it works. One minute you're walking in a straight line and then it all changes."

"I could have an abortion. Still just time."

"Don't even think of it."

"Thank you. If I killed this child I might as well kill myself."

"We're caught between two stools. Africa and America. We'll eat, pack and go. Life's complicated enough as one person. When you take a partner, it gets doubly complicated. What a shame. What a bloody shame."

"Are we ever happy, Phillip?"

"That's a question people have been asking themselves since the dawn of time. It comes and goes. It's life."

IT HAD all started on the banks of the Zambezi River where it had now finished. She had been through the hope and loss before. Was her life once more repeating itself? Martha hoped it wasn't just for the sake of the baby, but she wasn't sure. They packed without any enthusiasm. The bus started first time. She watched the sadness in Phillip's expression, his last look back at his camp making Martha want to cry. She had created a baby and killed the father's life. The winding dirt road went on and on as they drove out of the valley. They turned left onto the tarred road, a few miles short of Chirundu. Martha drifted back into her thoughts, into the story of her life. She thought of the old ranch and her father dying. Her mother's pain. The months of mourning while her mother tried to sell the ranch, her brothers gone. She had driven away with the whole world beckoning. There would be boys. Lots and lots of boys. Or men, Martha not sure then if she was a girl or a woman. Two years later she had met Jake, the love that she thought was to be the love of her life. Jake Tinklerot. Like so many names in America, his echoed a far-off place. His grandparents were persecuted Russian Jews who had fled to America. Jake was young, good-looking, popular with everyone, a man with so much charm it was impossible not to fall for him. The ranch had been sold for a good price. Looking back, to Jake, her family was rich. She had a job in an advertising agency and was making a good salary. He was everything Martha wanted: a passionate lover and a man with all the charm in the world. There was no thought in her mind other than happiness when Jake proposed. Only Martha's mother wasn't so confident.

"He's an odd-job man, Martha. No career. Little education he can use to support a family. All that charm will wear off."

"But I love him, Mother."

"Marriage is a big decision. The biggest in a girl's life. You're twenty-two with all those many years ahead of you. Mrs Tinklerot. Doesn't the name alone tell you something?"

"You're always so negative."

"I love you, Martha. I worry about the future of all my children. When I'm gone, you'll have to look after yourselves."

"The boys are looking after themselves. His grandparents were from Russia. In Russia, Tinklerot doesn't have the same connotation."

"But we live in America. He's a bum, Martha."

"I make a good living."

"That's my point. You're far too gullible. You believe what men tell you. Which is mostly what you want to hear when they're trying to get into your pants. Marriage is a whole different kettle of fish. You need a provider. A man who can earn himself a good living. Think before you jump, Martha."

"You never like my boyfriends."

"Maybe you're always picking the wrong ones. Think about it. The next minute you're going to get yourself pregnant and then who's going to earn the living? Odd-job Jake? I don't think so."

"I'm in love."

"Oh, we all think we're in love at your age."

"Weren't you in love with Dad?"

"That was different. He was also a practical man. He had the farm he had inherited from your grandfather."

"Money isn't everything."

"But it helps. And isn't Jake Jewish? He'll want you to change your religion."

"He doesn't follow his faith."

"He doesn't follow anything except a good-looking woman with a successful job and a mother with family money."

The first year while Martha was trying to get herself pregnant had been the best year of her life. They had a small apartment in downtown Kansas City. Jake said he was trying to get himself a permanent job and Martha had believed him. Most evenings when Martha came home after a hard day's work, Jake was still in his underwear on the couch in front of the television. She should have known then she was in a trap. Not even the washing up was done. He was all smiles, a beer bottle in one hand, a sandwich in the other. When Martha caught him cheating her world collapsed. The fog of love evaporated allowing her to see Jake for what he was: a low-life, lazy bum. Feeling lucky she hadn't got herself pregnant, she had thrown him out of the apartment, leaving her with a pile of his unpaid bills. She had given up the apartment and moved in with her mother. Three years later, she did it all over again with Jonathan Mann. Her mother was right. Each time she had chosen the same man. A charmer. When it came to charming, good-looking men who told her how wonderful she was, Martha knew she was a sucker.

"A penny for your thoughts. You've barely said a word since we left Chewore."

"I was thinking back on my life to all the mistakes."

"And hoping you haven't made another one."

"Something like that. Do you really have all that money from your grandfather? Craig doesn't look rich."

"We have different mothers. Not the kind of question I was expecting."

Two hours later, neither having spoken, the small bus entered the outskirts of Harare.

"Do you really think I want to marry you for your money, Martha? You were the one to deliberately get yourself pregnant. I'm the one throwing away the only life I have known. If you want, you can have one of your fancy American lawyers contact my bankers in Jersey. I'll authorise them to give you an up-to-date statement. Something I haven't asked from them for years. I'm not a money man, Martha. Provided I've got a roof over my head, good food and the occasional bottle of wine, money with all its showing off doesn't interest me. We don't really know each other. And if we don't trust each other to tell the truth now, what the hell are we going to do in the future? At this moment, that child in your belly is close to being brought up by a single parent. The wonderful new modern world they have in Europe and America where half the kids don't have families. Poor little bastard. Do you want me to take you straight to the airport?"

"Calm down, Phillip. You don't understand."

"No, I don't. And I'm not sure I want to. Right now I'm not certain that child in your stomach is mine. And stop crying. Women always cry when they can't get their own way."

"Are we having an argument?"

"Damn right we are."

"I'm so sorry."

"Heard that before."

"Can't we just drive through to the cottage? I was thinking of my ex-husbands who lived off me until I caught them cheating. We live in a different world in America."

"Damn right you do. And that's what scares the shit out of me. What we'll do is book into Meikles Hotel and do some dispassionate thinking. We've got to stop fooling each other. You're pregnant. You say it's mine. You don't believe I have my grandfather's money. Where the hell do we stand?"

"Then we only marry after our baby is born and I prove I'm not lying to you with a DNA test."

"You'll do that?"

"If I have to. I'm sick of people lying."

"Then we'll drive on to my cottage by the lake."

"Thank you, Phillip. Was your grandfather really the famous Ben Crossley?"

"Damn right he was. Why are you giggling?"

"It's better to laugh than to cry. I nearly blew it."

"That poor little bastard doesn't know what he's getting into."

"You're not going to dump me at the airport?"

"Not yet."

"Now you're laughing."

"There's too much at stake. Let's try and trust each other and be happy. Someone in this crazy world has to be trustworthy... Did they both live off your money and cheat on you? Poor Martha. I wonder if the new world isn't destroying us."

"We make the world what it is."

"God help us."

"Are you a Christian?"

"Church of England. Politics, religion, it's all one big manipulation. A bit like half the world's marriages. Maybe why I never married. Saw too many of my friends go down the drain. So here we go. I give you a bank statement. You prove I'm the father. And never, never lie to each other."

"And we can live in America?"

"Here we go again. You just want your own way."

"I want what's good for our child. Africa is wonderful and romantic. But it isn't practical. The blacks don't like you, Phillip. Don't you get it?"

"Not all of them."

"The ones with power. Bit by bit they'll steal your last cent and say it's all justified as you shouldn't have had it in the first place. That you colonials exploited them and everything in their country, from the minerals to the land. Black empowerment. Nothing wrong with it. Take from the rich and give to the poor. Robin Hood and his merry men. There's just one problem with it. Someone has to make the money in the first place. Create a tobacco industry. Find the minerals and dig them out of the ground. And manage the business afterwards. It's easy to steal and spend other people's money. Not so easy to make it. America respects the work and brains that go into creating a successful economy. We call it capitalism. And it works."

"Only history will tell. As President Mugabe has found, it's easy to manipulate a democracy once they've voted you into power. But you're right. The chances of this beautiful country of mine succeeding in the short run are slim. In the valley, I don't think about the future. I just enjoy the present. And yes, that has now changed."

"Aren't you bitter?"

"Not bitter. Just sad. There were so many lives destroyed, not just those of my family. Took Dad years to pay back the bank the money he borrowed to make the farm productive. All went down the drain. Dad didn't take a cent. You can't get money out of the country. Black empowerment."

"Come and live in America. That kind of thing will never happen in America."

"I hope not. I hope not for the whole damn world. I'm going to stop at the supermarket. There's no food in the cottage. America. Now I'm off to America. The poor old English are spread right round the world. Now England's filling up with Eastern Europeans. One Englishmen goes out, one Eastern European comes in. Damn that lion. You know there, for a moment, I was thinking of myself as an Englishman like my father."

Martha helped with the shopping, conscious of the ten thousand American dollars in one-hundred-dollar bills stashed in her handbag, thanks to her mother's advice. A girl had to be ready for anything. As she walked round the supermarket dropping food into the trolley, she wasn't sure where the next turn in her life would take her. At the till Martha insisted on paying the bill, the store manager smiling at her American dollars. The man, a white man, saw them right to the door.

"You think he'll pocket my dollars? Say we paid in local currency and put his own local money back in the till?"

"Probably. The only way to save money for the rainy day that's coming is to hold foreign currency."

"So you agree the white man's finished in Zimbabwe?"

"That was never my worry. I want to stay as long as possible thanks to Grandfather Crossley. And you never know. Hope springs eternal. Revolutions come and go. Man's been moving around the world since the dawn of time looking for something better to do with his life or running away from a catastrophe. Look at America. You were lucky. If the Red Indians had multiplied instead of dying from the white man's diseases, you might also be looking for somewhere else to live. Maybe the trick is to never get too comfortable. Never hope that if you work hard and build something you will have it for the rest of your life. Maybe those who bum their way through life have the answer. Spend what you've got. To hell with tomorrow. Like your charming husbands from what I hear. How are they, by the way?"

"Jake married a rich old woman."

"Good luck to him."

"Suits both of them. She gets a companion instead of living on her own. He gets his comforts. Her children hate Jake."

"Of course they would. He's spending their money. You want a banana? That lot should be enough to keep us going. Smile, Martha. The world hasn't come to an end."

"I love you, Phillip. I mean it. I really love you."

He smiled at her and went round to his side of the bus. She climbed up next to him. He was peeling back a banana and humming a tune. Haydn's Twenty-Eighth Symphony. Her favourite.

"You want me to play a cassette?"

"That would be lovely. Maybe our child will play the violin. Or jazz piano. One day I want to go to New Orleans. Wasn't that where traditional jazz began?"

"We're all right again?"

"We're perfect."

"Haydn's Twenty-Eighth?"

"What I was hoping for. We can always have his music wherever we are. What a wonderful gift. A man who lived so long ago giving us so much joy. Now that was a life worth living. They can destroy you and take away your money. But they can't destroy your music. That's a legacy worth leaving. How old is she?"

"Who?"

"Jake's wife."

"Seventy-two."

"My goodness."

THE BUS, well-tuned by Jacques, hummed its way out of the suburbs into the country. The road was long. The music played over the sound of the engine and the hum of the tyres on the road. Martha could see for miles. The occasional farmhouse with tobacco curing barns and sheds slipped by. There was no sign of life on the farms; Phillip had said it was the off-season, that planting tobacco started at the end of the month. At four thousand feet above sea level, the temperature and humidity were pleasant. The music and the thrum of the wheels on the tarred road sent Martha back into her reverie. The time after throwing out Jake was one of the best in her life. It was the end of the disco decade. A time when everyone partied in the clubs. Saturday night fever. They fucked it out of each other. Worked hard. Played hard. Enjoyed life to the full. But all good things had to come to an end. Hers came with Jonathan Mann, the old human call in Martha for immortality making her want a child. She had met him in a disco, the lights flashing, the music dancing her feet. He was the best dancer. Tall, thin, with perfect rhythm. She had fallen for him straight away. They had fucked the first night. But instead of fucking him out of her system she had fallen in love, her yearning for lifetime companionship and her desire for a child all-consuming. By then she should have known. Instead of remembering the example of Jake she convinced herself she had found the perfect man. As a lover he was perfect. As a dancer he was perfect. His charm was even better than Jake's. He had a job with an insurance assessor. He had money. An apartment of his own that he told Martha he had bought. Which he had, but with the bank's money. By then Martha had bought her own apartment, half of it paid for in cash. They had married. Martha had sold her own apartment and moved in with Jonathan, everything in the garden rosy. Or so she thought. Despite trying hard she again couldn't get herself pregnant. After a year of living high on the hog, the police arrested Jonathan and sent him to prison. The bulk of his money had come from his complicity in fraudulent claims. Like Jake, when it came to the accounting, Jonathan Mann was broke, the apartment she thought they owned under water. Every time the price went up, Jonathan had increased the mortgage to fund his lifestyle. Shattered for the second time, she had moved back with her mother. When she visited her husband in jail, he wanted a divorce.

"I'm a fraud, Martha. A thief and a fraud. You don't want anything more to do with me."

"I so wanted a child."

"I was never as good as the others so I had to steal to keep up with them. To keep up with you. The basic salary of a loss adjuster was nowhere near what you're getting. Many of my clients were happy to be complicit in getting more from the insurance company than their smashed-up car had been worth before the accident. So they gave me backhanders which has landed me here where I am. Now, I'll never amount to anything. The insurance industry will never employ a convicted criminal. Divorce me, Martha. Forget me. I'm no damn use to anyone, including myself. Go back to the good life. Give me a divorce. Are you still mad at me?"

"For lying. Cheating. For becoming a criminal. Of course I'm mad at you."

"Then let's have an amicable divorce. Maybe later, much later, when we're old, we'll remember those nights in the disco dancing to the music. The Bee Gees. You won't remember so much how it ended. Just those wonderful Saturday nights when everyone was happy. Just this once I want to do the right thing. I've destroyed my own life. I don't want to destroy yours."

SLOWLY, Martha pulled herself back to the present. She was staring through the windscreen seeing nothing but her memories.

"The tape has stopped, Martha. Don't you want to play another one? What a lovely day in Africa. Not a cloud in the sky. You were off into your dreams again. I hope they were good."

"Why does everything good in this life always come to an end?"

"Were you thinking of Jake?"

"No, my second husband, Jonathan. The one who went to prison."

"You didn't tell me."

"Not something you boast about. Maybe I'd better tell you."

As Phillip drove, concentrating on the road, she told him the full story of Jonathan Mann. At the end, she felt better. Phillip fell silent.

"How much further?"

"A couple of hours. We'll be at the lake before it's dark."

"Does it have electricity?"

"Of course it does. You'll love my cottage as much as I do. I'm hungry. What a terrible story. Poor Martha. Never met anyone who's been to prison. Can you look for the biscuits?"

"Did you ever see the movie *Saturday Night Fever*?"

"I loved it. The music. The dancing. The story."

"So did I. Those were good memories. Let's not make mistakes. I want to be happy. For you and our child. You'll get used to living in America."

Phillip smiled but said nothing.

2

The sun was shining above the trees when they reached the cottage, a small brick home nestling close to the water of the lake. The garden was overgrown, the path up to the garage next to the house full of weeds. The word dilapidated sprang into Martha's mind. But when it came to beauty, Phillip's cottage by the big lake was unbeatable.

"I put dust sheets over the furniture. Inside isn't so bad. I could employ a caretaker but it wouldn't be the same. The peace, the quiet, one man's perfect privacy. Every day when I'm here I walk round that lake. Takes me three hours. I take a backpack with food and a flask of tea."

"You don't have a boat?"

"Boats make noise. You saw that on the Zambezi."

"You could get a rowing boat. Are there fish in the lake?"

"Plenty."

"What do you do here on your own?"

"Think. Read. Walk the woods. Sleep peacefully. If only I had the talent to be an artist. Not all of us are that lucky."

"What would a child do by the lake?"

"Grow up peacefully."

"And education?"

"I'd teach him what I know."

"Not practical."

"I know it isn't. But which would be worse? Peace and simplicity like this? Or having to make all that money and ending up in jail?"

"Jonathan was unlucky. Many of them get away with petty fraud. They wanted to make an example of him. The insurance company's way of trying to keep the rest of the employees in the industry honest. The world you want to live in doesn't exist."

"Oh, but it did. Still does. Welcome to my cottage away from the crowd, Martha Poland. In the future, among the turmoil of modern life, you'll remember this place and wonder what went wrong with the human race. Greed. Wanting more. Always wanting more. Nobody satisfied. Help me unload the stuff out of the bus. Tonight we'll make a *braai* in the garden under the trees and listen to the lovely sounds of nature. We won't turn on the lights. Just the moon and the firelight. We'll talk quietly, so as not to disturb the African night... Give this old romantic a kiss."

"You're going to drown in Kansas City."

"No I'm not. Remember Clem? I'll make a new life for myself. It'll just be different. But I'll have a child. My life will go on. Maybe for centuries and centuries, if we don't blow up the planet."

"Is the bed made?"

"Matter of fact it is. All we have to do is take off the dust sheets."

"You're as mad as a March hare."

"Do you mind my being mad?"

"I love it."

"Welcome to utopia."

The sheets came off, the fridge was turned on and packed with food. The lake was silent, the fading light brushing the great sheet of water. Phillip lit a fire in the *braai*. From the cottage, he brought out a small folding table and two canvas chairs. Martha made herself coffee and Phillip tea, the argument in the bus forgotten.

"You'll need a sweater. Once the sun goes down it gets cold, even at the end of September. We're at five thousand feet above sea level."

"Why's it so quiet?"

"The crickets don't sing when it's cold. Rump steak. Spuds in the coals. No chance of rain. And all to ourselves."

"I can't see anyone's light."

"They're holiday cottages. People come up to fish. We'll see lights at the end of the week."

"What was that?"

"A bird. Sometimes you hear wild animals. There. How's that for a fire?"

"I have an idea for America."

"Tell me."

"To give you something to do when I'm working, you could become a venture capitalist."

"What's a venture capitalist?"

"At the birth of the internet many young people had brilliant ideas but no capital to develop them. The venture capitalist links good ideas with money and management skills, and takes a large share in the new company. If the idea works, as some of them have, the growth in the start-up and the value of the shares is ridiculous. They float these companies on the New York Stock Exchange. Think Microsoft and a host of others. They all started from small beginnings. You'd meet young people. Possibly make a fortune. It's risky, but you can spread the risk by investing in a number of ventures. You'd have some fun. Travel America. In my advertising career I've come across many people hungry for capital."

"I'll bet you have. I know nothing about business."

"That's my point. You do. You built a highly successful safari business and look after the money side like a professional. You have a degree. Most businesses are common sense. You think through each idea before jumping in the water. In LA, you were talking to all those travel agents. And it worked. Where that last group of tourists came from. It would be fun. And that's what's important in a city. It's not just making money. It's having fun making it. Sharing the excitement with other people."

"You've been thinking. Anyway, my degree was in history. No practical use to anyone."

"A girl's got to think. Life's not all bad in the big cities otherwise half the world wouldn't live in them. You can't just sit in a bar all day with the likes of Clem. You've got to have something to do. Something to think about. There will be time for holidays by the lake. Am I making any sense?"

Phillip got up and put more wood on the fire before sitting down again in his canvas chair next to Martha. He leaned forward to the flames of the fire, the palms of his hands held open to the heat, contemplating. Martha put on her sweater. When her head came out through the top she was looking up at the night sky, three layers of stars and a sickle moon. The surface of the lake reflected the heavens. No wind. No sound. The night held without motion. For a long while Martha looked out over the lake immersed in the silence, making a memory she wanted to remember for the rest of her life. So she could tell her children. The fire had burned down and the meat was cooking over the coals.

"Will you think about it?"

"I've been thinking about it."

"The night sky is so beautiful."

"The spuds will be ready in half an hour. We all eat too much meat in Zimbabwe... Would I need an office?"

"Probably not."

"Where do you find people with all the bright ideas?"

"Oh, they'll find us once the word gets out you want to be a venture capitalist... That's an owl?"

"And that's the bark of a buck. Just one single bark. A dog barks two or three times in succession. I'm hungry. I'm going to open a bottle of wine. Can't wait for you to have the baby and keep me company. There's nothing sadder than a man drinking on his own. The meat's nearly done. Are you hungry?"

"Starving. I'm starving, Phillip. And for more than meat."

"That will have to wait."

"Can I have a kiss?"

"Of course you can."

"I'm so glad we're not arguing."

"So am I. And if it works, what are we going to do with all that money?"

"We'll think of something. Kiss me."

"Better not. One thing leads to another... There. How's that for the perfectly cooked piece of steak? Crisp on the outside. Rare in the middle."

"Go get your wine."

The night sounds had begun from the bush surrounding the silent lake. The nearest house was half a mile away, surrounded by trees.

Martha had seen two of them before the light went. Again the bark of the buck. More a cough than a bark. The stars in the heavens were brilliant, the planets sparkling. A large bird flew across the moon, too far away for the slow flap of its wings to be heard. Martha watched Phillip sip at his wine. They were both smiling at each other, Phillip's face touched by the glow of the fire, his smiling eyes reflecting the light. Martha's life was in suspense, held by the night. Herself, a small, insignificant speck in the vastness of the universe. She was content. When they ate the meat it was delicious, the juice from the steak trickling down the sides of her face. When the potatoes came out of the fire they gingerly broke them open with their fingers and filled the fluffy, well-cooked centres with butter. Phillip had finished half of his bottle of wine. The fire and food had made them drowsy and ready for bed. Instead of making love they fell asleep enveloped in the silence. Martha dreamed all night. Happy unbroken dreams. When she woke it was daylight. The birds were singing. Phillip was still asleep. She lay, looking up at the ceiling, happy and content. It was all going to work out. In a cottage by an African lake on a peaceful morning, her child growing in her belly, her man sleeping next to her, she knew their lives were going to be happy. She got out of bed and walked to the window to look at the view over the lake. Near the shore, a duck was swimming with three little ducklings. A wind was ruffling the surface of the water, reflecting the morning light from a million ripples. He was right. It was utopia.

"It's perfect," she whispered.

"So are you, Martha. Come back to bed."

Phillip got up first, leaving Martha to contemplate, her back to the pillows, the lake visible through the open window. Outside, she watched Phillip put the cork back in the bottle that was still sitting on the table. She watched him walk towards the house. Heard him give someone a phone number, not quite understanding what was happening.

"Thank you, operator, I can wait."

The communication system in the wilds of Zimbabwe was something from her grandparents' generation. Her mind drifted away.

"Are you sleeping again?"

"Sorry. I dozed off."

"Craig and Jojo are still in England. Jerry Longhurst, our mutual friend, hasn't heard from them since they left Harare. Says no news is good news. I'm going for my walk. I'll take some breakfast. The best time to walk is early in the morning or in the evening. I don't need a gun out of the valley. No elephant, lion or rhino at five thousand feet. Will you be all right?"

"I'll miss you."

"You want to come?"

"Three hours of walking! You've got to be kidding."

"It's good for you. Exercise keeps us fit. Good for the kid."

"You won't walk too fast?"

"We'll stop regularly. There are two flasks in the cottage. We'll take one for tea and one for coffee."

"So we don't have to stop off and see your brother in Harare?"

"Straight to the airport where I'll leave Jacques the key to the bus. He can pick it up with Munya when he comes into town. When we go we'll be gone. Goodbye Africa. I'll cry. Silly, a grown man crying. But life goes on. Come on. Up you get. Your nice strong pair of walking shoes. We can skinny dip in the lake. No one will see us. No fishing today. Just you, me, flasks of coffee and tea, a large box of sandwiches and half a dozen oranges. Have you ever made love by the side of a lake?"

"It's worth trying."

"Have your shower and get dressed while I'm making the sandwiches."

"If we're going to swim bare-assed, I don't need a shower."

"You're giggling again, Martha."

"I know I am. I'm bursting inside with happiness."

"Ham, cheese and leftover beef from last night's dinner. How does that sound?"

"How long are we staying?"

"As long as you like. The time is ours. No one to dictate to us. Let's relish our solitude to the full. Who knows when we'll find it again?"

"Let the gods decide."

"Yes. Let the gods decide. They always do."

a week. One long, beautiful week. And then they left the cottage, its flowers gone wild in the long grass of what once had been a well-tended garden, a sad reflection, according to Phillip, of what once had been colonial Zimbabwe, or Rhodesia as it was known in those days. They drove straight to Harare Airport, after Phillip had carefully put the dust sheets back over the furniture.

"Are you quite sure you want to go?"

"What else can I do, Martha? What I had is past. A father has to be responsible."

When they landed at Heathrow Airport they were met by Craig and Jojo. They were to stay three days and fly to New York. Craig drove them to his father's flat in Chelsea where Martha was to meet her future in-laws. The block of flats was owned by Phillip's father and the woman who had once been Livy Johnston, Martha gradually picking up the Crookshank family history. Apparently, Livy and Phillip's father had once been lovers but Livy had not wanted to live in Rhodesia with its political turmoil. The story had made Martha smile. Nothing changed. History repeated itself. The world, and the people in it, went round and round. Martha had hoped she was going to meet the famous writer but Randall was still living as a recluse on the Isle of Man, writing his books. During the day they toured the sights of London one after the other,

Martha not sure if she had taken in the famous places she had seen to properly store in her memory. With luck, she would remember Admiral Nelson on top of his column in Trafalgar Square.

"I'm glad all my boys are out of Africa, Martha. He probably won't thank you now but he will later. So it's two of my children in America. Well, that's how it goes. Bergit and I will visit you. You don't mind if I don't see you to the airport. I'm always catching colds and the flu in England. Goes with the territory. Never happened in Rhodesia. Have a good life with my son. What are you going to call my grandson?"

"It may be a granddaughter."

"Of course. We always think our children will be boys."

"Will you come over for the wedding?"

"We certainly shall. A quick trip over the pond. Isn't that what you call it?"

"Nice to meet you, Mr Crookshank."

"Likewise. Call me Jeremy. We British aren't so stuck up as we used to be. At last my eldest son is getting married. Congratulations."

"We're going to be happy together. That's all that counts."

THEY STAYED two nights in New York for the fun of it and caught the flight to Kansas City. They were to stay with her mother until the tenant moved out of Martha's apartment. Two days later, on the Thursday, she called on Franklyn, looking for a job. Jasmine, ensconced in Martha's old cubicle, was happy to see her. Being an account executive, making all the decisions, wasn't as easy as Jasmine had thought. They all went out to lunch, everything back the way it had been.

"Three months' unpaid maternity leave, Franklyn. We'll share the clients, Jasmine. You'll still be an account executive. We'll work together. Grow the number of our accounts. I can't believe I'm home. You have no idea how good it is to see you all. I missed all my friends and colleagues. Give me until Monday. Wow, that went better than I hoped. One minute you're going, then you're coming. All that rush."

"When are you getting married?"

"When I've had this baby. Cheers, everyone. To the best friends and colleagues a girl could ever wish for."

"Where's Phillip?"

"In the pub, Jasmine. His friend Clem is on one of his visits again. They met up again yesterday. Can you believe the timing? Luck. You got to have some luck in this life. What Phillip needs. Friends. A couple of years and he'll be speaking with an American accent."

"Didn't you like Africa?"

"I loved it. But a girl has to be practical. Especially a girl about to be a mother."

"What's he going to do with himself? You can't run a safari business in Kansas City."

"Venture capitalist. When the market hears he's Ben Crossley's grandson and Randall Holiday's brother, they'll come running. Nothing like fame to get the word out. People like to know who you are before they'll do business. We'll pick through it all for the right ones. Both of us. Two heads are better than one... Are you in a hurry to get back to the office, Franklyn?"

"Not at the moment. Maybe you can use some of that fame to find Horst and Maples some new clients."

"The first new client is Phillip Crookshank. We'll be his publicist. By the time we're finished he'll be famous. Every newspaper and television show will want to interview him."

"Waiter. Bring us another bottle of that red wine. We're celebrating."

"If he finds another Bill Gates to finance we'll have a new client the size of Microsoft. And who knows how far that one is going? All you need is a good idea, money and the right people to do your marketing. This wine is going down so well I'm going to get tipsy. Doesn't matter. My lover is having fun. I know I shouldn't be drinking with a baby inside of me but this is special. Two family reunions in three days. Some say a little red wine is good for a baby. Who knows? One lot says drink, another lot says don't. Am I making any sense?"

"You're happy, Martha. Full of fire. Your old clients will be happy to see you. Three months' maternity leave. Jasmine stays in your old cubicle. We'll move Max down a slot and you can have his cubicle. Nothing like an open-plan office. Same salary as before, with one condition: within a year you double your billings... How's your mother?"

"Happy to see me. She gets lonely. I can't wait to get started."

By the time they finished the bottle of wine the Zambezi Valley and the cottage by the lake were forgotten. Martha felt a cold shudder go through her body. She would have died of boredom living at the cottage trying to write a book. No people. No television. Nothing but herself and Phillip to think about. There had to be more in life than trying to pretend she was happy. Her life had almost been taken away from her by the desire to mother a child. Forget the politics. In the wilds of Africa, among all the solitude and beauty of nature, she would not have had a life. Neither would her child. And in the end, when the politics exploded over the last colonial's head, neither would Phillip.

"Where've you gone, Martha?"

"Sorry. I was thinking of Phillip. Trying to kid myself I've done him a favour. Why are we humans so damn selfish?"

"How we are made, I suppose. Let's enjoy another bottle of wine. We're getting somewhere on the Ferndale account. Come back to us, Martha."

"Sorry. You have my undivided attention."

The waiter came with the new bottle and filled up her glass with the others. She had been so good in Africa not drinking with the baby. But business was business. She had to be part of the team. Not the odd one out. She had her job back. Her life back. Soon she would have her apartment back. The tenant had not paid the last month's rent. By the end of October, it would be paid from the man's deposit.

"If I give him back his deposit he might move out tomorrow."

"What was that, Martha?"

"Nothing, Franklyn. Go with direct marketing for Brindles. They're too small for television advertising. Direct mail. They'll get more for their buck. We'll need to do some research to compile a potential client list. Flyers will be a waste of money. Got to be specific. Target the right market."

"Didn't he pay his rent?"

"No, he didn't."

"Sometimes your worst enemies do you the best favours."

"He's not my enemy."

"He was living rent-free. Cheating you."

"You're right. People. It's always the money."

"I always pay my rent on time. Stop order."

"You're still young and naïve, Jasmine. You'll find out."

"I prefer to trust people. Not everyone is a thief. Direct mail. I agree with Martha. Be nice to get your apartment back so soon. Make sure he doesn't run off with the furniture."

"You're catching on, Jas."

WHEN SHE REACHED HOME after the lunch Phillip was talking to her mother in the lounge.

"We've planned the wedding for next month, darling. Come and sit down."

"I got my job back. Better wait until I've had the baby. The marriage will make him legitimate. America is different to England."

"Have you been drinking? What about my granddaughter?"

"Celebrating. Had to join in. I'm going to be a working mom. You have to juggle your life. No fast rules. A few glasses of red wine won't hurt. Three months' unpaid maternity leave. That's when we'll get married, Phillip. How was Clem?"

"Drunk. I didn't want to get drunk. He was a bit boring towards the end."

"What happens when you don't join in. I want to make a phone call to my tenant. With luck we can move back in over the weekend."

"Why are you so chirpy?" asked her mother.

"Because I'm winning, Mother. There's no better feeling than winning. Franklyn's going to help us look for prospects, Phillip. Horst and Maples are going to be your publicists. It's all happening... John Stone? Martha Poland. If I gave you back your deposit will you move out tomorrow? Splendid. Take you a day? Splendid. Sorry about your job. I'll come round for the keys at five o'clock tomorrow afternoon. Splendid. Have a nice day."

"That was quick."

"Poor jerk's run out of money. You know what? In for a penny, in for a pound as you say in England, Phillip. Let's crack a bottle of wine. Let's celebrate."

"Why not?"

"That's my Phillip. Got my job. Got my apartment. Got you. And I got a baby on the way. What more could a girl want? Let's celebrate. It's just so damn good to be home... Don't look so sad, Phillip. Be happy for us. Everything is working out fine. What's that frown for?"

"I was thinking about the dust sheets in my cottage. And Munya driving my bus. Now it's all so far away."

"That's the past. Think of the exciting future. You're a venture capitalist now. Not a safari operator."

"Of course. What was I thinking? Aggie, give me that bottle. If there's one thing I still know how to do it's pull a cork out of a bottle."

"Thank you, Phillip. I've invited Mrs Crabshaw to dinner. She's been such a good friend while you were away in Africa."

"Ah, Mrs Crabshaw. What a shame. I tried to write her story into a book. It didn't work. Who knows where we would be if it had? For a moment I quite fancied myself as a novelist. Why don't you ask Randall to come over for our wedding?" Phillip still looked sad.

"I can try. Do you want to give Mrs Crabshaw's story another go?"

"Don't be silly. I'm an account executive at Kansas City's most prestigious advertising agency. Give me a break."

"Sorry. A man can only hope. I'm homesick. You're home but I'm homesick."

"I'm sorry, honey. Bring that bottle and three glasses and come sit with Martha. Poor Phillip is homesick."

"Are you laughing at me?"

"Of course I'm not. Give us a kiss. Aren't you going to congratulate me for getting my job back?"

"What was I thinking? Well done, Martha. Have a drink. Now I've got someone to drink with... Cheers, Aggie. Cheers, Martha. Top of the morning to both of you."

"It's afternoon."

"Just a saying. Let's get plastered."

"You should be married before you have the baby."

"I know we should, Mother."

"Then why don't you?"

"Because if I told you the reason we'd have an argument."

"What's the problem, Martha?"

"I want to prove to Phillip with a DNA test that he's the father before we are married."

"You don't trust each other."

"Yes we do."

"Doesn't sound like it. What has the world come to?"

"There's nothing better than proof. Written proof. Isn't that right, Phillip? Have you written to your bankers?"

"Your mother let me use her phone. Their letter is on the way. Oh, and it's over five million dollars. Good investing in the global equity market."

"What with your money and my job we sure aren't going to be short of cash. Cheers, everyone."

"Down the hatch."

"Five million dollars!"

"Yes, Mother."

"That's quite a lot of money. Why does Phillip want to work?"

"To give him something to do."

"And what are you going to do with more money?"

"Spend it."

"You're all crazy. And what are you going to spend it on?"

"I have no idea."

"There was a man I met at a dinner party some years ago not long after we came to Kansas City. For some reason he fancied me. Horrible-looking man. Full of himself. All he could talk about was what he had done. How clever he was. How rich he had become. Told me all about his properties. A plush apartment in New York. A house in the best suburb of Los Angeles, a suburb I'd never heard of. A place in the South of France. And his ranch outside Kansas City that he wanted me to visit. Why he didn't use his money to buy a young whore was beyond me. Told him I was quite happy in this apartment and didn't wish to visit anyone's ranch as it would remind me of my late husband. Years later I heard he went broke. Committed suicide. Be careful of too much money, Martha. It rarely brings happiness."

"What was his name?"

"Fortunately I can't remember."

"He couldn't have been that bad. All that lovely money. You should have thought of your children."

"I hope you're not being serious."

"Of course I'm not. But it might have been fun. Extreme luxury can have its advantages."

"This generation is never satisfied. If you ask me it's all plain showing off. The man was horrible. All he had was money to compensate. Or so he thought."

"Didn't he have a wife?"

"Divorced four of them."

"And he was after my mother."

"Don't be rude, Martha."

"Just kidding. I'm high from all the excitement. It'll be fun for Phillip to find a nerdy geek and make him rich and famous."

"What's a nerdy geek?"

"A young man who wears glasses and can't pull women but has a brain the size of a full-grown elephant."

"Have you just finished a full glass of wine?"

"Yes, Mother."

"You did eat?"

"Yes, Mother."

"Never drink on an empty stomach. Phillip's been telling me all about Africa. Sounds the perfect place to be. I'd much prefer to live in a safari camp than with that dreadful man."

"Maybe he was murdered."

"Serve him right. Most of those rich people get their money by stealing it one way or another. I'd love to go visit Africa. Hear a wild lion roar in the night. Paradise. Like the old ranch. I miss it. I miss your father. I miss my young life."

"Mother, you're crying."

"Just being sentimental. Nothing wrong with an old woman looking back on her life. We were all so damn happy. Why did he have to die? I want a hug."

"My poor mother. Have you heard from the boys?"

"Not a word."

"Now you're sobbing."

"What do you expect? You go through all that bringing up of your children and then they go away. Never hear from them."

"They have their own lives. Their own problems."

"I know they do. You'll find out, Martha. You're going to be a mother."

Martha got up from sitting next to Phillip and went to her mother. Gave her a hug.

"Is that better?"

"Much better. Just be careful, both of you. Life's full of traps. Just get married and be happy."

Martha drank the last of the wine in her glass. No one offered her a refill. The problem with drinking once you really started was not wanting to stop. Most drunks drank until they fell asleep, leaving the consequences until the next morning. Martha hated drinking at lunchtime. But business was business. Now there was nothing else to do. What the hell. She leaned forward, picked up the bottle and filled up her glass. She was almost five months pregnant. One drink should not hurt.

"Don't look at me like that, Mother. It's going to be the last time until the baby is born. We'll have an early night. Get a good long sleep and go into the country tomorrow for a walk."

"What about Mrs Crabshaw?"

"You're right. Mrs Crabshaw. I'm going for a nap. Wake me when she arrives."

Putting the full glass of wine on the coffee table, Martha stood up, deliberately sticking out her belly. High from wine and excitement she walked out of the room and into the spare bedroom. She closed the door, took off her dress and got into the double bed. The sound of their voices floated through the door. Phillip was talking about the African bush. Telling her mother an African story, his voice excited. Poor Phillip. In life, you never got it all. The voices drifted away as Martha fell into a drunken sleep where the devil was waiting to greet her in her dreams. The devil was laughing at her. Making fun of her. Putting his hand on her swollen belly and making it hurt. The pain became excruciating, the devil laughing right in her face. When she woke the door was open and Phillip was standing next to her bed. She had screamed herself awake.

"The devil was trying to kill my baby! Hug me, Phillip. Why did I drink?... That must be Mrs Crabshaw ringing the bell. How long was I asleep? At least I'm sober. I wish I could stop drinking but you have to join in. Do you think we should marry before the baby? I'll still have the test. I know you're the father. Oh, Phillip, that was the worst dream I ever had in my life. He won't take away my baby, will he?"

"Of course he won't."

"Maybe we should get married in a church? Do it all properly. I'm still shaking with fear. He had his devil's face right in front of me. Laughing. Laughing. Laughing."

PART 5

OCTOBER 1993 — TO BE, OR NOT TO BE

1

*P*hillip was now the one in a nightmare far from his home. She had him, literally, by the balls. If she was prepared to marry him in a church before the baby was born she was certain he was the father. Before, Phillip had the niggling suspicion he was being used. There was an old saying he had first heard in university: 'You are sure who is your mother but not your father.' It was a warning to all young men in their relationships with women. His name was Fergal Kopple, Phillip's best friend at Rhodes University. As Phillip looked at Martha's swollen belly, the fear from her nightmare still visible on her frightened face, he remembered that conversation with Fergal Kopple.

"We chase women for the sex, the women chase us to find a husband and give them children. They all say they're on the pill, but are they? We all sleep with multiple partners. I scored a hat-trick last weekend. Three newies in two days. Not bad. Did I ask them if they were on the pill before I fucked them? Of course I didn't. I was drunk. So were the girls. And if I had three women, what's to say they did not have three men? And if they get pregnant they have no idea which one was the father. So what do they do in their panic? Look for the best husband material, that's what they do. Or tell the one with the most money he has to pay for an abortion. It's all one big game at university. But be careful, Phillip.

Can you imagine marrying some woman you barely know because you feel guilty? And bringing up some other bastard's bastard? She doesn't know. You don't know. Why they say you know who's your mother but never so sure of your father."

"I look just like my father."

"You're lucky. I have no resemblance to my father or his family."

"Have you asked your mother?"

"Don't be damned silly. Who's paying for university?"

"Don't you like your father?"

"Not particularly. He's an arrogant, rich drunk who hits me when he's pissed."

"You're big enough to defend yourself."

"One day I will. But only after he's paid for my degree and I can be independent. We all want something from other people, Phillip. Remember what I say, old pal. You're the first true friend I have ever had. Live your own life, buddy boy. Don't let it be controlled by others. Masters of our fate, what we have to be. Or we're wimps. Even fools."

The whole conversation came rushing back to haunt him, the devil in every thought. Was the reason Martha was happy to marry him in a church because it made the baby legitimate? Or because he had told her his bankers were sending him written proof of his wealth? At that point, as Phillip walked out of their bedroom to meet Mrs Crabshaw, he wasn't certain. In a strange apartment, in a strange city, in a country he had never once imagined living in, he was trapped, no longer the master of his fate.

"This is Martha's fiancé, Mabel. Phillip, meet my friend Mrs Crabshaw."

"Nice to meet you. Heard so much about you."

And there it went. The usual polite claptrap. When Phillip turned, Martha was coming out of the bedroom, composed and full of confidence. She gave Mrs Crabshaw a hug.

"So, Phillip. Apart from marrying the lovely Martha, what are you going to be doing in America?"

"I'm not quite sure."

"Of course you are, darling. You're going to be a venture capitalist."

"Of course I am, Martha. How stupid of me."

"What's a venture capitalist?"

"Why don't you ask Martha, Mrs Crabshaw? It's her idea. She knows all the details. It's something about using my money to make young people rich."

"You have lots of money?"

"Over five million dollars, Mabel. His grandfather was Ben Crossley, the Hollywood actor."

"My goodness."

"Just what I said myself... Would you like a glass of wine?"

"Just one. At my age I have to be careful. Or I won't live to be a hundred and get my telegram from the Queen of England."

They ate supper at Aggie Poland's dining room table. Most of the conversations were about money. People, especially Americans, were obsessed with it.

"Your brother Randall must have a lot of money?"

"Got it twice. From Grandfather and his books, Mabel. You don't mind me calling you Mabel?"

"Of course not. What does he do with it all? Must live like a king."

"Lives like a hermit on the Isle of Man, a small island off the West Coast of England. His passion is writing books, not showing off his money. In America, they swarmed all over him. His publishers, the media and the public. Randall said it drove him nuts. He hates his fame. Says it was like living in a glasshouse."

"Most people would give everything for fame and money."

"There must be something wrong with us. You can only eat one meal at a time. Sleep in one bed. We grew up on a tobacco farm in Rhodesia. Now they say tobacco kills more people than half the diseases on earth. Of course, they don't ban cigarettes. Too much tax money for the governments. We live in a wonderful world, Mabel."

"Indeed we do. Luckily, most of it is truly wonderful. I've had a wonderful life. Many are not so lucky. Are you bitter at being forced out of Zimbabwe by Mr Mugabe? I may be old. My hearing is going along with my sight but I still know what's going on in the world."

"More sad than bitter."

"Will you be a nice young man and see me back to my apartment? We can order a cab. I like someone to see me to my door."

"It will be my pleasure."

"Thank you, Phillip. We can chat more in the cab. Thank you, Aggie, for a wonderful evening. Now it's time for an old woman's bed. Wars, turmoil, pain. We've all been through it, Phillip. You and Martha are going to have a lovely life together. That's what's important. Family. Watching your children grow up. Trying to stop them falling in the same holes. None of us are very different. Neither are our lives. What happens today will happen tomorrow. Martha, be a dear and phone this number to arrange a cab for me. They will know me and the address... I've so much enjoyed the evening. Why did we British go to Africa in the first place, Phillip? You know I was born in England, like your mother and father. It's so nice to find out about other people's lives. They can be so interesting."

"The missionaries and the ivory hunters were first. When the missionaries got into trouble with the non-believers who wanted to still control their own people, soldiers were sent to protect them. The next thing, the country was a British colony. There's an old joke. When the converted were kneeling and praying with their eyes shut we British hoisted the Union Jack. Some say the missionaries and the church were used by the politicians for power and monetary gain. There was gold in them hills. I reckon politicians and priests go hand in hand. From what I learned from my studies, we're all as bad as each other. And the root cause is money. There are too many greedy bastards in the world. It's inherent in who we are as human beings."

Not sure why he had flown off the handle, Phillip shut his mouth. Mrs Crabshaw was giving him a puzzled look. There was nothing worse than blasphemy. Never good to criticise the priests.

"Do you believe in God, Phillip?"

"I try to. Sometimes it becomes more difficult."

"You must believe. Otherwise life on earth has no purpose."

Aggie stood up looking from one to the other. She was agitated. "Well, it's been a long day. Never does to be too serious. I just believe what I was told to believe. It's much easier."

"Aggie, you are so clever."

"I hope so, Mabel. Maybe we should all go down to the foyer and wait for your taxi. Martha can stay and clear the table. Lovely evening. I become a little uncomfortable when people question the Christian religion."

"I'm sorry."

"Don't be sorry, Phillip. We are all entitled to our own opinions. Shall we go? My friend is tired. So am I."

"At least so many in Africa are now Christians."

"Exactly, Mabel. God is far bigger than all of us. He shall prevail. Of that I am certain. And if anyone doesn't believe in this world they shall end up in hell. It's all very simple."

On the way down in the lift to the foyer all three of them were silent. At least the last of the conversation had not been trivial. The cab driver arrived as they reached the front door to the block of apartments. He helped Mabel Crabshaw into the taxi. It was difficult for the old lady. Phillip walked round to the other side and got into the cab.

"Is there something wrong, Phillip?"

"No, of course not."

Feeling uncomfortable, Phillip sat and said nothing. The old lady took his hand and held it. When they arrived at her apartment she was still holding his hand.

"Feeling better, Phillip?"

"Much, thank you."

"Responsibility affects all of us. Don't you worry about Martha. She's a good woman. Sometimes things come at us in a rush. Marry her in a church and you'll feel a whole lot better. Now, out you go and round the other side and help this old lady up to her bed. I've enjoyed meeting you. Martha is lucky. You think. Too many people don't think. There was a philosopher I read some years ago whose name I can't remember. He said, 'Most people in the world would rather die than think. And many of them do.' In twenty years, long after I'm dead, and your child is a grown-up person, the world will be very different. The politicians you hate will be touting a whole new set of solutions. We individuals get through life as best we can, avoiding the pitfalls and, if we have any sense, doing no one any harm. Be nice to Martha. Be nice to your children and friends. Being nasty never helped anyone... Thank you, driver, for coming so quickly. Please keep the change. There's enough there for your tip and the return journey for my friend... Come along, Phillip. Give me your arm. These old bones don't work so well these days. It was nice of Martha to try and write a book about me. Maybe I should tell your brother my story. Now that would be immortality. Driver, we'll be just a few minutes. What's your name again?"

"Harry."

"Such a simple name, Harry. It's my memory. Like my legs, my memory is fading. Thank you, Harry."

"My pleasure, Mabel."

"I'll bet it is." The old lady gave him a mischievous smile.

At the door to the apartment, Mabel kissed Phillip on the side of his face. Going up in the lift Phillip had had to support her.

"I'm all right now. Getting old isn't all it's cracked up to be. My first love was killed in the First World War. His name was Jimmie Hallingham. Died at the Second Battle of the Somme. Royal Dragoon Guards. I have a photograph of Jimmie in my lounge from all those years ago. Funny how I can remember that so clearly but not the name of the cab driver. I should have brought my walker. Silly of me. Thank you for your help. We all need help in the end. You go home and have a good sleep. You'll feel better in the morning."

The door closed behind him as Phillip walked down the corridor back to the lift. No wonder Martha had wanted to write the old lady's story. The idea of hearing more and trying to write it himself crossed his mind. Mrs Crabshaw's story was history. Something that once had been his passion. Downstairs the driver was waiting patiently.

"Thanks, Harry."

"My pleasure. She's a nice old lady."

"And tips well."

"That helps. It's a tough life making a living driving a cab."

Phillip sat in the back thinking. Thinking how lucky he was not to have to earn his living from driving a cab. At the entrance to Aggie Poland's block of apartments, Phillip gave Harry ten dollars.

"It all helps."

"Thank you, mister."

"Phillip. Phillip Crookshank from Zimbabwe."

"Where's Zimbabwe?"

"In the middle of Africa... Goodnight."

Going up in the lift to Aggie's apartment, all Phillip could think of was Jimmie Hallingham. Royal Dragoon Guards. Killed in the trenches in a war that now had no importance for anyone other than Mabel Crabshaw. In the apartment, Aggie had gone to bed. Martha was waiting for him.

"What's the matter now?"

"Losing a life so early. Poor Jimmie and Mabel."

"She's been telling her story?"

"From all those years ago. Let's go to bed and hope for happy dreams. Some of us are the lucky ones."

"Aren't you lucky, Phillip?"

"I know I am. She really is old. Don't think I want to live that long. And she wants to live to be a hundred."

Maybe one day he would have his epiphany and really believe in God. Feel it. Understand it. Know for certain. He really hoped so. To believe in God and an afterlife would make the sacrifices of people like Jimmie Hallingham worthwhile. And he would get to meet his mother, the mother the lions had taken from him making him a lonely man. Why he had never married. He leaned across and switched off the bedside lamp. The room was dark, the curtains drawn. Martha turned over without touching him. The noise of the traffic outside was constant. He was far from home in a strange bed with a woman he had not known six months ago. Who was carrying his child. A woman about to become his wife. He lay thinking, his mind running in circles. Even with the outside traffic he could hear the rhythm of Martha's breathing. An epiphany. That's what he needed. As hard as Phillip tried to imagine an afterlife, nothing happened. He was the same old Phillip lying in bed. One simple human among all the living billions. Hoping for something more. When he dozed off into a troubled sleep, Phillip was still not sure. All through the dark night he tossed and turned. The outside traffic never seemed to stop, the sound a far cry from the African bush, his cottage by the lake. But he wanted children. Someone to be with him when he was old. Not that it had helped Mrs Crabshaw. Four children and their offspring and she needed the help of a stranger to get her to bed. Around the noise of the traffic came the other sounds from a city. Someone playing music. A hard, beating sound that never changed, as if the musician had got himself stuck. No beauty, just the beat. The sound was sad. An aircraft flew overhead. There was a crash. Some fool full of alcohol driving into something. Or was it? Lying awake, Phillip had no idea. Had no wish to know. Worrying about other people's problems was useless. Instead, he took his mind back home. He could hear the flow of the river. The plop of a fish. The owl calling to its mate. The bark of a bushbuck. The sound of the crickets. The happy croaks of the frogs. He was where he wanted to be. A place of peace. A place with few people, far from the madding crowd. When he woke again it was daylight. He had been dreaming. Absently, he put his hand on Martha's belly. She was still asleep. Not sure if he was still dreaming he felt something move inside her belly. The excitement was overwhelming. The traffic no longer mattered. The true future of life was in Martha's belly.

"You want to make love?"

"I felt something move."

"You got to be kidding, if you'll excuse the pun." Martha was chuckling. "More likely last night's booze growling around in my stomach. I've got a hangover. I feel terrible."

"Poor Martha. Try and go back to sleep. Best thing is to sleep off a hangover."

"You know, you might be right. I do feel something. Can they kick at five months? I'll be blowed. Give your future wife a hug. It's all happening. My head is pounding."

"Go back to sleep."

"Easier said than done. Did you sleep well?"

"Towards the end. I was back in Africa in my dreams."

"Poor Phillip. My poor darling. What have we done to you? Don't worry. We'll soon be home. Back in my old apartment with all my familiar things. I'm so looking forward to it."

"Why's the traffic so noisy?"

"I don't notice it. Oh, my poor head."

This time when Martha went back to sleep, lying on her back, both hands over her belly, she was snoring. He heard Aggie get up and move around the kitchen, doing last night's washing up: the chink of china, the rattle of cutlery. With no chance of any more sleep, he got out of bed as quietly as possible and sneaked out to the loo. Wearing shorts and a shirt he went to the kitchen to make himself tea. He would have to get used to it. Maybe, one day, he too would not hear the sound of traffic. With a cup of tea in his hand, he walked out of the kitchen. Aggie was in the lounge watching the morning television. Barefoot, he walked quietly back to the bedroom, put the mug of tea on the side table and sat on the edge of the bed. What else could he do? Phillip sighed. He sipped his hot tea. There was nothing better than the first cup of morning tea. At least that was something. She was still fast asleep, hopefully working off her hangover. There was nothing worse than a morning hangover. The pleasures of life.

The next day they picked up the keys. Phillip's new life had begun, a lifestyle six months ago he would never have hoped for in his wildest dreams. The following day the storage van delivered Martha's personal possessions she had removed from the apartment. Everything else was in its place. The old lady on the balcony across the way nearly fell off her chair waving at Martha. People liked the familiar even though neither of them had met. The abstract painting Martha had been told would one day be worth a lot of money was put back on the wall. Phillip still thought a lot of painted squares of different colours on a canvas was a load of rubbish. The tenant had spilled something on the blue carpet making Martha furious, though the poor man was still out of work and glad to have his deposit back. To celebrate, Martha suggested they went out to dinner. She didn't want to cook. Didn't have to cook. They had the money. Phillip felt sorry for the evicted tenant. Where were he and his wife sleeping tonight? What were they eating? Vagrants lost in a big city if they didn't have friends. They went down in the lift to the second-floor basement. The car that Martha had wanted to sell when she packed up to go to Africa was in its usual parking spot. The battery was as flat as a pancake, obliging them to go back up in the lift to look for a taxi.

"No booze. Definitely no booze."

"You don't mind if I have a glass of wine?"

"Back to work on Monday. I can't wait."

"When do I get to meet a nerdy geek?"

"Don't be impatient."

"I won't be impatient, Martha. I might just be bored. There's nothing worse than having nothing to do."

"Don't tell me... Taxi! Come on. I got him. I feel like a good steak."

"Maybe I should look for a church. Find someone to marry us. Mabel said we should marry in a church."

"Get in, honey. The meter's running."

"Are there any churches around here?"

"None that I know of. You know I'm lucky. Not a trace of morning sickness. Most pregnant women want to throw up. I'm going to have to buy some new clothes. This dress is tight. I love my mother, but oh how nice it is to be back in my own apartment. Why do the English call an apartment a flat?"

"All on one level? I have no idea."

"We'll find you a geek. Don't you worry about it."

"I can't wait."

"Don't be sarcastic. You'll love being a venture capitalist."

"If you say so, Martha... I'll have to apply for some kind of permanent residence."

"That'll be easy, once we're married."

"Yes, I suppose it will."

EARLY MONDAY MORNING Martha went to work. She was smiling, happy as a cricket, the routine of her life back to normal. The door to the apartment closed leaving Phillip on his own. A cup of tea made no difference. At eleven o'clock he went out, his raincoat on, an umbrella in his hand. The streets were full of people all striding somewhere, all with a purpose. Clem had gone back to the ranch. Solly greeted him.

"You're early, Phillip. What can I give you?"

"Some information. She's gone back to work."

"At least you don't have to support her. Just kidding. I've had a few ladies who sit on their bums when I'm working. Expect me to pay for everything. So, what will you have?"

"Make it a beer. One of those American beers... You know any priests in this town? Any churches? We want a priest to marry us."

"Have you gone all religious?"

"It will feel better. Make the marriage ceremony significant. Have lasting meaning making an oath to God."

"Still doesn't stop half of them getting divorced. An old pastor comes in here on occasions. The owner of this bar is a member of his congregation. The pastor comes in looking for his monthly donation. Does good work. Looks after the down and out. Pastor Gregory. Usually stays for a couple of drinks. I like him. What denomination is your wife-to-be?"

"She doesn't have much to do with the church."

"And you?"

"Church of England. Does it matter?"

"Not really."

"Can you tell me how to find Pastor Gregory? Give me an address. Some directions. Did Clem leave all right?"

"Put him in a cab myself. I'll write it all down. Glad to have you back in Kansas City."

There were three other men down the bar. No women. None of the men looked happy. Phillip drank his beer in silence. Ten minutes later Solly handed him a piece of paper.

"You can give him my regards. Make a good contribution to his church and there shouldn't be a problem. You want another one?"

"Not now."

"Drop in on your way back."

The church, when Phillip found it, was small and neat, the building old, a relic of an earlier city.

"Can I help you?"

"I'm looking for Pastor Gregory. Solly sent me."

"What do you want, young man? I am Pastor Gregory."

"For you to marry me and my fiancée. She's pregnant. I was brought up Church of England. There are no C of E churches in America. I will be happy to make a substantial donation."

"Splendid. Come through to my office and give me the details. Are you a religious man, Mr...?"

"Phillip Crookshank. From Zimbabwe where I went to a boarding school that was run by the Church of England. The headmaster was a reverend. Taught me scripture knowledge and history. A special man in my life. I was confirmed by him at the age of fifteen when the doubts began."

"What happened? Take a seat. Monday mornings are quiet. How are you going to make a donation if you come from Zimbabwe?"

"My grandfather was Ben Crossley the Hollywood actor."

"Was he now?"

"Left me four million dollars. It's five million now. In a trust in Jersey under my full discretion. Towards the end of my confirmation, before the ceremony in the chapel, I asked the reverend if I would see my mother again. She was attacked and killed by a pride of lions when I was a small child. I don't remember her except in my dreams. Up till that point I was so happy to be confirmed into the church. I love the philosophy of Christianity and everything it teaches."

"What did he say?"

"He said he didn't know."

"But he was a reverend?"

"Oh, yes. Went on to become a bishop. I respected him so much. Maybe he didn't want to lie to me. I just don't know. But from that moment I've had no real faith. Only a belief in the rightness of the Christian way of life."

"We all want to be certain, Phillip. For some of us it can be very difficult. You're still young. Hopefully your time will come to see the light. I shall be most happy to marry you and your lady. How is Solly?"

"He's fine. Just fine."

"Splendid. Give me a date and we'll get the process started."

"How much do you want?"

"That's up to you."

"Solly says you do good work."

"We hope so. Not everyone is as lucky as you, Phillip. A grandfather of the stature of Ben Crossley. I've liked all of his films."

"Thank you, Pastor Gregory."

"Just call me Gregory. You live around here?"

"I do now. With my girlfriend. We met on a safari when she came to Africa."

"And you got her pregnant?"

"Exactly."

"And now you are doing the right thing?"

"Exactly."

"I would like to meet your bishop. Is he still alive?"

"No, he died. He never married."

"I'm sure he's in heaven."

"So am I. He was a very good man. I will never forget him."

"You should bring your lady to church on Sunday."

"Martha. Her name is Martha."

"Eleven o'clock service. I like to know who I'm marrying."

"We'll be there."

"Welcome to my congregation."

Feeling uncomfortable, as if he was using the man, Phillip slowly went back to Solly's Saloon.

"How did it go?"

"I'm not sure. He's going to marry us. I haven't said she's twice divorced. Can that be a problem?"

"You'll have to ask Pastor Gregory. Was she married in a church?"

"I don't know. She didn't say so."

"Then to the church, if she didn't, she was never married."

"Is that how it works?"

"I have absolutely no idea. You want a beer?"

"Six months ago my life was a whole lot less complicated."

"Women. Once you let a woman in your life it gets complicated. A wife and children. Now that's complications. Lots of them. I'm going to have a beer with you to celebrate."

There was nothing else to do but sit and think. The bar had been filling up. By the third beer Phillip was beginning to enjoy himself, that discussion with his headmaster twenty years ago no longer in the forefront of his mind. Would he have been a different man if the answer had been positive and he was going to get to know his mother in the afterlife? He didn't know. Solly was doing his best to keep his clients amused, get them talking to each other, getting them to stay. Why the bar was called Solly's Saloon even though he did not own the place. Martha would be working while he was drinking. The whole thing was ridiculous. A few more years of such behaviour and he would be an alcoholic. And where would that take them? Would he really become this venture capitalist she was talking about? He had never used a computer and didn't particularly care. But what else could he do but sit in a bar with the rest of the drunks? Just the dividends from his inheritance were more than enough to support him, Martha and a child. What was the point of getting into something he knew nothing about to make more money than he needed? And if the venture did not work and he lost his money, what then? He'd be like John Stone, the one-time tenant. No job, no home and no money. But he was having a child. In Africa, the chances of marrying were small. Any girl that wanted to marry him wanted to get the hell out of Zimbabwe with all its negative politics. His mind went round and round. It was a pity Clem had gone home to the ranch. They could have gone on a bender.

"Solly, give me another one. Let's get started."

"That's the stuff, Phillip. Do you know Billy?"

"Hello, Billy. I'm Phillip. You want a drink?"

"Lay it on. You got a funny accent. Don't matter. Man buys you a drink, nothing matters. What you do, Phillip?"

"Nothing. Absolutely nothing."

"All the time in the world to drink."

"You got it. Give him the same again, Solly."

"Coming up. You two enjoy yourselves."

"And what do you do for a living, Billy?"

"I fix things. You got something to fix and I'll fix it. Electrical. Plumbing. You name it. I'm a fix-it man. And what you do before you did nothing?"

"Ran a safari business on the banks of the Zambezi River."

"That's different. What brings you to Kansas City?"

"It's a long story."

"I'm listening... Thank you, Solly... Cheers. I like a good chat in a bar. Pleasant way to pass a day."

"Nothing to fix?"

"Not today. Well, go on. What's a safari?"

The man had no idea. Not that it mattered. Phillip steered the conversation away from himself. There was nothing more boring for the listener than a man talking about himself. The trick was to keep the conversation trivial. And get drunk together. When they were drunk what they talked about didn't matter. They wouldn't remember. A drinking companion. That's what he wanted. A need Solly understood. Why he was a successful barman. Like Clem's, Billy's life began to unfold hidden among the trivia, the bits and pieces of their conversation. By the time Phillip took a cab back to Martha's apartment he and Billy were best friends.

Drunk, uncomfortable, and not knowing what to do with himself, Phillip played music, slumped in a lounge chair and waited for Martha. He had not eaten lunch. He tried to read but was too drunk to concentrate.

"What the hell are you doing, you silly shit?"

The expletive and anger with himself did not help. He wondered if Munya and Sedgewick were back at Chewore. Despite the overpowering heat and humidity in the valley during October, he envied them. The rains would soon break. They could swim in the river. Not sure if it was the booze or the pain of loss in his stomach, he went to the toilet and was sick. The taste in his mouth was horrible. The fun from getting drunk with a stranger was not worth it. But at least he had done something positive by finding Pastor Gregory. Back in the chair he turned on the television, his mind barely concentrating. The programme was trivial, just what he needed. No need to think. He just had to sit. And watch. And change the programme when this one became boring. And the day passed. Another wasted day on earth. A day he had squandered because his girl was going to have his baby. When he woke up, the television was still playing. He got up and went to the kitchen and made himself a cheese sandwich. The sandwich was delicious. He felt better. When Martha came home just before the eight o'clock news, Phillip was feeling sober. The name Billy came into his mind. Who the hell was Billy? And then he remembered. Martha was smiling,

"You have a nice day, honey?"

"It was wonderful. On Sunday we are going to church. I've found someone to marry us."

"In such a hurry?"

"No time like the present."

"I've found you someone to talk to. He's twenty-three years old. Franklyn and I both think his idea is brilliant."

"How much money does he want?"

"Half a million."

"He doesn't come cheap."

"Good ideas never come cheap if you want to make them into something. I'm going to order in. What you fancy?"

"Two very large hamburgers."

"So, what else did you do with yourself?"

"Met a man called Billy. A man who fixes things for a living. How was your day?"

"Nice. I'm back in the rhythm. Hectic but nice."

"What's his name?"

"Marcin Galinski. From Poland originally. Schooled in America."

"Poland. How appropriate."

"I thought so. Can you phone for the food? I want to soak in the bath for a change. Everyone has been so happy to see me back."

"Has he kicked again?"

"I think so. My mind was so much on work I wasn't sure. You're to give him a ring tomorrow. I wrote down his number."

"What's his idea?"

"You'll find out."

"Does he wear glasses?"

"I've no idea. A client put me onto him."

"Where does he live?"

"New York. You really got to learn how to use a computer. We'll find you a trainer."

"Must I go to him or will he come to Kansas City?"

"For half a million, he'll go to the moon."

After her bath, a man knocked on their door with the hamburgers. Phillip paid him. It was all so easy. All you needed was money. Thankfully, Martha was back on the wagon. No red wine with the hamburgers. They ate and went to bed.

"Can you feel anything, Phillip?"

"Not this time. Tell me about your day."

Phillip only half listened. She was trying to get a new account. There was something wrong with her computer in the office. Something about a virus. Phillip thought a virus was something that attacked humans, not a machine. And all the time outside on the table was the piece of paper with the name Marcin Galinski and his telephone number in New York. When the day's story was over, Martha turned over and went to sleep, her interest in sex diminishing with the growth of the baby. Instead of lying awake, Phillip fell into a peaceful sleep. He was woken by Martha getting out of bed in the morning. Phillip's mouth felt like the bottom of a parrot cage. So much for the pleasures of drinking. Martha had gone straight to the bathroom.

"You all right, Martha?" She was being sick. He could hear the vomit going in the toilet from where he was lying in bed. "Must be morning sickness."

"Or a delayed hangover. I feel positively terrible."

Martha came back and started to dress. She was in a hurry.

"Don't forget that phone call."

"How could I?"

"Got to fly. There's so much work to be done. Have a nice day."

"I'll try."

All day Phillip avoided the piece of paper on the table. To try and be coherent on a hangover was as stupid as making the phone call in the first place. He moped about the apartment. Even thought of phoning his brother Randall on the Isle of Man. His father in England. He would have phoned Jacques if he was sure where he was but knew that that would make him miserable. Even Haydn's Twenty-Eighth Symphony did not take him out of his alcohol-induced misery. There was nothing worse than a hangover, the only cure, another drink, and a repetition of the cycle. Forcing himself to behave he tried to read a book. Apart from making a phone call to some twenty-three-year-old he had nothing to do. Would he understand what the young man was talking about apart from wanting half a million? Phillip doubted it. The computer age had a whole new language. That much Martha had told him in her discourse on the day's work. The man was a computer geek. Had some fancy degree from Yale University that was way over Phillip's head. When Willy and Beth in the apartment below started one of their arguments it made Phillip's day.

"What's wrong with people!"

Instead of feeling sorry for himself, Phillip went to Martha's kitchen. He was going to make one of his 'damn fine curries'. As he got into the swing of it he was happy. He had something to do. From below, there was a loud bang as the door slammed. Willy and Beth had finished their argument. Nothing ever changed. When he went through to the lounge and looked out the window the woman was back on her balcony. Phillip waved. The old woman waved. He was part of the family. Again he looked at the piece of paper on the table. He would phone the man in the morning. The curry-mix had boiled enough with the meat. He went back into the kitchen and put in the water with the rest of the ingredients. In an hour, when Martha came home, they would have a 'damn fine curry'. Only then would he put on the rice. He was enjoying himself.

"Maybe become a chef instead of a venture capitalist, old boy."

He went back to the lounge, sat in the chair, and waited for Martha. In Kansas City, he was always waiting for Martha. He was going to be the housewife instead of the husband. How it went in America. He would have to get used to it, if he wanted to be a father.

The rice went on at half past eight. They ate at nine. By half past nine they went to bed, Martha too tired to tell the day's story. A full day for Martha, a void for Phillip. She was soon sound asleep. No sex. Poor Martha. Poor Phillip. Long before the sun rose she was gone. At ten o'clock, Phillip picked up the phone and dialled the long number on Martha's piece of paper.

"May I speak to Marcin Galinski?"

"Marcin speaking."

"Phillip Crookshank. I believe you have an idea to tell me about."

"When can I fly to Kansas City?... Zimbabwe is such a beautiful place. Such a shame it's being ruined by President Mugabe. The country has so much potential. I've seen all your grandfather's movies."

"How much do you want?"

"Half a million dollars should get us to the point where we can launch the software. We need staff. Equipment. Computer engineers, good ones, are expensive."

"I'll bet they are. What's the bright idea?"

"You sound a little cynical, Phillip, if you don't mind my mentioning it. I can explain the workings of the computer industry when we meet."

"All of it?"

"Don't be silly. Algorithms and programming software are complicated. They require a great deal of time and work to understand. I wish to create computer software that will allow people to dictate to a computer instead of a dictating machine, and have the words printed as they speak. No secretary or typist required. You won't even have to be good at spelling. My programme will be able to check the grammar. Put in place the correct capitals. All they will have to do is talk. Much faster than typing. Developing voice recognition software is my ambition, Phillip. Words, spoken down a telephone, will be turned into computer language automatically. The applications are simply mind-boggling, as will be the profits. I'll turn your half a million into a billion in two or three years... Are you there, Phillip?"

"Thank goodness I didn't phone you yesterday."

"I don't understand. Can I come? Martha gave me the address. I spoke to her and Franklyn for the best part of an hour. Franklyn grilled me. That man's got brains. Picked up on my idea with a host of questions... Are you there? I believe you have a university degree?"

"In history."

"We are going to write history. May I come tomorrow? No time like the present. There are other companies already in the development stages of the software but I want to be first. My ideas are so exciting and all I need is money to leave my job and employ some co-workers. There are two from Yale that will be perfect. You have to know the right people. Trouble is, we are all very young and don't have any capital. Once we're up and running you can take me on a safari to Zimbabwe. How does your brother write his books?"

"In longhand."

"My goodness... Are you there? Can I come? It's so exciting. I can take a cab from the airport straight to your apartment. Martha Poland. And I was born in Poland. Now that is a coincidence. I'll phone you from the airport when I arrive. Martha gave me the address and phone number of her apartment. Franklyn's excited about marketing the finished product. So, is it tomorrow, Phillip?"

"Why not?"

"I'm so looking forward to meeting you."

"Do you wear glasses?"

"No. Why should I?"

"See you tomorrow, Marcin. I will be waiting. Until we have a deal you'll pay your own expenses."

"Of course. You only put in the money when we form the company. See you tomorrow."

The phone went dead at the other end leaving Phillip cynically smiling. When people wanted something they were always charming. The man had brains. So if it worked they would go on safari. It made Phillip laugh out loud.

"The tricks people play to get money. Anyway, the lad's paying his airfare. And who knows, we might just go on safari. That lad's clever in more ways than one."

3

---

*L*ater that day, at five o'clock in the afternoon, Phillip phoned Randall and told him the story.

"You do know I headed up a software recognition project for the Brigandshaws back in the eighties? I don't know what the outcome was... How are you, Phillip?"

"Bored out of my tree. How's your family and the new book?"

"Both are fine. I'm looking forward to meeting Martha. We all are. Poor Dad, he so misses the farm."

"Don't tell me about it. Don't you miss Africa?"

"Every day of my life. And who knows? One day everything will come right and we can all go home. When's the wedding?"

"Soon. Are you all coming over?"

"Of course we are. The whole bang shoot."

"Have you seen Craig and Jojo?"

"Not yet. The baby's due next month."

"And they are staying in England?"

"Who knows?"

"Are they married?"

"Not yet. You getting married should encourage them."

"Has Jojo spoken to her father?"

"Not a word. You know the African system. Poor Jojo. She misses her family, but you can't have the best of both worlds."

"Don't I know it. Give my love to Meredith."

With the phone down, Phillip was back to waiting for Martha. He had no idea what he was going to do. What the hell is an algorithm, he asked himself? That word was never in his history books. The whole thing was way over his head. He would have to talk to Franklyn and get his opinion. Lots of people's opinions. It was quicker to talk than type, that bit he understood. How many people had computers? How much did they cost? Was there a mass market or was it just a niche market? He could tell a lion from a cheetah at a mile's distance, but computers made no sense. He would have to learn if he gave him the money: ten per cent of his grandfather's wealth. Having money was a responsibility. Phillip looked at the clock on the wall. It was half past five. Three hours to go. What the hell. There was leftover curry or they could order in. He would make a lousy housewife. He put on his coat and left the apartment. It was cold outside. He walked to Solly's Saloon. Inside it was warm. Looking around, all he could see were strangers.

"What happened to you last night?"

"Give us a beer. Do you know what an algorithm is?"

"Isn't that an animal that lives in water?"

"That's an alligator, Solly. We call them crocodiles."

"Close. Beer coming up. Make yourself at home."

"Lots of new faces."

"That's a pub. One night you know everyone. The next they're strangers. Makes the experience more interesting."

"Do you know them?"

"Most of them. Hey, everyone. This is Phillip. He's from Africa. Tell you all about alligators."

"What the hell. Let's buy a round for everyone at the bar."

"The round's on Phillip."

A small cheer went up. Everyone at the bar was smiling. The two men on either side of Phillip moved closer. When the drinks came they lifted their glasses to him. Nothing better to make friends than buying drinks for a row of strangers.

"Anyone know what an algorithm is?"

"Matter of fact I do. I'm from New York on a business trip. Selling computers. Why you want to know? Cheers, anyway. Africa. Never been out of the States."

"A man wants me to invest half a million to develop his new software and I have no idea what he's going to be talking about tomorrow. He's flying in from New York."

"My name is Gordon. Gordon Blake."

"Phillip Crookshank."

"Nice to meet you... So, what's this new software? It's all happening in the computer industry. New ideas every day. I'm selling the latest personal computer you can use from home. They're calling it a laptop. Take it with you on a business trip. So, where you from?"

"The Zambezi Valley. I have a safari business."

"Then we've lots to talk about. You tell me all about the animals and I'll tell you what I know about computers."

"Do you believe in luck, Gordon? This is my lucky night. Tell me all that's happening in the computer industry. If I don't know what he's talking about tomorrow a hangover won't make any difference. You know Billy or Clem?"

"Don't think so. This is good. On business trips I often end up in a bar on my own. And there's nothing worse than drinking alone. What brings you to America?"

"My pregnant girlfriend. We're going to church on Sunday."

"Good for you. Religion is big in America. Are you not married?"

"Why we're going to church. The pastor wants to get to know us. What is an algorithm?"

"The mathematics of software, put simply. Where you going to get half a million?"

"From my grandfather's estate."

Smiling, Phillip sat on his barstool and listened. The man was off on his favourite subject, happy to tell his story. There was luck in life, Phillip told himself. Lots of luck. He was going to drink slowly and take it all in.

By the time he left the bar to go home to Martha he was less concerned about what he was going to hear from Marcin Galinski. Gordon knew what he was talking about. There was nothing better than a salesman who knew his product. Buying that round of drinks was money well spent.

"You doing anything tomorrow night, Gordon? Why don't you join us for supper? Meet Martha. I'll tell you more stories about Africa. You said you had another day's business in Kansas City. Maybe Jasmine from Martha's office would like to join us."

"You want me to meet Marcin Galinski?"

"Something like that. My luck meeting you may be your luck meeting me. He says he's going to turn my half million into a billion. Probably exaggerating. I don't know much about the business world, but a salesman who knows what he's talking about sounds pretty good to me. Seven o'clock. I'll write down Martha's address."

"One minute you're going happily in one direction in life and then everything suddenly changes."

To Phillip's surprise Martha was home cooking supper. It was half past seven.

"We're throwing a dinner party tomorrow, Martha."

"Who for?"

"Marcin Galinski, Gordon Blake and Jasmine Fairbanks. Gordon is single. Bright. Full of potential. Just what Jas is looking for."

"And who the hell's Gordon Blake?"

"A man I met at Solly's. Computer salesman. Told me all about the computer industry."

A deep smile spread over Martha's face. Almost a satisfied smirk. He had laid his own trap and now he was walking into it.

"Good boy. Now we're getting somewhere. I'll ask Jas. I'm sure she'll come. Sales and advertising go hand in hand. When's the genius arriving?"

"Said he'd phone me tomorrow from the airport."

To Phillip's surprise, that night they made love. The night's dream was full of strangers, blurred dreams making no sense.

At a few minutes past noon the phone went.

"Hello. Phillip Crookshank."

"It's me, honey. Jas would love to join us for dinner. Has he phoned?"

"Not yet. Gordon Blake will be here so it doesn't matter."

"What are you going to cook? Oh, and Franklyn is joining us too."

"Roast lamb with fresh mint sauce."

No sooner had Phillip put down the phone than it rang again.

"What's the matter, Martha?"

"It's Marcin. I'm on my way."

"Where are you staying tonight?"

"I have no idea."

Ten minutes after Phillip had returned with the shopping there was a knock at the door. A young man was standing outside, a broad smile on his face. He was tall, broad-shouldered, square-jawed. He looked more like a professional athlete than a computer boffin. They shook hands.

"Aren't you going to invite me in?"

"I'm sorry. You're not what I expected."

"I have two passions. Playing baseball and computers."

"Explains everything. Good. Here we are. You want some coffee? We're having a dinner party tonight. Give me your bag. I'll put it in the spare bedroom. No point in wasting money. I see you have one of those laptops Gordon was talking about. Instead of talking about the business why don't we get to know each other? Tell each other our histories. It's the person I will be investing in if all goes well. First and foremost we have to be able to trust each other. I'll let Gordon and Franklyn do the technical talking. I will listen."

"You don't know anything about the computer industry? And who is Gordon?"

"Absolutely nothing. Gordon is a computer salesman I met in a bar. But anyway people tell me I'm a good judge of character. And that's what I'll be studying. Do you have the proposal in writing?"

"Yes, in my briefcase."

"How long is it?"

"Two pages."

"My goodness. Half a million dollars for a couple of pages. Did you play basketball for Yale?"

"Yes, I did."

"I'll be asking a lot of people their opinions before I make up my mind. The big question I have to satisfy myself is whether voice recognition software, as you call it, really works. My brother Randall would be over the moon. He's the novelist Randall Holiday. Holiday is a pseudonym."

"Coffee would be nice. Do you have any photographs of Africa?"

"I have a few with me though I have a whole photograph album back in Zimbabwe from all the years of running my safari business... I'll go and get them... I try not to look at them."

"Why not?"

"It makes me want to go home. Let's start with your family. Tell me all about your parents and your siblings. You do have brothers and sisters?"

"My parents are ordinary people. Were it not for the baseball scholarship they would never have been able to afford my going to Yale. I want to make a lot of money to help them. Buy them a house. All the years of growing up we lived in rented apartments. I want them to have the American dream."

"Oh, we all dream. What keeps us going."

"Let me get out the proposal for you and then I can look at the photographs... My word, just look at that lion."

"A pride of lions killed my mother when I was a very small child."

"You're kidding."

"Unfortunately I'm not."

The man looked puzzled and sceptical. He put down the photographs and picked up his briefcase.

"There you are."

"Thank you."

"I'm so sorry to hear about your mother. I can't imagine life without my mother."

Shaking his head in disbelief, Marcin took a sip of his coffee. Phillip turned his attention to the words in front of him. He began to read. Twice he read the first page. Marcin was looking at him expectantly. Phillip read the second page. All of it was incomprehensible. A whole new set of words he had never before experienced made into sentences. He could as well have been reading Greek. He had no idea what Marcin Galinski was talking about other than wishing to employ lots of expensive people and requiring an investment of half a million dollars. And if he threw half a million of Ben Crossley's money down the toilet and went on to do it again and again, he would soon have neither a safari business nor any money. Would Martha really want to be married to a penniless man? The other two had been shown the door for lack of money. She'd go off with his son and leave a middle-aged man with no money, no country and no means of earning a living. Where could he go to teach history? There was always good old England. But what would his father say? What would Randall? They'd think him a fool for losing his money on ventures he knew nothing about. A fool and his money easily parted.

"You're shaking your head, Phillip."

"I don't understand a word of it other than the money."

"I'll try and explain."

"Please do. I doubt it will help. I am not of your age, Marcin. Not of your schooling. I read the classics. Not modern science. Better drink your coffee before it gets cold."

"So, what are you saying?"

"I don't know. I don't know. I'll listen to you all talking at dinner and see if I can make sense of the conversation. There are far too many words and sentences in your proposal that make no sense to me as I don't understand the language. I would be investing blind. Look, I'd be happy to reimburse your airfare. I've brought you on a wild goose chase. Pressure from Martha. Life is complicated. At twenty-three you're full of energy and excitement. You can't see life's pitfalls. The age of innocence. For you and Martha, if the project doesn't work, you will have lost nothing."

"But I'm confident it will work. We all have to take chances."

"But I don't. By the luck of birth and my grandfather's acting abilities I have enough money to last me my lifetime. I don't have to take chances. I'm not greedy. I don't want to impress strangers with my wealth and celebrity. You, on the other hand, must use your youth and ability to amass enough money to protect you from life's vagaries. Let's wait for the others. I'll make a final decision tomorrow."

"Isn't doing nothing rather boring? What's the point in life if we're not facing a challenge? It's not the money, Phillip. It's the excitement. Creating something and making it work. I want to have fun. Don't you?"

"I also don't want to end up a bum. Let's forget computers and software for the moment. We'll talk about playing sport. How does that sound?"

"Does it really make no sense? Explaining how it works in simple English is rather difficult... The coffee is nice... I'm always in a hurry. That's my problem. And before you know it, someone else will have got there first. Why I need to throw money at it to reach the finished product and have it patented. The world is moving fast. Especially in America. And we have to keep the pace going if we want to stay ahead."

.   .   .

BY THE TIME Gordon Blake knocked on the door they had become friends. The leg of lamb was in the oven, along with the potatoes. The mint sauce stood on the sideboard.

"Martha's not home yet. Come in and meet Marcin."

"The food smells good."

"Roast lamb and roast potatoes. We had sheep on the farm in Zimbabwe. A whole sheep on the spit. Now that was a party. How was the day's business? Can you do me a favour and read Marcin's proposal? I'll get the first beer. Marcin Galinski, meet Gordon Blake."

While Phillip went to the kitchen, Gordon sat down.

"There are two pages in my proposal, Gordon. See what you think. Phillip tells me you sell computers. Sorry. I'll let you concentrate."

The lounge went silent as Phillip basted the lamb. The trick, according to Phillip's stepmother, was not to overcook the meat. The vegetables were in the colander over the pan, ready to be steamed. Phillip took his time. When he came back with three cold beers, Gordon had finished reading, a broad smile on his face.

"Does it make sense to you?"

"Absolutely."

"And half a million dollars?"

"I've heard them say in the office it takes three years to make a new business viable. It's going to take time to make a profit, get the word out, start selling the product. The first year you make a loss. The second year you break even if you're lucky. The third year you make enough profit to pay back the first year's loss. Why a venture like this, with expensive computer engineers, requires so much start-up capital."

"Will the software work?"

"That's up to Marcin and his co-workers to perfect his basic concept. People talk differently. Different accents. Different languages. Here it says what Marcin already has. That the principle works. From what I see, it needs fine tuning. The big problem is marketing. Which is where the money comes in. Advertising is expensive. Ask Martha. Cheers to both of you. I'm excited. You need a brain the size of one of your elephants to work out something like this."

"So you understand what he's saying?"

"Absolutely. Of course, I can't verify the algorithms but I'll take his word for it."

. . .

THE OTHERS ARRIVED and by the time Phillip was standing up at the sideboard carving the meat, the five of them were sitting at the dinner table talking nineteen to the dozen, leaping over each other's words to add to the conversation. There was no discussion about the money, just the concept and the marketing. Jas, dressed to kill, had her eyes fixed on Marcin, Gordon doing his best. As Phillip put the last plate down in front of Martha he was the only one in the room not bursting with enthusiasm. They looked from one to the other with excitement, occasionally drinking. Phillip sat down with his food and said nothing, listening to the rapid-fire conversation, trying to make sense of it, small glimmers of comprehension occasionally penetrating the fog. Listening to tourists sitting round the campfire was a whole lot simpler. When the guests left, with Marcin ensconced in the spare bedroom, Phillip joined Martha in bed.

"That went well. When are you getting started?"

"I'm not sure."

"Don't be silly. It's all there. Franklyn said the proposal is the best thing he's seen in years. We'll handle the marketing. Marcin and his engineers will handle the software. All you have to do is put in the money and sit back. Franklyn said he'd put in the money if he had a half a million. So did Gordon. Did you see Jas flirting with the genius? My word. Brains and good looks. The perfect combination. Don't find that very often. Our houseguest is going a long way in life. I like him. He wants fun. Not just the money."

"But it is my money at risk."

"You can afford it, Phillip. What's the problem?... It's been a long day. The office was screaming. Can you turn out the light?"

Within a minute all Phillip could hear was Martha's breathing and the constant sound of the traffic. He turned over and tried to go to sleep. She had not asked him to feel her stomach to see if the baby was moving.

"Now what the hell do I do?" he asked himself softly.

. . .

WHEN HE WOKE it was morning. The day of decision had begun. Was it going to be the start of a whole new wonderful life or the beginning of a disaster? It was all up to him.

"Good morning, Martha."

"Good morning, Phillip. How are you feeling today?"

"To be honest, I'm not quite sure."

"Go make the tea."

"At your service, madam."

"Why is life such a rush?"

"You tell me. It never used to be."

"Welcome to America."

When Phillip went through the lounge on his way to the kitchen Marcin was sitting fully dressed at his computer. He did not turn round. Barefoot, Phillip went through and put on the kettle. In the fridge were the remnants of last night's dinner. Phillip took out a cold roast potato. There was nothing better than eating cold roast potatoes. When the whistle blew on the kettle he poured boiling water into two mugs with tea bags and one with instant coffee.

"I didn't hear you get up. When I'm working I don't hear very much."

"I've made you a coffee. Sleep well?"

"Out like a light. That Jasmine is nice. I'll be catching the twelve-thirty back to New York. I've said all I can say. There are a couple of others that might be interested."

"You want me to drive you to the airport?"

"I'll take a cab. Have you come to a decision?"

"Not yet."

"The others liked it."

"But it's not their money."

"I understand."

"Would you invest a fortune in a safari business in the middle of Africa?"

"Probably not. The politics would put me off."

"Forget the politics."

"I don't know anything about wild animals."

"Each to his own."

"You're an investor, Phillip. Not a computer analyst. Leave that part to me. At least we've got to know each other. How long do you want before I look elsewhere?"

"A couple of days should be sufficient. Help yourself to cold potatoes in the fridge. I'll let you get on with your work. You're lucky to have a passion for your work. Let me drive you to the airport. Martha was going to sell her car but luckily she didn't."

"Thank you. Whatever else, let's stay friends. That Franklyn certainly knows advertising. So do Martha and Jas. All those ideas last night blew my mind. If we go ahead, you think Gordon would like a job?"

"I wouldn't be surprised."

"Enjoy your tea. Say good morning to Martha for me. I'm still hoping one day you'll take me on a safari and show me your Africa. Now that's going to be an experience. I'll keep my fingers crossed. Who knows, I might even get you to a baseball game. Back to work. When you got an idea running you got to hold onto it. There are many more ideas in my head other than voice recognition software. That's just the beginning. Can you even imagine what a team of hungry youngsters can get up to? Bouncing ideas off each other."

"Don't forget the roast potatoes."

"I'll try not to."

With a mug in each hand, Phillip pushed open the bedroom door with his knee and inside, kicked it shut without looking back.

"What was all that about?"

"He's as good a salesman as Gordon."

"All in one package."

"I've two days to make up my mind. Can I use your car to take him to the airport? Afterwards, I need time on my own to think."

"That was quite some dinner party."

"Yes, I rather think it was. You all looked to be enjoying yourselves."

"Everything is going to work out just fine. The little bugger's kicking. You want to feel him? Thank goodness I didn't drink. Give me your hand. There. You feel him? You're very pensive. What you thinking?"

"There's a good chance I will pour my money down the drain."

"I have an idea. Would it help you make up your mind if I put in fifty thousand of my own money?"

"Would you? Then you really think it's a good project?"

"Didn't you listen to us last night? Got to go. Time never stands still.

Don't look so worried. It's only money. When's that letter arriving from your banker?"

"Soon. Depends on the speed of the post. You still don't believe me?"

"All this prevarication can make a girl think."

Trust. Such a small word. Life all came down to trust. Trusting. Being trusted.

"There are cold spuds for breakfast. Have a nice day."

"I'll try."

"You don't believe I have the money?"

"Seeing is believing."

"Trust has to be built."

"I'm trying."

She kissed him on the forehead and left. Marcin was still in the chair up at the desk, oblivious to everything around him.

"What time do you want to leave?"

"Half past ten. Can't afford to miss the flight. This is the most important period in my life. I want to take my future now. In both hands."

"I'll leave you to it."

"How does she get to work?"

"By cab. It's easier. No parking."

"Always take the easy route."

"I'll try."

"And that doesn't mean going back to Africa. Just kidding. Got to have a sense of humour."

PART 6

OCTOBER TO NOVEMBER 1993 — THE WEDDING PLANNER

1

*D*ownstairs Martha hailed a cab and gave the man the address of her office. The traffic was building up to the rush hour. With luck she would not be late for her first appointment. A new client was coming round to the office to view the artwork that had been prepared by the art department, everything in a hurry. In the back of the taxi her whole feeling of life was uncomfortable and she only had herself to blame. There she was on safari deliberately letting a stranger impregnate her thinking wrongly she was infertile. But who was this Phillip Crookshank? All she knew was what he had told her. Was his grandfather really the famous Ben Crossley? Or was it another of his stories for the campfire? Did the father of her child have five million dollars? Or was it all one big lie to get into America and live off her salary like the other two? Everyone round the dinner table, except for Phillip, had quickly grasped the extraordinary opportunity that was being offered. Why on earth was the man hesitating? He had made a million since he had inherited. Or so he said. It was his money. She couldn't see the problem. Opportunities like the one being offered by Marcin Galinski came once in a lifetime. The two were a perfect match. The money and the brains. The only thing Martha could think of was the money was fiction. By the time the driver dropped her off outside the office she was fearing a life on her own. Of bringing up the baby without a father. If he had lied to her, she could lie to him. Tell him he was not her only lover. That she was pregnant before she met him. For some people life was one big lie. A means of getting what they wanted.

"Have a nice day."

"You too."

When she turned to go into the building her client was standing next to her, smiling. Switching her mind away from her personal life, Martha got down to business.

"Good morning. What perfect timing."

"You can say that again. Was there something wrong?"

"Of course not. Our campaign for you looks really good. The art department have been working overtime."

"I appreciate it."

"All part of the service, Claude. Come on. It's all waiting for you."

They entered the lift and stood, neither of them talking. The pause, as Franklyn liked to call it, before the closing. People gathered around them. The lift rose. The day's work had begun.

It took Martha an hour to close the deal. She shook hands with Claude, the artwork spread out on the boardroom table. She saw Claude to the lift. Back in the open-plan office she waved at Jas before going to Franklyn's office.

"Signed and sealed."

"I'm so glad you're back. I enjoyed last night's dinner. Has Phillip agreed?"

"Still hesitating. Got me worried. I suggested I put in fifty thousand of my own money but it didn't make much difference."

"Sit down and relax for a moment. I've been asking around. Repeating what I saw in that proposal and what I heard at dinner. The maths can be checked by a friend of mine at the university. He's a professor of economics. The rest is marketing. We can generate the income once we offer the software to a wide public. The use is universal. Anyone with a computer is a potential client. I'm not much of a gambler but I'll put in fifty thousand. Better than wasting money on the lottery. If you can talk Phillip into giving us a fifth of his equity I'll come in with you. Why don't you go home and talk to Phillip?"

"He's taking Marcin to the airport right now. There's too much work on my desk. I'll try tonight. Said he wanted time to think."

"Have you checked his credentials?"

"Not really. Is Randall Holiday really his brother?"

"That's easy. I'll phone his publishers."

"Of course. Silly of me."

"Marcin Galinski. Whatever we do or don't do we're going to hear that name again. Do you know the name of Phillip's bankers in Jersey?"

"Royal Bank of Canada."

"That's interesting. Give them a ring. Get a bank reference. Go through the company bank. Better still, phone Geoffrey Ardel and ask him to do a confidential check-up."

"I'd be going behind his back."

"If you don't he'll miss the best opportunity I've ever seen. He's got to move fast. That young man isn't going to sit around. There's plenty more money in the country looking for somewhere to go. He likes us because we know how to do his marketing. Merchandise, money, management, market and manpower. The five Ms. Get them together properly and it works. The unbreakable links in the chain. You got to have all them links or it don't work. And last night I think we got 'em, Martha. But you've got to be quick. You want me to phone Geoffrey?"

"You're more than a good boss. You're a friend."

"Everyone's a friend when they see a lot of money. The American way."

The working week was over before Martha had time to catch her breath. Villiers Publishing had confirmed Randall Holiday's real name was Randall Crookshank. The Royal Bank of Canada would not confirm they had a client by the name of Phillip Crookshank. Jersey bankers, like their counterparts in Switzerland, refused to divulge client information. Phillip had still not made up his mind despite the expiry of the two-day deadline. The deal was slipping away, Martha's frustration building. Even Franklyn's fifty thousand offer had made no difference. He wanted time to think. Phillip always wanted time to think. Tired from work and her personal problems, Martha left the office at six o'clock. Jas was still working.

"You and Noah still good?"

"Why you ask?"

"The way you were chatting up Marcin at my dinner party."

"Don't be silly. Just impressing a future client with my charm."

"Don't lie to me, Jas. Your hormones were jumping all over the dinner table."

"You can look. So long as you don't touch. When I got home I screwed Noah's brains out. He loved it. He looks at other women. Be something wrong with him if he didn't."

BACK AT THE apartment there was no sign of Phillip. An opened letter from the Royal Bank of Canada was sitting all by itself on the dining room table, listing the current value of Phillip's global equity funds along with cash held in the bank and giving a total, the number well over five million. Having to verify her lover's credentials made Martha happy and sad. It was a miserable life when you didn't believe another person's word. The heading just below 'Dear Sir' was The Ben Crossley Family Trust. Martha poured herself a glass of wine and sat drinking. She waited an hour, looking at her watch. She had drunk three glasses of red, the wine giving her courage. When she walked into Solly's Saloon, Phillip was sitting up at the bar drinking on his own.

"I'm sorry I doubted you."

"So am I... You want a drink?"

"Wouldn't mind."

"Solly, meet Martha. She'll have a glass of red wine."

"How did you know?"

"You've been drinking. All we have in the flat is red wine."

"You look pensive."

"I am. I phoned Marcin before I came to the pub. We're in. All three of us."

"Oh, Phillip. I'm so excited. You're really going in?"

"The other choice was running away... Thanks, Solly."

"You're on your own. Why aren't you talking to the other people?"

"Sometimes it's nice to drink on one's own. Think on one's own. How was work?"

"Hectic. Can I phone Franklyn?"

"Be my guest. We'll need Horst and Maples's lawyers to write up a contract and have all the parties sign. Form a new company. Marcin will fly back once the contract is drawn up. He's already talking to his friends from Yale. It's all happening."

"You happy with it?"

"Like a ten-ton load off my shoulders. Cheers, Martha."

"Your bankers wouldn't talk to us."

"I know they wouldn't. They told me an American bank was making enquiries. I had a call from Randall. His editor phoned me."

"I'm sorry."

"In reality, we barely know each other. English and American cultures are miles apart, despite the common language and history. If I'm going to spend the rest of my life in America, I'll have to get used to it. Man's been getting used to changes through all the centuries. How it works. They call it evolution. I'll just have to evolve. And don't forget, we're going to church on Sunday."

"I love you, Phillip."

"Careful, darling. Don't throw words around too glibly. Only say something when you really mean it. Not when you've just heard what you want to hear."

"Can I give you a kiss?"

"Only on the cheek. We're in public and I'm descended from a long line of Englishmen who would sooner be dead than be seen kissing in public."

He was smiling at her. When he put a finger to the side of his face, Martha leaned forward and gave him a peck on the cheek.

"You two have a good evening."

"I think we will, Solly. Don't you agree, Martha?"

"We're going to celebrate."

"That's my girl."

"Can we eat in this place?"

"We can have a feast fit for a king. If we're sober enough."

"Let's get drunk and forget our troubles."

"What about the baby?"

"Didn't your mother drink when she was pregnant? In those days they weren't telling us what to do and what not to do. We did what came naturally. Tonight I feel like drinking with my lover. Celebrating. We worry too much in the modern world. We should relax more and enjoy ourselves. Live for today. Worry about tomorrow when it comes. Eat some potato chips and peanuts to counter the effect of too much alcohol. Why they have them on the bar. Right, Solly. Fill 'em up."

The barman smiled at her. The man on Martha's right smiled at her. The music was playing. People were laughing. She was thirty-seven years old and still had most of her looks. And she was going to have a healthy baby with both parents to look after him. Or her. She drank the last of the wine in her glass. Solly was waiting, the bottle at the ready. Phillip gave her a quizzical look. A mix of hope and resignation. Or was it alcohol-induced pleasure at having his drinking companion? Whoever knew? Did it matter? She was rambling in her mind. Not caring. Friday night. No work tomorrow. Let the gods decide. He had committed. He was going to be staying in America. A venture capitalist. And when it worked, as it would, who knew how rich they would be? Let the gods decide. And the day after tomorrow she was going into a church for the first time since she had left school.

"What's this pastor's name again?"

"Pastor Gregory."

"Is he nice?"

"He will be when I donate to his church."

"Ah, the old game of money. What are you and Marcin going to call the company?"

"Linguare."

"Your idea or Marcin's?"

"Oh, it's his. All I do is put in the money."

"There'll be more. Much more."

"I hope so. Can't stay drunk in a bar for the rest of my life."

"Let me phone Franklyn the good news."

When they went home they were helping each other into the taxi, both of them having a fit of the giggles. Martha couldn't remember when she had enjoyed an evening more. She had forgotten her worries. Tossed them out of the window. From now on she was going to stop her worrying.

"We should do it again, Phillip."

"Remember joining the mile-high club?"

"Do I ever. That's quite some bar."

"You can say that again. We're laughing, Martha. How we started."

"And now we're going on. A life full of laughter. You know the most beautiful thing on this earth? It's the sound of children laughing."

They went to bed, Phillip too drunk to make love. Martha slept right through the night. When she woke, Phillip was putting a mug of coffee on her bedside table.

"You got a hangover?"

"Not sure. But I'm hungry."

"We should have eaten more than those sandwiches. What do you want to do today?"

"Go shopping. Stock up the fridge. Hire a boat and go out on the river. Talk about anything but business. Just you and me together."

The hangover didn't seem to matter for either of them. A picnic lunch on the boat, a day of idle fishing, excitement when she landed a fish. A day they would both remember. No arguments. No tension. Just two lovers on a boat enjoying themselves. They did not drink, Martha thinking of her baby. Of all the things she wanted, she wanted most to be a mother. Part of her own family. A normal life. With happiness and laughter. Sitting on a wooden bench at the boat's stern, her line in the water, the sun dappling through the trees, she could see it all ahead of her.

"You've shown me happiness. Thank you, Phillip. And don't give me that look. How I feel today has nothing to do with your commitment to Marcin. We're going to be together for the rest of our lives. That's what made me smile."

The sunset through the trees was spectacular, a flood of red brushing the horizon. Phillip said it reminded him of Africa, making him look content. They dropped the boat back with the hirer and went home with their fish. They were physically tired. Martha made them supper of grilled fish, the classical music playing. They went to bed and fell asleep in each other's arms.

THE CHURCH WAS QUIET, and a feeling of peace flooded over Martha. They took their seats in the third pew from the back. Phillip knelt down, clasped his hands in front of him and half closed his eyes. When she looked at him he smiled.

"Are you praying?"

"I'm not sure how to pray. Been such a long time."

They were whispering. At the front of the small church with its high ceiling a few people were sitting, waiting for Pastor Gregory to appear. One old woman was praying, her mouth moving. She looked old and frail. From outside the church came the hum of the Sunday morning traffic. When a man appeared in all the trappings of the church the service began with a prayer. By Martha's watch it was exactly eleven o'clock. With the clergyman, a group of children had filed into a pew facing the congregation, all wearing white surplices down to their feet. After the prayer, Pastor Gregory began to preach, Martha barely listening. The old woman was listening intently. At the end of the service everyone filed out, Pastor Gregory waiting for them to shake their hands. His face lit up when he saw Phillip. Phillip gave him an envelope.

"Thank you so much, Phillip, for your donation. The poor people who need our help will be so grateful. This must be Martha. Hello, Martha. I'm Pastor Gregory. You are getting married in our church, I believe?"

Once he had gone back inside, Martha looked back at the small church nestled between two high-rise buildings.

"How much did you give him?"

"Ten thousand dollars. Are we going to set a date?"

"How does the first of December sound? A nice easy date to remember."

"What day will it be?"

"I'll have to look at my calendar. Did you enjoy the service?"

"The church was very peaceful. I'm beginning to get excited."

"About the marriage or having your baby?"

"Both. Hold my hand."

Smiling, happy, they walked down the road towards the park. Half an hour later, invigorated by the cold, fresh air, they were back in the apartment. Martha checked her calendar. The first of December was a Wednesday.

"Can we change the date to the fourth? It would be better as it is a Saturday. And Pastor Gregory can start reading the banns next Sunday. Do I tell him about my previous marriages? I can phone him."

"The fourth is perfect. There shouldn't be a problem with your marriages."

"You know about the men in my past. What about the women in your past? Was there anyone important?"

"That's something you'd like me to neither answer yes or no. So I'll say nothing. Our lives together started when we met on the banks of the Zambezi River. Let's leave it at that. I don't want to know about Jake and Jonathan, so let's leave our past alone."

"There must have been someone. You're a great lover. Great lovers have great affairs. Why didn't you marry, Phillip? You're thirty-seven. That's a long time to be single."

"She didn't want to go back and live in Rhodesia. I didn't want to stay in England. Like you, I was young and naïve. And selfish. We had met at Rhodes and become lovers when we were nineteen. When we graduated we went on a holiday to England, my father's graduation present. Dad had his money from the Chelsea block of flats he had bought with Livy Johnston. We went for a month and stayed for six. Henrietta loved England, loved being away from all the apartheid nonsense in South Africa. She hated apartheid. As an Afrikaner of French descent that was unusual. Many were rabid racists like her father. Henrietta du Plessis. That was her name. Do you really want to know about my past affairs?"

"It's best to tell each other. To have a perfect future together, we must be able to share our pasts. The good and the bad. What happened to Henrietta?"

"I don't know. After England, I went back to Rhodesia. She went back to South Africa. Probably has a family. Married another Boer. Her father hated me. Said I was a *kaffir* lover like his daughter. That he should never have let her go to an English-speaking university."

"What's a *kaffir*?"

"It's the 'n' word. The man was a bastard. Once, staying on the farm, when Henrietta took me to meet her family, a small generator went missing. It was one of her father's employee's children. He'd stolen it for a friend in the black township. A boy of sixteen. Instead of going to the boy's father and have him punish his son, he went for his gun and shot at the boy. Luckily missed him. Literally made the boy shit in his pants. Soon after, Henrietta and I left for England where she wanted to get a job teaching English. She had her degree in English literature. She wanted to run away. Wanted me to teach history in a prep school, both of us working in the same place. You see, through Dad's birth in England I have the right to British citizenship. Without a marriage to me she couldn't get permanent residence in England."

"What a horrible world. So she wanted to marry you so she could live in England. Were you in love?"

"We were lovers. Maybe in love. I just couldn't handle the English weather. The smallness of everything. Everything on top of each other."

"A bit like Kansas City."

"Don't let's go down that path again. I've made up my mind. But the one thing from my past you must understand, Martha, is my love for Africa. That passion will never fade. Hopefully, I will also come to love your country. And no, I'm not using you. If I had wanted to run away from the troubles in Zimbabwe, I could have gone to England without any problem. Rhodesia became Zimbabwe two years after I returned home from England. Democracy. People were excited. Trouble is, very few got what they voted for in all the political corruption. You want to ring Pastor Gregory or shall I?"

"Will he spend your ten thousand on charity?"

"We can only hope so."

"Put on the kettle and I'll give him a ring."

When Martha made the call, her divorces proved no obstacle.

"Now you will make your vow before God, Martha. Your marriage to Phillip will be permanent. When you come on Sunday you'll hear me read your banns of marriage. Saturday, fourth of December at three o'clock in the afternoon. Invite all your friends."

"I'm pregnant, Pastor Gregory."

"Then it will give me joy to baptise your child in my church. I am on my way to the hospice to give them Phillip's ten thousand dollars. His money will feed many hungry people. It is one of God's blessings to be able to help the less fortunate. Only when a person has experienced abject poverty do they understand the importance of charity. Have you ever gone hungry, Martha?"

"No, I haven't."

"You are lucky. There are many in this world who have not been so fortunate. Enjoy the rest of your day."

Feeling squeamish at her previous bad thoughts, Martha put the phone down. Phillip offered her a mug of coffee.

"What did he say? Is everything on?"

"Everything's fine. He's a good man. A really good man. Three o'clock in the afternoon on the fourth of December."

"He got to you."

"Yes, he did. In a nice way. He wants to baptise our baby."

"A church wedding. What are you going to wear?"

"A long, expensive white dress down to my ankles. My previous marriages were in dressy suits. Are you going to phone your relations in England? They've a little more than a month to prepare. Are we just inviting relatives?"

"If we're going as far as a church wedding let's do it properly. You'd better phone your brothers. I'll phone Myra and Julian. Who's going to give you away?"

"I'll have to think. Probably Hugo or Ford if they can find the time to come. They don't think much of modern marriages."

"We want all the pomp and ceremony. One big grand wedding. Everything, Martha. Including a cake the size of the Empire State Building. Bridesmaids. You'll need bridesmaids."

"Can we organise all that in six weeks?"

"Why not? We'll invite Mrs Crabshaw. She'll love to go to a wedding. Everyone loves a wedding. A nice flowing dress and they won't see you're pregnant. One grand day never to be forgotten. When we're old and in our wheelchairs, we'll still be talking about our wedding day. We'll need more than an organist and a schoolboy choir. A black revivalist choir and a band. People shouting with joy. All dressed in their best. A big, big reception in a big, big hotel. I did mention the cake. The best food available in America. Lobster. Oysters. Caviar. You mention it. The most expensive caterers I can find. Celebrity caterers. How does that sound? My goodness, we'll have a big Hollywood star in my brother-in-law. A famous writer in my brother. Randall can bring his American publisher, Julian his Hollywood friends."

"Aren't you getting away from yourself?"

"How does it sound?"

"Fabulous."

"Then let's get started. Phone your mother. All your friends. Everyone you like at work. We'll invite the genius. I'm only getting married once in my life, Martha. We're going to do it properly. From now until the fourth of December we're going to chase up one hell of a wedding."

"You're insane."

"Does it matter? I'm about to get married. We have a life. At last we have a life."

First out of the blocks was Hugo, the brother who worked for the federal government. Three calls and she tracked him down in Tokyo. No, the fourth of December was not possible, his work schedule clashing with the date. Ford came next and said he had the kids but could he bring them and give the bride away? Phillip spoke on the phone to Randall on the Isle of Man. The day rushed by, one phone call after another, the lists growing on Martha's desk and the coffee table in front of Phillip. Then he was talking to Craig.

"She's just had her baby!"

"Who, Phillip?" asked Martha.

"Jojo. It's a boy."

"Are they married?"

"Are you married, Craig? No, they are not."

"Are they coming over?"

"Can't get away from work. All that fundraising. Talk to you later, Craig. It's Martha asking all the questions. Dad and your mother are flying over. Can't you make a plan? Good lad. It's going to be one hell of a wedding. You and Jojo should get yourselves married now you have a son. What are you calling him? Harold. I like Harold. Very formal. Look after yourselves. Got a piece of paper? Good. Now write down these details and repeat them back to me. Don't want any mistakes. I'll pay your airfares and hotel bills, of course. Of course I'm excited."

After Phillip finalised his brother's visit, Martha began phoning her old friends. By suppertime she had fifteen confirmed invitations on her list, a man to give her away, and one of the bridesmaids. She was exhausted from all the excitement.

"How many you got, Phillip?"

"Twenty-one definite. How does that sound? Julian says he will bring a couple of his friends. Not sure how many. Randall is phoning his publisher. They all love a wedding. Tomorrow I'll spend all day on the phone while you're working. And I want to visit that hospice and see what they're doing with my money. Clem is coming. Says he's going to find his Martha and bring her along."

"One can only hope."

"You're right. Can you feel the bugger moving in your belly with all the joie de vivre? His parents are getting married."

"Her parents are getting married."

"Whatever. I'm going to have a drink. From now until he's born you're not allowed to drink booze. Responsibility for both of us starts right now. Are we going to stay in this apartment? It doesn't have a garden. Kids love a garden. Love a farm. The whole damn Zambezi Valley."

"Slow down. You're going to explode."

"Why not? Nothing wrong with a little explosion. A man doesn't arrange his own wedding every day. On second thoughts you'll have to arrange the venue. You know the right places. So, there we have it. It's all happening. No going back. No changing our minds. In less than a year this safari operator will have come out of the bush to be a husband, a father and a venture capitalist. Life really can change on the turn of a tickey."

"What's a tickey?"

"A South African coin. The smallest. Enjoying every moment of it. The about-to-be Mrs Crookshank. That's who you are. Let's go and see your mother. Then we'll call on Mrs Crabshaw."

"Aren't you going to have a drink?"

"The drink can wait."

By the time they went to bed they were both exhausted, their minds still racing with all the excitement.

"Let's make love, Martha. Good sex makes us sleep."

Gently, Phillip stroked her swelling belly.

"I can feel him. Our whole future is in your stomach. Let's sleep. Let him sleep. Our whole lives are ahead of us."

"Do you love me, Phillip?"

"With all my heart."

"Make love to me. Gently. I want to be as close to you as is physically possible. I want part of you inside of me. Oh, Phillip. Our lives together are going to be so wonderful. I have wanted a family of my own so much. Yes, my lover. Thank you, my lover. Oh, yes! Yes!"

TRYING to concentrate on her work and not on her wedding, Martha sat at her desk and picked up the phone. There was a message to call the advertising manager of Brindles, one of her clients. Within an hour her day was in overdrive, her mind concentrated. Martha enjoyed her work. The satisfaction of getting it right. Seeing her various campaigns come together. The morning flew by. She ate her lunch at her desk. At three o'clock in the afternoon, Franklyn called her into his office. With him was Jas.

"You want to be a bridesmaid at my wedding? We're inviting everyone. The biggest wedding you've ever seen. Brindles are happy with our work. They gave me the name of one of their clients to contact. Nothing better than a recommendation. What can I do for you, Franklyn?"

"Sit down, Martha. We have a new company to launch in which we both have an investment. I want to talk about promoting Linguare. Publicising Marcin and his product. Build the hype. We won't give them a launch date for the software as Marcin doesn't know it himself, but he's found premises on the East Side and his two friends from Yale have gone on the payroll. He's opened a company bank account. All three of us are to transfer our funds at the same time. Marcin Galinski as CEO will have sole signature for amounts up to fifty thousand dollars. Anything over requires Phillip's approval. Your future husband will be doing a lot of commuting between here and New York. Later, he may have to move there. You can't control your money at arm's length. We've been thinking of opening a Horst and Maples branch in New York for some time. This may prove to be the final catalyst. You must start preparing a media campaign so by the time of the launch the whole world knows about the product."

"We can start by inviting the local media to our wedding. Julian Becker and Randall Holiday will be there. So will their friends. We can link them to Phillip and Phillip to Marcin Galinski and to the product."

"You don't waste time, Martha. You and Jas are going to be in charge of the account. Celebrity names are good but that is only a beginning. Jas will be arranging interviews for Marcin on television. Get his face known. Get him telling the public the benefits they can expect from voice recognition software. I want a million sales of the software the day we launch. They'll be given a week's trial run for free. Then they must pay one hundred dollars to use the software, the figures came in from Marcin on the phone this morning. They're moving camp beds into the new offices so they don't have to go home at night. They say they don't need much sleep. The pleasures of youth. The energy of that man is mind-boggling. Now, let's go through the rest of the details."

"Are you going to be my bridesmaid, Jas?"

"Only a pleasure."

"Just keep your eyes off the genius."

"I'll try. When's the wedding?"

"Fourth of December. It's a Saturday."

"Thank goodness. How's the baby?"

"Kicking. Just a little. I can feel her."

"Ladies. Please. We are preparing to launch a product."

"Of course you're invited, Franklyn."

The thought of moving fifty thousand dollars from her hard-earned savings account made Martha's stomach flutter. With a conscious effort she brought her mind round to the day's business. By six o'clock they were finished. It was time to go home to Phillip.

"Are you really happy putting all that money into Linguare, Franklyn?"

"Nothing ventured, nothing gained."

"My money is in blue-chip American companies, not some start-up. No wonder Phillip was hesitant."

"You can live an ordinary life never taking a risk and die of boredom. Or you can go on an adventure with all the excitement. Part of an adventure is the risk. Maybe we'll lose. Who knows? Your husband-to-be's father went from England on an adventure to Africa. Yes, in the end it failed. But I'll bet he wouldn't change any of it. Didn't he end up owning half a block of apartments in London? He didn't lose all of his money. And what a life that must have been in the wilds of Africa. Wish I'd had the chance. I love my job but it's still sitting behind a desk. Every working day of my life. The night of your dinner party Phillip talked about their farm in Africa. Made me downright jealous. Like taking the wagons into the Wild West. Now that was an adventure. And that's what we're doing with Marcin. If it works and we do an IPO and the shares take off like Microsoft we'll have more money than we can even imagine. I'll travel the world. Go to Africa on a holiday with Phillip. Never have to worry about money for my family. With money, real money, there are so many opportunities out there. We only have one life. Got to make the best of it. You take a calculated risk and take your chances. We're still comparatively young with years ahead to save for our old age."

"Thank you. I feel a little better."

"Get your money ready to transfer. I have. You'll need the fifty thousand liquid by Wednesday. It's been a good afternoon's work from both of you. See you in the morning."

Martha had to smile at herself. It was all so different when it was your own money. She was looking at the whole big picture of venture capitalism from a different direction. Her direction, not Phillip's. As the picture grew so did Martha's smile. They were both on the same page. Both taking the same risk. And Franklyn was right. What was the purpose of life without an adventure?

Down in the street, happy as a cricket, Martha hailed a cab. When she opened the apartment door, Phillip was still on the phone, three pages of names on the coffee table in front of him. She went across and kissed him on the side of his face without interrupting his conversation. In the kitchen, she put on the kettle. It was time to make her lover a cup of tea.

Back in the lounge, with her mug of coffee next to Phillip's mug of tea close to the lists of guests, she smiled at Phillip, happy with her day. When he finished talking on the phone he added two more names to one of his lists.

"Can you have the money ready by Wednesday? I'm selling shares tomorrow. Franklyn's ready. Did you go to the hospice?"

"One of them is going to kill the other."

"What are you talking about?"

"Willy and Beth. It's been going on all day. They weren't just arguing, they were fighting. I heard the furniture go over. For a moment I thought I'd better go down and see what was going on. Decided to mind my own business. By the sound of it both of them are out of jobs. Never interfere in others' marital affairs. Don't we marry for better or worse? Why do people end up hating each other? Arguing won't help. They should get out of each other's way. Oh, well. Thankfully, it's not our problem. Tell me where to send it and I'll phone the bank details to Jersey. Pastor Gregory wasn't there. The man in charge of the hospice knew all about my ten thousand dollars. Gave me the grand tour. Not that the place was grand. We should thank our lucky stars every day of our lives for having financial security. Gave him another cheque. That man is dedicated to helping poor sods who can't help themselves. Made me feel good my money was doing good. How was your day? Do you know, this is my sixth cup of tea today?"

"It's a mug of tea. Franklyn's all over Linguare now he's putting in his own money."

"Concentrates the mind, risking one's own money. What the hell do you do when you don't have any money and you can't find a job? There was one woman living in the hospice with a two-year-old. They'd brought her in off the street that morning. She was dirty. Filthy is a better word. So was her little boy. Neither looked as if they had had a bath for weeks. When Colin put food in front of them they shovelled it down their throats nearly choking, the poor buggers were so hungry."

"Who's Colin?"

"The man in charge of the hospice. I invited him to our wedding. Said he'd prefer a donation instead of my spending money on him. That invitation cost me ten thousand dollars. Money well given. Lucky I had my chequebook in my pocket. I can still see their dirty, hungry faces shovelling down the stew. There's a whole world out there I know nothing about. Never seen before in my life. The Crookshanks have always had money as far back as five generations... That's as far as Dad can go in our ancestry. It's become a hobby of his... You take money for granted when you're born into wealth. Those two hours made me think. Just hope I don't lose my money with Marcin. If I don't and it works, I've promised myself I will create a charitable foundation and run it myself. Do the job properly. Like Colin. He looks as poor as a church mouse, the way he was dressed. He lives in the hospice. No fancy salary for doing good. I've seen charities in Africa where the managers have fancy cars and live like rich people from the money donated to their NGO. Some of those non-governmental organisations are a way of avoiding tax. They're one big business for the organisers. And then they tell the world how much good they're doing. If half the donated money gets to the people who need it I'll eat my hat."

"Where will you run your charity?"

"In Africa, of course. Colin and Pastor Gregory have made me think. There's more to life and money than spend, spend, spend on useless luxuries. Buying bloody great diamonds that have no other use than to show off."

"So I'm not getting an engagement ring?"

"A ring, yes. With a tiny, tiny diamond. Just as valuable. It's the intention that counts. Have you added any more names to the wedding list? We're all hypocrites. Twenty thousand to the hospice and God knows how much on a wedding."

"I don't understand you, Phillip."

"I don't understand myself."

"Should I go visit Willy and Beth?"

"Leave them alone."

"We could invite them to our wedding?"

"Don't be ridiculous. They start one of those fights and it will ruin the whole damn thing. You can't help everyone."

Not sure she wanted a tiny, tiny diamond for an engagement ring, she drank her coffee quietly. Phillip was back on the phone. No sooner had she finished her coffee than a loud thud followed by a scream resounded from the apartment underneath. The scream was terrifying. A woman's scream. Phillip had stopped talking.

"Got to go, Josh. Problems. Right. That's it. I'm going downstairs. What number are they?"

"Nine-o-six. I'm coming with you."

"No you are not."

"Yes I am. We'll walk down the back stairs."

Phillip knocked on the door, both of them pensive, not sure what to expect. Willy half opened the door on the second loud knock.

"Can I help you?"

"I'm from the apartment above. What's going on?"

"Mind your own damn business."

"Willy, it's Martha. Is Beth all right?"

"Why shouldn't she be? Why can't people mind their own business?"

"Martha, please help me?" Martha recognised Beth's voice.

"Do you want me to call the police?"

"No. Don't do that. Can I come up?"

The door opened wide, Willy turning his back. The side of Beth's face was bleeding. She was crying. She flew into Martha's arms.

"We've lost all our money and we can't find jobs. We just got the eviction order this morning. It's not Willy's fault. We're desperate."

"Don't you have family?"

"We can't ask them for money."

"What are you going to do?"

"That's what we've been fighting about all day. I want to get a job as a maid. Willy won't hear of it. Says he won't have a wife who's a house servant. I tell him he should sweep the streets if necessary but he won't. He's too proud. His company closed down six months ago. They're doing the manufacturing in China. They've all been laid off. He was the works manager. Good salary. Lots of experience. Now all that knowledge is worthless. At fifty he can't start learning a new career."

"Didn't they give him severance pay?"

"Not a cent. The company went bankrupt. The money he put into the pension fund for all those years has gone as well. Twenty-five years of contributions."

"That doesn't sound right."

"None of it's right, Martha. Instead of trying something, all we're doing is taking our frustration out on each other. How can this have all happened? A year ago our whole lives and futures were perfect."

"Don't you have any kids?"

"No. We never had kids. I can't have kids."

"Do you know anything about computers?"

"I know how to use one to enter data. What are we going to do?"

"Shoot those bastards who bankrupted my company."

"Willy, shouting won't help."

"You'd better leave us alone, Martha. Willy and I will work something out. We didn't always argue. Married twenty-eight years. At least we have each other. Thanks for coming down."

"When are you leaving?"

"On the fourth of December."

"The day of our wedding."

"How it goes, Martha. Some have luck. Some don't. Have a nice wedding. We've got to solve our own problem or our lives will be finished. Hopefully, in a while, we'll look back and laugh at today."

"Both of you come up if you need me."

"Thank you, Martha. You're a good neighbour."

"We have a spare bedroom."

"You're so kind."

The door closed, leaving them in the corridor looking at each other, both of them uncomfortable.

"Doesn't get worse than that."

"Oh, it does. You should have seen that woman and her two-year-old son. They've got a long way to go before they end up in the hospice."

"We'll never do that to each other, whatever happens in our lives."

Walking back up the stairs, the tiny, tiny diamond didn't seem so bad after all. And they both had money. Their children were going to be lucky, the Poland and Crookshank legacy passed down the centuries. Back in her apartment, Martha stood by her window listening. It was all quiet down below. Phillip poured himself a drink.

"After that I'm breaking the rules. I need a drink to calm my nerves."

"Are you sure?"

"You're never sure by the look of it. He must have nearly knocked her head off."

Across the way, there was no sign of the old lady who liked to wave.

"You just don't know how lucky you are."

Phillip shrugged, picked up the phone and dialled a number.

"We're going to have one hell of a phone bill."

"You can say that again."

"Marcin? It's Phillip. Your money will be in the bank on Wednesday. Latest Thursday. How's it going?"

Martha turned on the hi-fi. Soon enough she started to feel better. Classical music always calmed her nerves. She walked into the kitchen and poured herself a glass of red wine. It tasted delicious. If she was content it would be good for the baby. She was rationalising. Back in the lounge, Phillip was listening to Marcin who was doing most of the talking. Phillip was smiling. If half a million dollars went down the drain on an idea that did not work she would never forgive herself. They were going to have a child to support. Marcin had his youth and it wasn't his money at risk. Her mind went round in circles. She got up and went back into the kitchen. Downstairs Beth and Willy had started arguing again. This time Beth was doing the shouting. They had done their best. She filled up her glass and walked back to the lounge. Phillip was still talking to Marcin, his face animated. Whatever he was hearing was good. What would they do if the couple downstairs took up her offer of the spare bedroom? The shouting and swearing would be right next to them. Their lives interrupted. She was glad she had made the offer but feared the consequence. There were so many people in the world with problems. She couldn't help all of them. She thought of the young woman and her starving son while she sipped at her expensive wine. Phillip put down the phone.

"If he doesn't start building revenue by the end of next year he'll need more venture capital. There are still some minor glitches in the system. Trouble is, one small glitch can make the software unworkable. The three of them are working on it eighteen hours a day."

"How much will they be paying themselves?"

"Fifty thousand dollars a year."

"Sounds good for them. All the marketing in the world won't help if the product doesn't work."

"That's our gamble. Why have you gone negative?"

"I'm thinking of Beth and Willy. Just listen to them."

"I'll turn up the music."

"Good idea."

"How's that wine going down?"

"Another glass or two and I won't give a shit. Did we really meet in the middle of Africa? Seems like a century ago."

"A lot's happened since May. What's for supper?"

"I'm too upset to cook. I'll phone for a takeaway."

"Fine by me. Let's relax. If Marcin doesn't get it to work by the end of next year he'll have to look somewhere else for money."

"And let the next investor reap all the benefits?"

"If worst comes to worst and we run out of money we can go back to Africa and you can help me run a safari company."

"Is that a threat or a promise?"

"Better than what's happening down below. Just listen to them. Are they really going to live in the spare bedroom?"

"I hope not. Two jumbo hamburgers each. Will that be enough?"

"Should be. Makes me think of elephants. I miss my elephants. Miss all the animals."

Instead of listening to Phillip's reminiscing she picked up her phone and ordered the hamburgers. Half an hour later when the doorbell rang she was immersed in the pleasure from her wine. The music of Beethoven was loud. The Ninth Symphony, 'The Choral'. She could no longer hear them arguing in the flat below. She picked up her purse and went to the door. A young boy was waiting patiently. She paid him, giving him a good tip, and put the box of food down on the coffee table in front of Phillip. He finished what he was writing, opened the box and took out a hamburger.

"Nothing wrong with America, Martha. All you have to do is make a phone call and pay the bill."

"Was she an immigrant?"

"Who are you talking about?"

"The woman with the two-year-old living on the street."

"Probably. I don't know. She had a dark complexion. Probably Mexican."

"Did you hear her speak?"

"Too busy shovelling food down her throat. This burger is perfect. Just wish I had a bigger mouth."

"An illegal immigrant. Can you imagine having to run away from your own country?"

"You're talking to a man with first-hand knowledge."

"You'll get used to America."

"I'm getting used to this hamburger. Did they originate in Hamburg?"

"I don't think so. The Germans eat sauerkraut."

"We're beginning to talk rubbish."

"Nothing wrong with a bit of rubbish in life. I could employ a wedding planner."

"If we can't organise our own wedding we really are idiots."

"We need a venue, a cake maker, a caterer, a wine merchant. All takes time."

"Find me the names and their phone numbers and I'll do the rest. Wedding planners. That really is the limit."

Martha smiled inwardly as she ate her food. The music had stopped. There was no argument coming up from down below. Putting the half-eaten burger down in the box, Martha began making her list. She was happy. She had a fiancé with enough money to pay for the most expensive wedding money could buy. She was lucky she wasn't an illegal immigrant. Instead of waiting for the noise to start again from down below she found Haydn's Twenty-Eighth Symphony and restarted the music.

"What are we going to call him, Phillip?"

"Sebastian. After the first of the Brigandshaws who went to Africa. Without the Brigandshaws I would never have been born in Africa. Never got you pregnant on the banks of the Zambezi River."

"Very old-fashioned name."

"Wasn't then. They called him Seb."

"I want to call her Kimberley."

"They'll call her Kim."

"What's wrong with Kim?"

"Nothing. I just so love that music."

"So do I. We're a perfect match. To the rest of our wonderful lives together, honey. There you are. You can phone them all tomorrow and get their prices. Ask around. Ask the hotel who they recommend to do the catering."

"Won't they do it themselves?"

"Maybe. A wedding planner would know the right people at the right prices. Save us money."

"You win. Find a wedding planner."

As Phillip sank his teeth into his second hamburger he winked at her. In America, everything was easy provided you had the money. A flutter at the thought of losing fifty thousand dollars on Wednesday ran through her body, arguing with the beautiful music and the pleasure from the wine.

"I just hope we don't lose our money."

"So do I. And, not to start a Beth and Willy argument just now when we're enjoying ourselves, don't forget it was your idea."

"You'll only blame me if it doesn't work?"

"Something like that."

"Why did you go ahead?"

"I summed up Marcin. Liked what I saw and heard. He was happy to explain the pitfalls. Wasn't giving a whole lot of bullshit. In a situation like that you can only judge the person, not the product when the product has not been perfected. I'm investing four hundred thousand dollars in Marcin Galinski. Not Linguare."

"Who taught you that?"

"My father. And his father taught him. Life is all about judging people if you wish to succeed."

"Have we had time to judge each other?"

"We don't have that privilege. We made a child. But luck was on our side. What I see, Martha Poland, the soon-to-be Martha Crookshank, is perfect."

"Is that the booze or the hamburger talking?"

"It's the truth. I've got to know you like no other person."

Martha got up, walked round the low table and kissed him on his mouth, both their mouths half full of food. As quickly as possible they swallowed the food before they began to laugh. When Martha sat back and picked up her glass of wine she was exquisitely happy. There was nothing better than the sound of happy laughter. It did not have to come from children. They were going to have the perfect life together. Every person's dream. Enjoying the company as much as the bottle of wine they chattered nonsense, both of them content. When the wine was finished, Phillip opened another bottle and the evening went on. Down below, Willy and Beth were quiet. Martha thought of them. Tried to imagine what it would do to a person's mind who had no money, no job and no home. It made her appreciate everything she had. From now on, she told herself, there would be no taking for granted. She would pray in Pastor Gregory's church and thank God. Thank God for her wonderful mother. The man smiling at her from the opposite couch. The child growing in her belly. The comfort of having money. Her friends at work. Her clients who appreciated all her hard effort. Despite losing her father, she had had a lucky life.

"We're so damn lucky, Phillip."

"I know we are. My luck came when we seduced each other, and you became pregnant. We'd better go to bed before we drink the rest of the wine. On second thoughts, to hell with it. We're enjoying ourselves. Cheers, Martha. Cheers to Kim or Seb. Have another glass of wine."

"I probably shouldn't. But what the hell, honey."

"I'm going to send out written invitations to those who say they're coming. We don't want them changing their minds or getting the dates wrong. Ink or print is better than the strongest memory. We want a perfect wedding with all our friends. Tomorrow, while you're at work, I'll go downstairs again. All those jobs moving to China. Makes you think. I'm still hungry. You want a sandwich?"

Trying not to think of life's pitfalls, Martha changed the music. She found a tape by Abba which she played. There was never any point in worrying. Her mind went back to her work and what she had to do the next day. Before she made any decision in her client's advertising she thought it through in every which way. It was important to picture the advertising on television from the viewer's point of view, not just the client's. 'Think, think, think,' she always repeated to herself when she was orchestrating a campaign. Phillip was smiling at the music, a plate of sandwiches now in front of them when she came out of her reverie.

"What are you frowning about, Martha?"

"My work. There's so much to do. Never stops. Always somewhere in my head. You want to make love, Phillip?"

"Won't make any difference. You're already pregnant."

"Stop laughing. Eat your sandwich. I do so love you, Phillip."

"You think Beth could be our wedding planner?"

"Wouldn't know where to start."

"Maybe she would. Now that would be luck. There's another old saying: 'Your worst enemies sometimes do you the best favours.' A year or two down the line Beth could have a highly successful business. Money to buy their own apartment. Why don't we give her a try? Willy was the works manager. Must know how to organise. We can all help each other. What neighbours are for. What happened in Rhodesia. Stuck out in the wilds of Africa you had to help each other if a community wished to succeed. A country. Why America works. Everyone is proud to be an American. How it used to be in England before they all started emigrating after the war. What's Willy and Beth's surname?"

"Hardcastle."

"Sounds English. We must help, Martha. Get them started. If that business were to succeed I'd be happier than if the genius makes us a fortune. How's my sandwich?"

"You make a good sandwich."

"I love Abba. There was just something special about them. If she agrees to be our wedding planner the first thing I will do is pay their rent. It's a win-win. I don't know my way round the American marketplace and you don't have the time. We'll save money instead of me being taken for a ride by all those caterers. And Beth will be earning a living. We won't feel so guilty wasting all that money on a wedding."

"It won't be wasted."

"Of course. I forget. It's everyone's dream to be able to show off their wealth."

"We want to make a memory."

"And we will."

"Spending money isn't bad. It helps everyone. Keeps the economy growing. How success in the world works. If we were all miserly with our money the country would collapse."

"There's always two ways of looking at anything, Martha. Let's drink to Beth Hardcastle, the successful wedding planner."

"To Beth's success."

"To Beth's success. How much does a wedding planner get paid? Must be a percentage of the caterers' bills."

"I'll find out."

"It's all part of being a venture capitalist. There's another old saying in life: 'The mushroom is on your doorstep.' A cliché wouldn't last in our minds down the generations if it wasn't true. She could take wedding planning a step further and expand into party planning. Functions. That sort of thing. Who knows, she might get herself famous mingling with all those rich celebrities. Why are you smiling?"

"Every now and again you get away from yourself."

"It's probably the wine. Expands the mind."

"Better go to bed. It's work tomorrow. Thanks for making the sandwiches."

"Always my pleasure."

Downstairs it was still quiet. Hoping she had not drunk too much wine, Martha went to bed, Phillip following, turning off the lights. Whether he would do anything for Willy and Beth only time would tell. Stranger things had happened. She took off all her clothes and got into bed. Under the sheets she watched Phillip come into the bedroom from the bathroom and get into bed. His body was still lean and hard. Walking the trails in the wilds of Africa kept a man fit, reminding Martha to go back to the gym as soon as possible after the baby was born. They snuggled up, both of them lying on their backs content with the world. When they fell asleep with the bedside light on they were still holding hands. She was soon back in her dreams.

When Martha left for work in the morning Phillip was in bed, a mug of tea on the side table next to him.

"Have a good day, wife-to-be."

"You too, honey."

THE DAY'S race had begun, the hours rushing past her. In one brief quiet moment she phoned three of the local wedding planners she found in the Yellow Pages. One said they charged a basic fee of fifty dollars per wedding guest. Another charged ten per cent of the catering, stating that through their expertise and knowledge they saved their clients money as well as giving them the perfect wedding reception. Martha smiled to herself. It was all about making money and selling, the lifeblood of Horst and Maples. And tomorrow she was going to the races to back a horse with her fifty thousand dollars. She was out of her mind.

"What a world."

"What's that about, Martha?"

"Business, Jas. It's all about business. See you in the morning."

On Thursday morning the money passed into the new company's bank account, Martha no longer confident she had done the right thing. Beth had accepted the idea of starting a business as a wedding planner. And why shouldn't she once Phillip agreed to pay their rent? Like Marcin, Beth had nothing to lose. Phillip, despite Martha's negativity that she kept to herself, was full of enthusiasm. The wedding invitations had been printed, Martha giving him her list of acceptances with the postal addresses. In between driving Beth around Kansas City he had written out the envelopes and posted the invitations. Beth and Willy had stopped fighting. On the Saturday morning, Martha went to see her mother.

"Hugo won't come. Says he can't get away from his work."

"I'm not surprised. My eldest son is sanctimonious. He and his wife tell the world they took an oath to remain married for the rest of their natural lives. Makes me want to laugh. She's been having affairs behind his back for years. He wouldn't dream of coming to his sister's third wedding. Has nothing to do with his work schedule. That's an excuse. He never visits me either. Ford only visits when he wants something. Children. But I shouldn't complain. They have their own lives to live. So, Ford's going to give you away? Sit down. Stop hovering. What's the matter?"

"I threw away fifty thousand dollars."

"You wish to explain?"

"Not really. Did you drink when you were pregnant with us children?"

"All the time. As well as every night when your father came in from the fields and you children were tucked up in bed, your father and I sat in front of the log fire and drank a glass of whisky. In the summer, we sat out on the lawn under the chestnut tree."

"How much did you drink?"

"I can't remember. As many as we wanted. Your father worked hard all day. The evenings were our special times together. The bonus for all our hard work. Three kids were quite a handful. And now look at the boys. They ignore their mother."

"How do you know she was having affairs?"

"A mother can see these things. It was the way she treated Hugo. I never liked that woman."

"Any more than you liked my husbands. Do you like Phillip?"

"He's rich, Martha. At least he has money."

"Maybe not forever if the new ventures don't work."

"Oh, they'll work. Money makes money. Not that I have any idea what he's doing."

The poor woman was lonely. For an hour, trying not to make an excuse and go about her day, Martha sat like a dutiful daughter and listened to her mother's complaints, her mind wandering.

"You're not listening, Martha."

"Of course I am."

"What did I say?"

"You were talking about Mrs Crabshaw."

"No, I wasn't."

"Mother, please. You're not the only one with problems."

"I'm going to telephone that Hugo and tell him to come."

"Thank you. I want as many of the family there as possible."

"Now, where was I?"

By the time Martha returned to her apartment it was five o'clock in the afternoon. Judging by the smile and hug when she left, her mother had enjoyed her visit. Promising herself to do it more often, she let herself in. A smiling, exuberant Beth was sitting on the couch, words gushing out of her mouth. Next to her sat Willy. The middle-aged couple were holding hands. Phillip, sitting back in the opposite settee across the coffee table, had his right hand stretched across the top of the couch. He too was smiling, his fingers loosely on the material, not tapping as Martha might have expected. She went into the kitchen and came back with an open bottle of wine. In among her fingers hung four glasses. She put it all down on the table. When Beth saw the wine she stopped talking.

"You are both so kind, Martha."

"Did you know Beth is a devotee of Constance Spry?"

"Who is Constance Spry, Phillip?"

"An Englishwoman who in the twenties turned flower arranging into a profession. Beth wants to put flowers all over the church and do the arrangements herself. Big, beautiful bowls of flowers in the church and in the reception room of the Alameda Plaza where we're having our reception. Have you ordered your wedding dress? Beth says she wants to help. She loves white wedding dresses, don't you, Beth?"

"Please pour the wine." Martha was quietly shaking her head as she spoke to Phillip.

"My pleasure. It's all happening. Beth and Willy are so on top of it."

"Have you heard from Marcin Galinski?"

"Not a word. Far too busy."

"I thought he might phone and thank us for our money."

"It's more important to concentrate on perfecting that software than being polite. Don't be nervous, Martha. Everything is going to work out fine. My Uncle Paul and Aunty Beth are coming over. Her father was Harry Brigandshaw, Sebastian's son. Paul runs the Brigandshaw family business in England. He's stinking rich. There's an American branch of the Brigandshaw company run by Tinus Oosthuizen. The Brigandshaws and the Oosthuizens have been involved with each other since Sebastian's early days in Africa."

"I have no idea what you are talking about. Are you going to wear a suit?"

"Of course. A safari suit with a wide-brimmed bush-hat and a rifle slung over my shoulder. It'll remind me of the tropical sun and everyone will know where I come from."

"Be serious, Phillip."

"I am."

"Including the gun."

"I'll leave the gun at the church door. Sit you down next to me and come and enjoy a glass of lovely wine. How was your mother?"

"Lonely. Seriously, what are you going to wear?"

"Maybe my birthday suit."

"Phillip, you're quite impossible."

"Do you like the idea of the flowers?"

"I love flowers. Otherwise, Beth, how's it going?"

"I'm going to every caterer in Kansas City for quotations. With the prices in front of me I will then judge the quality of their produce. I've asked each of them for references which I will follow up before giving them an order. I'm so happy, Martha. Phillip, bless his heart, has given our landlord three months' rent in advance. And now, thank you for the wine, Phillip. To a wonderfully successful wedding."

"I'll drink to that."

"And thank you both. You've saved our lives. Now, how about tuna fish with a sauce touched with a taste of ginger..."

Martha sat back and listened, a smile coming to the corner of her mouth, her hand joining with Phillip's on the top of the back of the couch. The woman seemed to know what she was talking about. Once again her future husband was right: the mushroom, indeed, was on their doorstep. Despite the thought of her fifty thousand dollars sitting in a New York bank out of her control, it seemed they were not wasting money employing Beth Hardcastle as their wedding planner. For a brief moment the picture of Phillip in a safari suit at their wedding appeared in her mind making her laugh. She squeezed his hand and brought her mind back to concentrate on what Beth was saying. Willy winked at her. The sparkle was back in his eyes, making Martha feel good inside. She sipped comfortably at her wine. When the neighbours left to go downstairs to their own apartment, Martha knew she no longer had to worry about her reception. It was being taken care of professionally. Martha smiled. There was nothing like the threat of poverty to concentrate a person's mind.

"So, what you think?"

"Are you taking a share in the business?"

"Thirty per cent. I'm a venture capitalist, thanks to you. We're calling the business Reception Perfection. We're already talking to Solly, asking him to spread the word. Nothing better than word of mouth to promote a local business. Come on. We're going to Solly's for dinner."

"Really, what are you going to wear?"

"I'm still thinking. You think a dark suit? Never worn one in my life."

"You should wear a bow tie."

"Now it's you that's being ridiculous."

"Is your aunt's name really Beth? What a coincidence."

"Not really. Elizabeth is a common name. There are so many diminutives. But yes, maybe the name Beth caught my attention when it reminded me of my Aunty Beth. It's Saturday night, Martha. Let's go and enjoy ourselves. We won't hear them arguing anymore which will be nice. I can't imagine what it must be like to be on the bones of one's arse."

"Where do you English find these expressions?"

"Pretty universal. More explicit than down on your luck."

"What's Willy going to do?"

"Help his wife. What marriage is meant to be all about. Shall we walk or take your car?"

"Let's walk to Solly's. If it's raining when we come back we'll take a cab. My mother drank when she was having me so why shouldn't I?"

"So you're off the wagon?"

"In moderation."

"That's my girl. Tuna fish with ginger. Sounds delicious."

"Hold my arm."

"We're going to be so damn happy, Martha."

"I know we are. I love chatting with you. You make the little things in life sound exciting. Love does so bind people's lives. Makes life have a constant purpose. I'm never bored anymore. My thoughts are always positive. Before, on my own in the apartment, dark thoughts came over me and made me depressed. It's not good to live on one's own. Ask my poor mother. She brought up three children and all she has for company most of the day is herself."

"I'm glad you're happy. Makes me happy. Wrap that scarf round your lovely throat. It's cold outside."

"Do you miss Africa so much?"

"There's another of those old sayings that springs to my mind: 'You can't have your cake and eat it.' Or, more simply, you can't have it all at once. We'll go visit when our child is old enough to appreciate the wilds of Africa. It'll be his first great adventure. The lights of Solly's bar. Now what could be better than that?"

PART 7

NOVEMBER TO DECEMBER 1993 — A MAN HAS TO WORK

1

Ten days before the wedding Phillip flew to New York. The first of the guests were due to arrive on the following Thursday, his father and stepmother from England, his sister Myra and Julian Becker from California, and Jacques Oosthuizen, his business partner, from Zimbabwe. From the airport, Phillip took a cab to the new offices of Linguare on the East Side. He walked into the lobby of the tall building and searched the noticeboard. At the bottom of the list of tenants he found what he was looking for. Linguare were on the twenty-seventh floor. It was at four o'clock in the afternoon, unannounced, that Phillip walked into the office of the company that would not have existed without his money. A familiar face looked up with surprise: it was Gordon Blake, the computer salesman he had first met in Solly's Saloon. Behind him in small cubicles were people working at their screens. Along the walls were camp beds, the blankets and pillows tossed casually. Hard rock music was blaring.

"My goodness, it's Phillip Crookshank. What are you doing in New York, Phillip?"

"Are you working here?"

"I sure am. When I said I wanted to resign, my old company let me go immediately. I supplied Linguare with all their computers. Marcin didn't mention you were coming."

"I didn't tell him. Can you turn the music down a bit? Don't they make their beds when they get up in the morning?"

"Marcin! It's Phillip."

"Wow. So it is. What are you doing in New York, Phillip?"

"Checking on my money."

"Where are you staying tonight?"

"I have no idea."

"There are a couple of spare camp beds if you want to stay with us. This is a pleasant surprise. We've been so damn busy I haven't had time to think of anything but work. Come and meet the others. Guys! It's Phillip. Our money mentor. The man from Africa. Everyone take a break, and Gordon, make us some more of your lovely coffee. We wouldn't survive without Gordon's coffee. Aren't you getting married a week on Saturday? Can't make it, I'm afraid. We're on a run. When the brain's on a run you don't stop for a break. Unless it's a cup of coffee to keep you awake. This is Penny. The best brain I ever met at Yale. Meet Greg. He's good. Larry. He's good, too. How you like our office?"

"Looks more like a dormitory."

"What's wrong with that? This way we don't interrupt the flow."

"Are you any nearer to completion?"

"Two brains are better than one. Four are brilliant. When we've had our coffee together and I've brought you up to date, Gordon will look after you. Can't stop the flow. Later, why don't you and Gordon go out to dinner? He'll tell you everything to put your mind at rest about your money. You want to sleep on the floor?"

"Better find a hotel. Glad to find you all working."

"Why didn't you phone?"

"I was hoping to find exactly what I'm looking at."

"Without a warning?"

"Something like that. Gives what I'm seeing true substance."

"How long are you staying?"

"I'll be gone in the morning now I have nothing to worry about. I'm impressed, Marcin. You're fulfilling your side of the bargain. Just sometimes in life it's better to see than rely on a telephone conversation. If I've hurt your feelings, I'm sorry."

"You have every right to check on your money."

"You all look so young."

"I like your jacket. What's it made from?"

"Buffalo hide. Don't forget that safari I'm taking you on when the software is successful. That's a promise I want to keep. So, here we are. The modern world of computer software."

Going round the room, Phillip shook hands with each of them in turn. For ten minutes they clustered round Gordon's front desk as they drank their coffee. One by one they went back to their work, most of their technical conversation unintelligible to Phillip.

"With a bit of luck, one of these days I'll understand what you guys are talking about. Good to meet you all. Don't let me interrupt what you're doing. There's plenty of time in the years ahead for me to get to know you."

It was all a world apart from the Zambezi Valley. Hoping he had not put Marcin's nose out of joint by arriving unannounced, Phillip wished them well in their quest. Gordon had found him a room in the nearest hotel. Carrying his small suitcase, Phillip left smiling, secure in his feeling that Martha and Franklyn had not wasted their money. At seven o'clock, half an hour before Gordon was due to join him for supper, Phillip phoned Martha the good news.

"That's a relief."

"You can say that again. See you tomorrow night."

"Can't wait, honey."

Gordon arrived on time. The dining room of the hotel was full. Phillip ordered the wine.

"You didn't sit around, Gordon."

"What a bit of luck it was meeting you that night at Solly's Saloon. I'm going to be offered shares when they go public."

"How much are they paying you?"

"The bare minimum. Marcin didn't have to buy me the way he had to bring the computer engineers to Linguare. There's big competition out there for the likes of Larry, Penny and Greg."

"Are they going to win?"

"Probably. Take time. If they knew all the answers they'd have launched the product already. They work eighteen hours a day, seven days a week. You can't believe the enthusiasm. Nothing better than being passionate about your work. Good to see you again, Phillip. I owe you a big one."

"I hope so."

"How's Jas?"

"Still living with her boyfriend."

"Her name comes up in Marcin's conversation."

"You ready to order?"

"How long are you staying in New York?"

"I have one more job to do in the morning. Now, tell me everything in a language I will understand."

"I can't stay out late. Business again tomorrow."

"This is business, Gordon. You work for me and the other shareholders. One bottle of wine only. When you've told me what I want to know we will end the evening."

"Employer and employee?"

"Something like that."

"Good. How it should be. I've been listening carefully to their conversations. Here's the gist of it. When they get it right, which they will or I wouldn't have thrown away my previous job, there are literally hundreds of applications. The product is going to blow people's minds. You can ask questions over the phone and have a robot give you the answer. Let me try and explain."

By the time Phillip went to bed his mind was saturated. He was excited. The fog was beginning to lift, the basic concept of what they were after becoming more comprehensible. It would take him days to think back and process all the new information.

"Not bad for a man with a degree in history, Phillip Crookshank."

He was smiling as he began to fall asleep, the noise of the traffic no longer disturbing. He was getting used to it. Getting used to living in America. Later, in his dreams, he was visited by the wild animals.

At the reception desk in the morning Phillip paid his bill.

"Where's the nearest jewellery shop, kind lady?"

"There you are, sir. All I need is your credit card. Thank you for staying with us."

"It was my pleasure."

"Out the door you turn left for two blocks. There's a jeweller on the corner."

"Is it good?"

"Everything is good in New York, or they wouldn't still be in business."

Outside it was cold. Still wearing his buffalo jacket, the small suitcase in his right hand, Phillip looked to his left among all the people and traffic, unable to fully comprehend he was on the streets of New York, a possibility that would not have entered his mind six months earlier. Putting his best foot forward, Phillip strode out onto the pavement. He was going to buy his future wife a diamond. Not a tiny, tiny diamond but a big one, his unlimited American Express card waiting in his pocket.

"Good morning, everyone." His thoughts were spoken out loud. No one took any notice. They were all too busy going about their own business. The words of Frank Sinatra flooded Phillip's mind: 'New York, New York, it's a wonderful town.' He could hear the words. Hear the song. Hear the music. And it made him happy. Giving his feet a skip to the music, Phillip quickened his pace. Life was for living.

"Look out with that suitcase."

"Sorry, old boy. It's just such a lovely day."

When Phillip turned his head to look back, the man was shaking his head. New York indeed was a wonderful town. He found the jewellery shop and walked inside. The place was a vision of wealth and glitter. A man, clasping his hands together by the tips of his fingers, came towards Phillip. He had that ingratiating smile on his face, the smile false but understandable for a man hoping to make a big sale.

"Can I help you, sir?"

"I hope so. I wish to buy an expensive diamond engagement ring for my fiancée."

"What sort of figure did you have in mind?"

"I thought something in the region of one hundred thousand dollars."

"Expensive diamonds are half a million dollars. Let me show you, Mr...?"

"Crookshank. Phillip Crookshank from Zimbabwe. Show me what you've got."

"How does this tray look?"

"Brilliant. In every sense of the word."

Ten minutes later, still carrying his suitcase, Phillip walked out of the shop with a four-carat diamond in a box in his right pocket. The salesman had called him a cab.

"To JFK please. How long will it take to get to the airport?"

"Depends on the traffic."

Sitting comfortably in the back seat, his suitcase next to him, Phillip could see the salesman standing on the pavement, his hands still held in front of him, the tips of his delicate fingers touching, the same smile fixed on his face. Phillip waved. The man broke his clasp and waved. A small, tenuous wave.

"Not a bad day's work."

"You talking to me, mister?"

"Not really. If I go on this way I'll have spent all my money by the time I'm forty."

"Welcome to New York."

"If I'm lucky, and all goes well, I'm going to be living in New York."

"Only place to live in the whole wide world."

"I hope so."

"I know so. What time is your flight?"

"In an hour and a half."

"No problem."

It was the game of life. So far as Phillip could see, the velocity of money was what kept the world going round and round. When it stopped, the world economy would sink into the abyss like the economy of Zimbabwe where the people generating the money were being kicked out of their own country. Not sure if this line of thinking made him happy, Phillip stared out of the window as the taxi passed on through the city. If nothing else, spending all that money would make Martha happy. She would have glaring wealth on her finger for everyone to see. Wealth cocking a snook at the sods without enough money to buy themselves food. It made Phillip sick. But that was the way of the world, he told himself. As the cab made its way to the airport, Phillip's mind wandered back to Africa and his life in the bush surrounded by nothing but nature. It made him sad. He was committed to another life and would have to put up with it the best way he could. Life was always a journey. The ring, his expression of love for a woman, was in his pocket. In a few months' time a new life would begin its journey to who knew where. Did he know where he was going? He doubted it. He was born and one day he would die, no wiser for the experience.

2

---

*W*hen Phillip arrived back at Martha's apartment, it was six o'clock in the evening. He put Martha's spare key into the lock and opened the door and walked inside with his suitcase. In the lounge, on his way through to their bedroom, he saw someone sitting on the settee with their back to him. It was too early for Martha to be home. When a man turned round, a big grin on his face, it was Phillip's second big surprise in two days.

"Randall! My God, it's you. Where's Meredith?"

"In the bedroom feeding the baby. You have no idea how much milk he can suck from his mother. Three months old and demanding. How are you, old cock?"

"You're a week early."

"Thought we would use the trip to spend some time with our publishers. They want Meredith to make some changes to *Talking to the Animals*. Kids' books can be tricky."

"How's *Love Song* selling?"

"Not bad. Villiers are happy. How was New York? Is your money safe?"

"Who knows? The world of finance is no different to the Wild West. What did you call him in the end?"

"Douglas. For where he was born. The small town of Douglas.

Despite all the characters I have named in my books, my mind went blank. What are you calling yours?"

"Sebastian or Kimberley. How did you get into the apartment?"

"Your wife-to-be had left instructions downstairs after I spoke to her on the phone. We arrived two hours ago."

"Have you eaten?"

"On the plane. We're all going to be together again next week. The whole Crookshank family. I'm so excited."

"Are you writing?"

"All I ever do. Not much else you can do on the Isle of Man in winter. The weather is lousy. I so miss Africa."

"Join the club... Meredith! Let me look at my nephew. Randall gave me a fright. Thought a stranger had broken in. No, I won't hold him. Might drop him. Hello, little Douglas. It's all happening. We can all sit and have a drink and catch up on each other's stories. I miss you, brother."

"Miss you too. I will always miss my family and those wonderful years growing up in Rhodesia. Only when you look back do you realise how lucky you've been. We lost our mother but we still had a family. Now look at it. We're all having our kids at the same time. You, me, Craig and Myra. The next generation has begun. I just hope they'll be as lucky as we were. These days there are too many disturbed families facing one crisis or another. You and I are lucky to have money. Something we should never stop being thankful for. Now, tell me all about this venture capitalism."

"Do you really want to hear?"

"Of course I do. Just look at him. He's positively gurgling. You know Uncle Paul and Aunty Beth are coming out?"

"You find some bright spark with a new idea and sink your money into the venture. If it works, you multiply your money. You can also lose the lot. It's one big pond with everyone swimming around trying to survive, the strong swimmers getting rich. They say you have to make your money work if you want to keep it. Only time will tell. Do you know anything about computers?"

"Some, from my time at Brigandshaws. I write in longhand with a pen, not with a typewriter."

"What we are developing will blow your mind. The opportunities are endless. When I asked you to the wedding I mentioned the voice recognition software."

"You did. When's your baby due?"

"Four months, if all goes well. When do you see your publishers?"

"Monday. They want me to go on the *Late Show with David Letterman*. In New York. It's the side of my writing I truly hate. Promoting oneself. Villiers Publishing would far prefer for me to live in New York so they can use me for regular promotions. They don't understand you can't write a novel with your head muddled up with all that twaddle. Anyway, for five days I'm at their beck and call. For a working week I'm Randall Holiday. I always hoped my books would sell because they were good and not through publicity stunts. The talk shows need celebrities to keep them going. They think every writer is happy to have his life talked about in order to sell his books. I hate it. I'm not frightened to talk to David Letterman in front of a camera, I just hate losing my privacy. One minute they're building you up, the next minute you do something wrong and they're tearing you to pieces to increase their ratings and their advertising revenue."

"Welcome to America. It's all about money."

"The whole world's about money."

"Easy for us to talk when we've always had it. For generations. You ever gone hungry?"

"Not likely. Hold him, Phillip. He won't break."

"How are you, Meredith?"

"Happy. There is nothing more precious than being a mother. There you are. Say hello to your Uncle Phillip, Douglas. When's Martha due back from work? She told me to move into the spare bedroom and make ourselves at home. Your Aunty Martha can't wait to see you, Douglas. How does he feel?"

"I've never held a baby in my life before."

"Better get used to it. Soon you'll be changing nappies."

"He's all wet."

"Oh, dear. All that milk. You'd better give him back."

"Beer or wine, Meredith?"

"Wine for me. I'll just go and change him. You brothers have so much to talk about. A woman called Beth came round. Something to do with her new business."

"Beer and wine coming up. You want a beer, Randall?"

"Of course."

"What did she want, Meredith?"

"For you to go down and see her. Said she's a neighbour. Planning your wedding."

"Was she in a hurry?"

"Don't think so. Had a big smile on her face."

"What are you writing at the moment, Randall?"

"I hate talking about a book until it's finished. Until then it stays in my head. It's easy to muddle a story with too much talk. Dad hates living in England. Pines for the old life on the farm. There's still nothing happening on World's View. The new owner has no idea how to grow Virginia tobacco. He's a politician, not a farmer."

"In this lovely age of democracy, it's the politicians who make the most of the money. The world's corrupt."

"Always was. They call it bribery and corruption. How's the Zambezi Valley?"

"Perfect. Always was. Always will be if man leaves it alone... Is this beer cold enough for you? Feel the bottle."

"Perfect. Don't need a glass. Cheers. To a wonderful wedding. To a wonderful family reunion."

"To the next generation. Cheers. Your wine's on the table, Meredith. Can you hear me?"

"Coming. The little bugger pooped in his pants."

For an hour they talked of themselves, Phillip not sure if Meredith or Randall had any interest in hearing about venture capitalism. They both politely listened, adding bits about themselves when the opportunity arose. When he finished his own diatribe Meredith talked about her baby in every detail, a permanent smile on her face, Phillip's mind wandering back to his own problems. Randall looked distracted, the smile coming back when the conversation turned to himself. It made Phillip smile. They were all happy when talking about themselves, the streak of selfishness permanent in the human condition. But he would have to stop being cynical even when he wasn't showing it. No one liked a cynic – or was it the truth?

"Where have you gone, Phillip?"

"Sorry. My mind wandered. What were you saying?"

"Who's giving away the bride?"

"Her brother, Ford ... Here comes my wife to be. What you are about to see now is pure theatre. But I think she will love it."

"Hello. You must be Randall and Meredith. I'm Martha... Phillip! What on earth are you doing down on one knee? I want to see the baby."

"You'd better wait."

"Oh, my God. It's a little box. Phillip! It's enormous!"

"Let me put it on your finger."

"Look, everyone. My engagement ring. It's so big. Is it a real diamond?"

"I hope so."

"Oh, Phillip. Thank you. I can't wait to show my mother."

With her left hand outstretched, Phillip watched Martha show the ring to Randall and Martha in turn.

"You want to hold my baby?"

"I would love to."

"I've just changed his nappy."

"Why don't you and I go into my bedroom while I change from my work clothes? What a day. It never stops."

The girls walked away, the baby their centre of attention.

"Where were we, Randall?"

"You tell me. They'll be talking baby talk nineteen to the dozen."

"We can have another beer. The Crookshank brothers once again together. Been too long. Good to see you, Randall. Tell me more about Dad. Are you going to live on the Isle of Man permanently? Do you like the cold?"

"The mountain is covered in snow at the moment. I look across at it through the window when my hand begins to ache from too much writing. The writing lets me go wherever I want to go. I live in my head. We have cats and dogs. The house is cosy. Big log fires for winter. We're happy away from the crowd. People can suffocate you. No, we'll stay on the island unless sanity returns to Zimbabwe. Then who knows? Underneath it all, we're Africans. She's nice, your Martha."

"Are we going out to dinner, Phillip?"

"Don't shout, Martha. What's Meredith going to do with the baby?"

"We're going to leave him with my mother."

"There's a thought."

"Got to celebrate this ring. Thank you so much, honey. Even a tiny, tiny diamond would have made me happy. This one has blown my mind."

"Dinner for four. Solly's?"

"Why not? Everything happens at Solly's Saloon."

"Beth came round."

"What did she want?"

"I wasn't sure."

"We'll drop by on the way out. Maybe they'd like to join us at Solly's. One big party to celebrate my engagement ring."

"Aren't you working tomorrow? It's Friday."

"I won't drink too much. This baby is so cute. Can't wait for my own. You'd better give Solly a ring and book a table. This is all so much fun. How was Gordon? That must have been a surprise."

"Gordon was fine. Says we're all going to make a fortune. He's going to get shares when the company goes public."

"Told you it would work."

"Time will tell. Time always tells."

SOLLY'S WAS full for a Thursday, not a barstool empty, the same soulful stares from those drinking alone. Phillip felt sorry for them. There was nothing worse than drinking alone even when surrounded by people. Instead of going up to the bar they went straight to the table, Solly waving from his post behind the bar. A young waitress showed them the way.

"You're new. I'm Phillip Crookshank. I booked the table."

"Sonia. College student."

"What's your subject?"

"English literature."

"Meet my brother Randall Holiday. The writer."

"Shut up! I loved *Masters of Vanity*. The book and the movie. You're kidding. How can he be your brother? You have different names."

"I write under Holiday."

"Why are you here at Solly's? It's not the kind of place I'd expect to find a famous author. Is the table all right?"

"Perfect. We need a drink first. Everyone, tell Sonia what you want.

Tonight's on me. If you watch the David Letterman show, Sonia, you will see Randall being interviewed."

"Go on. That's awesome. I so want to be a writer. I want to be famous. I'm so blown away. A famous author! Wait till I tell my friends."

"Do you like my new ring? It's an engagement party."

"So awesome. Wow. That's big. Is it real?"

"We hope so."

"What you all want to drink? Randall Holiday. I can't believe it."

Watching his brother cringe, Phillip sat back and studied the menu smugly.

"Did you have to do that?"

"Probably not, Randall. So, Beth, what did you want to tell us? How's our wedding coming along? We're nearly there. Another nine days."

"I've been given two more weddings to plan. Pastor Gregory loves the idea of lots and lots of flowers. He's spread the word."

"See what happens when you get something right?"

"If it goes on like this I'll have to employ staff. Willy and I are running our feet off."

"I'm pleased for you. There's nothing better than a plan that works. Give me all the details."

Only half listening to Beth, Phillip watched the girl go off with the drinks order which she gave over the bar to Solly. There was no sign of Clem or anyone else up at the bar that Phillip recognised. Had Clem found his Martha and invited her to the wedding? Or was his Martha a figment of his imagination, the one thing in Clem's life that he wanted but had never found? Across the small table, Meredith and Martha were still talking babies. Randall had his faraway look, back in his mind in the new book he was writing. Willy was holding his wife's hand on top of the table, not a sign of an argument between them. At least there, he told himself, he had done some good, the picture of the Linguare office coming to his mind. It was the time in the evening the takeaway food was delivered. Martha caught him looking at her and showed him her ring, a big smile on her face. They all looked happy around him. Dinner with friends. A pleasant evening for everyone. His mind drifted away despite the noise and bustle in Solly's Saloon. His thoughts were back in the bush with the animals.

"You've drifted away again, Phillip. Where were you?"

"Zambezi Valley by the big river."

"Lucky bastard."

"Where've you been?"

"In the Congo. Kinshasa. Or Zaire as it is now called. On the banks of the Congo River. The whole country is about to explode. I spend a lot of my time in Africa when I'm sitting at my desk among the cold of Europe with the snow on the mountain outside my window. It warms me up. It's my way of escape. We have the same genes, Phillip. Why our minds do the same things."

"I wish I could write. You're so lucky. Martha wanted to write."

"I wouldn't mind running a safari business in the steaming hot Zambezi Valley. What a place."

"But you wouldn't want to be a venture capitalist?"

"Probably not. Will Douglas be all right with your mother-in-law?"

"She was a good mother. And she's only my mother-in-law to be. You couldn't imagine a better babysitter. Here comes the booze. Family. What would we ever do without family?"

"Glad you're getting married at last."

"So am I."

"To two fathers."

"To two fathers."

"We haven't got the drinks yet."

"In our minds."

"Of course. You can do anything you want in your mind."

Martha was looking at Randall, waiting for her opportunity to butt into the conversation.

"Will you show me how to write, Randall? I sat for weeks in a tent writing in that valley you two love so much. Each morning when I read back the previous day's writing I threw it away. How do you do it?"

Sonia put the full drinks tray down on the table.

"Practice. It's amazing when you practise anything how much better you get. Read good news journals written by journalists who know how to use English. Find their rhythm. But, most of all, find a good story. And never give up. It's the flaw in many people's lives. When it doesn't come easy they give up... Sonia, thank you... I couldn't do your advertising job, Martha, without a five-year apprenticeship. It's the same with learning to tell a story. Good storytellers are not all writers.

They tell stories in bars, around the fire at home to entertain their families. In those days far back in history the storyteller was the only entertainment they had. Many people couldn't read. No TV or radio. All they had was a storyteller if they were lucky. The good storytellers were always welcome in the home and told stories for their suppers. Many of the stories had been passed down from generation to generation. Others were new from a storyteller's own experience, from his travels. When the only light was the fire burning in a dark room, a story of a faraway place became real. The same way a book can transport people with written words to faraway places. You need experience of life to tell good new stories. Some say you can only write a good tale after you have reached forty. Don't give up the idea, Martha. There's more to writing than making money. It's a solace. A place to go when the world gets on top of us. If you write, Sonia, you too will find out. Not now when you're young but as you get older. When the drinking and parties stop. Forget the idea of fame and money. It's the process of writing that is joyful."

"But you're not forty and look at your success." It was Phillip's turn to butt in.

"Phillip, myself and our family went through a lot at an early age. Losing our mother to a pride of lions. The bush war in Rhodesia. I didn't go into grown-up life with the idea of being a writer, however much I wanted to write. I got a degree at the London School of Economics so I could make money and survive. I used all of it in business, an experience that I used in writing my stories. I started my adventure through life at an early age. And there's much more to be done. One day I'm going to decide I've written all I know about life. Then I'll start another adventure. Won't we, Meredith? We'll travel. Teach Douglas his letters on the road. All the time I'll be looking for new stories to tell like those storytellers of old sitting round the winter fires."

"Have you got a title for your new book?"

"*What Happened to Chivalry*. I'll probably change my mind. Sonia, you'd better take our food orders. That man behind the bar is waving at you."

"Thank you so much."

"My pleasure. I hope it helps you and Martha. Now I'm going to let someone else talk before I become boring."

"You want to order another beer, Randall? That one's going down quickly."

"Why ever not, brother? Maybe I'd better wait for the wine. We are having wine? Make mine the rump steak, Sonia."

"Your order will be ready in twenty minutes. Enjoy your evening."

"Thank you, Sonia."

"My pleasure."

Martha and Meredith were still talking about babies, Beth listening with a faraway look. When Martha got up to phone her mother to ask about Meredith's baby, she looked both sad and envious. Willy sat back in his chair, enjoying his beer. He was relaxed, the financial worry of the immediate past gone from his face. The food came with two bottles of wine and the evening went on, a mixture of chatter and quips. The noise and laughter increased with the intake of alcohol. When they went home they were happy, a pleasant evening had by all. Phillip had paid the bill with his American Express card. It was all so easy. The cab Martha ordered took them first to Aggie to collect the baby, Martha again showing her mother the engagement ring. Willy and Beth had gone home separately, happy to walk. The evening was cold but it wasn't raining. Willy had said he liked the exercise. When Phillip got into bed he was pleasantly tired. Once, during the night, he was woken by the sound of a crying baby. Then he slept right through to the morning. He was another day closer to his wedding. Another day closer to becoming a father.

THE NIGHT before the rest of the family were due to arrive, Phillip sat on the couch looking at the television watching his brother squirm on the David Letterman show. Next to him sat Jacques Oosthuizen, his suntan in deep contrast to everyone else's pale skins. Letterman praised Randall as the best-selling author and Randall said how much he enjoyed being on the show. Phillip cringed for his brother. Letterman dug back to Randall's early days in Rhodesia. Randall praised President Mugabe as the liberator of Rhodesia from colonial rule. The audience clapped. Phillip laughed out loud in unison with Jacques. The rehearsal and indoctrination for David Letterman had gone well. There was nothing more important on an American talk show than to denigrate British colonialism, despite the new American hegemony which Phillip saw as being little different to British imperialism. Wasn't Vietnam typical of a colonial war, he asked himself? The fight was capitalism against communism. Russian world domination or American. When the show finished they turned off the television, Phillip feeling sad for his brother. There was nothing worse than having to sell one's soul on television. But it sold books, got good ratings for the talk show and told people what they wanted to hear. Provided no one criticised America, they were happy.

"Goodnight, Jacques."

"Did you hear that crap? Doesn't your brother know the country is headed down the toilet? In a couple of years the Zimbabwe dollar won't be worth shit."

"All part of the game."

Phillip went into the bedroom he shared with Martha and climbed into bed. At that moment he wanted more than anything to run back to Africa and live in a tent, no care for the value of the Zimbabwe currency or the political state of the country. He wanted to hide from all the claptrap. To get away from the world.

"What's the matter, honey? Last-minute nerves?"

"Something like that."

"Everything will be just fine when we're married and our child is born. I envy him his tan."

"So do I. Made me homesick."

"Poor Phillip. You've got a big day tomorrow with so many relatives arriving. Are you going to the airport?"

"Told them to take a cab here. Too many arriving from different places. Dad's going to phone when he lands. Are you going to be working on Friday?"

"Probably. Beth's got everything under control. Your brother did so well on the show."

"Did he? I thought he made a fool of himself. They were using him."

"What are you talking about?"

"We were wrong. And shouldn't be proud of it. Every moralist says the three hundred years of the British Empire was wrong. When you lose your power you lose your legitimacy. America has always wanted the demise of the British Empire so they could take over running the world.

Randall understands the way the American world works. Why he was doing what he was told tonight. He has an American publisher. It has nothing to do with who is right or wrong in politics. It's about money. About selling books."

"Don't be silly, Phillip. Your old Rhodesia is finished."

"I know it is. So is Zimbabwe. For everyone. Black, white and khaki."

"Sleep well, honey. Give me a cuddle. She's kicking. You want to feel? Don't be sad. Your life is going forward. In five years' time you'll become an American."

"You want me to change my accent?"

"You can try."

"You're right. He's kicking."

"Now you're smiling. Turn out the light and cuddle up, honey. There are three of us in this bed. I'm completely exhausted."

"And you don't have time for a honeymoon?"

"Can't do everything. Franklyn would kill me if I tried to take time off after the wedding. It's going to be bad enough when I have the baby. Do you love me?"

"I certainly hope so. We're getting married on Saturday."

Phillip tried to laugh, the laugh getting stuck in his throat. As he dropped off to sleep his last thoughts were for Randall.

THE BIG BUILD-UP to the wedding started after lunch the next day. The first to ring the doorbell was Julian Becker, the man towering in the doorway with ten-month-old Shoona in his arms. Myra stood next to him.

"I can't believe you're getting married, brother."

"Neither can I, Myra. You remember Jacques, my safari partner."

"Envy your tan. Julian, give Phillip the baby to hold. Where's Randall?"

"In New York until tomorrow. Didn't you see him on the Letterman show last night?"

"My brother was on the Letterman show last night? I don't believe it. Where's the bride-to-be?"

"Martha's at work. Come in. Dad and your mother are due any minute. Is your hotel okay?"

"The best that money can buy."

An hour later, with the conversation still gushing, the doorbell rang again. Phillip opened the door and shook his father's hand, Bergit running past them to hug her daughter.

"Have Craig and Jojo arrived?" While hugging her daughter, Bergit had turned her head back to look at Phillip.

"Not yet."

"This is all so exciting. We're a family again. Where's Randall and the baby? Oh, Myra, I've so missed you all. The worst part of being a mother is having your children grow up and fly the nest. Suddenly everything is so empty. How are you, darling?"

Phillip shepherded his guests through to the lounge.

"Who wants a drink? Dad, you want a beer? Randall's still in New York. Be here late tomorrow."

"You got everything ready for the wedding?"

"Best wedding planner in America. Good to see you, Dad."

"Good to see you, son."

"Why didn't Craig fly with you?"

"We all have our own schedules. He has to work for that charity. Do what he's told. He's flying in before dawn on Saturday with baby Harold. The family is expanding so fast it takes my breath away. How are you, Phillip?"

"Missing Africa."

"Aren't we all? Who's the old lady across in the flat over the road waving at me?"

"We don't know her name. We always wave at each other. Is the beer cold enough?"

"Just right. It's the English weather that's just horrible. But I shouldn't complain. Lucky I bought that block of flats when I could get my money out of Rhodesia. Julian, how are you, son? Watched your latest movie the other day. Myra, give your old man a hug. Just look at my granddaughter. Little Shoona. And now Phillip's going to be a father. Life never stops."

"You want to sit down?"

"Let's all sit down. There's so much to catch up on, I don't know where to begin. Has your Uncle Paul arrived?"

"Not yet."

"We were going to fly together but Beth persuaded him to take a holiday in Jamaica to get away from the London winter. We all live our own lives. This is a nice flat. Nice and warm."

"They call them apartments in America."

"So, Phillip. Tell me everything."

"Where do you want me to start?"

"At the beginning."

"Well, I'm now what they call in America a venture capitalist..."

When Martha came home the lounge was full of happy people, the drinks fuelling the flow of excited conversation. When Uncle Paul arrived with Beth the crescendo peaked. Phillip found extra chairs for them to sit on from the bedroom. By the time he took them all out to dinner at the Alameda Plaza where his family were staying, Phillip was mentally exhausted. A babysitter had been organised by Myra at the hotel. By ten o'clock the travelling caught up with them and they went to their rooms, the plans for the next day's fun being shouted down the corridors. Martha, Phillip and Jacques went back to the apartment.

"And this is Thursday. Can you imagine what it's going to be like on our wedding day? You were clever, Martha. You didn't drink."

"Had to keep my wits about me. Tomorrow night is a party with my family and friends."

"Can you tolerate an evening with your family?"

"I hope so. Goodnight, honey. Sleep. All I crave is sleep. Weddings! What would we have done without Beth and Willy?"

Lying back in bed in the dark Phillip listened to the constant sound of the traffic. There was no sound from Jacques. Martha fell asleep next to him. Still on his back, Phillip drifted off into his dreams.

WHEN CRAIG and Jojo arrived on the morning of the wedding, going straight to the Alameda Plaza where Phillip had paid for their room, the family reunion was complete. To Martha's surprise her brother Hugo had arrived the previous day in time for the Poland family reunion at Aggie's apartment. Aggie had twisted his arm. At two o'clock they were ready to drive to the church, Martha resplendent in her white wedding dress. Beth had hired Phillip a suit. At Pastor Gregory's church, the organ was playing a piece by Haydn at Phillip's special request. Sitting in the front pew with Randall next to him Phillip realised there was no escape.

Everywhere in the church were bowls of flowers. The organ changed to Mendelssohn's 'Wedding March' as the bride came walking down the aisle on the arm of her elder brother, Ford. All the guests stood up. Looking down his church from the altar, Pastor Gregory was smiling. In a trance, Phillip did what he was asked to do and took Martha Poland to be his wife. He put the ring on her finger and they were married, the organ blaring. Phillip and Martha were first out of the church. Phillip drove them in her car to the Alameda Plaza in a stunned silence. The wedding ceremony had overwhelmed both of them. In the function room, Beth, the wedding planner, was waiting. The reception was soon in full swing. When Martha went to change, half the guests were on their way to getting themselves drunk. Never before in his life had Phillip imagined spending so much money on a party. When they drove back to the apartment they were man and wife. Mr and Mrs Crookshank. For better or for worse. For good times and for bad.

The next day the families began dispersing. It was all over. Phillip had hoped to spend the Sunday on the river, alone with his bride but it was raining, a constant, driving rain. Instead, they spent the one day of their honeymoon talking to family. On the Monday Martha went off to her work leaving Phillip in the apartment. As the day progressed, his family arrived. By Tuesday they were flying home, the memory of Phillip and Martha's wedding all that was left. Craig, Jojo and little Harold were the last to leave. Phillip drove them in Martha's car from the Alameda Plaza to the airport.

"Have you made up with your family, Jojo, now the baby is born?"

"He doesn't want anything to do with me. He won't reply to my letters. He doesn't have a phone in the village. So far as my father is concerned, I no longer exist."

"How sad. Do you enjoy living in England?"

"We have our jobs. We have a home. I go back to work in two months' time. We're happy, so it doesn't really matter, I suppose."

"Are you going to get married?"

"Probably. Maybe. We don't know. People don't get married in England anymore. There's no stigma to living together. Most of all, we'd like to go back and live in Zimbabwe but my father has made that impossible. We're grateful for what we have. The baby is healthy. In a few years we'll grow used to England. That was a splendid wedding. Thank you, Phillip, for paying all our expenses. We don't get much of a salary from a charity."

"You're welcome. It's been wonderful seeing the three of you. Now it's all over and life goes back to the old routine."

"What are you going to do today with everyone gone?"

"Go to Solly's Saloon. Find a friend to talk to. There's not much for me to do in America. A venture capitalist puts in his money and then it's up to the rest of them. We'll see. So much of life is waiting to see. I'm so sorry about your father."

"So am I."

"Thanks for coming all this way."

"Do you feel any different?"

"Time will tell. It all happened so quickly."

"And then there's the baby."

"Exactly. It's all about having the baby."

Sad, lonely and bored out of his mind, Phillip drove Martha's car back to its parking bay in the basement of the apartment. He then walked to Solly's Saloon. Driving back drunk was not on his agenda. It was eleven o'clock in the morning. Two men on their own were up at the bar, Solly was on a barstool behind the counter reading the morning paper.

"Aren't you on your honeymoon?"

"Martha has to work."

The two men at opposite ends of the bar turned to look at Phillip before staring back at their drinks. Solly brought Phillip his usual beer, pouring the contents slowly into a glass.

"Have a good wedding?"

"They're all much the same. At least our baby will be legitimate."

"There is that. Do you think it's important in this day and age?"

"We think so. We both wanted to be parents. Do you ever miss a shift? You're here first thing in the morning and when the bar and restaurant closes at night."

"If you don't control the till, you don't control the money. Other people own your business."

"Not everyone is dishonest."

"Most of them. There's too much cash. A professional barman thinks taking his cut is all part of the business. When I've made enough money

I'm going to buy a farm and get the hell out of the way. Enjoy your beer. Reading the paper, you see all the problems in this lovely world. I want to find sanctuary."

"I know how you feel. Sorry to interrupt your reading,"

By the fourth beer Phillip had forgotten his worries. Three more men had arrived to sit up at the bar, each of them sitting alone. Phillip stared into his glass. One minute he was surrounded by family and mayhem, the next he was sitting at a bar drinking all on his own. There was nothing lonelier than drinking alone.

"Why aren't you on your honeymoon?"

"Clem! Goodness gracious me. Why didn't you come to my wedding? Couldn't you find your Martha?"

"She doesn't exist. All part of the bar talk. A figment of my imagination. Sometimes one's imagination is better than reality."

"Solly wants to buy a farm."

"Good luck to him."

"You want a drink?"

"Can we make today a bender? When did you start?"

"This is my fourth."

"I'm single and you're married and we're both up at the bar. Give me a shooter, Solly. Got to catch up. So, how are you, my African friend? Make it two shooters for me and then we'll get started. A bender with an old friend. What more could a man want? To all those lovely wedding bells. They did play wedding bells?"

"They always play wedding bells."

"Let's talk about your days in Africa. I love your stories. Why don't you write a book like your brother?"

"I can't write. I can only tell stories when I'm drunk."

"Give my African friend a shooter. Let's get started. Well, well, well. Didn't expect to see you so soon in the bar. Tell me a story."

Phillip put on a smile. The man nearest turned his head to listen. Solly turned a page of his paper.

"Well, it was years ago. I was nineteen years old. Her name was Mona. That trip, there were eight of us..." And the story went on.

"That was one hell of a story. My name's Bill. You mind if I join you? There's nothing better than a good storyteller."

"You come right here and sit next to me, Bill. My name is Clem. This is Phillip, my African friend."

"Can I buy you two a drink?"

"You certainly can. We've decided to go on a bender. So, what's your story, Bill? What brings you to Solly's Saloon?"

"I'm a salesman. Only had one call to do today. Went much quicker than I expected. Big, fat order. Nothing else to do so I came to celebrate. I'm a commission salesman. The bigger the order, the more I make."

"What you sell?"

"Women's underwear. You want to see my range? Fly back to Chicago tomorrow. Where they make all them knickers."

"My friend's from Africa."

"So I gathered."

"Just got himself married."

"Just got myself divorced. For the second time."

"You want a shooter?"

"I'm paying."

"Who cares who's paying? We're on a bender. Tell us more stories, my African friend. Good old Phillip. What would we do without a good storyteller up at the bar? Ladies' knickers. Now that's a product."

The bar filled up as the three of them drank, the slippery slide of drunkenness not far away. At Phillip's suggestion, they ate a plate of Solly's sandwiches to delay the inevitable. At least he wasn't bored and having to behave himself as he had been with his family. He finished a second story about his life in Africa and let the Americans talk. By five o'clock, when the bar filled up to capacity, they were all talking gibberish and none of them cared. They were having fun.

"Better get home in case my wife doesn't stay late at the office. Remember, the worst thing in life is a drinking companion with a memory. Nice meeting you, Bill. See you tomorrow, Clem."

Outside it was raining. Phillip stood in the doorway and waited for a passing taxi. When he got back to Martha's apartment the place was empty. By the time his wife came home from work, he was sober. They were both tired. Naked, Martha's belly was big and round. They got into bed, both of them quickly falling into their separate worlds of sleep. Phillip woke in the middle of the night and couldn't get back to sleep. They hadn't made love for a week. He had a creeping hangover that was giving him a throbbing headache. He felt awful. Daylight came and he was still awake.

"What's the matter, Phillip? Got to go. See you tonight. Try not to drink. It's not worth the hangover."

When the phone rang Phillip was sitting in the lounge, his hands on his knees.

"Phillip Crookshank speaking."

"Marcin Galinski. We've cracked it. We have the formula. It works. Penny found the flaw. All those months I spent on my own trying to find out why it didn't work and Penny has cracked it. Can you believe it? We're so excited. Running around the office like ten-year-olds. Wanted to let you know. Gordon's going to launch his marketing programme next week. We'll need more staff, of course. Marketing, according to Gordon, requires people. Feet on the ground. Should have enough money for a few more months. Looking at it now, solving my problem was so damn simple. You want to see this place. It's chaos. You want to come and visit us? Join the fun? Got to go. Gordon's brought in a bottle of French champagne. Wow, this really is something. Didn't you get married?"

The phone went down before Phillip said a word, the good news making his hangover feel worse. They were all so young. All so damn happy. Dejected, he went into the kitchen and put on the kettle. Someone had left a note under the front door. He picked up the folded piece of paper.

'Two new weddings and a function! Have a nice day. Love Beth.'

By eleven o'clock he was back up at the bar waiting for Clem.

"I don't think he's coming today. After you left last night the two of them got really drunk. Made a fool of himself. Take a while to get it out of his head. My guess, he went back to the farm. How are you today, Phillip? You want your usual? Place is quiet."

"Anything new in the paper?"

"Same old scams. Same old exposures. Same old scandals."

"Why do you read it?"

"Something to do. Sitting behind a bar all day, you got to have something to do when it's quiet."

"I hate hangovers."

"Don't we all? Some of my best customers say the only way to cure a hangover is to have another beer. The sooner the better. One nice cold beer coming up."

"What do you do when you've got too much money?"

"Never happened to me."

"They've cracked the code in New York. Now, instead of needing a typist or a telephonist or anyone else to process your words, you can talk into a computer and the software will do the work. And we have the registered patent on its way."

"Sounds good... Enjoy your beer."

"Thanks, Solly. You're a friend."

"What friends are for."

Watching Solly go back to read his morning newspaper, Phillip felt depressed. He had everything there was to have in the world. A wife, a baby on the way, and money. And here he was, up at a bar on his own.

"What's it all about, Alfie?"

The old song he had first heard as a child on the farm in Rhodesia kept playing in his head, the same words repeating themselves: 'What's it all about, Alfie.' Phillip had no idea. By the fourth beer he was feeling better. The headache had gone. The bar was beginning to fill up.

"You mind if I take this seat?"

"Be my guest."

"My name's Dick."

"Phil. I'm Phil."

"Hello, Phil. Nice to meet with you. You got a funny accent. Where you from?"

"Africa. A place called Zimbabwe."

"Give us both a beer, Solly. I hate drinking on my own. So, Phil, what's your story?"

"Not much really. Why not tell me yours? I much prefer other people's stories."

"Well. Let me see. Where shall I start?"

---

he days that should have been his honeymoon, Phillip spent at
the bar talking to strangers. Most nights it was ten o'clock
before Martha came home, stressed from her work. Franklyn had gone
to New York to see Gordon Blake, driven by the business from a new
client and his fifty-thousand-dollar investment in Linguare. Together
they were preparing for the launch of the marketing campaign.

"You know Gordon went to see Randall in New York after he saw him
on the Letterman show? Found out where he was staying from Villiers
Publishing. Said he was a friend of the family."

"I didn't, Martha. Should you be working so hard? Won't the stress
affect the baby?"

"The baby's fine. I'm fine. I love my work. Did you go to Solly's
again?"

"Not much else to do on my honeymoon without the bride."

"Poor Phillip. I'll make it up to you. Randall doesn't mind Gordon
using his name in your publicity campaign. Gordon and Franklyn are
also going to use your grandfather's celebrity in their campaign to get the
media's attention. The first job is to go to every broadcasting station and
television studio and demonstrate the new product to the staff. After that
they will go to the newspapers and publishing houses. With everyone
caught up in the excitement, the public will be ready to ask for a free trial

in their millions. Then the cash will begin to flow. We found a good one in Gordon. That company is going to make us all so much money we won't have any idea what to do with it."

"That's the problem."

"I was only kidding. I've got a slight pain in my lower belly. Time for bed."

"Shouldn't you see the doctor?"

"Baby pains. Quite normal. Lucky I don't have morning sickness. Oh, and we're working on Saturday when Franklyn gets back from New York. With Randall's publishers having agreed to let some of their staff test trial the voice recognition software we want to get all our ducks in a row for a nationwide campaign. And he's looking for offices in New York. Did I tell you that?"

"No, you didn't."

"Well, he is. Who knows where our baby will be growing up? Beth phoned. Another function. Two new weddings and two functions in a week. You have the Midas touch, honey. Come to bed. Look happy. The whole world is opening up for us. The world is our oyster. Anything interesting in the news today? Oh, well. The office is so busy you can't even imagine what's going on. Jas wants to live in New York when we open an office. Oh, and when the publicity is in full swing Gordon is going to get you on the Letterman show to talk about your grandfather and your brother. That way you can bring up Linguare to millions of viewers across the nation. By the time we've finished the voice recognition app will be part of daily life, and Linguare a name known right round the planet. It's all in the advertising, honey. Always was. You can have the best product in the world but without advertising, it won't get known. That fifty thousand dollars in Linguare is the best investment I ever made. Franklyn says there are so many venture capitalists trying to get on the bandwagon, the value of each share in our initial investment has trebled. That's what the new investors are prepared to pay now the formula is proven. Life in America. Takes your breath away. When they see money to be made it's a stampede. Oh, and Beth's taking on staff. You're so lucky to have had your grandfather's money. My husband is not only going to be stinking rich but he's going to be famous. Oh, and as your publicist I suggest you look to charities to support. Charities that chime well with the public. A rich, famous venture capitalist must look generous. It's all about appearances. There's a drought in the horn of Africa. People starving. Send them a boatload of food. The media love filming food going to charity. They get pictures at the other end of all the starving children. One in ten children under five is dying. You can make yourself look like a hero. Great for Linguare's image. Nothing better than charity-driven free advertising. It's a whole new world through television and I bet the internet too. The power of instant communication."

"So you do something good to gain publicity. Isn't that hypocritical?"

"How it works, honey. Got to use every tool available. Did you enjoy your day? All that new money on its way makes my head spin. You must concentrate on what we are going to spend it on. Damn. That pain again. Into bed. It goes away when I lie down. I'm so proud of you, honey. It seems like a lifetime ago we met, so much has happened. Do you know how many appointments I have tomorrow? I love it when business is booming. Can you turn out the lights? My body is exhausted but my mind's still racing. Give me a hug. The Crookshank Foundation. That's what we'll call it. All those new investors in Linguare can contribute. They call it leverage. Every dollar you give to the charity, nine more will come from givers who want to be part of our publicity. Where's the horn of Africa?"

"Somalia and the surrounding interior. A lot of it is desert. Drought is common in North Africa. Why the people are always trying to emigrate. I'm worried about your stomach. You should see the doctor."

"Don't have time. Anyway, we shouldn't run off to a doctor every time we have a little pain."

"Do you want to make love?"

"Not really. I'm too pregnant. I thought a fat belly would turn you off. Good night, honey."

"Good night, Martha. Sweet dreams."

Longing for the peace and quiet and solitude of his safari camp in Africa, Phillip tried to go to sleep. In his mind he was on the bank of the big river. He wondered how Munya and Sedgewick were getting on. It was time for both of them to find themselves wives. Have some children to look after them in their old age. Solitude and loneliness were so different. He had never been lonely on his own in Africa. Maybe Jacques, he told himself in his ramblings, would find himself a wife. They would all be happy. Could a man be happy sitting in a bar all day? He doubted it. Let alone all the repercussions from drinking too much alcohol. With all the new money, would Martha consider living in the wilds of Africa? He doubted it. She wanted excitement. Permanent attention from other people. The rush of doing business. The lady he had just married was a city girl, despite growing up on a farm. He and his new wife were as different as chalk and cheese and there was nothing he could do about it. Many times he had heard the old adage 'opposites attract'. He wondered why. Wouldn't similar interests make for a happier life? She was asleep. He could hear her steady breathing. If he knew what to ask he would phone the doctor himself. There was no point in worrying. He had no idea what it would feel like having a live baby in his belly. Maybe the baby gave the occasional kick which caused Martha's pain. At least she went for her monthly check-up. His mouth was dry from all the beer he had drunk in Solly's bar. Dick had had his problems. They all had problems or they wouldn't be sitting alone in a bar. Maybe listening to other people talking about their personal problems was being kinder than giving money to charity, the way rich people liked to salve their conscience: you gave a bit, felt better, and kept the rest. Was a poor man unhappy? Was a rich man always happy? Phillip doubted it. Then again he had never gone hungry. All night, Phillip tossed and turned. When he finally fell asleep he was home by the flowing Zambezi River. When he woke in the morning he felt happy. He got up and went to the kitchen to make the tea. His wife was still sleeping peacefully. He put the mug of coffee down on the small table next to the bed, leaned forward and gave her a kiss. When her eyes opened she smiled up at him.

"It's nine o'clock in the morning."

"I'm late!"

"I just phoned Jas. She said heavily pregnant mothers have every right to be late. She's covering for you. Relax. Enjoy your coffee. I'm making breakfast."

"I slept so well."

"That's good for both of you."

"What are you going to do with your day?"

"I have no idea. I'm sick of bars and other people's problems. It's not raining. When you go to work I'll go for a long walk. Exercise. I miss my exercise. I've done a husband's job. I got you pregnant and by the sound of it made enough money to last the rest of our lives."

"Are you bored?"

"It'll pass. Everything passes if you let it. The trick is to take life as it comes. One day at a time. Bacon and eggs coming up. After breakfast you can take your shower."

"I love you so much, Phillip."

"I love you too. In three weeks it's going to be Christmas. I'm going to get a tree and decorate it with a million things. All those lovely coloured lights that keep winking. We'll invite your mother and Mrs Crabshaw for Christmas lunch and put their presents under the tree. Just as we did it on World's View."

"All those missed appointments."

"There are more important things in life than doing business. Jas is covering. Stop worrying. All that stress is bad for you and the baby."

Doing his best, Phillip went back to the kitchen. Being nice to his wife made him happy.

Martha went to work with a smile on her face. Phillip walked to the window. Rainwater was dripping down the outside of the big glass pane. Across the way there was no sign of the old woman. Down below he could see the morning traffic. A siren blew, followed by an ambulance trying to make a fast track through the traffic. Some poor sod had a problem. Suspended ten storeys up it all seemed far away. Like watching television. He looked at the clock on the wall. It was only ten o'clock in the morning. He went back to the couch, turning on the television. The channel was broadcasting the news. A reporter was interviewing the Zimbabwe president who was castigating the British. It made Phillip nostalgic. The brief interview changed to the Middle East and Phillip lost interest. He put his head back and half listened to the usual problems. He sat up and switched programmes, getting nowhere.

"What's the matter with you?"

With the car key in his pocket Phillip went down to the basement and drove Martha's car to the river. It was a perfect day for a walk. All morning, Phillip walked and walked, pushing the previous day's booze out of his system. By lunchtime his mind was thinking more positively. On the way back to the apartment he stopped at a supermarket and bought himself six ballpoint pens and a pack of A4 white paper. In the flat he unwrapped the five hundred sheets of paper, sitting up at Martha's desk. He tapped six sheets together and placed them down on the desk in front of him. He cracked open one of the packs of pens. At the top of the first sheet Phillip wrote 'Memoirs of a Game Ranger' and put down the pen. For a long while he stared at the blank sheet of paper, his mind still polluted by the previous day's alcohol. For three days in a row, Phillip walked the banks of the Missouri river, cleaning his brain. On the fourth day it was raining. Phillip sat back at Martha's desk. Within a minute the four walls had gone. He could not hear the sound of the traffic. He had left America. The story of his life on the banks of the Zambezi River flowed. He was there, back in the African bushveld. Two hours later, Phillip came out of his trance and into reality, getting up from the desk to make himself a cup of tea. Three of the pages were covered in his writing. He was happy, skipping his feet, knocking over one of the kitchen chairs in his excitement. He had found his escape. A way to go home and still be with his pregnant wife in America.

That night Martha told him that Franklyn was opening an office in New York and, if they wished, they could go live in the Big Apple. She had spoken to Marcin. They were going to give Phillip a desk in the Linguare office to encourage his visits. Encourage him to help with all the publicity they were building for the company.

"What's this on my desk?"

"My escape."

"Oh, my goodness... You mind if I read?"

"Be my guest."

Stressed at the possibility of Martha finding his writing a load of rubbish, Phillip went to look out of the window at the lights in the apartments across the way. Holding his breath, he waited. From behind there was only silence.

"You've captured the smell of it, Phillip. I can see it all as it was on my trip. All these anecdotes. People who have never been fortunate enough to visit the African bush will have a true-life experience. It's all fact, not fiction. Wow. This will sell. But you weren't a game ranger but a safari operator."

"I have ranged through the African bush all my life looking at the wild animals. Even Mugabe can't take away all those wonderful memories. So you like it?"

"I love it, honey. Let's take ourselves out to supper and celebrate. When are you getting the Christmas tree?"

"Tomorrow."

"Give me a hug."

"How's our baby?"

"She's been quiet. No pains. Oh, Phillip. I'm so happy for you. Having nothing to do all day must have been awful."

"If a man doesn't work he has no worth."

"Are you going to tell Randall?"

"Not until it's finished."

"How big will the book be?"

"Big. Very big. I'm going to drag it out as far as I can. Now I've started, I want the writing to last as long as possible. Forever. Now how about that hug?"

PART 8

DECEMBER 1993 TO FEBRUARY 1994 —
RETRIBUTION

1

Martha would have preferred to go to bed. What with the child growing in her belly and the stress of the office, all she wanted to do when she got home was eat, go to bed and sleep. But Phillip had a problem. With nothing to do all day, sitting in Solly's Saloon would have turned him into an alcoholic. Not exactly what she wanted for her child. Martha had no idea if anyone in America would wish to read about the African bush. And how did you conduct the marketing to reach the few that did at a cost that made the publishing profitable? It was certainly not a book for everyone. But it kept him out of the pub. So they would celebrate. It had been her idea to suggest a desk at Linguare for Phillip. There was no way they were not going to move to New York. Franklyn had been adamant.

"It was a chance in a million, Martha. We must have an office in New York. And you must go and be close to our investment. I want you on top of the marketing. Nothing is going to slip through our fingers. We've got to make it work by hands-on management. Nothing left to chance. Your future and my financial future are in this new technology. Horst and Maples will be able to justify a New York office, the leg-up we've been looking for, for years. With one big account to pay expenses any new business will make our company a good profit. We'll become a national advertising agency with a foot in the technology business."

In all the excitement the only problem was finding something for Phillip to do. He was bored with Kansas City. That much to Martha was obvious. She'd plucked him from a totally different environment and plonked him down in a city. In life, a girl had to think or the dream came crashing down. The thought of herself spending her life at home as a housewife made her laugh. She understood Phillip's problem. Soon after the baby was born they would employ a live-in girl to take care of the child. A girl with little or no sexual attraction. She had it all worked out. Between them they had more than enough money for a servant. One of those nice girls from South America who loved children. Sitting comfortably in the passenger seat she studied Phillip's face as he kept his eye on the traffic. His jaw was clenched, his whole demeanour stressed.

"You're driving the wrong way for Solly's, Phillip."

"I'm looking for a different restaurant. Any ideas?"

"That one over there. It's Italian. Eaten there a couple of times."

"Then we're in luck. We won't stay too long. I know you're tired. Did you really like my writing?"

"I certainly did."

"Everyone wants to be able to write."

"They just want to be famous. Or get themselves rich. You're writing for your own pleasure. Why it works."

"We shall see."

"You can park over there."

"Thanks for leaving me the car during the day."

"My pleasure."

"Walking. It clears the mind. Cleanses the body. Italian. I love Italian food."

"Let's go celebrate."

"Except for one thing. I'm not drinking."

"Better for both of us."

"Anyway, I'm writing tomorrow. Can't write with a hangover. Can't do much at all with a hangover except go to the pub and drink."

Keeping her mouth shut, Martha took his arm. They were going to be all right. She had not married a fool. Hugging his arm, they walked inside the restaurant where it was warm and full of people sitting down at the tables.

"Any chance of a table for two? My wife and I didn't book."

"Come this way."

"Our luck is in. Some days you win. I like this place. We'll come again. Why are you smirking, Martha?"

"I'm happy. Happy for both of us. It's our lucky day."

Confining the conversation to Phillip and his new book saw them through the meal. To counter her inner tiredness, Martha drank two glasses of red wine. Her mind kept wandering back to their wedding. The brief explosion of family. Ford walking her down the aisle in place of her dead father. Hugo finding the time to come. All the relations telling their stories, more interested in themselves than her wedding. So many children. Her mother had cried. That was something. And then it was over. The job done. A pregnant woman with a husband. Had they made a worthwhile memory? Martha wasn't sure. All that money spent to say, 'I do'. At the end of the meal, Martha having declined coffee in case it kept her awake, she felt the sharp pain in her stomach. It was like a stab with a knife in the gut.

"What's the matter?"

"Nothing. We'd better go home."

"Of course. Thanks for listening to my stories."

By the time they reached the car, the pain had gone. She was feeling normal. In the passenger seat of the car she hugged her stomach. The stab had made her frightened. There was so much to giving birth to a child she did not know.

"You think Mrs Crabshaw will live to receive her cable from the Queen of England? She was quite bubbly at our wedding."

"Of course she will. It's her sole purpose in living to a hundred. You're hugging your stomach. Is everything all right?"

"Everything is going to be fine. *Memoirs of a Game Ranger*. I like the title. I'm so tired I'm ready to drop."

"You shouldn't work so hard."

"Randall made such a good speech. Far better than Ford."

"All that practice. His life is words. Must be freezing at this time of the year on the Isle of Man."

Expecting her pain to come again at any moment she sat quietly while Phillip drove them home. Nothing more happened. They went straight to bed. For a long while pretending she was fast asleep, Martha lay awake worrying. If something was wrong with the baby, was there anything her doctor could do? In the morning she would make an appointment. The whole reason for getting married for both of them had been to have a baby. Create their own family. Have a future. It was late when Martha finally fell asleep.

IT TOOK the doctor half an hour to complete all the tests. Martha was tense as she waited for the verdict. When it came, Doctor Hamlyn was smiling.

"Nothing wrong I can see, Martha. Everything on course. You should have a healthy baby in two months' time. Don't worry. The worst thing for a pregnant mother is stress. Try to relax. What I would recommend is you stop working. Stay at home and relax."

"It was a sharp, stabbing pain."

"We all get the odd pain. If you weren't having your baby you wouldn't worry about it. Nothing wrong I can see. Go home and relax."

"I have an appointment in the office in twenty minutes. We're very busy."

"Probably your problem."

"I can't stop work."

"You asked my opinion and I've given it. Are you drinking?"

"A little. Sometimes a little too much."

"Drink can sometimes give you the cramps. Better not to drink when you're pregnant. For a lot of my patients it's better not to drink, period."

"Thanks for seeing me on such short notice."

"My pleasure, Martha. Always my pleasure."

Her gynaecologist walked her to the door of his surgery. Outside in the waiting room three women were sitting impatiently. The man was always busy. Always that confident look. He was now smiling at the other women, Martha no longer making him money. A doctor's practice was like any other business: it was all about making money. Whatever his friendly diagnosis, she had still had a stab in the gut.

Back at the office, she sat at her desk in her cubicle, her head down, unable to concentrate. The client was late, leaving Martha time to worry about herself. Ever since she could remember, she had wanted a child. If something now went wrong she would not have another chance, the luck of falling pregnant again after thirty-seven less and less likely. And without the baby, would there be a lasting bond to Phillip? Or would he run back to his first true love, the African bush? Everything depended on the baby: her life, her marriage and their future. Martha sat rigid, fear paralysing her mind and her body. Should she tell Phillip? Should she tell Franklyn she didn't want to work until after her baby was born? Or was she worrying for nothing?

Fighting her panic, Martha brought her mind back to where she was sitting, motionless at her desk in the cubicle. She looked around the office. Everyone's head was down, concentrating on their work. Instead of going to see Franklyn and asking him for leave, she turned on her computer. The doctor had said not to worry. She would try and do what he said. When she looked up again, the client was waiting, business back to normal.

When she reached home at seven o'clock Phillip was standing in the lounge decorating their Christmas tree. The fairy lights and tinsel were twinkling, and he was hanging small coloured baubles to the branches. Instead of telling him about the stab of pain, she walked into the kitchen and poured herself a large glass of red wine.

"You said you weren't going to drink, Martha."

"Just one glass to relax after a hard day at the office."

"You're home nice and early."

"I love the tree."

"There's nothing better than a Christmas tree. Reminds me of my childhood. I've made supper so we don't have to order in. Lots of lovely green vegetables to go with the fish."

"How was today's writing?"

"Wonderful. I'm so happy. All day I've been back in Africa in my mind. You quickly forget the cold of winter. The man Solly told me to ring delivered the tree at four o'clock. Just when I'd finished writing. Now. How does that look? The glass baubles reflect the fairy lights so beautifully."

"They want us to transfer to New York after Christmas. I'm going to put this apartment on the market."

"Can you just imagine our baby in a crib under that tree? It would make everything just perfect."

"Last time, letting the apartment was a disaster. If we want to go live in New York we must make the commitment."

"As you wish, Martha. It's your flat not mine. Now, just look at it. The perfect Christmas tree. Have you invited your mother and Mrs Crabshaw for Christmas lunch?"

"Not yet."

"Come here, wife. Give your husband a kiss."

"I love you, Phillip."

"Maybe I'll join you in one glass of wine. Then I'll put on the fish."

"What are you going to buy Mrs Crabshaw for Christmas?"

"That's easy. A portrait of the Queen of England."

"And where in Kansas City are you going to find a portrait of the Queen of England?"

"That is a bit more tricky."

"My mother wants a fur coat now she knows how much money I'm making with you and Marcin."

"She'll have all those animal rights activists splashing paint on it. Fur coats are definitely out of fashion at the end of the twentieth century. Makes me laugh. They eat and fish but that doesn't count. Hypocrites the lot of them. All they want is media attention. Someone to take notice of them. The brief flash of fame."

"Some of them are passionate about saving the animals. Saving nature."

"A nice portrait of the Queen of England in all her fancy regalia. Americans love the royal family. Why the media are so paranoid about celebrities. They don't have a king. Terrible job. Wouldn't have it for all the tea in China."

"Being a celebrity or being the King of England?"

"Both. You'd never get any peace. Did you see them chasing Julian at our wedding? He hates it. Randall's lucky he writes under a pseudonym and keeps his face away from the media by living on the Isle of Man."

"We need all the publicity we can get for Linguare."

"Money. All we think about is money."

"What else is there to think about?"

"Happiness. Peace. A life of contentment. A life of fulfilment. Self-worth. Most rich people have screwed someone to make their money."

"The poor are rarely content, Phillip."

"Better to be poor and honest than be a thief. Don't these people have consciences? All they do with their ill-gotten gains is flash it to show off."

"Are you going to form the Crookshank Foundation?"

"Probably. Were it not for the baby, I'd pour my money down the sink. Money has no real value. It's a book entry in a bank account. Now you see it and now you don't. I'd love to have lived in Africa in the old days. Before the white man brought with him his materialism. Life in the kraal. A round hut with a hole in the roof to let out the smoke from the cooking fire. Cattle. Growing one's own food. Dependent on no one but oneself. Everything you have in a city is dependent on the good behaviour of other people. What if the government goes bust? No, life in the kraal is my dream. With the drums playing. Make your own alcohol and then have a party."

"You're nuts."

"Probably. They didn't have Christmas trees. Let's have some supper. Right there, under the tree. A crib with our peacefully sleeping baby. Imagine it."

"They didn't have doctors."

"Of course they did. Witch doctors. Good genes survived. Made healthier future generations than the modern way of keeping us all alive, defeating the course of nature. Or God, however you look at it."

"You're a romantic."

"Nothing wrong with being a romantic. Even if it's a dream. You know what I fancy now? Some beautiful music. I'm going to put on our favourite. Haydn's Twenty-Eighth Symphony. Now that's a legacy to leave mankind. To give people true pleasure hundreds of years after you die. That's wealth. Lasting wealth. There we are. Haydn's Twenty-Eighth. Cheers, Martha. Here's to you and our baby. To happiness. To family."

Forgetting supper, they sat washed by the music, Martha having no idea why it was so beautiful. Why it made her feel happy. The slow, beautiful notes of the flute, a tune but more than a tune, taking away her worry. Her wine tasting good. Christmas lights all a-twinkle. A man holding her hand in peace. A child almost ready to come out and see what life was all about. If she had been a cat she would have purred. When the music finished, they sat in contented silence. After what seemed like an hour Phillip got up.

"I'm starving. Can't just live on music, however beautiful. Thank you, Mr Haydn, whoever you were. For coming into our room. For becoming part of our lives. And our child will enjoy his music in years to come, as much as we do, Martha. Isn't that a lovely thought? Maybe one more glass of wine. It's so good to be happy."

They ate at the dinner table, Phillip having cooked the fish to perfection, the flesh juicy and sweet in the middle, the vegetables just right, crunching in Martha's hungry mouth. The material world outside had gone for the moment, Martha glad she had not had to grow her own vegetables. Despite growing up on a farm, she preferred to have money and go to the shops to get her food. Married life was good, the banter of simple conversation making her smile. Phillip had put on a Mahler symphony that went on and on, cocooning them up at the table, keeping the outside world at bay. How she wished life could always be so peaceful, away from the noise of traffic and the shouts of quarrelling people. It made her feel good thinking of Willy and Beth, now successful entrepreneurs. Helping other people gave Martha deep satisfaction: a client with a marketing campaign that worked, saving their company. Seeing Jas promoted in the company. Making Franklyn the kind of money that would secure him a comfortable retirement. Waving at the old lady across in the opposite block of apartments and making her smile, taking away that look of loneliness for one brief moment. The meal over, Martha took the dishes to the kitchen. She had left some of the vegetables on her plate which she scooped into the bin. Phillip's plate was clean as usual, not a morsel of food gone to waste.

"I threw away some of my food."

"I saw. Leave it on the plate and put it in the fridge. There's nothing better than a cold potato eaten in one's fingers. You Americans have had it too good for too long. That's the problem with never learning from our mistakes. Rampant consumerism never ends well. Look at the two world wars. The next bout of self-destruction will likely be financial. Everyone borrows too much to sustain their lifestyles these days. The democratic governments make promises to the public in order to get themselves elected and borrow the money to fulfil their pension and health care obligations, leaving the generations to come in a pile of debt that will swallow them whole. The democratic system only worries about the next four or five years, depending on how long the politicians will get themselves elected. Nice game, making your grandchildren pay for your pension instead of your own money. It all looks good when the economy is expanding. In *Hamlet* Shakespeare has Polonius say, 'Neither a borrower nor a lender be'. Countries of the democracies should think about his warning before it's too late. The philosophy of democracy sounds a lot better than its practice. Politicians don't have to be responsible when they can borrow money. They don't even have to know what they're doing. A good politician has to be able to debate, talk his way out of a problem. Most of them in this lovely new world couldn't organise a piss-up in a brewery. They're just good at talking to get themselves elected. You want another glass of wine? Better not. Let's go to bed. The washing up's done."

"You think America could run into problems?"

"All countries and empires run into problems in the end. How it works."

"Do you think there is something wrong with democracy?"

"What we now call a democracy is rotten to the core. It's corrupt. All jaw. And everyone expects too much. It's more a tyranny than a democracy. But who am I to say? I'm just a safari operator from the outback of Africa. In the bush you have plenty of time to think. Too much thinking can warp a man's mind, so they say. Who knows who's right? Only history will tell. New York. That's going to be something new for a simple man from the bushveld."

"Are you looking forward to going?"

"If it makes my wife happy, it will make me happy."

"I can't wait for our baby."

"Neither can I."

In bed, content, trying to convince herself her husband was talking nonsense, she lay quietly thinking. To say modern American democracy was a tyranny was a load of rubbish. All you had to do in America was work hard to be rich. The few that slipped through the capitalist system needed help. It was called charity. And there was nothing wrong with borrowing money from the bank to develop a business or the infrastructure of a country. What banks were for, to put idle money to work in exchange for paying the lender interest. How would Marcin Galinski have succeeded without their money, creating new wealth for everyone: Phillip, herself and Franklyn, Marcin and his staff, the people who would use voice recognition software to improve their businesses and their lives? Everyone was a winner. And they all paid taxes which paid for the welfare of the less fortunate. And not all politicians were idiots or America would never have prospered for so many generations while so much of the world stayed mired in abject poverty, including Phillip's beloved Africa. But what Phillip had said so adamantly wouldn't quite go away. Like the thought of the stabbing pain in her stomach coming back again, the idea of a tyrannical democracy that had got out of control would not stop nagging at the back of her brain.

When she slipped into sleep the nightmare began, a wide universe with Martha floating away out into space, watching the earth below her disintegrate, her baby screaming to her for help. When she woke in the night she was sweating. She could hear the clock ticking from the lounge and the sound of the city's traffic, the horn of a car, the sound of an aeroplane, the shout of someone's voice. Martha wasn't sure if what she heard was real or still part of her dream. Phillip was sound asleep next to her, one of his legs touching hers. The baby was kicking inside of her. She was in her own bed, in her own home, in her own beautiful country. She was back in her mind, arguing with Phillip's prognosis of a disintegrating world. By the time she went back to sleep she was happy America was free of any lasting problems, that her future, and the future of her baby was secure. She was dreaming again, dreaming of the farm, seeing a new-born calf struggling to its feet, nuzzling its mother's udder, all the world content.

When Martha woke in the morning to the sound of the rain beating on the windowpane she forced the nightmare from her mind. Phillip brought her a mug of coffee and went back to the kitchen to make them breakfast.

"Did you sleep well, Martha?"

"Never better." Sometimes in life it was better to lie.

By the time she reached the office of Horst and Maples, her mind was back to the problems of the day, everything normal, everything as it should be on a working day in Kansas City. To start her day, she phoned her realtor and put her apartment on the market. If she found an immediate buyer they would go to New York after Christmas. She would have her baby in the Big Apple. There would be a new gynaecologist to replace Doctor Hamlyn. Without the daily stress from her clients, it would be better for the baby. All she would have to do was move into new business premises. Look around. Employ some staff. Get the feel of the place. Concentrate her business mind on the marketing programme for Linguare. In America, everything happened quickly. By the time Kim was born they would have a branch office in New York, a new apartment, a whole new life full of excitement.

"The market is slow at the moment, Mrs Crookshank. Everyone is thinking about Christmas. If you want the right price you have to wait for the right buyer. Are you sure you wish to sell your apartment this time?"

"My company is opening an office in New York for me to run."

"Well, that is different. Last time you were going to live in Africa."

"I'm married now. And pregnant."

"Have a nice day."

"You too."

And the day went on amid the bustle of doing business. At six, Martha took a cab back to the apartment. She was going to slow down. In the lounge, below the abstract painting she had never been quite sure of, was a portrait of a young Queen of England, a surprisingly beautiful woman. On the couch, his feet stretched out on the blue carpet she had bought when she first moved into her apartment, Phillip sat smirking.

"Painted just before her coronation."

"She was beautiful."

"Prince Phillip would never have fallen for an ugly woman just because she was one day going to be Queen. I'm going to wrap it in brown paper and put it under the tree. Have you bought your mother's fur coat?"

"Where and how did you find it?"

"Luck. Pure luck. After I'd phoned every art gallery in Kansas City."

"How was the writing?"

"Not so good. Christmas was on my brain. Not that there's any problem having Christmas on the brain. Are we having a turkey? Mince pies? You always have to have mince pies for Christmas."

"What on earth for?"

"Dad said it was a relic of the war. Mincemeat was easier to get with the rationing. Anyway, we always had mince pies on the farm for Christmas."

"Come here, honey. Give your wife a kiss."

"How's our baby? Can I feel him?"

"It's a girl."

"You could find out from Dr Hamlyn if you wanted to."

"But I don't. I want it all to be the most wonderful surprise. There. Can you feel a kick?"

"Not a thing. Roast turkey with all the trimmings. She's going to love that portrait. Hang it in her lounge so the Queen can watch as Mrs Crabshaw moves up to her hundred. It'll give her that extra encouragement."

"You are nuts, Phillip."

"You must never take life too seriously. Life must be fun."

"Did you make supper?"

"Of course. I'm the perfect househusband. I've made a steak and kidney pie. Made the pastry myself."

"Where did you learn all this cooking?"

"From Bergit. With a bit of help from the cook."

"You had a cook?"

"Lots of servants on a Rhodesian tobacco farm. Like one big family. You like the portrait? I felt it! A kick. The little bugger kicked. One life stops and another beautiful life begins."

"We can all go back again for a holiday."

"That would be grand. You want to try my steak and kidney pie?"

"Where did I find you?"

"In New York we're going to lots of classical concerts and listen to Beethoven. The New York Philharmonic. We'll be going to the best theatres in the world. Have a chance to meet and talk to some of the best brains in the world. That wonderful variety of restaurants. So much fun. When we buy our new apartment, it's going to be right on top of a tall building so we can look out over the lights of New York with a glimpse of the Statue of Liberty. I'll encourage Marcin to take Linguare to the top of the IT market. Become the most valuable company in the world, bigger than General Motors. Technology. That's the future for the world. And all the money we make out of voice recognition software we'll use to research the next big thing in technology. They're all young. Lots of energy. We'll invent things that will boggle the mind. Give a million new opportunities for everyone on the planet. We'll use our minds to expand the universe. We've been to the moon. With all the new technology we'll go to the planets. Into another galaxy. Give Seb and his generation the opportunities for the kind of excitement experienced by that young

Sebastian Brigandshaw. What's the matter, Martha? Why are you grinning?"

"I'm hungry. Where's that steak and kidney pie?"

"Coming up. I'm going to have a glass of wine. To hell with my new rules. Are you going to join me?"

"Why not, honey? Why not? You've got me really excited. A whole new, wonderful world."

"Adventure. Life must always be an adventure going forward. In a hundred years' time who knows what our son's grandchildren will be looking forward to? Maybe not a telegram from the Queen of England, but something equally exciting to fire their imagination. Keep them wanting to go on living. Then, of course, they'll be living to a hundred and twenty. Working right up to the day of their hundredth birthday. A full and productive life that has helped everyone. That's going to be the life for our great-grandchildren."

"And if it's a girl?"

"She'll live long enough to play with her great-great-grandchildren. Tell them stories of far back in history when one of their ancestors was a safari operator who roamed the African bush. She'll be able to show them my book. I'll talk to them from the pages, showing them a world that no longer exists. They won't be sitting in a three-roomed apartment in a city staring at the blank walls. They'll be off to the furthest planet of a far distant galaxy taking man's knowledge and experiences with them. It won't be colonisation. They'll have some new fancy name. Planetisation. Hoisting the star-spangled banner and looking up at the moons, not one, not two, a whole host of smiling moons... Do you think babies can hear what you're saying when they're still in the womb? If you can hear me, son, get ready for a life brimming with excitement. You and I, Martha, are so lucky. In that child in your womb we both have a future. Our genes will never die. Our lives will have had a purpose. Isn't it just so exciting? What now? Oh, of course. My wife is hungry, poor darling. First, a glass of wine and a toast to the Queen of England."

"What did you pay for the painting?"

"Not much. No one in Kansas City is interested in a young Queen Elizabeth. They were glad to get rid of it. A portrait of Thomas Jefferson would have cost me a fortune."

"Is the kidney pie ready?"

"It's in the oven on a low heat. Don't want to overdo my cooking. Two months. That's all it is. A child for Mr and Mrs Crookshank. And without that magic meeting in the heart of Africa it would never have happened. There. How does that look? A nice glass of wine. To our good fortune, Martha. To the Queen of England. We're going to have one beautiful Christmas."

"Cheers, honey."

"On Christmas morning with Mrs Crabshaw and your mother we'll go to the morning service at Pastor Gregory's church. Pastor Gregory, a man I admire, a rare, good man in a world of greed, will tell us the truth as it was once preached by Jesus Christ. Then we'll come back here and open our Christmas presents. Have a few drinks. Eat the roast turkey with all that lovely stuffing. What's the matter, Martha?"

"I'm starving!"

When it came the steak and kidney pie was well worth waiting for. They sat up at the dinner table eating their supper in companionable silence, leaving Martha to think. In her mind she was planning for her baby: the big cot and the big pram. The car seat to take her child in the car. A rattle. She would have to buy a rattle. All babies lay in their cots with a rattle so they could smile and rattle up at their parents, lying happily on their backs, covered in all those little embroidered blankets, their heads on a little pillow. A sweet, young, innocent-eyed face surrounded by the softness of pink. The picture for Martha was perfect. Mentally scratching her head for what else she was going to buy on Saturday, she barely listened as Phillip went back to talking. Did he ever mean all the things he was saying? Martha doubted it.

"What's for pudding, Phillip?"

"You weren't listening."

"Yes I was."

"I talk a load of tripe."

"Not always, honey. Just keep off religion."

"Apple pie. I had some of the pastry left over. When are you going to stop work?"

"Soon."

"The sooner the better. We both want a healthy baby. I'll get the pudding. Tomorrow, I'm going to try and write. There are two things taboo in a pub. Talking politics or religion. Sometimes I forget. There's a little piece of kidney pie left on your plate."

"I'm so sorry."

"When you've finished it you can have your apple pie."

"Thank you, Dad."

"That sounds so good. Dad. I like hearing the word dad."

"How many nappies do you think I should buy?"

"Don't ask me. I've only ever done it a couple of times."

"You'll change our baby's nappy, won't you?"

"Do you know, my father never changed my nappy."

"How can you remember?"

"Never changed a nappy in his life."

"Saturday, I'm going shopping after I've made my list. Will you come, Phillip?"

"Wouldn't miss it for all the world. You know, in the old days they washed the kids' nappies and used them again. Hung them out in the sun to dry. Not the wasteful world of throw away then. Bergit told me."

"You had servants. What a horrible job. The American system is far better. We'll make a tour of all the baby shops. This apple pie is lovely."

The chatter went on until they went to bed, both of them smiling, Phillip touching her hand. And, all the time, all Martha could think of was baby clothes. Step by step, she planned everything in her mind.

"You want to make love tonight?"

"Not until I've had my baby. It's too big. Uncomfortable. I can't believe I still turn you on."

"Some women stay randy right up to the night of delivery. I didn't want you to think a fat stomach put me off. Well, that's settled. Sex is off the table until after our baby is born."

"Are you mad at me?"

"It's all new to me."

"All new to both of us."

---

2

*W*hen Martha drove them all to church on Christmas morning it was raining. They had first picked up Mrs Crabshaw and helped her down to the car, the old woman using her walker, Martha with a hand on her elbow, Phillip holding up the umbrella to keep off the rain. Mrs Crabshaw was wearing a hat. Outside Pastor Gregory's church people were congregating in the rain, wishing friends a happy Christmas.

"Why aren't you wearing a hat, Martha?"

"Is it obligatory, Mother?"

"Of course it is to go to church."

"It's been a long time. Do you go to church, Mother?"

"Not very often. Not since your father died and we came to the city. I'm going to make a New Year's resolution to go to church more often. Are you all right, Martha? Your face just twisted. Are you in some kind of pain?"

"It will pass. Here we are. We can sit at the back."

The choir was singing a carol, their white surplices down to their feet, the sweet, high alto voices of the boys making a perfect welcome to the service. Happily for the smiling Pastor Gregory, who greeted them as they came in, his church was almost full, more people walking from both directions along the pavement towards the big open door. They took off their raincoats and sat down in a pew, putting their wet raincoats on the floor in front of the hassocks where they knelt down to pray. Martha closed her eyes and prayed for her baby, asking God to deliver her safely. There were tears in the corners of her clenched eyes from the pain. Kneeling down had been difficult, her mother and Phillip helping her down. When Martha pulled herself back into the wooden seat, the pain in her stomach had eased. Her mother was looking at her.

"What's the matter, Martha?"

"I'm fine. Just cramps."

Mrs Crabshaw, sitting on the aisle next to Phillip, had her eyes shut and was praying, the old, tired lips moving. She was sitting on the bench, her head bowed, too old to kneel down. Pastor Gregory walked up the aisle to the altar and began the service. As the service progressed, Martha's pain subsided. Inside the church it was warm from the underfloor heating. The sermon was about the inner goodness of people, Pastor Gregory's sincerity making Martha believe what he was saying. An hour after the stabbing pain, the service was over, the congregation beginning to mingle, Phillip going off to have a talk with Colin, the man who ran the hospice funded by Pastor Gregory. Martha saw Phillip give the man a cheque, which made him smile. They shook hands for longer than necessary, Colin pumping Phillip's arm. When they all left the church, the rain had stopped. Slowly, with Mrs Crabshaw in the middle, they walked to the car.

"How much did you give him?"

"Another ten thousand. When we set up the Crookshank Foundation he's to receive five thousand dollars every month. Give him a regular income so he can budget."

"It was a nice service."

"You're going to have to tell me what's going on, Martha."

"I will when they go home after Christmas lunch."

They were standing back from the open door of the car to let her mother ease Mrs Crabshaw into the back seat, handing her walking stick and gently closing the door before walking round. Over her shoulder, she looked at Martha. She had heard.

At the apartment, Phillip took the presents from under the tree one by one, giving the first to Mrs Crabshaw. When she tore off the brown wrapping paper she squealed with delight. With all the presents open they sat at the dinner table while Phillip brought in the turkey. Everyone was laughing and smiling.

"Is there something to be worried about, Martha?"

"Of course not, Mother. Early birthing pains. Cramps, Doctor Hamlyn calls them."

"I never had cramps. Not with any of you. You sure you're all right?"

"I'm fine."

"My goodness, Phillip. That bird looks good. This is really Christmas. Both of you, thank you for my present. I've always wanted a fur coat."

"Tell anyone who asks it's a fake. Not the fur of an animal. Some people get excited."

"Should I feel guilty?"

"It's the way of life. We're about to eat a turkey. In my mind, I can't see the difference. Do you like the breast, or would you like a slice of the brown meat from the leg?"

Martha looked over her shoulder at the chinchilla fur coat draped over the back of the sofa. The soft grey of the fur from all those squirrel-like animals from South America made the perfect coat. But Phillip was right. People were self-righteous hypocrites. The thought of all those beautiful little dead animals made Martha uncomfortable. She had a conscience. They all had a conscience. Trying not to think of a dead bird, Martha tucked into her lunch. Instead of Christmas carols, Phillip had put on a Brahms symphony. Martha recognised the music.

"Which one is it, Phillip?"

"Brahms's *Symphony Number Three*. What would we do without beautiful music?"

"Should you be drinking, Martha?"

"A glass of red wine with Christmas lunch shouldn't do any harm, Mother. You said you drank when you were pregnant."

"My portrait looks so beautiful. I'm going to hang it in my bedroom. Not long now before I'll receive that telegram. I do so love Christmas. Thank you all for inviting me. Judith is coming round tonight to make me dinner. Won't want much food after this turkey. It's delicious."

"Why didn't she want to come to lunch?"

"Two's company, three's a crowd."

"There are four of us, Mrs Crabshaw."

"Call me Mabel. You know what I mean. She doesn't know you, Martha. Christmas is for friends and family."

"She's your daughter."

"You know what I mean. Tonight we can talk about our family without boring everyone. She's going to love my portrait of the Queen. You're all so good to an old lady. If it weren't for the telegram she'll be sending me on my hundredth birthday I wouldn't see any point in living. At my age the whole body aches. Sometimes I envy my old friends who are dead. Do you really think there is something after this? Oh, well. Silence is golden. Nothing wrong with this turkey. Maybe a little drop of red wine in my glass won't make me drunk, Phillip. In the old days I could drink until the cows came home. Now, with one glass of wine my memory goes completely. Can't remember a thing. Thank you, kind Phillip. I give you all a toast. To the Queen of England. You don't have to stand up, Phillip."

"Why ever not?"

"Happy Christmas to all of you. Thank you so much for befriending such an old woman."

"We'll still be with you on your hundredth birthday."

"I know you will, Aggie. To friends. What would we do without friends?"

"When we've finished eating you must come and look at the baby things in the spare bedroom. Everything is ready. Mother, why are you shaking your head?"

"Wait till they can talk back to you. Sometimes, you three arguing, being a mother wasn't so pleasant."

"Right now my baby is hoping her mother is going to be a good cook. I'm sure we all thought in the womb. We just don't remember. Did you know some people can remember their previous lives?"

"People say such things to get attention."

"Was being a mother that difficult?"

"It wasn't easy. Ask Mabel. Babies grow into little people. People are never easy."

"A French philosopher said, 'Hell is other people'. Jean-Paul Sartre I think was his name." All three women stared at Phillip in silence.

"Without the child inside me my life would have had no point. Everything now is lovely."

"Hope springs eternal, Martha."

"Would you prefer not to have had us, Mother?"

"Don't be silly. What's life without an argument? Life's a mix of so many feelings. Love. Happiness. Argument. Even hate. Why life in all its facets is so exciting. The good and the bad. We all have our ups and downs. Mostly we remember the ups and forget the downs. It's human nature."

Martha, her plate of roast turkey finished, sat back and listened. She loved her mother, despite their occasional difficulties. Her mind wandered away from the lunch table. For a long, sweet moment she was back in her childhood with her two brothers. Even then it was so easy to pull their legs.

"Penny for your thoughts, Martha?" Her mother was regarding her with that look of disapproval.

"I was thinking of Ford and Hugo. They were so easy to manipulate. Putty in my hands. When they argued with each other it ended in a physical fight. They weren't allowed to hit their sister."

"How many children are you going to have?"

"As many as possible."

"Hugo didn't even phone me for Christmas."

"He's such a louse. He's likely phoning you now. When you get home you'll find a message from Tokyo on your answering machine."

"I'm full to bursting. Now what I need is a nap. Would you like to nap, Mabel?"

"Not right this moment, thank you. That little drop of wine has gone straight to my head. What a lovely Christmas."

BY THE END of the first week in January, Horst and Maples were in overdrive. All the phones were ringing, account handlers were back at their desks, the holiday season was over. Time to work. Time for America to make money. Jas had volunteered to go to New York to help Gordon Blake with his marketing programme. Martha was more convinced she was after the tall, good-looking Marcin now swimming in money. For Martha, whatever people did, they had a motive. A reason. Often selfish. Women, like men in business, threw out the line hoping what they were after would take the bait. The man was young, full of fun, and going to be richer than half the population of Kansas. Looks faded. Money stayed. The principle of a successful life in the twentieth century. In a city, there was no sitting back looking at the view, as Martha had done so many times growing up on the farm. In a city, every experience that was pleasurable cost money; the more money, the greater the pleasure. In her mind Martha wished her friend the best of luck: in life, never miss an opportunity. In just one week, Martha had signed up two more clients, her career back in top gear. Even the memory of thinking she was going to spend her life in an unstable Africa made her shudder. She had found what she wanted. Been given what she wanted. And Phillip, despite his nostalgic yearnings for a life that no longer existed, was far better off in America. She had done him a favour by getting herself pregnant and giving him a life in the States where in Linguare the sky was the limit. Later, when they were older without a business incentive, they might have enough money to buy a ranch half the size of Texas. Putting her conscience aside with that slight niggling feeling she was being selfish, Martha picked up the phone. Her life was all go. A life never dull. A productive life full of reward. Only when she had finished the conversation with her client did she feel the tearing pain that coursed through her stomach, her mind stopping, both hands gripping the desk, eyes clenched, her world blanking out. When her head hit the desk, Martha passed out. When she came to, Jas was standing over her in the cubicle.

Two hours later she was sitting up in the hospital, Phillip by her side, Doctor Hamlyn standing at the end of the hospital bed.

"What happened to me, doctor? I passed out."

"You need to go home and rest. The combined stress of work and your baby caused you to faint."

"There was terrible pain. Am I going into labour?"

"Not yet. Your baby is due in six weeks. You need rest. You've been overdoing it, Martha. Too much work and too many drinks. Having your first baby not long before your thirty-eighth birthday is more difficult for you than it is for a girl of twenty. Go home and rest. Everything is going to be fine."

"Are you sure? You have a worried look on your face."

"You'll have the best medical attention money can buy. Your husband not working is a blessing. He'll be with you all the time, won't you,

Phillip? When the contractions begin he'll bring you straight back again."

"But what caused the pain? Why did I pass out at my desk?"

"It's your first baby. Everything in life is more difficult the first time as you don't have the experience. Inside you, your baby is fine."

"Thank you, doctor."

"Phillip tells me you're trying to sell your apartment and move to New York. Leave everything until your baby is born. Tell the realtor to take the apartment off the market for the moment. Otherwise, how do you feel?"

"At the moment I'm feeling normal."

"Good. Now go home and go to bed."

Not feeling the same confidence as her doctor, Martha dressed and went home with her husband.

"Everything's going to be fine."

"Are you sure, Phillip?"

It was always the same with other people. When it wasn't their problem everything was going to be fine. Men had the fun that went with impregnation, not the nine months of carrying the baby. The doctor said she was fine. The nurse who had put her in the bed in the hospital room had said everything was going to be fine. And now Phillip. Martha wasn't so sure. When Phillip left the bedroom to go and make the tea, her mind went into panic. What would she do if she lost her baby? How could she live? Would her marriage last? They had married because they were going to have a child, not because they were in love. Love, she had hoped, would come later in the process of rearing a family. Happiness would be a family, the binding cord that would keep them together. Without the baby who were Phillip and Martha? Would there be lasting love between two people without purpose?

Taking a deep breath, she tried to calm down. It would be good to try and sleep but it wasn't possible. The worry kept going round and round in her head. She felt her stomach with both of her hands, trying desperately to hold onto her baby.

"Oh, baby. Please don't leave me," she mouthed.

"You'd better phone Franklyn and tell him you're not going back to work. I'll call the realtor and temporarily take the apartment off the market. How are you feeling, Martha?"

"Terrible. Bloody terrible."

"Is the pain back in your stomach?"

"The pain is in my head."

"I'll bring you an aspirin. You want a sandwich?"

"I'm not hungry."

"What do you want for supper?"

"I can't eat I'm so frightened."

"My poor wife. Life has its ups and downs. Remember what your mother said at Christmas. This is a small down neither of us will even remember in six months' time."

"Are we going to love each other for the rest of our lives?"

"Of course we are. We're going to have a baby. We're going to be a family. Good. The kettle's boiled. You'll feel much better after you've had a nice cup of coffee."

"Please don't leave me, honey."

"I'm right here by your side."

When Phillip went to his desk to write his memoirs Martha tried to go to sleep. All the will in the world would not make her relax. All she could hear in her mind was 'everything is going to be fine'. It was a taunt. Life mocking her. All the bad things she had done in her life seeking retribution. The worry of past indiscretions came back as if they had happened yesterday. She tried to rationalise each one of them. Wasn't marrying a man and throwing him out when he no longer paid his way right? When he no longer turned her on? Why did she have to carry a load that was no longer profitable? Good old Jake and Jonathan. What had happened to them? Did they hate her for being so incredibly selfish? Would either marriage maybe have found an equilibrium? It most likely wasn't either of their faults that she hadn't fallen pregnant. She had used both of them and then tossed them out. She was a horrible person and did not deserve a baby and a happy family life.

'Retribution.' The word kept echoing through her mind. Taunting her. Laughing at her. The word knew every nasty thing she had done in her life. For all her sins she was going to end up a lonely old woman where all the money in the world would mean nothing. Did rich people have friends because they were nice people or because they had money? A source of income for all those people saying how nice you were, hoping for a handout? She would be buying favours, the whole world laughing behind her back. Talking about her. Mocking. Saying all those nasty things when they knew she could not hear. The time now for Martha, lying in her bed, her mind full of black thoughts, was retribution. She was going to get her comeuppance. She was going to lose her baby, the thing she wanted most in her life. She was going to lose Phillip. Lose everything except her money. But what was the point of having all that money without being happy? What was going to be the point for the rest of her life?

Swamped by misery, Martha began to cry silently, her mental pain every bit as terrifying as the stabbing pain that had left her unconscious face-down on her desk. She could hear the sound of the traffic. Hear the sounds of distant people. Everything that once had made her feel comfortable. Desperately, she hoped Phillip would come in from the lounge and give her comfort. She willed him to come but nothing happened. She was alone. All on her own. No one in the world caring the slightest about Martha Poland. For everyone out there she might as well be dead.

When she woke from troubled dreams, more nightmares than dreams, Phillip was standing over her, a look of distant sympathy on his face.

"Are you real?"

"You were making funny noises in your sleep. Broke my concentration. It was so lovely being back in the bush. I was writing the story of a lion cub we found abandoned next to her dead mother. We never found out what killed the mother. When the cub grew big she walked away into the bush. Never saw her again. We'd called her Baby Girl. Could that cub drink milk! Believe me. Ate anything. Ran round and round the camp having fun with us until she was big enough to enter the world of lions. I often think of Baby Girl. It was so lovely back there writing about her. I wonder what happened to Baby Girl? Must have met a lion. Lionesses always meet their lion in the end. Have you been crying, Martha? Your pillow is all wet."

"Please hug me, Phillip."

"You want me to get into bed?"

"That would be wonderful."

"You want me to get you anything?"

"Just get into bed. I love you, Phillip."

"I know you do. There. How does that feel?"

"Wonderful. Phillip, you're horny!"

"You're telling me."

"Make love to me, Phillip."

"Are you sure?"

"Never been surer, honey."

Slowly, gently and from behind, Phillip made love to her, the climax coming to both of them at the same time. With his arms around her Martha fell into a trouble-free sleep. When she woke she was feeling a whole lot better. She was feeling positive. They were right. Everything was going to turn out just fine.

Doing what she was told by the doctor, Martha spent her days in bed, hoping the good behaviour would make up for the stress and too much drink. On Sunday morning, Beth came for a visit. Phillip had gone for a walk. A plot walk as he called them. Walks that cleared his mind and let him think what next he was going to put in his memoirs. Jas had called twice from New York, Phillip taking the calls.

"You take no phone calls, Martha. I don't even want you to think about your business. For the moment it is none of your business. Your business is giving birth to a healthy baby."

"What did she say?"

"None of your business."

"Seriously."

"I am being serious."

"Are we making lots of money?"

"Probably."

Beth, when she arrived, was full of smiles, a small bunch of roses in her hand.

"Do you have a vase? Willy's having a sleep-in on his Sunday. Never worked so hard in our lives. Sorry. Not allowed to talk business. On the phone, Phillip told me the rules. No business. No talking money. No getting you excited. I'm so envious of you having a baby. How are you, Martha?"

"They're lovely. You'll find a vase in the kitchen cupboard under the sink. I'm not allowed out of bed except to go to the bathroom. How's your marriage coming along? Not one squeak of an argument so far as we can hear."

"Did you hear us arguing?"

"All the time."

"We were bored. That was why we argued. That and lack of money. It's not much fun knowing you're about to lose the roof over your head. But now with something productive to do with our lives, we're both happy. Don't you get bored doing nothing all day?... Don't know what we would have done without Phillip. He's such a lovely man. Where is he?"

"Gone for a walk."

"He knew I was coming."

"Doesn't want to talk business. The rules of Phillip. Never break them."

"So, everything is all right?"

"Everything is just fine."

With the vase of yellow roses on the dressing table at the end of the big double bed, Beth pulled the stool out and sat down next to her. For an hour they talked girl talk, the trivial chit-chat they both found so comfortable. They even had a fit of giggles when Beth described how Willy got drunk and fell in the empty bath when he was trying to have a piddle.

"He couldn't get out. We were both drunk. Couldn't stop laughing. It's so lovely to be happy again, Martha. Now you're giggling."

"How'd you get him out?"

"Pulled him out by the back of his trousers."

"I don't believe it."

"You should have seen it."

"What did he do when he got out of the bath? Lucky it wasn't full of water."

"We had another drink. You know that expression 'legless'? Now I know what it means. His feet wouldn't work. All we could do was giggle."

"Your flowers look so lovely. Thank you, Beth. I've really enjoyed your visit."

"What neighbours are for. You keep your pecker up, neighbour. Got to run. You never stop when you're running a business. Give Phillip my love. Promise him I will not talk business next time I visit. He doesn't have to get out of the way. Nice to visit with you. Everything is going to be fine."

"Give my love to Willy."

"I'm going to pull him out of bed. We have work to do. Just look at that. The sun is shining in January. I love Kansas City. I'll miss you both when you go. Glad you like the flowers. Now you look after yourself."

The front door closed leaving Martha alone. For the first time in a long while she felt hungry. When Phillip came back from his walk she would ask him to make her some pancakes.

"You'll love pancakes." She was talking aloud to her baby. Holding her stomach she could feel the baby move against the palms of her hands. The sound of the outside traffic was pleasing. No honks or sirens, just the sound of vehicles moving. Sunday in Kansas City. They were all coming back from church. Relaxed and grateful for what she had, Martha dozed, not sure if she was awake or asleep. The front door opened and closed bringing her out of her reverie.

"Have a good plot walk?"

"There's so much story to be told."

"Can you make me some pancakes? I'm starving."

"How was Beth?"

"We had a giggle."

"That's my girl. Pancakes coming up."

BY THE END of January everything was ready for their baby. Phillip had taken her to church, driving her car right up to the door. It was the first time Phillip had let her leave the apartment. He helped her out of the car into the hands of Pastor Gregory. They were all smiling. The baby felt heavy, the weight in front making Martha walk leaning back. The pastor took her straight to the pew near the front. The church was empty except for three worshippers down on their knees on the hassocks praying. The boys' choir had not yet come to sit in the pews close to the altar.

"Things are pretty quiet after Christmas. People think they have done their duty to God by coming here on Christmas Day. Many of the people attend church at Easter and Christmas. Better than nothing. When's your baby due?"

"Next month."

"Everything all right?"

"I hope so."

"I'll pray for you and the baby. What's it going to be? A boy or a girl?"

"We've deliberately not looked at the scans. Want a surprise. All I want is a healthy baby."

"I'm sure everything will be just fine."

The choir, when it sang, outnumbered the congregation. Pastor Gregory delivered his sermon on the merits and responsibilities of bringing up a family, Martha smiling as he spoke. At the end of the service, Phillip drove her home and put her back into bed. She was tired, the baby kicking. Martha wanted the birth of her child to be over. Phillip brought her a cup of soup.

"Are you all right?"

"Tired, honey."

"You poor women. You do all the work and we have all the fun. Do you know some mothers had ten children back in the days of Queen Victoria? That's ninety months of pregnancy. My poor great-grandmother. She got married to my great-grandfather when she was seventeen."

"Was she a Crookshank?"

"No, she was a Taylor. I have cousins all over the world I have no idea about. My grandmother told me the names of some of them. They were mostly girls. Only four of them married and had children."

"Why didn't they marry?"

"Two died young. The rest I don't know. I have a photograph of the family taken in 1875. They look a loving family."

"Ten kids! She must have been out of her mind."

"In those days women didn't have much say in the matter."

"All that washing and cleaning."

"They had servants."

"Of course they did. Were the servants in the photograph?"

"You're being silly. The class divide."

"They should have come to America."

"Some of them did. Why we all lost contact. No phones. No aeroplanes. A whole different world."

"He's going to pray for me."

"Who?"

"Pastor Gregory. I feel so much more peaceful. If I lost the baby I'd kill myself."

"Don't say such things. You frighten me. Relax, take it easy and everything is going to be just fine."

"Give me a kiss."

"My pleasure. When's your mother coming round?"

"Tomorrow morning. If it isn't raining you can go for a plot walk. How's the book going?"

"I'm enjoying writing it. Whether it will be of the slightest interest to anyone I have no idea. Eat your soup. It's good for you."

"Packet soup. What would we do without packet soup?"

"Welcome to America where life is easy."

"Do you like living in America, honey?"

"Provided I have you. Look after yourself. I'm going to my desk."

"It's my desk."

"Not anymore."

BY THE TIME her mother came round, Phillip had taken the car and gone to the river. Outside it was drizzling. Martha was still thinking of Phillip.

"Looking at the river will remind me of the Zambezi. Have a nice chat with your mother. The door's on the latch. You won't have to get up to let her in. Only days now, Martha. Only days."

Sitting up in bed, Martha watched the drizzle dripping down the outside of the bedroom window. She was agitated, her mind making her body feel uncomfortable. Negative thoughts from the pain in her body. The fear was back again. When the doorbell rang Martha tried to come out of it.

"It's open, Mother."

"My goodness. Do you leave your front door open? That's being silly. Always lock your door."

"Phillip doesn't want me to get out of bed. The pain is back again. What is it? I'm terrified."

"Very soon it will all be over. Where's he gone?"

"To the river to think. He still hankers after Africa. The river reminds him of home."

"I've decided I'm going to move into your spare bedroom until the child is born. I'm your mother. To me you are still my baby. Mothers worry about their babies. I'll feel better being close to you."

"Did you bring some clothes?"

"Everything is in my suitcase I left by the door."

"What would I ever have done without you, Mother?"

"For one thing, you would never have been born. How bad is the pain?"

"It's niggling. Comes and goes. When I think everything is all right it comes back to remind me that something is wrong."

"Even more reason for me staying here. If it gets any worse I'll drive you straight to the hospital. You don't have a temperature. Your forehead is cool. Lie back and try and relax. What do you want to talk about?"

"The baby."

"Right now it's better you don't. Don't dwell on it. If there was anything wrong I'm quite sure Doctor Hamlyn would have put you in the hospital. It's not as though you can't afford it. You do have medical insurance, Martha?"

"All employees of Horst and Maples have medical insurance. And a pension plan. It's all part of the package."

"There you are."

"Any news from the boys?"

"Not a squeak. They usually only phone when they want something. Why are we all so selfish?"

"All part of being human. You'll have to move the baby things off the bed."

"That's better. Now you have a smile on your face. A year ago, I had no idea I'd be sitting on the side of my pregnant daughter's bed."

Trying hard to relax and ignore the niggling pain in her stomach, Martha listened to her mother's talk, all of it trivial. When her mother went to the kitchen to make coffee, the niggling pain had gone. She closed her eyes, quickly falling asleep.

When Martha woke it was lunchtime. Her mother was sitting on a chair reading a book wearing her reading glasses. Among the sounds of the traffic from the street ten storeys below a horn was honking. Far away was the sound of a siren.

"You're a good mother, looking after me."

"You're my daughter. Did you sleep well?"

"Like a baby. Is Phillip home?"

"He's writing. I'm going to make the lunch."

"What are you reading?"

"*Masters of Vanity*. By Randall Holiday. Phillip gave it to me."

"He's Phillip's brother. Do you like it?"

"The author draws you right into his world. No wonder he sold so many copies. You forget we all met at your wedding. What do you want for lunch?"

"You could have sat more comfortably on the sofa in the lounge."

"And upset Phillip's writing? They're quite a family, those Crookshanks."

"Yes, they are."

"What are you doing?"

"Getting up to go to the bathroom."

"At least that's normal. When I was having you I spent half my life going to the toilet. So, what's it to be?"

"Pancakes."

"Your favourite."

MARTHA'S WATERS broke a week after Aggie moved into the spare bedroom. Mother and daughter were alone in the house. Phillip had gone for a walk. The sun was shining, a thin, pale February sun. They drove to the hospital, the labour pains coming every five minutes. Martha walked into the hospital, her teeth gritted. A nurse put her into a bed in a private room. Doctor Hamlyn paid her a visit an hour after her arrival. When he finished feeling, poking and listening through his stethoscope he was smiling. He touched his hand on her shoulder and left. Phillip arrived ten minutes after Doctor Hamlyn. The hours of waiting began, her mother in a chair on one side of the bed, Phillip on the other. Four hours later, Doctor Hamlyn returned. When he left to consult in private with the hospital doctor he was not smiling. There was no comforting hand on Martha's shoulder. The labour pains had stopped coming. For four more hours they were left on their own. Aggie had fallen asleep. Phillip was sitting reading a book. The contractions were back again, now three minutes apart. When Doctor Hamlyn left he put his hand on Martha's shoulder. He was smiling. The man behind the smile looked tired. It was three o'clock in the morning. Half an hour after he left, the contractions stopped. When the two doctors came back at eight in the morning, neither of them was smiling.

"We're going to do a caesarean section."

"There is no other way?" Phillip was standing up as he spoke to the doctor.

"No, we will need to cut open her stomach to deliver your baby. A common procedure with a difficult birth. I have performed many such operations. Nurse, please bring a trolley and wheel Mrs Crookshank into the operating theatre. I will go and scrub up with Doctor Hay."

"May I watch the operation?"

"Not in the theatre, Mr Crookshank. There is a round window in the door to the theatre. You may both watch the operation through the window."

"Is everything going to be all right?" Aggie's voice choked when she spoke.

"I hope so, Mrs Poland. Only when we open her stomach will we find out. Be calm, Martha. It's important for you not to stress. You will be given sedatives before the operation."

"Is my baby all right?"

"I hope so."

"You're not sure?"

"No, I'm not sure."

"Oh, my God."

"Please, take it easy, Martha."

"Now you tell me."

The man turned his back and left the room with the house surgeon. The nurse came back with a flat-topped trolley. With her mother and Phillip on either side, Martha was wheeled down to the operating theatre where she was lifted onto the centre table. She was given pills and then an epidural anaesthetic. She could see Phillip's face through the small round window. When he moved, she could see the face of her mother. Neither of them was smiling. There were three doctors and two nurses surrounding her. Doctor Hamlyn began to cut her open, a nurse holding Martha's shoulder to stop her leaning up to look at what they were doing. When they held up her wet baby, Martha could see her son. He was not crying. Both doctors shook their heads. Her baby was dead. Martha lay back hoping she was dying, half losing consciousness. She could see the body of Sebastian on a bench next to the operating table, his face looking up at nothing. They had not covered him up. He was just lying there. Discarded. The trolley was brought back and Martha was moved off the operating table. They wheeled her back to the private room. The baby was left behind. Phillip tried to hold her hand. She wanted to be dead. There was no point in living. They had taken her baby, stitched her up and sent her back to her room. Martha closed her eyes. There was no crying. No tears. All she wanted was death. Instinctively, she knew what had happened. It was retribution. The final retribution for all the horrible things she had done to other people. Losing her ability to think, she lost consciousness.

EPILOGUE

*a*ll Phillip could see was what was in his mind: the house doctor's outstretched hands holding his son under the arms, the rubber gloves wet with the liquids from inside Martha's body. The long legs hanging down, the small eyes closed, the body dripping wet. There was no crying. No sign of life. The man put the baby on its back on a bench behind the light-drenched operating table. Watching, waiting, Phillip expected a cry. There was nothing. When the doctor shook his head looking at Doctor Hamlyn, Phillip knew Sebastian was dead.

In the private room, both of them standing, too upset to sit down, they watched Martha pass out. Phillip thought she was dead. The elderly matron took Martha's pulse.

"She's sleeping. The sedative has taken effect. I'll leave you all alone. I'm so sorry for your loss."

"What have they done with the body of my son?"

"Tomorrow, when your wife is stronger, you will be taken to the mortuary to see the body. It's important for you both to look at him. To know what happened. Initially, the shock makes a mother believe someone has stolen her baby. Hospital procedure."

"How long will she sleep?"

"As long as possible. I'll send you both some lunch."

"You're hard as nails."

"I can't change what just happened."

"Of course you can't. I was being rude. I'm sure you all did everything right. Will there be an enquiry?"

"The child's dead. Don't torment yourself. Do you want lunch?"

"No I damn well don't."

"The nurse will keep an eye on your wife."

"That's so kind of her."

The woman gave Phillip a pitiful look and left the room, leaving the door open. Phillip closed the door. Aggie was standing rigid. He put his arms round her. They were both crying, sobbing, their bodies shaking.

The lunch came, uninvited, an hour later. Martha was still sleeping. Phillip and Aggie ate in silence. All afternoon they sat next to the comatose Martha, waiting for her to wake. Phillip had no idea what he was going to say. When Martha woke in the evening her eyes were strange, unable to focus. She said nothing. Aggie took her hand. The eyes rolled in Martha's head.

"Am I dead?"

"No, you're alive."

"The baby is dead?"

Neither of them was able to reply.

"I want to die. I was dying. Let me die."

"Don't be silly."

"It's not silly. What purpose do I have in living?"

The nurse came back and gave Martha a sedative. The unfocused eyes closed. She was asleep.

"Is she going to die?"

"Of course not."

"The doctor hasn't been back."

"There's nothing wrong with your wife, Mr Crookshank. It's a terrible thing that has happened. I've seen it before. Your wife will get over the loss. You'll have another baby. Ah, here comes your supper."

"I'm sorry for being rude to the matron."

"She's been doing this job a long time. She understands. Be strong. For you and your wife. I'll bring some blankets if you wish to spend the night in your chairs."

"Do you have children?"

"No children. Why I understand your pain. Ring the bell if you need anything. You're not American?"

"I'm African. From Zimbabwe. I met my wife on safari."

THE NEXT DAY when they were shown the body of their dead baby in the mortuary, they hugged each other, both of them shaking. The day after, Pastor Gregory conducted a funeral service in his church. After the service, the body was taken in the small coffin to be cremated. Phillip, Martha and Aggie left the church in silence. When they reached Martha's apartment they were alone. Aggie had asked to be dropped off at her own apartment.

"What are we going to do, Phillip?"

"Life goes on."

"Are you going back to Africa?"

"Do you want me to?"

"I don't know. Can you leave me alone? I want to think on my own. Go to Solly's. Get yourself drunk. I'm not good company."

"Will you be all right?"

"I hope not."

"My poor Martha."

"All the sympathy in the world will change nothing. Get out. Leave me alone. Go, Phillip. Please go."

"Are you sure?"

"Absolutely bloody certain."

"Don't you love me anymore?"

"We don't love each other. We never did. We were using each other."

"You'll feel better later."

"I doubt it."

Martha had gone to the window, her back to Phillip. He wanted to go and put his arms around her. Instead he turned and left the room. Outside in the corridor he stood on his own, never lonelier.

"Now what do I do?"

Phillip walked to the lift and pressed the button. The lift took a long time to come. It was stuck on the thirteenth floor. He wanted to go back. His feet were heavy, stuck to the floor. The lift door clanged open.

"Are you getting in?"

The man was pressing the button, the door opening and closing.

"Sorry. Thank you."

Downstairs in the street the sun was shining. Unable to think straight, Phillip found himself walking. When he reached the entrance to Solly's Saloon he stopped. The fog cleared in his mind. He knew where he was but not the time of day. Inside, the pub was empty of customers. His son was dead. Martha did not love him. Never had.

"You all right, Phillip?"

"No, Solly. I'm not. We lost the baby. Martha hates me. She says we were just using each other."

"Were you?"

"I don't know. Probably."

"You want a drink?"

"A double whisky. Any old whisky. I want to get drunk."

"What about your wife?"

"She told me to get out. To leave her alone."

"She'll get over it."

"Will she? We'll have to see. Some things when they are spoken can't be taken back."

"What are you going to do?"

"There's certainly no point in relocating to New York. The only reason I came to America was because Martha was pregnant."

"Did she do it on purpose?"

"She said not."

"Why wasn't she on the pill?"

"I have no bloody idea."

"Would you have married her had she not been pregnant?"

"It was a one-night stand in the African bush. A safari operator pleasing one of his customers."

"You must have had fun."

"Perks of the trade. Before, the women looked after themselves."

"You should have used a condom to be sure."

"In the future I will. I damn well will."

"Enjoy your drink."

"Will you mind if I get drunk?"

"Not one bit. Just don't get into an argument."

Lifting the glass, Phillip drank down the double whisky. In his mind, he could still see his dead son lying on the bench through the round window in the door of the operating theatre. If he was feeling like this, what must Martha be feeling? She had grown the boy in her stomach for nine months, whatever the motive for her pregnancy. And both of them had wanted a child. A family. A future. He couldn't stay in America on his own. What would be the point? And if she had never loved him how could he stay with Martha? With his mind going round in circles, Phillip signalled for another drink. Solly had retreated to a barstool at the other end of the empty bar. They were all leaving him alone. He would have to go back to his Africa. The season would be in full swing. The game of life would go on. Poor Martha.

"Same again?"

"If you will."

"Take it easy, Phillip."

"I'll try."

With his life shattered all he could think of to do was drink. Would it ever be the same back in the bush, putting up with tourists, being polite to strangers? Before, it had been a life. Now Phillip was not so sure. There was a hook in the whisky when he drank. Not even drinking booze was a pleasure. He downed the whisky and ordered a beer. Solly went back to his seat on the barstool at the other end of the bar. The beer tasted better, the whisky taking effect. Tears pricked at the back of his eyes. There were no tears. Even tears wouldn't come. Would she kick him out of her apartment in her misery? Where would he go? He couldn't just run away. He had no friends in America. No one to turn to. Should he go to England and cry on his father's shoulder? He had lost his mother and now he had lost his son. Was he going to spend the rest of his life without being part of a family?

"Is this seat taken?"

"I don't think so seeing I'm the only customer."

"What's the matter?"

"My son just died at birth and my wife hates me."

"What happened?"

"Stillborn. He didn't make it. She's blaming me."

"Can I take this barstool?"

"Of course. What you doing in a bar so early in the morning?"

"Women. They always want to blame someone for their problems.

My mother was the same. When something went wrong it was always my fault. Never my sister's. Sometimes I think women hate men. They only stay with us because they need someone to pay the bills. When my wife has a go at me I get out of the house. No point in arguing. After a while she calms down."

"How long have you been married?"

"Twenty-seven years."

"And you still argue?"

"Never stopped. We've got three kids. The last one, Hank, is due to leave home next week. He can't wait to get out of the house. Hates all the bickering."

"Have you enjoyed your marriage?"

"I suppose so. It wasn't all bad. When my wife gets what she wants she can be absolutely charming. All smiles and friendly. The trick is to tell her how good she looks. Loves praise. Loves to be told what a good mother she's been to the kids. When I try that tack, Hank raises his eyebrows."

"Are the other two boys or girls?"

"Both women. Just like their mother. Both are married with kids. My poor sons-in-law. Both my girls are good-looking so they put up with it. Once Hank goes I don't know what I'm going to do. Do you know a place far, far away?"

"Matter of fact I do."

"What can I get you, sir?"

"A beer, Mr Barman. And one for my friend."

"Call me Solly. You new in the area?"

"Just moved into a one-bedroomed apartment around the corner. Never had enough money to buy my own place. Never had the deposit. My wife and children spent all my money. What's your name?"

"His name is Phillip. He's from Africa. Two beers coming up."

"My name is Cory, Phillip. Where you from in Africa?"

"Zimbabwe."

"Never heard of it."

"It's far, far away."

"Just the place I'm looking for. She can get herself a job and pay her own rent. I never read the newspapers or listen to the news. Too depressing. Sorry about your son. Life's full of shit."

"You'd leave your wife after twenty-seven years?"

"Freedom. Nothing better than freedom. Tell me about this place you call Zimbabwe. Where is it?"

"Southern Africa. You ever heard of Robert Mugabe?"

"Never heard of him."

"You're lucky. Real lucky. Once there was a farm in Africa called World's View..." With the four tots of whisky soaking his brain, Phillip went off on a story. It took his mind off his son, his guilt at having left Martha in the apartment on her own. He went on and on, the man called Cory happy to listen.

"Now it's your turn, Cory, before I bore you stiff. Want another beer?"

"Thought you'd never ask. Let's you and I get drunk and forget the rest of the world."

"Now you're talking. Have a shooter to catch up. So, what's your story?"

WHILE PHILLIP WAS GETTING drunk with his new friend, Martha was drowning in her depression. How could she ever face Phillip after what she had told him? And they had both used each other. Lied that they loved each other. Tried to make something out of nothing to have a child. They were strangers from different worlds. Now she was nothing. All the money in the world wouldn't make her life worthwhile. Making up her mind, she took a chair from the kitchen and carried it through the lounge to the glass door that opened onto the balcony. Even the sun shining outside made no difference to her mood. She opened the door and pulled the chair through to the railing, the open seat of the wooden chair facing her. Hatred and bitterness soaked in the depths of her depression. She stood up on the seat of the chair, the top of the back of the chair level with the top of the iron railing. She put her right foot on the railing feeling the pain in her stomach from the incision. In her mind's eye she could see him lying on the slab in the mortuary. With her eyes wide open she looked straight across the way, not looking down the ten storeys to the traffic in the street far below. The old woman saw her and smiled, then waved, happy for that moment to have company. Martha teetered. The old lady's hand went to her mouth. Instead of bringing up her left foot from the chair, Martha stood back.

Fear, and the wave from the old lady, had stopped her from killing herself.

"You don't have the guts, Martha Poland. You're worthless."

Disgusted with herself she got out of the cold, back into her apartment, closing the balcony door. The old lady was still standing on her balcony across the way, her hand clasped over her mouth, looking appalled. Martha went into the kitchen and took out a bottle of red wine. She pulled out the cork. Took a glass.

"Now what the hell do I do?"

She took the wine bottle and the glass into the lounge and sat down on the couch. She pressed the button on the hi-fi. She recognised the music as Mozart. She was crying. Tears flooded down both sides of her face as she began to drink. She had called herself Martha Poland. Who was Martha Crookshank? She was still finished, despite not having killed herself. She was a worthless, gutless, selfish bitch and nothing was ever going to change that. After the third glass of red wine, the music of Mozart began to seep into her mind. The old lady had stopped her jumping from the balcony. Mozart and the wine began eating away at her depression.

"Poor Phillip. What am I going to do? You can never take back the truth."

With the curtains drawn and the music playing, Martha went on a drunk. After the second bottle of wine the depression had mostly lifted. She was drunk. Well and truly drunk.

When Martha woke in her bed in the night she stretched out her hand for Phillip. She was alone. He had not come home. Her husband had left her. She got up, went into the kitchen and opened another bottle of wine. Then she put on the music. Haydn. Haydn's Twenty-Eighth Symphony. It was their favourite and all she could do was cry.

An hour later when Phillip let himself into the apartment she was back in the depths of her depression, her eyes tight closed, black worms seething in her eyeballs, and bent forward on the couch. She ignored Phillip. The music had stopped.

"What's the kitchen chair doing on the balcony?"

He put a hand on her shoulder. Martha snatched it away.

"If you're going to jump off the balcony think of the poor sods underneath. I can't help if you won't talk to me. He was my baby too, Martha."

"You didn't have it in your belly for nine months. Get out."

"I'm not leaving you alone."

In the rage fuelled by her depression Martha lurched up from the couch, picked up the wooden cow her father had carved when she was ten years old and threw it with all her might and pain at Phillip. Phillip ducked, the cow shattering the glass of the abstract painting on the wall. Suspended in hate, she watched Phillip pick up the cow, walk across the room, and put it back on the shelf where it belonged.

"Your Dad's cow isn't broken."

"Get out. I told you to get out."

"You're not going to jump off the balcony?"

"I tried. I don't have the guts."

"Thank God for that."

"Get out of my apartment, Phillip."

"You want me to pack?"

"I said get out didn't I?"

"Lucky I can get a room at a hotel. I'll pack a small bag and leave the rest. And don't shout. I've got a hangover. Have you been drinking all night?"

"You weren't home in the night when I needed you. Get out before I go to the kitchen and get a knife."

"It's not my fault. It's not your fault."

"It is. I drank when I was pregnant. You'd better leave. I want to suffer alone."

She went back to the couch and sat with her back to Phillip, hoping he would ignore her abuse. She waited, her eyes closed tight. The black worms had gone. There were sparks. Violent sparks. She heard the door to the apartment close gently. When she opened her eyes all she could focus on was the carved cow in its place on the shelf. She looked back at the painting: the top corner of the glass was shattered. Still in a rage, she walked into the bedroom. He had not packed his small bag. Relieved, she walked back into the lounge and put on some music and poured herself a glass of red wine. It was Frank Sinatra. Another of her favourites. It didn't help. Tears, tears and tears. All she could do was cry.

PRINCIPAL CHARACTERS

~

The Beckers

Julian — A famous American actor

Myra — Craig's sister and wife of Julian

Shoona — Julian and Myra's baby daughter

The Crookshanks

Bergit — Craig and Myra's mother

Craig — Phillip and Randall's younger half-brother

Douglas — Randall and Meredith's baby son

Harold — Craig and JoJo's baby son

Jeremy — Phillip, Randall, Craig and Myra's father

Jojo — Craig's Shona girlfriend

Phillip — Randall's elder brother, central character of *The Game of Life*

Randall — Central character of *Look Before you Leap*

The Polands

Agnes (Aggie) — Martha's mother

Martha — An American woman Phillip meets on her safari tour

Ford and Hugo — Martha's brothers

Other Principal Characters

Clem Wesley — A man Phillip meets in Solly's Saloon, Kansas City

Colin — Runs a hospice centre in Kansas City

Doctor Hamlyn — Martha's gynaecologist

Franklyn — Martha's manager at Horst and Maples Advertising Agency

Gordon Blake — A salesman Phillip meets in Solly's Saloon

Jacques Oosthuizen — Phillip Crookshank's safari business partner and cousin to Barend Oosthuizen

Jasmine (Jas) Fairbanks — Martha's advertising assistant

Mabel Crabshaw — An elderly friend of Agnes Poland

Marcin Galinski — A Yale graduate looking for a venture capitalist

Munya — Sedgewick's assistant

Noah Hughes — Jasmine's boyfriend

Pastor Gregory — The pastor who agrees to marry Phillip and Martha

Penny, Larry and Greg — Computer engineers who work for Linguare

Sedgewick — Phillips's safari driver and assistant

Solly — Barman who runs Solly's Saloon in Kansas City

Willy and Beth Hardcastle — Martha's downstairs neighbours who constantly argue

DEAR READER

~

Reviews are the most powerful tools in our kitty when it comes to getting attention for Peter's books. This is where you can come in, as by providing an honest review you will help bring them to the attention of other readers.

If you enjoyed reading *The Game of Life*, and have five minutes to spare, we would really appreciate a review (it can be as short as you like). Your help in spreading the word and keeping Peter's work alive is gratefully received.

Please post your review on the retailer site where you purchased this book.

Thank you so much.
Heather Stretch (Peter's daughter)

ACKNOWLEDGEMENTS

~

Our grateful thanks go to our *VIP First Readers* for reading *The Game of Life* prior to its official launch date. They have been fabulous in picking up errors and typos helping us to ensure that your own reading experience of *The Game of Life* has been the best possible. Their time and commitment is particularly appreciated.

Agnes Mihalyfy (United Kingdom)
Daphne Rieck (Australia
Hilary Jenkins (South Africa)

Thank you.
Kamba Publishing

Made in United States
Orlando, FL
28 May 2023

33573837R00193